P9-EGN-035

Praise for *The Moon in the Palace*

"*The Moon in the Palace* is a colorful and vibrant journey into the grandeur of the Tang Dynasty. Weina Randel weaves a captivating tale about the intrigues of the inner court through the eyes of the woman who would become the most infamous empress in Chinese history, finding a human story of love and hope amid bloodshed and treachery. I couldn't stop reading this exciting debut novel."

—Jeannie Lin, *USA Today* bestselling author of *The Lotus Palace*

"With fresh, lyrical prose and a true storyteller's flair, in her novel *The Moon in the Palace*, Weina Dai Randel brings seventh-century China to vibrant life. Through the eyes of Mei, a name meaning simply *sister*, given to the middle daughter of the household of her birth, we are submerged into intrigue of the imperial court, where wives and concubines fight for positions of power beside the Emperor, and where men fight to take the Emperor's throne. A story of courage and daring, in *The Moon in the Palace*, a girl without a name takes her destiny into her own hands. A shining jewel of a novel."

—Christy English, author of *The Queen's Pawn* and *To Be Queen: A Novel of the Early Life of Eleanor of Aquitaine*

"With elegant, modern prose and vivid details, Randel's gorgeous debut novel seductively pulls back the curtain to reveal the heartbreaking world of harem politics in Tang Dynasty China. Exploring the early years of the legendary Empress Wu when she was still a concubine struggling to survive the whims of the man who ruled her, the book's brave and clever heroine finds herself at the center of intrigue and civil war. This is a page-turner that will transport you in time and place. Bravo!"

—Stephanie Dray, author of *Lily of the Nile*

"Randel writes with a fresh, poetic style, bringing to life a time remote from our own, yet filled with the same intrigues, power struggles—and love affairs. For those confined to a claustrophobic existence in the palace, to offend the wrong person was to risk a horrible death. Yet strong women could bend the intrigues to their own benefit—if they dared. This is history, but also a stay-up-all-night read."

—Mingmei Yip, author of *Secret of a Thousand Beauties* and *Peach Blossom Pavilion*

"An astonishing debut! Weina Dei Randal spins a silken web of lethal intrigue, transporting us into the fascinating, seductive world of ancient China, where one rebellious, astute girl embarks on a dangerous quest for power."

—C. W. Gortner, bestselling author of *The Queen's Vow*

"I absolutely loved Weina Dai Randel's *The Moon in the Palace*, which is a truly immersive experience and a rare and beautiful treasure. All I want now is to read the next novel!"

—Elizabeth Chadwick, *New York Times* bestselling author of *The Summer Queen*, *The Winter Crown*, and *The Autumn Throne*

"Mei is a triumph of intelligence and passion, cunning and courage. Randel has provided a strong cast of supporting characters, successfully resisting stereotypes of eunuchs and concubines; in the end, we realize they are all victims of the crucible that is the Imperial Court. Even though I know Mei will prevail to become Empress Wu, I can't wait for the next book and more of Randel's gifted storytelling."

—Janie Chang, author of *Three Souls*

"A must for historical fiction fans, especially those fascinated by China's glorious past."

—*Library Journal* Starred Review

THE *Empress* OF *Bright Moon*

a novel *of* Empress Wu

WEINA DAI RANDEL

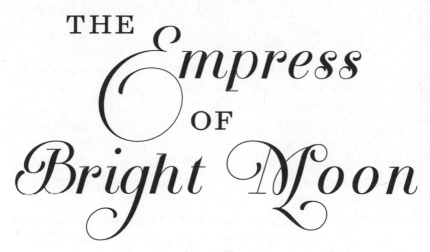

East Baton Rouge Parish Library
Baton Rouge, Louisiana

sourcebooks
landmark

For Mark, as always.

Copyright © 2016 by Weina Dai Randel
Cover and internal design © 2016 by Sourcebooks, Inc.
Cover design by Laura Klynstra
Cover images © Allan Jenkins/Trevillion Images, Molostock/Shutterstock, 100ker/
Shutterstock, tomertu/Shutterstock

Sourcebooks and the colophon are registered trademarks of Sourcebooks, Inc.

All rights reserved. No part of this book may be reproduced in any form or by any
electronic or mechanical means including information storage and retrieval systems—
except in the case of brief quotations embodied in critical articles or reviews—without
permission in writing from its publisher, Sourcebooks, Inc.

The characters and events portrayed in this book are fictitious or are used fictitiously.
Apart from well-known historical figures, any similarity to real persons, living or dead,
is purely coincidental and not intended by the author.

Published by Sourcebooks Landmark, an imprint of Sourcebooks, Inc.
P.O. Box 4410, Naperville, Illinois 60567-4410
(630) 961-3900
Fax: (630) 961-2168
www.sourcebooks.com

Library of Congress Cataloging-in-Publication Data

Randel, Weina Dai.
  The empress of bright moon / Weina Dai Randel.
    pages ; cm
  (pbk. : alk. paper) 1. Wu hou, Empress of China, 624-705—Fiction. 2. China—
History—Tang dynasty, 618-907—Fiction. 3. Empresses—China—Fiction. I. Title.
  PS3618.A6423E47 2016
  813'.6—dc23

                                    2015022864

        Printed and bound in the United States of America.
                VP 10 9 8 7 6 5 4 3 2 1

AD 649

The Twenty-Third Year *of*

Emperor Taizong's Reign

of Peaceful Prospect

LATE SPRING

WOULD HE DIE TONIGHT?

The thought flickered in my mind as I dabbed at a brown stain on the Emperor's chin. He did not respond, not even to twitch his lips or blink. He lay there, his mouth open, his gaze fixed on the ceiling. The right side of his face was a ruinous pool of skin, and his good left eye was opaque, like a marble that the light of candles failed to penetrate. Now and then, there seemed to be a spark in that eye, as though his old valor was struggling to come to life, to surface, to fight the fate that conquered him, but the light flashed like a fish in a murky pond. It was there, swimming, but it did not come up to the surface, not even for a breath of air.

He did not see me. He was gone, I could tell—a once-powerful whirlwind of wrath and will, now a bag of slackened skin, a shell of vaunting vanity.

I straightened, and an ache shot through my back. How long had I been kneeling at the bedside, watching him? I could not remember. All of us—the Talents, the Graces, and the Beauties, once the bedmates of the Emperor—had been his caretakers for the past ten months. Every day, we took turns feeding him, cleaning him—for he had long ago lost the ability to control his fluids—and carefully we watched him, listening to his every labored breath and every painful groan.

When the Emperor had announced Pheasant as the heir of the kingdom last year, he had been frail, and he had collapsed a few days later, shaken by the mysterious hand that had tormented him all these years. Writhing, gushing white foam from his mouth, he fell out of a stretcher on the way to his bedchamber and had not wakened since.

The water dropped in the water clock beside me. Nine. Where were they? They must hurry...

I rose, patting the side of my Cloudy Chignon, the elaborate hairstyle I had finally mastered. A few strands had fallen on my shoulders, and the loose knot that should have sat on top of my head had slumped sadly to my right ear. I wished I could make myself look more presentable, but we were not allowed to leave the chamber. The physicians had ordered me and the other Talents to stay with the Emperor at all times. I had not bathed for two months, looked at myself in the bronze mirror, or put on my white face cream. My hair, which had once been soft and fragrant, now felt heavy and lumpy on my neck, and the green robe I wore had turned brown, stained with splashes of herbal remedies.

The thought whispered to me again. I peered at him. What if he died tonight? What would happen to me and the other women who served him when he did die? I quickly smothered the thoughts. I should not think of those questions, for it was treason to ponder on the Emperor's mortality...

But all the titled women in the Inner Court must have wondered about their fate these months while he lay there unresponsive. After all, it was the unspoken law that we, as the Emperor's women, should never feel the warmth of another man's arms again after the Emperor's death. There must have been a plan for us. Yet no one openly talked about it, even though the ladies gathered together in the courtyard every morning, whispering, their eyes misty with tears.

I wished I could listen to the Duke and the Secretary, the two highest-ranking ministers, when they came to visit the Emperor. But they had many important matters to discuss and did not seem to pay attention to us. And Pheasant. He was busy too, and I had not yet had an opportunity to ask him about our fate.

But no matter what the plan was for us, I knew one thing was for sure: after the Emperor's death, Pheasant—my Pheasant—would be the ruler of the kingdom. He would look after me and my future.

And he had promised... *The empress of bright moon*, he said...

My heart warm with joy, I glanced at the doors. Pheasant and the Duke should have arrived by now. I wondered what the delay was.

A soft drizzle fell outside, light, persistent, carrying a pleasing rhythm that reminded me of the sound of baby silkworms devouring mulberry leaves. It was the fifth month of the year, a good time to have some rain. I yearned to go outside, feel the raindrops on my face, and smell the fresh air, for the bedchamber was veiled with the thick scent of incense, ginseng, musk, clove, dried python bile, and the unpleasant odor of death. I had been inside for so long, I supposed I smelled just like the chamber. I knew my fellow Talent, Daisy, did, as well as the others who yawned in the corner. Each time one of them passed me, I could name the herb in her hair.

Footsteps rose in the dark corridor, and red light from many lanterns poured through the doors. Finally, Pheasant and the Duke entered the chamber, their wet robes clinging to their chests. The physician, Sun Simiao, followed behind.

I retreated to the corner, giving them space, as they had asked each time they came, although I wished to stand right beside them and listen to what the physician had to report. When he examined the Emperor earlier, he had sighed heavily.

The men whispered in low voices, their eyes on the Emperor. The Duke sighed and sniffed, running a hand over his face. Pheasant, surprisingly, looked somber, although his eyes glittered.

"Crown Prince," the physician said, stepping aside to the screen, and Pheasant and the Duke followed him. "We have done the best we could. But I'm afraid I must tell you the dreadful news. The One Above All will not see the dawn's light."

My heart jerked. I tried to remain motionless.

"I understand." Pheasant's voice was soft and sad, and I stole a look at him. His eyes sparkled in the candlelight near the screen. His face was thinner, his jawline more refined than ever, and he had grown a beard.

I remembered how grief-stricken Pheasant had been when he learned the Emperor had become ill last year. For days, Pheasant had stood by the bedside, with us women scurrying from the physicians' herb chamber to the courtyard, carrying bowls of medicine. When we fed the Emperor, Pheasant, careless of his own life, would taste

5

the liquid first, to ensure it had not been mixed with any pernicious ingredient by a vicious hand. When some of us fell down in
fatigue after days without sleep, he would tell us to rest and watch
the Emperor himself. He was a dutiful son, and I was not sure the
Emperor deserved him.

"If there is anything you need, Crown Prince," the physician said,
"we're here to serve you."

"You have my gratitude, Physician Sun." Pheasant nodded solemnly. His gaze swept over me. A swift look, but long enough to
warm my heart. We had seen each other more often recently, as he
came to visit his father almost every day. Sometimes, when the other
Talents were not watching, he would brush my arm or hold my hand,
and sometimes, when he went to use the privy chamber, I would
follow him. There we would share some precious private moments,
and it would be the highlight of my day. "Uncle?"

The Duke bowed slightly. "Nephew."

The old man looked his usual self, his face long and hard and his gaze
arrogant. I wondered how the Duke managed to stay in good health.
He was the Emperor's brother-in-law, and they were the same age, but
while the Emperor was in the throes of death, the Duke still stood strong.
For the past three years, he had been the Emperor's close assistant, taking
direct orders from him, writing edicts for him when he lost control of
his arm. Since the Emperor had become ill the year before, the Duke
had acted on the Emperor's behalf, giving orders to the ministers. At the
moment, he was the most powerful man in the kingdom.

"I must prepare for the inevitable," Pheasant said. "I would like
you to arrange a meeting with the astrologers, Uncle, and report to me
the auspicious dates for burial in the coming months. Also, summon
the mausoleum's mural painters for me, as well as the craftsmen who
will build the four divine animal statues for the burial. I would like to
examine their works and make certain all matters regarding the funeral
are taken care of."

His voice was loud and steady, full of command and authority. I was
proud of Pheasant. During the past months, he had shown a strength
that was unknown even to himself. He had learned the rituals of wor-
shipping Heaven and Earth and the judicial and penal processes, and

familiarized himself with the governments of the sixteen prefectures of the kingdom. He had gathered ministers together, charmed them, and even won the support of the General, the commander of the ninety-nine legions of the Gold Bird Guards, who safeguarded the palace.

"Of course, Nephew," the Duke said, looking hesitant, "yet I would advise you not to tell the women of this devastating news at the moment."

"Why?" Pheasant looked surprised.

The Duke coughed, and when he spoke again, his voice was so low I had to strain to hear. "For the women are most petty minded and troublesome… If they know their fate…"

"What fate?"

"Naturally, your father's women shall never be seen or touched by any other men, and he has ordered that those who have borne him children must dwell in the safe Yeting Court for the rest of their lives."

Pheasant frowned. "I see. But what about the women who have not borne a child?"

"They will be sent to the Buddhist monasteries around the kingdom, where they will pray for the Emperor's soul. This is for the best and a fine tradition that dynasties follow."

I froze. Buddhist monasteries? He was banishing us. He was demanding we become Buddhist nuns, the ones who severed their secular ties to the world, the ones who forsook joy and desire, the ones with only past and no future. If we were banished there, scattered to the remote corners of the kingdom, we would hear nothing but the sound of misery, feel nothing but sorrow, see nothing but death. Our lives would end.

A chill swept over my body. The Emperor's death would be my noose.

"Buddhist monasteries?" Pheasant sounded shocked. "You can't mean that."

"Yes, it is their duty. Our Emperor, praise him, who is most merciful, told me of this tradition some time ago. This order shall be effective once the unfortunate moment arrives."

"But there are so many women…hundreds. He wants all of them to spend the rest of their lives in monasteries, praying?"

I could feel Pheasant's eyes on me, and the Duke's too. I turned away and fumbled among a pile of clothes I had worked on earlier. I found Pheasant's coronation regalia, which I had embroidered during many nights while tending to the Emperor. I had put my heart and love into every stitch, imagining how splendid Pheasant would look when he sat on the throne. My hands trembling, I clutched the silk fabric tightly.

The Duke's voice rose. "In old times, these women would have been buried alive in the mausoleum."

Pheasant was quiet for a moment, and then he said, "I am glad that was in the ancient time only, and yet banishing them to the monasteries still seems to be a dated tradition. I shall not agree to that." His resolute voice calmed me. Of course Pheasant would not let such a terrible fate befall me.

"You must, Nephew," the Duke said sharply. "As the future Emperor of the kingdom, you have a duty to fulfill your father's wishes and continue carrying out the tradition."

I did not like the way the Duke spoke. He sounded so assertive, as though he were the Emperor himself. Perhaps he thought he was. He was used to the power he had acquired over the past years.

"Uncle." Pheasant sounded calm. "I believe, as the future Emperor of the kingdom, I am also entitled to make exceptions to the rules."

There was a sharp intake of breath from the Duke, as though he could not believe Pheasant's open defiance. "Nephew!"

This was not the first time Pheasant and the Duke had disagreed. Last night, I had heard them arguing about who should conduct the Emperor's burial rite when the moment came. The Duke insisted on Taoist priests, as he claimed the Emperor would have wished, while Pheasant favored Buddhist monks.

"I shall consent only if they express their wish to live in the monastery, Uncle. Otherwise, I would rather my father's women spend the rest of their lives with their families. They have lived away from them long enough," Pheasant said.

That would be marvelous. And merciful. The ladies would be overjoyed. Some must have been separated from their families for more than twenty years. As for me, however, I had no home. My father, a wealthy governor who had believed I would grow up to be a ruler and bring my family glory, had died protecting me. After his death, I had lost my family's enormous fortune, my ancestral house, and even my sisters. Now my mother, a cousin of a late empress, was destitute and homeless, a nun living in a dilapidated Buddhist monastery far away from the palace.

Would the Duke send me to the same monastery where Mother lived? That would never happen, I realized. The Duke wanted us to die in loneliness, not to rejoice in family reunion. He would certainly send us to monasteries far away from Chang'an if he had his way.

"Living with their families? And have them seen and touched by other base men? This is most unconventional and outrageous! Your father would not agree to this. None of the ministers will agree to this!"

"If you wish, Uncle, we shall discuss the matter with the Secretary." Secretary Fang, I knew, was on Pheasant's side, and he would defend him against the Duke. "Come. They are waiting outside." Pheasant waved and headed toward the bedchamber's door. The Duke followed reluctantly.

I put down the robe, went to the door, and peered out. In the dark corridor, a group of ministers waited. Rain showered their long robes, and their faces were painted red by the light of lanterns hung from the eaves. Secretary Fang was speaking with Sun Simiao. He straightened as Pheasant approached. When Pheasant spoke to him, he glanced at the bedchamber and nodded. The Duke threw up his hands.

Daisy came to me. "What's going on?"

"I'm not sure," I said, hesitant to tell her too much. "The Duke wants to banish us to monasteries."

Daisy's eyes widened. "Why?"

A wave of voices burst forth as the other Talents gathered around me.

"We will have to become nuns?"

"Did our Crown Prince order that?"

They buried their faces in their hands and sobbed.

Oh, women. What else could we do but sob when our fate was in other people's hands? But I would not cry. Not ever. "Our Crown Prince will not banish us."

Pheasant was still talking to the Duke and the Secretary. The Duke gestured vehemently, shaking his head. Pheasant held up his hand and walked toward the entrance to the courtyard. The Duke looked frustrated. He opened his mouth again and turned toward the entrance, where a large figure loomed near the gate. The Duke froze.

Even though it was too dark for me to see the man's eyes and the purple birthmark on his face, the way he held his sword was unmistakable. The man near the gate was the General.

He had long ago been promoted to command the ninety-nine legions of the Gold Bird Guards and all the cavalry in the kingdom. He had been the Emperor's loyal servant, and after the Emperor's death, he would serve Pheasant.

Pheasant greeted the General. The Secretary followed after him, and together they walked to the end of the corridor, where they tipped their heads together and spoke quietly, sheets of rain falling on their shoulders.

The Duke stood stiffly, and the ministers around him left to join Pheasant and the Secretary as well. The Duke was alone, standing under the eaves, the lantern light casting a long shadow near his feet. For the first time since the Emperor had fallen ill, I could see that the powerful Duke, the Emperor's assistant for more than three years, was losing his influence.

It was for the best. Since the Emperor was about to die, the Duke had to go too. I had never liked him. He was cruel—like the Emperor, devious, and also a man lusting for power.

I liked Pheasant's merciful plan for his father's concubines. People would be overjoyed once it was announced. But what about me? I had no home to return to. Since I came to the palace at the age of thirteen, I had been living here for almost eleven years. The palace was my home now.

I went to the Emperor's bedside. He looked the same, his mouth open, his gaze fixed on the ceiling. A sound, half gurgle, half groan, rose from his throat, as though he was having trouble breathing, then ceased. Was he dead? My heart stopped. But then his chest rose again.

The Duke appeared on the other side of the bed. "Ungrateful son, ungrateful, ungrateful!" He gritted his teeth and cursed, his hawkish nose shining in the candlelight like a honed blade. There was something ferocious and calculated in his eyes. Something furtive and disturbing. He caught me watching him and gave me a cold stare. I lowered my head.

When I dared to look up again, he had disappeared.

A hot wave of unease rushed through me. The Duke must not be ignored. I had to warn Pheasant. He was not crowned yet, and he had to be cautious, for the death of his father could create a crack in the ladder of power, and if he did not watch it carefully, the crack could expand, the rungs could split, and the entire ladder could collapse.

IT WAS MIDNIGHT. THE ROOM WAS DARK, THE ONLY LIGHT coming from the two candles near the Emperor's bed. Near me, the other Talents dozed in the corner, but I was sleepless. Several physicians came to examine the Emperor again.

I took the opportunity to slip to the door and peered out the window. The courtyard was masked in darkness as well, and no one seemed to be there. I searched and found the Secretary on the other side of the corridor. He was talking to several ministers under the lanterns. The Duke and the General were not around, and Pheasant was walking toward the privy chamber.

Quietly, I made my way to the Talents in the corner and shook Daisy's shoulder. "Daisy, wake up," I whispered to her, my eyes on the physicians standing around the bed. "Watch the physicians and let me know if anything happens."

Yawning, she nodded.

I took the robe I had been embroidering and hurried down the corridor. Some eunuchs appeared near the compound's gates. They wiped their wet faces and turned toward me, probably waiting for the news of the Emperor's death. I put my nose in the air, holding the robe above my chest to show them I was on an errand. When I reached the privy chamber, I glanced around to make sure no one was watching me and pushed the door open.

The chamber, filled with the scent of camphor and frankincense, smelled more pleasant than the Emperor's rank room. Pheasant was washing his face near a basin.

He raised his head toward me. "I'm glad you came, Mei. Did you hear what the physician said?"

I nodded and put down the robe on a nearby table. "I did, and I am sorry, Pheasant."

"It is perhaps for the best." He sighed. "My father has suffered enough."

I turned around to fetch a towel for him. "But, Pheasant, I have to tell you this. Your uncle came to see your father while you were talking to the General."

"You look worried. Why?" He took the towel from my hand and wiped his face.

"I wish you could have seen his expression," I said. "I am afraid for you to anger him, Pheasant."

"You heard what he suggested, didn't you? To banish the ladies? I do not care about tradition, and I have my own plans for the women of my father's court. My uncle belongs to the old world. Remember what he suggested about the horses?"

The Duke had wanted to sacrifice them—all two hundred stallions, including the Emperor's favorite horse, Brown Grizzle—at the mausoleum so they would keep the Emperor company in the other world. Pheasant, a horse lover, was disgusted. He had spared the horses and ordered the artists to build sculptures of the horses instead.

"I do," I said and put my hand on his arm. "But he is still a very powerful man. You will need him when you come to the throne."

Pheasant shook his head. "He needs me more, Mei. When I become the Emperor, I will choose my own counselors, and my uncle will not be among them. I have decided to replace him with the Secretary, and my uncle can retire."

"I see." I was pleased to hear his plan. If the Duke left the court, his influence would wane, and Pheasant would not need to fight him each time he made a decision. "May I ask you, my emperor," I said, and raised my head to look into his eyes, "what is your plan for me?"

Pheasant swept my hair aside, and I tried to smile, for I knew how wan my face looked without rouge, but he did not seem to mind. His brush was tender, his gaze affectionate. "You understand you will not go home again."

"Oh, that is sad." I feigned disappointment, but I was so relieved. Of course he would let me stay beside him.

"I have talked to the Secretary about you too. He has no objection to you staying in the palace."

"Really?" I was surprised but also glad. After all, I was the Emperor's concubine, and even though I had not given myself to the Emperor, my relationship with Pheasant, his son, would cause a stir in the palace. Many people would consider it immoral and even incestuous. If the Secretary did not object to me, then those voices, those furtive looks of disapproval, could be stopped. "What about your wife? Will she approve of that?"

A few years before, Pheasant had married Lady Wang, daughter of the prominent Wang family, by the command of Emperor Taizong. As Pheasant's chief wife and the highest-ranking woman in the court, Lady Wang had moved into the Eastern Palace after Pheasant was announced as the heir. She had also immediately assumed the duty of overseeing the silkworms in the Imperial Silkworm Workshops and begun enjoying her new status. I had seen her, a plain-looking woman with a colossal frame like a wrestler's, a broad face with two eyes set too closely together, and a nose thick and stubby like an ornate candleholder. Her unattractiveness could not be masked even by her glittery silk gowns, and I would have mistaken her for a peasant's daughter if not for the many maids trailing behind her.

But Lady Wang carried a certain menace with her. When she came to visit the Emperor, she often gazed at me, her eyes dark and filled with suspicion. She was unfriendly, unapproachable, and definitely not a woman whom I wished to antagonize.

"You don't need to worry about her. She won't object." Pheasant shrugged. "And I want to tell you, Mei: I will not disappoint my father, my mother, or my people. I was told that I would give my kingdom great prosperity and much happiness when I reign." He smiled, raising his chin, his eyes sparkling in the candlelight. "I have just met this great monk, who has returned safely from India. He brought many scriptures in Sanskrit back home—"

I stopped him. "Tripitaka?" The monk who had predicted my

future? Mother had mentioned him when I visited her in the monastery, saying he would soon return from a journey to India with the true words of Buddha.

"Yes. After fifteen years of travel, he has returned. Imagine that! He's now staying in the Great Maternal Grace Pagoda. You remember it, don't you? I requested Father build it to honor my mother, and it will house Tripitaka, his disciples, and all the scriptures. Do you know what Tripitaka told me? A great era is coming, he said. Greater than my father's and my grandfather's, and one that will not be surpassed for centuries! Isn't that astounding? This could be the beginning of glory for my kingdom and my people."

His voice was firm and filled with excitement. I clasped his hand. Pheasant had been a boy when I first met him, and now with the weight of the kingdom on his shoulders, he had transformed into a man, a righteous and benevolent ruler.

"Do you think I will be a good emperor, Mei?"

I smoothed the front of his garment. He would look glorious in the ceremonial robe I had embroidered for him. "No," I said, shaking my head. "You will be an *extraordinary* emperor."

He pulled me close, his breath warming my forehead. "And you, my love. You will be here. You will be mine. Once my enthronement ceremony is finished, you will be my Lady, my Most Adored. Remember what I promised you?"

My heart sang. He had not forgotten. "You mean it?"

"Every word, my empress of the moon."

I smiled happily. Everything—his face, his words, and the splendid future he promised me—enticed me. I stood on tiptoe to kiss him.

"Crown Prince!" A shout, rough and desperate, came from the courtyard. "Crown Prince!"

"Physician Sun." Releasing me, Pheasant dashed to the doors.

My heart tightened, but I waited until he had left the corridor, and then I tidied up my robe and ran out.

It was still raining outside, and the courtyard was brightly lit by strings of lanterns hung from the eaves. The corridor near me was crammed with many titled women—Lady Virtue, Lady Obedience, the Ladies-in-Waiting, the Beauties, the Graces, and the others, and through the compound's entrance, many ministers and eunuch servants rushed in, shouting, waving their arms.

"Oh, the One Above All!" someone wailed near the Emperor's bedchamber.

All at once, the women around me screamed, their hands striking the ground, their heads dipping and rising.

The Emperor was dead.

I dropped to my knees beside the ladies, joining the mourning, although I wanted to be with Pheasant. He had entered the bedchamber with the physicians, and I could see him through the chamber's open doors. Standing over his father's body, he was wiping his eyes. My heart pounding nervously, I watched him intently. Pheasant was the Emperor of the kingdom now. He had much to do. He had to summon the Minister of Rites, order the palace to strike the funeral bell, and command the kingdom to start the mourning for his father.

But the chamber was eerily quiet. I did not hear any orders from Pheasant or see any movements from the physicians. What was happening?

Finally, Pheasant appeared at the chamber's threshold. His hands trembling, he faced us in the courtyard. Beside him stood the Duke, his shadow stretching menacingly like a vulture spreading its wings.

I did not expect to see the Duke there. He had left the Emperor's chamber earlier, I remembered. He must have returned while I was seeing Pheasant.

"All kneel!" the Duke ordered. His voice, loud and sharp, drifted toward me and echoed across the courtyard. Pheasant hesitated but fell to the ground to obey the order, and all the other people—the Secretary, the other ministers, and the servants—knelt as well.

An ominous feeling seized me. The courtyard fell silent as a graveyard.

"Crown Prince, ministers, and the women of the Inner Court," the Duke said. "It is with a heavy heart I inform you that our most venerated sage, the One Above All, the Emperor of Great China, has passed away. I hereby give you my command that I shall now release his will, which he wrote last year prior to his illness." He held up a scroll.

I frowned. The Emperor had not been able to hold a calligraphy brush for a few years, and I had never heard him mention a will.

There would have been no point in keeping one, since he had already announced Pheasant to be the heir of the kingdom.

"He wrote a will last year?" Pheasant looked surprised too.

"Indeed, before he fell ill." The Duke spread the scroll. "Now, all of you, listen!"

Pheasant lowered his head. I could not see his face, but he seemed calm, staring straight ahead of him.

I tried to remain calm too. Perhaps the will would not say anything meaningful. After all, Pheasant was the known heir, the kingdom recognized him, and the Emperor, a sensible ruler, certainly would not have wanted to throw the kingdom into turmoil with a change of heart.

"On the seventeenth day of the seventh month of the twenty-second year of the Reign of Peaceful Prospect, I here now write my will," the Duke read. "I now declare the Grand Duke, Changsun Wuji, brother of my late Empress Wende, the faithful friend of mine, to be the Regent of the kingdom, who has the right to examine, supervise, assist, and oversee any decisions made by my heir, Li Zhi. This is my will, written by me, the One Above All, Emperor Taizong of Tang Dynasty, the Conqueror of the North and the South, the lord of all land and the seven seas. I now announce it effective upon my death."

I felt the strength drain out of me. Li Zhi was Pheasant's formal name. He was still the heir, the ruler of the kingdom, but the will had just taken away all the power the throne had granted him and given it to the Duke.

Was this truly Emperor Taizong's plan? I did not believe so. It must have been the Duke's. He was the Emperor's assistant, drafting his edicts and keeping possession of the dragon seal. He would have had many chances to write the Emperor's will. Or to forge it...

The only sound in the courtyard was the patter of the soft drizzle, seeping through my robe, chilling my skin like a cold, stealthy hand.

"Regent? Regent?" I heard Pheasant's voice, filled with surprise and confusion. "Why? I am a grown man. I don't need a regent to oversee my decisions. Why did he do this? He believed in me. I thought he believed in me."

"Nephew, your father always knew what was best for the kingdom."

"But…he never mentioned his will to me."

"He did not need to." The Duke paused. "And here, you have it. His will. Do you disobey?"

"I… I…" Pheasant's voice cracked, and my heart broke for him. He had always loved and respected his father. He would have no choice but to follow and honor his father's will. "Of course not."

"It is my duty now to advise you, Nephew, on the matters of importance regarding the kingdom. I shall obey your father's wish, may his soul rest in peace."

"I know… I know…" Pheasant's voice was faint and hollow, and I wanted to weep. A kingdom, gone in a moment. Was there anything crueler than that? Pheasant covered his face, his shoulders trembling.

"Ministers," the Duke said to the Secretary and the others, who were still frozen in shock, "now that you have heard the will of our most-venerated Emperor, I must follow his wish and command all of your attentions. Send a servant to strike the bell—"

"Wait." The Secretary snapped upright. "Was the will witnessed?"

The Duke turned abruptly toward him. "Secretary Fang, you know I am the only witness the Emperor needed."

"But—"

"Have you heard Emperor Taizong's will?"

"Yes, but—"

The ministers around him raised their heads as well. Someone cleared his throat.

"Guards!" the Duke shouted before anyone had a chance to speak, and suddenly the courtyard swarmed with shadows. Their arms stretching long, they dove toward the ministers. "By the power Emperor Taizong conferred on me, I command you to escort these ministers outside and await my further notice."

My heart leaped to my throat. He was going to arrest the ministers by force! He must have planned this. He must have planned every-thing—the will, the guards. Perhaps he would kill us too if any of us dared to put up a fight.

The Secretary cried out as two guards clamped their hands on him, and more guards rushed toward him and the other ministers, pushing them to the entrance.

"Stop, Uncle." Pheasant stood. "Stop, Uncle. Do you hear me?" But the guards did not back away. "General! General!"

I craned my neck, looking toward the compound's entrance. The General was our only hope. Now that the Emperor was dead, he would serve Pheasant, and he would use his sword and restore Pheasant to the throne if the Duke dared to resort to violence.

But near the entrance, the ministers stumbled, groaning and cursing, and the General was nowhere to be seen.

"He has left, Nephew," the Duke said, his voice cold.

"Left where? He was just here! I talked to him a moment ago!"

"I have exiled him. He was required to leave the city the moment the Emperor died. It was your father's order."

"What? Why?"

"The General has an army. He is a dangerous man."

"But…but…" Pheasant staggered backward, crashing against a pillar.

I closed my eyes and wept. Poor Pheasant was all alone. No one would listen to him. No one would obey him.

"Now, you." The Duke waved more guards into the courtyard. "The women must be sent to Buddhist monasteries. Take them away."

"No, no!" Hysterical cries burst around me.

My head spun. The Duke would have his wish. He would banish us all.

"Uncle!" Pheasant's voice, desperate and familiar. "You must not do this. Do not do this!"

"Nephew, I am following your father's will. Do you dare to disobey him?"

Two guards stepped to him and held his arms. Pheasant struggled, trying to free himself. "Then make one exception. Just let one stay, let me tell you. Just one!"

"Who would that be?" The Duke was already looking at me, his gaze cold.

"Yes, yes," Pheasant said. "Let her stay. I beg you, Uncle!"

"Nephew, how can you reign over a kingdom if you forget how to behave?"

I could not hold up my head. I hated the Duke. But I prayed for him to let me stay. I had spent eleven years, all my best years, in the palace. I could not live anywhere else. I could not leave Pheasant. And I did not want to spend the rest of my life in a monastery, praying and yearning for Pheasant. I would rather have been buried alive in a mausoleum.

"Uncle—"

"She is your father's concubine, and you wish to bed her, Nephew? Will you start your reign with a scandal and bring your kingdom eternal shame?"

I did not wish to stain Pheasant's reign in any way, but would I have to spend the rest of my life in a monastery? No, I could not. Let people laugh at me. Let them call me a harlot, as long as I could stay in the palace.

"Guards, take the heir away." Pheasant was fighting against them, his face wracked with grief, his arms thrashing, trying to get to me. I wanted to go to him too, to hold him so no one could pull us apart. But the Duke's lean figure appeared in front of me. "Talent? Will you disobey the Emperor's order?"

Tears stung my eyes. I turned my head away. Why must I obey? The Emperor was dead! Why must I end my life for him? I was only twenty-three years old. I had dreamed of a different life, a splendid life in the palace, with Pheasant.

But what else could I do? Scream? Shout? Fight? It was pointless. It would not change anything. Pheasant could not save me. No one could.

I turned to look at the other women in the courtyard. Some wailed, pounding the ground; some flailed their arms, screaming; some stumbled near the gates, weeping. I felt dazed. All these years in the palace. All these months of serving and nursing the Emperor. In the end, I was only as good as one of his horses, and like his horse, I was ordered to be sacrificed upon his death.

A large frame appeared a few paces from me. She had a broad face painted in stark white, her eyes closely set, and her nose large and stubby. Her chin raised, she looked down on me, and even though it was dim, I could see the relief and happiness on her face. It was Lady Wang, Pheasant's wife. She must have heard the news of the Emperor's death and rushed here from the Eastern Palace.

My face chilled, I looked away and searched for Pheasant. But he was gone. Only his screams—"Take your hands off me, take your hands off me!"—burst from the other side of the corridor. I felt the thick rain-drops lashing through the air and pelting my face, and although I could not feel my lips or hear my own voice, I said, "I shall obey."

✦ ✦

The next morning, before dawn arrived, before the priests came to keep vigil for Emperor Taizong, before my hair had dried from the rain, I was taken to the Xuanwu Gate in the back of the palace, where many of the palace ladies waited. Wearing white, plain gowns, their faces pale and streaked with tears, they looked like roaming ghosts ready to depart the world. One by one, they climbed into wagons that would take them from the palace.

The ladies who had borne the Emperor children had already been sent to a secluded compound inside the Yeting Court, I heard, where guards and high walls would thwart any fantasies of leaving or escaping, and those of us who had not given the Emperor children would be sent to various Buddhist monasteries scattered around the kingdom, the dark corners where only the outcast would set foot.

Although the Duke said it had been Emperor Taizong's order to exile the General at his death, the General had been banished before the Emperor died. The cunning Duke, fearing the General would resist him, had taken one hundred men and surrounded the General when he went to piss in the garden. Hearing he was to be banished, the General, whose loyalty was bound to the Emperor more tightly than his sword fit its sheath, lowered his head, packed his belongings, and left the city without a word. The Duke also exiled Pheasant's older brother, Prince Wei; the Noble Lady's two sons, Prince Ke and his brother; several other princes; and all of the princes' aides and assistants, claiming it was the Emperor's order as well. But it was clear to me that the Duke had seized this opportunity to eliminate any potential threats to his power.

Rumors said that Secretary Fang had a long talk with the Duke right after he exiled us. The Duke allowed the Secretary to remain in his position, and the two parted amicably, but when the Secretary went home, his carriage overturned in a ditch. When his servants found him, he was already dead, his neck broken.

A wagon, pulled by two donkeys, stopped before me. A guard waved at me. "You. Time to go."

I could not move. I tried to think of something to say, but my mind did not belong to me. It drifted like the pear blossoms from the trees beside me, their white petals laden with rain, their last scent washed away, trembling, falling helplessly to the ground.

A bell chimed in the distance. The Emperor was dead, and now the whole kingdom knew. The sound lingered in the air, filled up the sky like dark clouds, and then faded.

A tattoo of drumbeats followed, urgent and steady. The coronation ceremony had started in Taiji Hall. Pheasant would be proclaimed as the third Emperor of the Tang Dynasty, Emperor Gaozong, and begin the Reign of Yonghui, the years of Eternal Glory. He would ascend the throne, garbed in his golden regalia, the very robe I had embroidered and smoothed many times. Standing beside him would be Lady Wang, wearing the phoenix crown, who would be hailed as Empress Wang.

But Pheasant would rule in name only, for the man who held the dragon seal would be the Duke, now formally titled the Regent, who stood beside him.

The guard in the wagon shouted again, his voice so harsh it pierced my bones. I shivered. Someone lifted me into the wagon, where Daisy and the other Talents already sat, and the wagon lurched, throwing me back. Behind me, the palace shook too. Then it steadied, and slowly it wavered away from me, step by step, growing smaller and smaller, like a paper house sailing away in the wind.

I stretched out my hand, but no matter how far I reached, it slipped through my fingers.

I BROUGHT NOTHING WITH ME. NO SILK GOWNS, NO FRAGRANCE
sachets, no gold hairpins. I left just as I had come to serve Emperor
Taizong eleven years ago: with empty hands. And an empty heart.

I did not know where I was being carted either. Our escorts rarely
spoke to us, and one drank his way out of the city. Sometimes, after
he had drunk too much, he would bare himself to me. His member
shook like an avaricious rat, and he shouted, "Want to suck my cock?
Suck it. Suck it, *biaozi*!" Then he laughed. "But you can't. You can't,
biaozi. You're the dead Emperor's woman. You can't touch men.
Men can't touch you! What a waste! A whore in a tavern has more
fun than you."

I squeezed my eyes shut, crouching in the corner of the wagon
with Daisy. The man began to hum. His broken tunes pricked my
ears like thorns, and his voice hung on my skin like rough leather,
wrapping tight around me, choking me. I pressed closer to Daisy,
wanting to cover my ears. I wished he would stop and leave me alone
so I could have blessed silence.

But I did not know the true meaning of silence then. Silence
would not feel like rough leather. It would not smell like a corner of a
stinky wagon that reeked of horse dung. It was like nothing I had ever
imagined. Silence, as I would find out later, bore no color, no edges,
and no scent. But it had a name. It was called Grave.

✦ ✦

The abbess had a slight figure and a face like crinkled oil paper. She was ancient, like the mountain, like the monastery standing behind her. When the wagon stopped and I tumbled out after the other Talents, she pressed her hands together to greet us. She did not say anything, did not look kind or threatening. She simply stared at me, as though I were no different from a pole near a well where people hooked their buckets.

Behind me, the guards, shouting raucously, drove the wagon down the hill. Daisy and the others began to sob and walked toward the monastery. I did not wish to join them, but I did not know what else to do. I did not greet the abbess either. I pretended I did not see her. If I did not allow myself to see her, perhaps she would disappear. Perhaps I would disappear. Perhaps the monastery would disappear.

But it stood in front of me, a pitiful thing. Its dirt walls had collapsed on one side, and on the top of its roof stood a statuette of a rooster with a broken leg. Engraved at the entrance of the building were the words *Ganye Miao*. Monastery of senses. How ironic. What senses could I possibly have in a monastery? And how far was this place to Chang'an? A hundred *li*? A thousand? But I did not need to ask, for even if I could have measured the span from Earth to Heaven, the distance from Pheasant to me still would have been immeasurable.

Holding on to the wall, I stumbled inside the monastery. Before me, clouds of pale smoke drifted, and many figures, wearing ash-colored skullcaps, circled around the hall, their gray stoles swaying slowly like tired moths.

"Sit," the abbess, holding a pair of scissors, said beside me. "It will not take long."

I could feel the sharp edges of the scissors on my scalp, and I trembled. My hair. My long hair. She intended to cut it.

"No." I shrank back, holding my head. Since entering the palace, I had never cut my hair. Black and sleek, it fell near my knees and swayed behind me. It was a part of me, my charm and my identity. If she tonsured me, what would I become? Would I still be a woman? Would I still be able to love and be loved?

My hair was not simply an adornment either. It contained the threads of my memories, the stories of my past, and the essence of the moments I had spent with the people I held dear. If I let my hair go, would I still have memories? For I remembered those moments well. I remembered the hair falling in front of my eyes while I played tug-of-war with Big Sister behind me and my father laughing on the other side. I remembered Mother brushing it, greasing it with lance-shaped thoroughwort leaves, smoothing sunflower seed oil onto my head, and twisting braids near my ears. I remembered my friend Plum laboring behind me, piling loose strands on top of my head and powdering my Cloudy Chignon with fragrances. I remembered leaning against Pheasant's chest, my head close to his heart, my hair brushing his skin…

I pushed the abbess away and staggered toward the door. Voices called me back, and some other Talents screeched as the scissors cut their hair, but I did not care. I did not belong there. I needed to find Pheasant, find the palace. He would fight for me. He would make the Duke change his mind. He would take me back to the palace.

I passed the nuns, dashed across the dirt courtyard, and ran out of the monastery. Before me, walls of white birches glared like bleached bones, sharp rocks jutted out threateningly, and deep valleys cut through the slopes and stretched into the distance like a serpent's broken spine. The cold air sent a chill down my back.

In the distance, I saw a wall of fences, a small shack, and the two guards standing near the path, their swords in their hands. Beyond them, mountain after mountain piled into the air and reached toward the sky. I shuddered.

I could not escape. If I were caught, I would be hanged. Mother and all my blood-related family would be killed as well. And even if I could escape, where would I go?

Oh, Pheasant.

If only he had fought harder. Did he really love me as he claimed? Perhaps I had been wrong all these years. Perhaps I had meant nothing to him. Perhaps I was no different from the other girls he had dallied with. He was a lie coated in honey, a rotten trickery wrapped in silk. He had given me up. Now he sat on his throne, and I was here.

I returned to the monastery. The abbess came to stand before me, the scissors in her hand.

I turned around, showing her my back. "Do it."

She mumbled something and tugged at my hair. The scissors screeched as clumps of dark threads dropped to the ground beside me. It made no sound, but it battered my heart nonetheless. I clenched my hands, standing still.

More hair fell, rapidly, urgently, like a torrent of black blood. Then a cold edge pressed to my scalp, chafing at my forehead, around my ears, and the nape of my neck. I shivered.

The abbess wobbled away, trampling on the pile of hair that used to be a part of me, and a nun with a grim face hurried over with a broom and pushed the pile into a corner. There, my hair hunched like a frightened ghost, hopeless, helpless.

The nuns marked my head with incense and smeared ash on the burned spots to prevent infection. Later, the abbess offered me clothes to change into. I took off my silk gown, folded it, placed it near the pillow on my pallet, and put on the thin, gray stole that reeked of smoke and incense.

I lay down on my pallet and stared at the crack of the dirt wall. I tried not to think, to listen, or to feel, and when my eyes began to sting, I closed them and fell asleep.

✦ ✦

In the dark, I felt Daisy's warm arm against my back and heard her gentle breathing behind me. I was back in the palace! My heart leaping in joy, I bolted upright. But then my hand touched something bristly—Daisy's shorn head. I shrank back. All at once the pain of leaving the palace and arriving at the monastery stormed through me. I lay down and covered my face, but I did not cry. I could not cry.

Some time passed. The abbess entered the small room and beat a round, wooden block with a stick, startling me. Dawn had not yet arrived, but the nuns rose, dressed themselves, and lined up against the wall, their legs crossed. For a long time they meditated.

I continued to lie there, and the other Talents did not rise either. Perhaps they were still asleep, or perhaps they simply could not face the day. The monastery was enveloped in still silence. There were no eunuchs' voices answering orders, no clopping noises from high-heeled wooden shoes striking the floors, no tinkling of jewels from ladies' girdles, no gentle knocking of lanterns against the eaves. There was no laughter, no singing, no music of flutes or zithers. It was so quiet, it seemed the monastery had dropped into an abyss and would never see the light again.

An animal shrieked in the woods. The sound was so shrill, it ripped through the stillness and yanked at my heart.

A sliver of pale light crept to the gap between the threshold and the door. Dawn had arrived. The nuns stood and filed into the chanting hall. I did not move. They would need to drag me if they wished me to participate. I hated the sight of them. I hated their chanting, and I hated the hall with the big Buddha statue that reminded me of Tripitaka. And I hated him too.

I had believed in him, and Father too—had believed in his prediction of my destiny, that I would have the power to rule over all of China. But Tripitaka had been wrong. Look at me now, whipped by the storm of misfortune and trapped by its treacherous wind.

I dozed off and slept for what seemed like centuries, but when I awoke, the nuns were still chanting. The other Talents awoke too. Touching their shorn heads, they screamed and wailed in dismay. I turned away, my eyes moist.

The abbess came in and told us that the morning meal had been served. When none of us replied to her, she sighed and left us alone.

I could not stay in that room any longer. I would go insane if I spent one more minute watching the Talents weep. I rose from the pallet and staggered out to the courtyard.

Before me, people rushed about in a flurry of activity. Some swept the floor while some shined the hemp-oil lamps; others cleaned ash out of the incense pots. A slim nun balanced two buckets of water from a pole on her shoulders.

The nuns glanced at me without saying a word, and I hid my hands in my stole and looked away. I went to the backyard and stared at the melons, eggplants, cabbage, and green beans growing in the garden. I thought of the fragrant wine and roasted meat I had enjoyed at the palace. Perhaps I would never feel juicy bites of meat in my mouth again.

Near noon, the nuns arranged another meal. They served only two meals a day, they said, and afterward another session of chanting followed. Kneeling on black cushions, they rocked back and forth, their voices punctuated by the sound of a stick beating the wooden block. A thick scent mixed with smoke, oil, and incense wafted through the hall. I felt sick smelling it.

When the last light of dusk disappeared on the horizon, the abbess struck the wooden block again, and the lights in the monastery were extinguished. We sank into the darkness.

I stared at the dark ceiling and thought of Mother. I was like her now, a nun. A mother and a daughter. Two lives. One destiny. When I had seen her a few years ago, I had thought I was ready to walk down my own path. I was wrong.

And Pheasant. What was he doing? Did he think of me? Would he recognize me now, with my head shaped like a potato covered with dirt?

Perhaps, when I awoke tomorrow, he would stand before me, his head cocked to one side and his eyes twinkling with mirth, smiling at me. Perhaps he would push open the monastery's gate just as I stepped outside, giving me his hand, surprising me.

Perhaps…

I should not think of him. I should not dream something like that, for I knew what tomorrow would be like, and I knew what night after night would be like. And I told myself to sleep, and I hoped I would never wake up again.

But that was my life now—every day, it began with the same sound of the stick beating the wooden block, the same chants, the same incense fragrance, and every night, it ended with the same silence and the same darkness. I woke and slept. I slept and woke. I walked through the monastery, plunging into the fume of incense, but I did not know where I was going. I heard the loud chanting, the alien sounds around me, but I did not know what they meant. And I passed the nuns, their gray stoles, their wrinkled faces, and I turned my face away. I knew, though, that I looked like them, I smelled like them, and I felt like them.

The days lengthened, expanded, engulfed the void between the mountain and the sky and became void again.

Sometimes I went to the other side of the monastery and stood on the top of the mountain. I scanned the world beneath me. The scenery was the same every time I looked. Craggy rocks. Deep valleys. Massive trees spreading far and beyond.

The palace was out there somewhere, but it was not mine anymore—I would never be allowed to set foot in it again. My dream was there too, a cold moon, eclipsed by a cloud of treachery and death. It might shine again, gleaming with a faint light, but it would not warm me, and I would never again be part of its celestial dream again.

Unless the Duke changed his mind. Unless Pheasant came for me.

But months passed. He never came. And he would never come. I knew that.

Life was a cruel trickster. It had given me to Emperor Taizong only to let me fall for Pheasant, and now Pheasant was the Emperor, and I would spend the rest of my life in loneliness.

I cupped my hands around my mouth and shouted, "Why? Why? Why?"

Why—Why—Why—Why…

The mountain shouted back, faithfully, like a devoted lover. Tears welled in my eyes. I would live in the monastery until the last day of my life. I would grow old there. My face would become wrinkled; my back would become stooped; my breath would fade into the wind; my tears would seep into the ground, mingling with the dead leaves and rotten roots; and yet the man I loved, the man who had promised to stand by my side, would never hold me again.

✦ ✦

One day, after the midday meal, I was staring at the sunlight glittering at Buddha's shining feet when a shriek came from the woods near the backyard.

Daisy, my dear friend. She had hanged herself.

The nuns scrambled to untangle the white sash around her neck and pulled her down. I bent over her, touching her cold face, feeling her stiff hands. I could not contain my tears.

We buried her at the edge of the woods, and long after everyone else left, I sat there, my arms around my knees, keeping her company. I wished to speak to her, telling her memories of our life in the palace, comforting her spirit, but I could not find my voice. There was no point. Sooner or later, we would all end up buried in the same place.

The sun was setting, and the wind blew at my face. In the distant sky, the moon hung, pale, weak, and lackluster, like a bowl of tears. I remained still, watching the night's shadow emerge. Dark and feathery, it crept to the edge of the small mound, crawled to the top, slithered lower, and swallowed it all.

I rose. Suddenly, I understood. I could hang myself like Daisy and erase the agony, or I could ignore the pain and survive.

The next day, I hiked through the woods, striking back thick bushes with a branch. I grabbed on to a protruding rock and climbed. The rock under my feet rubbed my skin raw, but I did not slow down or look back. I had to climb; I could not stop. For when I ascended to the top of the mountain, I could breathe normally, I could see the world beneath me, and I would be happy again.

At the monastery, I learned to keep busy. I hunted for wild mushrooms, tender bamboo shoots, and fresh ferns. I tilled the garden to loosen the soil and planted vegetable seeds. I watered them every morning before sunrise and weeded every afternoon at sundown. When the plants grew, I made wooden frames to support the green beans and eggplants. The thought of meat became unappealing to me, and when I thought of the rich food in the palace, the fatty mutton and the greasy grilled ribs, I found it hard to imagine I used to covet it.

Sometimes birds came, and I threw leftover rice to feed them. I watched them peck at the grain and stretch their necks, their wings flapping at their sides as they swallowed. This was a small action, a basic survival instinct, but somehow it was majestic, reminding me of the joy of being alive, the joy of having a desire and fulfilling it.

When I cleaned Buddha's statue, I studied him. He sat there, his eyes half-open, his fingers spreading. Unlike Confucius, Lao Tzu, or Sun Tzu, he was not Chinese. The nobles did not worship him; only the weak, the lower class, and helpless women followed him. I wondered how he made people believe in him. I began to listen to the nuns' chanting and asked the abbess its meaning. It was part of

Diamond Sutra in Sanskrit, she explained to me, which was one of the scriptures brought by Tripitaka, whose very name meant Three Treasures in Sanskrit.

I thanked her, and when the nuns meditated, I crossed my legs and closed my eyes as well. Perhaps meditating would help me find inner peace, as it did for them. But when I meditated, my thoughts wandered like wisps of smoke. It was easier to chase a rabbit on the Steppes than to find so-called peace.

Oftentimes, I found myself thinking of Pheasant. I remembered his tearful eyes, his face contorted with grief, his arms reaching out to me. I thought of his pain.

He had done his best to keep me; he wanted me. But he was not in control. A filial son, a newly made emperor, and a young man with the kingdom on his shoulders, Pheasant had to honor his father's will. And then there was the Duke—no, the Regent. He had outfoxed Pheasant and seized the kingdom from his hands.

I asked the abbess of the recent news in the palace whenever I could. She heard many messages from the incense vendors, and she also regularly went to the city to perform Buddhist rituals.

The Regent, she said, had put many ministers who sided with Pheasant to death and exiled the ministers who had expressed criticisms about the Regent's actions. He then appointed his two brothers-in-law, Han Yuan and Lai Ji, as Vice Chancellors and decreed his servant, Chu Suiliang, a brainless man I had met a few times while Emperor Taizong was ill, to be the new Chancellor. With his own men in top positions, the Regent then gave the Secretary's post to Empress Wang's uncle, Liu Shi, and a few other important positions to her family members, no doubt to placate the Empress and her family.

I could see how alone Pheasant was, surrounded by all the men who bowed to him but had their ears turned toward the Regent.

And indeed, Emperor Gaozong was not much of a ruler, the abbess said. He was not requested to attend to the daily audience where important events were discussed. The Regent sat in the Audience Hall instead and took care of all the petitions. Pheasant was ordered to select one hundred maidens from the kingdom so he could complete his household, and soon, the Inner Court was packed with

Empress Wang, Four Ladies, and many titled women, all intended to serve Pheasant.

But Emperor Gaozong showed no interest in them, the abbess said. He had grown depressed, and his temper flared easily. He also started to drink every day, sending the urgent horse rally to the northwest border to fetch rare grapes to make grape wine, wasting the kingdom's resources. During the Lantern Festival, he had ridden utterly inebriated on a float on the Heavenly Street. He fell out and broke his arm.

When I heard the news, my heart wrenched in pain. Poor Pheasant. First he had lost me, and now he had lost himself.

More tales of his decline circled the city. He had built a pool filled with wine, where he indulged himself with many of his concubines, the rumor said, and he had also created something called the Firefly Game, where his concubines, all naked, danced around to catch fireflies. Whoever caught the most insects would win a night with Pheasant, who announced her to be his favorite, and then the next night, he discarded her, making another favorite and then another.

I wept, not in sadness that Pheasant had forgotten me, but in utter commiseration for him. For I knew him well, and this pleasure-seeking man was not the Pheasant I so loved. But when your heart was broken, when all your hopes died, what else could you do to continue living, other than numbing your heart?

✦ ✦

Spring arrived, the ice thawed, and the mountain was loud with trickling springwater.

Almost three years had passed since my exile. Four Talents, who had grown sick over the years, had died in this last cold winter, and now there were only four of us from the palace remaining.

One day, I was tilling in the garden when I heard yelping from the woods where Daisy was buried. A mastiff with lumps of red fur, matted and muddied, was whimpering there. His left front leg was broken, and he was missing two claws. With the abbess's permission, I brought him to the kitchen and bathed him in warm water. After cleaning him, I tied a wooden spoon to his leg to help him heal. At night he slept with me on my pallet. He breathed noisily, his body warm and comforting as the wind wailed outside.

I named him Hope.

When he was able to walk again, Hope followed me when I hiked. I was faster, for he limped, unable to run, and I had to wait for him. When I reached the top of the mountain, I inhaled the humid air, familiar and refreshing, and told Hope of the palace and Pheasant. Hope wagged his tail, gazing at the distant land, his large eyes filled with understanding.

Sometimes we sat and watched the clouds together—some rolled up like a scroll, some tiered like a ladder, and some flowed slowly like streams of tears. We watched the sun too, which always looked distant and weak even at its height. At sunset, though, it became wicked as it cloaked the mountain with an orange veil, and then it receded to the edge of the horizon and dimmed. I felt anxious and vulnerable at the moment like that, but I hugged Hope, feeling his warmth and soft fur, and I knew I was not alone.

Once I caught my reflection when I crossed a creek with Hope. I saw how I had changed. My skin was tanned, my face was taut, my cheekbones were sharpened, and my eyes looked wider, clouded by a veil of thoughtfulness.

Meditation began to calm me. Every morning at dawn, I sat against the wall, my legs crossed, my eyes closed. I wound my thoughts together, turning the wisps of smoke into a thick rope, and I grasped the rope, stepped onto the trail it led, and glided farther and farther. What lay ahead of me? I did not know, yet I felt no fear or anxiety. I only walked, farther and farther, to a chamber glowing afar, through which the sunlight, the opaque moonlight, and the warm air poured.

But I was not free, and my thoughts burned weakly, like the tip of an incense stick, because at the end of the door, I could always see the lean, tall figure of Pheasant.

One day, the abbess returned from the city with a message. "The Emperor will conduct the third death anniversary of his father, Emperor Taizong, at the Great Maternal Grace Pagoda on the fifth month of the year."

The death anniversary ritual was usually conducted at the Altar

House inside the palace, attended by many imperial relatives and high-ranking ministers. But this year, she said, Emperor Gaozong had insisted on having it elsewhere, and the Regent had agreed to have the ritual there.

"That's Tripitaka's pagoda, isn't it?" I stopped wiping at the grease on the hemp-oil lamp, my nightly chore, which included cleaning the lamps, tables, and pillars that had turned black with soot and smoke. I remembered what Pheasant had told me before my exile: the pagoda was built to honor his late mother, and it was located at the edge of the city.

"Yes, that's the one."

That night, I could not stop thinking about the ritual. Would it be possible to see Pheasant, since he would be out of the palace? Would it not be wonderful if I saw him again?

But perhaps this was only another dream. I would not be able to leave the monastery. I had been banished, and I would be hanged if I were caught escaping. It was open defiance of the law.

Besides, Pheasant had probably forgotten about me. After all, it had been three years. He must have been accustomed to seeing his fragrant concubines dancing around him, and I was twenty-six years of age, an old woman, and with my shorn head and patched stoles, I could not compete against those painted ladies in rainbow gowns. He would not even recognize me.

But Pheasant might never hold the death ritual outside the palace again. This would be my only chance to see him, and perhaps when he saw me, he could find me a way back to the palace.

I agonized for days. I could not meditate or tend to the vegetables, and in the end, I decided to take the risk of being caught and hanged. I had to leave. I had to see Pheasant again.

I packed some food when no one was looking, smuggled out a bowl, and hid everything in a sack I sewed in secret. One night, when the moon was high, I slipped out of the room where I slept. I wanted to say good-bye to the abbess, to whom I had grown attached. She had grown fond of me too, and during cold nights in winter, she often called me to her pallet, sharing with me her warming stove. But I decided not to tell her. If I were caught, it would be better if she did not know anything.

Hope stirred, scratching in his sleep. I wished I could take him with me. He was a good dog, a faithful companion. I would miss him, but it was better for him to stay there. The nuns would take care of him.

In my nun's stole, with wooden beads around my neck, a gray skullcap on my head, and a sack on my back, I closed the monastery's door and went downhill.

The mountain was silent, and the white birches shimmered like clusters of stars. The crescent moon hung above me, following me, stopping when I stopped, gliding as I sped. I traveled carefully, climbing over hills and stepping over the hard ground covered with twigs and rough rocks. The ground had hurt my feet three years ago, but now my soles had become accustomed to the roughness, and my breathing was even and unhurried. I did not know how far it was from here to Chang'an City, how many days it would take to reach there, but I did not feel discouraged. As long as I could walk, I would get there eventually.

When I reached the foot of the hill, I saw a section of high fences before me, a shack where the guards slept, and two horses in a stable.

The night wind swept my face. I stood still, holding my breath. Gripping the sack, I waited. Everything was silent—the shack, the horses, the moon, and the wind, like good, conspiring friends. Carefully, I went down the path, opened the latch that bolted the fence, and slipped through. Once the fence was behind me, I ran.

AD 652

The Third Year *of*
Emperor Gaozong's
Reign *of* Eternal Glory

SPRING

ON THE SECOND DAY OF THE FIFTH MONTH, I ARRIVED AT the Great Maternal Grace Pagoda, a five-story building with many banners in red and yellow fluttering near the eaves. The imperial ritual had not started, so security was not yet in place, for which I was glad. Once the day of the ritual came, it would be difficult to approach the building without being stopped and questioned.

It took me forty-eight days to reach the pagoda, during which I walked day and night, stopping only for a few hours of rest when I needed to. The travel was less eventful than I had expected. Since I was a nun, few people harassed me, and most were willing to provide me with food and directions when I asked.

When I knocked on the pagoda's door, a young monk in a patched saffron-colored robe answered. I bowed, telling him I was on my way to Luoyang and needed a place to stay. I had to lie to him, for my own protection. The monk nodded and told me to follow him. We crossed the central hall, where monks and devout laymen sat chanting in front of a giant statue of Buddha. All the monks wore tattered robes. Several had no shoes, and they looked gaunt and tired, like the nuns in my monastery. I lowered my head and passed them quietly, but I hoped Pheasant would bestow on the people some much-needed funds on his father's special anniversary.

The monk led me to a row of buildings behind a well, and there, I stopped. Near an ancient paulownia tree, on a porch of a low building, sat another monk. He looked serene, back erect, legs crossed, hands on kneecaps, while beacons of sunlight sifted through the blossoms of the tree and shone on his shorn head.

Tripitaka. The monk who had risked his life to seek the true words of Buddha. The monk who had predicted my future when I was five years old. He had said I would rule the kingdom that governed many men and would mother the emperors of the land but also be emperor in my own name.

I could not move. During my journey to the pagoda, I had heard many tales about him. Tripitaka, people said, had translated many precious scriptures from Sanskrit into Chinese, loosening the knots of the ancient wisdom and smoothing the wrinkles of misunderstandings over Buddha's words. I had also heard that his journey had been most fascinating. Once he traveled through a kingdom where there were no men, only women, who became pregnant by drinking the water from a special river. Another time, he passed a lair full of spider spirits and nearly died. I would have liked to ask him in person more stories about the foreign lands.

But, most of all, I wished to tell him his prediction about my destiny was wrong.

He had a pleasant, oblong face, his forehead broad like mine, and his skin was tanned and taut. I had been only five years old when I first met him, and I did not recall any of these facial features. I remembered only his eyes, bright and fierce, like twin moons glowing in the distance, but now they were closed.

I had told him we would meet again, and indeed, here we were after all these years. Would he remember me?

"Come, my child," he said. His voice was calm and steady, carrying a warm echo, like the sound of a bell calling the arrival of dawn.

I looked around to see if he was speaking to anyone else. The monk beside me nodded and gestured to me to step forward. I suddenly grew nervous. I did not know why Tripitaka called for me, and if he knew I had come for Pheasant, he might expel me. Gingerly, I knelt before him.

"I have been expecting you," Tripitaka said. His eyes remained shut.

I did not know what to make of that. Did he know I was a nun? How did he know who I was without seeing me? "Enlightened One, it is my honor to meet you here."

His face remained serene. "You have come a long way."

Perhaps he was referring to the travel plan I had told the monk earlier. "I still have a long way to go." I pressed my hands together.

"Indeed," he said. The corner of his mouth curved up, but he still did not open his eyes. "And what are you seeking, my child?"

"Enlightenment," I lied.

He opened his eyes and gazed at me. Oh, those eyes. They were just as I had remembered. So bright and fierce. They seemed to see right through me. I had once looked into Emperor Taizong's eyes, and there I had glimpsed power and supremacy that could not be defied. Tripitaka's eyes held power too, but of a different sort. They were vast, unimaginable, mysterious, like two mirrors that held the forbidden secrets of the past and the future.

I was mesmerized, but then the look in his eyes changed...and became familiar. I remembered that look. He had stared at my father like this years ago, as though he were watching a man drowning but was unable to help.

"The fire of grief shall set ablaze a thousand trees. But remember, only virtue will bear the fruit of your trees," he said.

I snapped upright. "What do you mean? What grief?"

I recalled the conversation he had with Father so long ago. "How could a woman become a ruler?" Father had asked Tripitaka.

"She must endure deaths," he had replied.

A few years after our meeting, Father had died.

Fear ran through me. I shivered. Whose death was he talking about this time?

He only sighed. "Remember, my child, virtue, not vengeance."

I stared hard at him, trying to read his face, trying to understand what virtue he meant. But I should not believe him. He had been wrong about my destiny, and he would be wrong again. I calmed myself, and taking a deep bow, I said, "I am honored to meet you, Enlightened One." And I hoped, with all my heart, that I would never see him again.

He looked as though he wanted to speak more, but he sighed and closed his eyes. The monk beside me bowed and gestured to me to follow him. We eventually came to a courtyard with two low buildings. It must have been the quarters where weary travelers lodged. I thanked the monk and sat on a mat against the wall, clearing my mind with meditation.

I had to forget Tripitaka and his words. I had to stay calm.

I would see Pheasant very soon.

✦ ✦

Five days before Pheasant's arrival, the monks grew busy. They swept the vast yard and corridors, dusted the eaves, polished the pillars, and cleaned the trash from along the road outside the pagoda. I made an excuse that I was ill and unable to travel. The monks kindly agreed to let me stay for another week.

Soon, loads of tributes were sent to the monks. Pig heads, whole goats, salted cow legs, and many barrels of oranges, apples, pears, beans, and rice, all offerings to the late Emperor's spirit. The guests would feast upon the meat after the ritual was over, but the monks would not touch it even if it had been blessed. The beans and rice, however, would be given to the pagoda as gifts.

Excited and nervous at the same time, I imagined what Pheasant might be doing every day. He would start fasting; he would purify his body; he would be on the way to the pagoda! He would bring many palace guards with him—that was for certain—and perhaps some high-ranking ministers. The Regent would come too.

I could not request a formal meeting with Pheasant. The palace eunuchs would interrogate me about my birth and the purpose of the meeting, and then they would hang me if they discovered who I truly was. Seeing Pheasant in private was the only option, but still difficult, since he would have guards surrounding him at all times. But no matter how hard it would be, I had to find an opportunity.

On the day of Pheasant's scheduled arrival, all the monks, wearing saffron-colored stoles, with wooden beads in hand, lined up at the gate, chanting and waiting for the delegation. By noon, the monks' lips were parched and their faces had turned crimson in the heat. My eyes grew sore after gazing intently at the roads all morning, and the imperial procession still did not arrive.

Tardiness was certainly an imperial family's privilege. But when the rays of the sun began to weaken, I started to wonder if Pheasant would come after all.

Then, with the ringing of a loud gong, the central yard came to life. Four guards carrying standards bearing the signs of imperial delegations rushed to the corners of the yard, and another procession of guards wearing maroon capes took their places at the north, south, east, and west sides of the yard. Another gong rang out.

My heart pounding nervously, I hid behind a door across from the entrance and peered out. A carriage with a blue roof stopped in the center of the yard, and two eunuchs ran up and pulled aside a red curtain.

I could hardly breathe. After three years, I would finally see Pheasant again. What should I say when I faced him? Should I address him as the Emperor? Should I kneel? Should I cry?

Would he remember me?

A red shoe with a curled tip stepped out. Then an enormous figure, wearing a sparkling phoenix headdress and cloaked in a voluminous white gown, strode into the yard.

The woman was tall and heavyset, with broad shoulders and hips, and her face was wide and flat, her eyes set closely. Lady Wang.

No.

Empress Wang.

My heart dropped. Of course she would come too, but with all my thoughts on Pheasant, I had forgotten about her. I had always known she was not a woman I wanted to fight with, and still, seeing her after three years, the memories haunted me. She knew Pheasant's feelings about me. She had been glad to see me exiled, and she must have hated me because I, Emperor Taizong's concubine, had seduced her husband.

If she saw me, she would certainly fly into a rage and order my death.

Tripitaka greeted the Empress, and all the monks lowered their heads and chanted. Empress Wang did not nod or reply. She passed them without a glance, walking toward the altar, where three incense pots sat before the statue of Buddha.

I should have hidden, but I could not look away. She had changed since I had last seen her. She looked pale. Her steps were unsteady, and she walked strangely, her back stooped as though she was ashamed of raising her head. She took some incense from a eunuch's hands and waved the servants away. Alone in front of the statue, she held the incense between her hands and knelt on a cushion before her. Her lips moved as she prayed silently.

I knew what she was praying for. A son. Undoubtedly. Before my exile, I had heard whispers of her being barren, for she had been married to Pheasant for almost four years without becoming pregnant. Now, after another three years, she was still childless. No son. No daughter. It was a great shame for any woman, whose chief duty was to give her husband a son who would carry the family's name, and for the Empress, it must have been a disaster. She must have been humiliated, desperate, and angry.

The Empress wiped her eyes. She was weeping. The Empress of the kingdom, kneeling before Buddha's statue, wept and begged for a child.

I wanted to sigh. This was perhaps the saddest thing that could happen to a woman like her. She had everything—the servants, the title, and the crown—but could not bear an heir. Pheasant must have been very disappointed with her barrenness.

More people filed into the yard. Some palace women, their braided hair standing up from their heads like rabbits' ears—the titled ladies—entered, followed by maids carrying trays of fruits and jugs of water. Behind them were the eunuchs, lugging chests that must have contained the Empress's personal items.

Not one face looked familiar to me. They all must have been new servants summoned to serve Pheasant and the Empress in the Inner Court. I was certain they would not know me if I told them who I was. Three years could be such a long time. One reign ended. Another began. The old players lay beneath their tombstones, new faces danced to fame, and I was only a servant of the late Emperor, the dust of a faded reign.

I shook my head. This was not the moment to be sad, and I had yet to find Pheasant. I craned my neck, watching the entrance. A guard strode forward to close the gate, Tripitaka struck his wooden block, and the monks began to chant.

I was stunned. Pheasant was not coming. After my escape, months of travel, and the monks' preparations, he was not coming.

The noise in the yard became deafening, pounding in my ears. My legs heavy, I pulled away from the door and headed toward the back of the temple. I kept walking until I could no longer hear any chanting or footsteps, and I went to the large paulownia tree. Shrouded in its tent of pale indigo blossoms, I could no longer contain myself. I buried my face in my arms and wept.

"What's the matter?" a man's voice said behind me. "Why are you crying?"

I hurried to dab my eyes, remembering where I was. I needed to leave as soon as possible, lest anyone discover my identity. "Oh, nothing at all."

A figure in a white robe stood before me. "Nothing?"

I raised my sleeve to shield my face, but as I looked up, I caught a glimpse of the man's face. The face that had become etched in my mind, the face that I had dreamed to see. I dropped my arm. "Pheasant?"

There he was, standing right in front of me, although his once-well-defined face was swollen, and his skin was pale. His chiseled jaw had lost its sharp edge, and there were layers of skin under his chin, and shadows and fine lines under his eyes. And his eyes, once beautiful, limpid, were now gloomy and heavy. He looked like a middle-aged man who had suffered a long illness and still had not recovered. My swelling happiness subsided. *Oh, Pheasant. What have you done to yourself?*

He stepped back, his jaw loosening, his eyes wide in shock. "You..." he stammered. "You...are..."

I nodded wildly, unable to keep back my tears. "Yes, it's me."

"You... It is you," he croaked. "Heavens! It is you..." Indeed, he had aged, in a way I did not expect, and his voice was scratchy, almost hollow.

A guard standing behind him coughed. "Your Majesty?"

Pheasant spun around. "Leave me. All of you!"

The guards hesitated, glancing at me, and I shrank back, hiding myself behind the tree. Finally, they turned around and left.

"Mei..." Pheasant came to me. He was trembling, but joy flooded his eyes, and it seemed he would burst into tears. He gripped my shoulders. "I thought I would never see you again."

He still loved me. My heart softened, and my eyes moistened. "I didn't think I would see you again either." Or hear his voice. Or stand in front of him. Or talk to him. I wanted to tell him how much I had missed him, how I often thought of him while I stared at the mountains as the days slowly went by.

"Oh heavens!" He pulled me into his arms and started to sob. "I will never let you leave my sight again! Never, never!"

I wanted to cry too, with joy and relief, for I could see how much he had loved me all these years, just as I had loved him.

"They didn't tell me where you went, Mei. I searched for you. I went behind the Regent's back and ordered two hundred guards to search for you. They went around the kingdom for months. They told me you were dead."

"They did?"

"I did not believe them. I told them to search again. But the Regent found out and stopped it." He closed his eyes for a moment, and when they opened, they were heavy with defeat and helplessness. "I couldn't do anything, Mei. I gave up. I was weak. I hate myself."

Standing on my toes, I reached out to dab at his face. "I'm here now," I said gently.

He smiled wanly. "I never forgot you. Do you believe it?"

"I believe you."

"Three years."

It felt like a thousand.

Gently, he brushed his hand against my cheek, my chin, my nose, and my ears. "So what is it like to be away from the palace? Do you like being a nun?"

"Sometimes," I said.

"Liar." His touch was light, his finger warm, as always. "You've lost weight."

"I hike on the mountain every day."

"Your skin is darker."

"I am often outside."

He gazed at my gray skullcap. "And your hair…"

With shame, I remembered the palace ladies' elaborate hair,

perfumed, thick, and long and how unattractive I was with my shorn scalp. I covered my head with my hands.

"Don't worry. I'm not going to steal your cap," he said.

I laughed, and he grinned too. He was himself again—handsome, youthful, and cheerful. A current of warmth coursed through me, thawing my cold memories of the monastery and dispelling the fog of despair that cloaked my heart. "I'm so happy to see you, Pheasant."

He squeezed my hand. "I will never let you leave again, I swear it. I want you to come back to the palace with me."

He sounded so natural, as though I had never been exiled. I was on the verge of tears again. Yes. I would love to return to my home and to be with him. "But it's not that simple, is it? What if the Regent finds out?" He would no doubt view my return as an open defiance. "Is he here?"

"He's coming. But I promise you, he will not know."

I turned to peer at the guards. I could see only their legs and their maroon capes waving near their feet, and with the large tree trunk between us, they could not see me either. But I was certain they must have been wondering why the Emperor would spend so much time talking to a nun.

"But your wife…"

Pheasant's face darkened, and I wondered what had happened between him and the Empress. "I saw her, Pheasant. She looked… She will not like to see me. She will tear me apart before I set foot in the palace again."

"She will not know either." He gripped my shoulders hard. His eyes were bright, and within them I saw my own refection, like a seed—radiant, hopeful—spark before me. "We'll find a way to get you back, sweet face. I promise. I will find a way."

IN THE END, PHEASANT DECIDED TO SMUGGLE ME INTO the palace.

On the second night in the pagoda, after Pheasant attended the ritual for Emperor Taizong and while the other imperial members were still dining on the blessed meal, I climbed into a chest filled with garments and returned to the palace in a carriage under the moon and stars. Once I entered the Inner Court, I was carried to the garden where Pheasant and I used to meet in secret. The garden still looked abandoned, with overgrown weeds and cobwebs in the pavilion, but a house had been swept clean for me. There was simple furniture—a table, two stools, and a bed covered with a red quilt. Apricot, a maid who had a tendency to blush and speak in a whisper, waited there for me. More servants would come to serve me, Pheasant said, but I told him one was enough.

The Empress was still in the pagoda, praying to get pregnant. I imagined how surprised and angry she would have been if she knew a concubine of the late Emperor's was living in her palace. But Pheasant was careful. He appointed two guards at the garden's gate and two eunuch servants, whom he said he could trust, to deliver food and water for me. As long as nobody knew who I was, I could live in peace in this corner of the palace.

I was fine with the arrangement. I relished every moment in the garden, strolling down the winding path covered with round pebbles and lingering in the shaded corners of the bamboo groves. When the sun was out, I sat on the warm stone stools near the pavilion and enjoyed the sunlight on my face, its rays much stronger than they had been on the mountain. I was mesmerized by the myriad of voices coming from other parts of the palace, the rhythmic songs of cicadas, the gentle sound of the lanterns swaying under the eaves, and the faint trill of the flutes from the distant halls. The music of life.

What more could I ask for? I had been given a second chance, a gift given to me by Heaven.

I spent many hours working on the flower beds. I weeded the grass, pruned dead branches, dug into the soil, and planted many asters, roses, peonies, azaleas, chrysanthemums, and orchids—anything Apricot gave me. The scent of dirt seeped into my clothes and lingered on my fingers as I went to sleep. I filled the pond with blue water lilies, added rocks around the edge, and poured carp and goldfish into the water. When the breeze sailed through the garden, bringing me the sound of trickling water and the scent of algae, I knew I had built this place, and I knew this was where I belonged.

I enjoyed Hope's company too—Pheasant, upon my request, had sent his men to the monastery to fetch Hope without telling anyone of my escape. I was so glad to see my dear companion. In the monastery, Hope's fur had tended to become matted, but in the palace, his coat was loose and fluffy, and when he ran, chasing bees and butterflies, the thick fur bounced back and forth like waves, making him look like a fierce lion. Hope seldom barked in the garden, as though he was aware of the need for secrecy. I took him with me when I strolled around the garden, I talked to him when I got dressed, and he paced around me as I worked on the flower beds.

Pheasant came to me at night, climbing over the wall into the garden as though he was still young. Together, we rode, he on a white stallion and I on a black one. The garden was not vast, but it had enough space for us to roam. We passed the groves of bamboos and birches. We hiked on the small hill at the back of the garden. We laughed. We shouted. We chased each other. And when the moon was high, when the breeze was warm, I took off his robe and then mine. We gazed at our nakedness and embraced, so naturally, as though we had never parted, as though we were two seeds sown together.

A long time ago, we had been close to each other, and we had explored each other with youthful passion and desire. We yearned for each other with the fierce passion of the sun, lured by the veiled temptation of the moon. And now we *were* each other; we were passion and desire; we were lovers bound by temptation. As the night went on, the moon our lantern, the garden our bed, we tempted each other, we let our love flow, and we drank each other, again and again.

When dawn came, we played polo. Our robes loose, our sleeves flying in the air, we chased the scarlet ball. I was not skillful, but all the same, the dawn sport was captivating. Soon, the sun rose; the warm rays brushed my moistened face. Smiling, I watched Pheasant as he struck at the ball, and it soared like a bird set free to the sky.

Sometimes Pheasant mentioned troubles near the border with the Tibetans. Their old king, Srongtsan Gampo, had died, and the new king had discarded our peace pact and ransacked many towns on our border. I asked Pheasant how serious the matter was, and he gave a heavy sigh. The Regent had dispatched the cavalry, Pheasant said, his head dropping low. Then he added that he was not requested to attend the daily audience, so he did not know the details.

I nodded in silence, but I could not forget his helpless tone and the pain in his eyes. I remembered how confident he had been the night when his father died. Pheasant would have been an extraordinary emperor if he had not been robbed of his chance to rule.

Oftentimes, Pheasant brought me gifts, baskets of sweetmeats, honeyed cakes, and dried persimmons rolled in powdered sugar, which I gave to Apricot. I used to enjoy these treats, but after living in the monastery, my tastes had changed considerably. I did not fancy meat or sweets. I did, however, crave chilled lotus roots, water chestnuts, and pickled plums.

Two months later, I told Pheasant I had a gift for him as well.

"It's about time." He put his hand on my stomach. "Do you think it is a boy or a girl?"

"Do you wish for a boy or a girl?"

He looked thoughtful. "A boy, if you don't mind the trouble."

I understood what he meant. A girl could live quietly in a walled garden, but a boy with Pheasant's blood could never live in peace, especially since we all knew the Empress was barren. Apricot, my bashful maid, had told me Pheasant had two sons. I knew of one, named Zhong, who must be at least eight years old now, borne by Rain, a court etiquette teacher during Emperor Taizong's reign. And Rain, Apricot said, had conceived again during my exile but had died in childbirth. The other son of Pheasant's was named Sujie, borne by a woman now known as the Pure Lady, one of the Four Ladies in Pheasant's Inner Court.

So if I had a son, he would join the battle of heirship whether I liked it or not. Before my exile, I would have welcomed the possibility with thrill and hope, but now I wished for nothing but a quiet and peaceful life.

"A girl then," I said.

I soon felt the first flutter inside me, the pulse of life, gentle but profound. My appetite increased. I devoured the food placed in front of me, while my body craved to breed more bountifulness of life. I also suffered moments of mystery, when tears came to me unbidden and words eluded me, no matter how hard I searched, but those moments always passed quickly.

I thought of my family. Big Sister must surely have been a mother as well, and Mother would have been happy to have a grandchild. She would have talked to me, from one mother to another, teaching me the taboos of pregnancy and tips for having a healthy child. We would have shared a mother's pain, joy, and pride. We would have laughed and cried. The thoughts warmed my heart, and I wanted to ask Pheasant to have Mother visit me. He would have given me permission, I had no doubt. But then people in the palace would have talked, and the Empress would have known someone was hiding in the garden. I could not risk being discovered.

Mother had to wait.

When winter came, I felt bloated. My hands grew larger, my fingers grew thicker, and my stomach became round. A sweet ache followed me each time as I tried to rise or when I stood for too long. When I looked at my reflection in the pond, I could see myself walk in an amusing gait, strutting, my shoulders thrown back, my stomach protruding like a well-fed duck on the way for a good swim with ducklings. I smiled. I would soon have my own duckling, and I would lead and protect like a mother duck.

My back hurting, I sat on a warm garden bench to rest. Hope leaped into my arms, and I leaned over him, stroking his fur. The red peonies and pink roses near me had lost their blossoms, but the bushes stood strong and proud. From the pond, silver carp and goldfish splashed across the shiny water. The wind blew across the garden, brushing the tops of the trees, sending the scarf on my head dancing behind me. I felt sleepy and happy.

And I prayed, every day, that tomorrow would not change. But even though I tried not to think, even though I tried to remain calm, I knew the Empress had returned to the palace months ago, and sooner or later, she would find me in the garden.

◆ ◆

I was taking a nap in my bedchamber when I heard a sharp voice coming from the garden's entrance.

"How dare you deny my entrance? Who said it was the Emperor's order? I would like to take a walk in the garden."

I leaned on my elbow, my drowsiness gone.

Finally, she had come. The Empress. She must have heard the eunuchs or the guards gossip about a mysterious guest in the garden, or she simply suspected something from Pheasant's behavior. Nothing escaped her eyes.

Apricot raced into my chamber, fear mapping her face. "My lady…"

I nodded slowly. "I will go." I turned to the side and rolled out of bed. I was seven months into my pregnancy. Simple movements like rising and getting out of bed had become rare challenges.

I covered myself with a rabbit fur coat Pheasant had given me. The Regent's voice rang in my ears. *A scandal…* He had exiled me on that account, and what would the Empress say when she saw me? She would whip me with a tongue of thorns, I was sure, but I had to face her. She would find me anyway.

I stepped into the yard outside my chamber. It had snowed last night. The air was chilly, and a thin veil of snow spread on the flower beds. Gingerly, I crossed the ice-covered trail near the pavilion. Pheasant had told me many times not to walk there, worried that I would slip.

Hope followed me, growling as if he sensed danger. I passed the stone lamps and a cinnamon tree with snow-powdered branches, heading toward the moon-shaped entrance. There, the two guards posted outside my garden scratched their heads. Standing near them were the Empress and a group of maids, craning their necks.

I stopped, growing nervous. If only I could turn around and hide in my chamber.

"Where is the Emperor?" Empress Wang pushed the guards aside and strode into the garden, her large feet crunching over the pebbles. She was wearing the ceremonial phoenix crown, even though it was a casual day. "Is he here? I would like to see what he has been doing here every night. Announce my arrival. He shall be glad to see me—" She stopped dead when she saw me.

Blood rushed to my head. For a moment, I did not know what to do. Trying to stay calm, I folded my sleeves over my stomach and bowed—it was difficult with my large belly, but I had to show my courtesy. "Greetings, Empress. You have just missed the Emperor. He was called to receive a group of foreign messengers this morning."

"Who are you?" She was thinking, or perhaps remembering. "You are... I know you. You are the late Emperor's concubine."

I could feel the curious stares from the maids behind her, and I knew my peaceful life in the garden was officially over.

"He's hiding you? You? All these nights, sneaking around? For you? But you were banished," she said, stepping closer to me, her face dark with confusion. "How did you come here? Did he summon you back? Why didn't I know this? Why didn't he tell me?"

"Empress..." I did not know what to say.

She was as tall as Pheasant, and I could barely reach her shoulder. But with her massive phoenix crown, she looked even taller, towering like a giant. I drew back despite my will, feeling like a dwarf. But I could see clearly how she had changed. Her forehead, carved with wrinkles, looked like a newly plowed field, her candleholder-like nose jutted out on her flat face like a rocky ridge, and her closely set eyes, which had been small and gloomy, seemed round and bulging, like those of a startled fish. She was still big boned and strong built, with broad shoulders and wide hips, and there was a thick herb odor around her, a sign of her effort to conceive.

She grabbed my wrist and twisted it, forcing me to look up at her face. "You!" she shouted, and her voice changed from being confused to furious. "No wonder he would not want me. No wonder he hates me. You seduced him. You took him away from me."

"No. It's not like that." I shook my head. "With your permission, Empress, I would love to explain—"

"I do not need your explanation. Seven years of marriage, he would not look at me. It's all because of you. You!" Her grip was so strong, I thought my wrist bone would shatter, and my back hurt from being forced to twist my shoulders. "You should not be here. You do not belong here."

My fur coat slipped to the ground. "Let me go—"

"Let you go? Do you know who you are? You are his father's concubine. You seduced my husband when his father was still alive, and now you are back to seduce him again. I will not allow it!"

She tightened her grip on me, and a pain shot from my wrist. "You don't understand—"

"You seduced him! What is there to understand? You seduce my husband, and now you are hiding in my house." Her voice rose higher, piercing my ears. I could not bear it.

A growl came from beside me, and Hope lunged toward the Empress. She shrieked, stepping back, and the pressure on my wrist disappeared. I panted in relief. Hope bared his teeth, ready to attack again.

"Stay still." I bent over, pulling him back clumsily. I was still hurting from her grip, and it took me a while to make Hope sit. When I faced the Empress again, she was staring at my stomach.

Instinctively, I put my hands on my belly, worried she would strike again.

But she did not move, her mouth open, her eyes frozen. Then she turned around and staggered through the moon-shaped entrance, her maids following.

Apricot laid the coat over my shoulders and tied the strings under my chin, but I was still cold. And I was deeply concerned. I had surprised the Empress with my presence and wounded her, no doubt, with my swelling stomach, but I had not intended for it to be this way. I did not wish to threaten her, mock her, or take Pheasant away from her. But she certainly would not believe me, and she would not let me rest in peace.

Suddenly, I felt sad.

I no longer desired the crown. That kind of power was a distant dream to me. I wished only for a corner of peace, a pocket of happiness, with Pheasant and my child, in this palace. Nothing more.

But I did not think it was possible now.

6

"I WILL STAY HERE TOMORROW." PHEASANT STOOD BESIDE his horse, holding a polo mallet. Usually, he was eager to mount his horse and play polo. Not today. The guards had told him of the Empress's visit, and he had rushed to her quarters and ordered her to leave me alone. He was still angry, frowning, swinging his mallet.

"I don't know." I picked up a polo ball from a bench beside me. Pheasant was worried about me, but there was nothing he could do. "You can't stay here with me every day."

"She will not leave you alone," Pheasant said. "She will come back and give you a difficult time."

Hope sniffed at the ball in my hand, excited. I tossed it away, and he chased it, yelping. "I have Hope, and he will protect me," I said. "But I think the Empress has changed a great deal." Her appearance, of course, but also her demeanor, changing so swiftly. Had she been like that three years ago? I could not be sure.

"Has she?" Pheasant shrugged.

"Have you summoned her on full-moon nights these past years?" Pheasant was supposed to follow the same bedding schedule as Emperor Taizong had. Since my return to the palace, however, Pheasant had stopped summoning many ladies. He still had to see the Empress, so she would not grow suspicious that he was hiding me.

"I think so. I do not remember." Pheasant shrugged. "I drank a lot those nights. But now that she knows you're here, I do not need to summon her anymore."

"She will not like that." Hope returned with the ball in his mouth and placed it near Pheasant's feet. Raising his head toward me, he wagged his tail. I smiled, scratching his head. I was proud of him.

"Well, she's barren. Everyone says so. There is nothing I can do."

"But—"

Pheasant positioned himself in front of the ball. "Sweet face, you know Empress Wang and I have nothing in common. When I married her seven years ago, it was only to obey Father. My mother would not have liked her, to tell you the truth. But Lady Wang was already very difficult to talk to. I avoided her whenever I could... She is not the type of girl I like... She is different... She is a cold, cold woman." He struck the ball. "And cruel."

I watched the ball flying through the air. Hope, yelping in excitement, chased it again. "Cruel? Did anything happen between you and the Empress while I was exiled? What did she do?"

"She did many awful things."

"Such as?"

"Two years ago, when Rain was in labor, she refused to summon a midwife for her. That's why she died."

Pheasant was talking about the other child Rain had conceived, I realized, but I had not known the Empress had played a role in Rain's death. Of course Pheasant would not forgive her for that. "What else did the Empress do?"

"Was that not enough? Only a cruel woman would sit outside a chamber, listening to a woman in labor groaning for two nights. Yes, that was precisely what she did. She sat and did nothing. She did not allow a midwife or a servant to help Rain, and she let her suffer. When a eunuch tried to inform me, she threatened to beat him." Pheasant knocked his mallet on the ground. "Rain could have had another child, but instead, she bled to death, and the child died with her."

A chill ran through me, and I put my hand on my stomach. I could not bear it if anything happened to my child.

"I do not wish to have a wife like her."

"I know, but—"

"She is also unkind to the other ladies. Each time I summoned a lady, she would torment her." He straightened. "I will not allow her to torment you, Mei. I will add more guards."

I looked at the entrance to the garden. The guards were nowhere to be seen, but I knew even if Pheasant put an army there, it would not help. To them, I was only an exiled concubine who had seduced the Emperor. None of them would offer their loyalty to me, and none of them would protect me against the Empress. I thought of Sun Tzu and *The Art of War*, the book I had studied so dutifully as a child. I wished the master had good advice for me. But I had forgotten most lines, and I did not have a copy of the book.

"Or I could move you to a different location, if you like."

I sighed. That would not help either. The whole court must have heard of me hiding in the garden by now—the Empress would certainly make sure of that—and no matter where Pheasant kept me, they would find me. "I will not hide from her, if that is what you are suggesting."

He looked around. "You are right. You are not hiding anymore. Next week, on the first day of the first moon, we will have a feast in your name, and you will meet all the women in the palace. Officially."

I was alarmed. "Officially?"

He nodded. "I have made up my mind. I will have you sit by my side. I shall declare you are mine and let all the gossip cease once and for all."

His words brought me memories of the time when I had competed for the honor of sitting beside his father against the conniving Jewel, who had risen to prominence only to die in disgrace. It would bring me so much joy if I sat next to Pheasant, for it to be known I was his and his alone, but the thought also troubled me.

I turned around to look for Hope, who was still searching for the ball in the woods behind the pond. "I don't know. I don't think it's a good idea."

I was not strong enough—I had no ally or protection, save for Pheasant, and once the Regent heard of my return, Pheasant would face pressure from all sides. The Regent was too powerful, with those high-ranking ministers serving him.

"I thought you said you did not wish to hide from her."

"I do not." I turned my head away so he would not see how

worried I was. What would the Regent do to me when he discovered I had returned? "I just don't think this is the time."

"But—"

"No feast in my name," I said firmly. "And don't look at me like that."

Pheasant took a deep breath, put down his mallet, and came closer to stroke my stomach. "He's my son."

He always said that, although I hoped for a girl. "You don't know that."

"But you know you must be part of the palace, don't you?"

A movement fluttered inside my stomach, as though the infant was responding to Pheasant's question. I covered his hand with mine. It was true. I was happy living in this garden, but my child, be it a boy or a girl, could not stay hidden forever. What would I do to protect him when the Empress tried to hurt him?

I needed to build a wall of protection for my child, even though I was not ready to stand before the Empress. And that meant Pheasant had to be my shield and armor.

I raised my head. "You mentioned the war against the Tibetans earlier. Did our cavalry win, Pheasant?"

He sighed. "The Tibetans routed us. Again. It's getting worse at the border. You know, Mei, had my father been alive, we would not have faced such shame, and now everyone in the kingdom blames me, cursing my impotence." He laughed dryly. "Even though I have done nothing. Absolutely nothing."

I felt his pain. "What is the Regent's plan?"

"He sent another twenty thousand men to fight, but the situation does not look promising." Pheasant picked up his mallet again. "The governor at the border has abandoned his post and fled. My uncle put his entire family to death. Now the ministers are frightened, and people are fleeing. They are worried the Tibetans will soon break through the border and attack Chang'an."

I frowned. The situation was worse than what I had imagined. "Perhaps you should attend the audiences, Pheasant." He turned to me in surprise, and I continued. "I know the Regent did not request your attendance, but he cannot stop you if you decide to go."

"I went there a few times, before your return." Pheasant looked down at his mallet. "I was…not helpful, and anyway, after I heard the news of your death, I did not see the point."

I put my hand on his arm. "You do see the point now, don't you? And when you go to the Audience Hall tomorrow, you will summon the General and send him to fight the Tibetans."

The General was still in exile, but his name was too great for the others to forget, and I was certain if he led the army, he would crush the Tibetans. But I had another motive for wanting him to return.

When the General succeeded in defeating the Tibetans and returned to the court, he would owe Pheasant his eternal loyalty, and with the General behind him, Pheasant would no longer remain powerless.

"Summon the General from his exile?" Pheasant looked surprised. "It's not possible."

The law forbade an exiled man to be recalled. But then, the Emperor made the laws. "You must make it happen."

"Why do you think the Regent will listen to me?"

"Because he does not have a better man to send." Twenty thousand cavalry, and still the governor had fled. When the General had attacked Koguryo six years before, he'd led five hundred men, fought against fifty thousand in the Koguryo army, stomped them all, and left ten forts as rubble. He was a legend on the battlefield, and I was certain he could repeat his feat if he were given a chance. "Mention his name when you go to the Audience Hall tomorrow, and see what the ministers think."

Pheasant shook his head. "They will not agree. And my uncle—"

"Would they rather let the Tibetans attack Chang'an?" I looked into Pheasant's eyes. "This is your chance, Pheasant. Remember what you wished for the kingdom? A long time ago? Before your father died? Remember Tripitaka's prediction that a great era, more splendid than any emperor's reign, is coming?"

"I shall never forget."

I squeezed his arm. "Then take what belongs to you, Pheasant. Take it when you have a chance."

He stared at the ground, and I could see the deep longing in his eyes—the longing to rule, and rule alone. "You don't think it's too late?"

"Too late? Of course not. You're still young. You have many years ahead of you."

"But my uncle... You know I bear him no ill wishes... He is only obeying my father's will..."

His voice, thin and quiet, hung around me like the delicate web the silkworms spun, but underneath it, I could also hear pain, dangling like a weighty insect struggling to survive. Pheasant, I realized, still paid great respect to his uncle. "You do wish to be the emperor, the real emperor, don't you?"

Nodding slowly, he looked sad. "Yes. I do. How could I not? It's my family's dynasty. My mother would love to see me rule. My father wanted me to rule too. He taught me so, even though he changed his mind before he died. Yes, it would be glorious if my dream could come true. Do you know that when my father was my age, he had already ruled the kingdom for five years on his own?"

For the first time since my return to the court, I heard bitterness in his voice, and I realized how much he had wanted to become a true emperor. I was certain we must gain the General's help to restore Pheasant's power in the court. It was not only for me, but for him as well. "You will rule, Pheasant, and remember—the Regent will not live forever."

He smiled a brilliant smile. "I shall attend the audiences from now on. And I shall fight to summon the General." He squeezed my hand. "I'm happy you are here."

I was glad too, and somehow I believed he would succeed. Perhaps soon, I would no longer need to fear the Empress.

Hope yelped joyously from near the pond and raced toward me with the ball in his mouth.

"He's a good dog," Pheasant said, watching Hope nuzzling against me. "I'll trade you for a horse."

"Can't do it." I smiled, holding Hope close to me. "He protects me. He almost bit the Empress the other day."

"Almost? He needs to do better next time."

I laughed. Pheasant was so transparent. His love and hate dwelled within him like fire and water. "I used to think horses were the most precious animals, but now, I'm not so sure."

"How fast you've changed your heart!"

I laughed again, but I would not argue with him. I would always love Hope more than any horses. Pheasant would not understand. He had a weakness for horses, especially fine breeds, the type whose sweat turned red like blood.

"But I still think you need someone who can stay with you in case she comes back," Pheasant said.

"To protect me?" It would not be easy to find someone who would be loyal to me and also powerful enough to stop the Empress if she tried to attack me.

"A companion, Mei. Let me think…"

"Pheasant—"

He coughed. "I shall ask my sister to stay with you."

I frowned. I would not expect a princess to be a congenial companion—many were arrogant, spoiled, and often looked down on concubines. I had encountered a few while I nursed Emperor Taizong, and they rarely glanced at me or spoke to me. "Which one?"

Pheasant had four sisters and seventeen half sisters. When Emperor Taizong was alive, they had lived with their mothers and rarely participated in the palace affairs. Now most of them were either married or lived in their own quarters in seclusion.

"Gaoyang."

It meant "high sun," an unusual name for a girl. "Is she one of your half sisters?"

Pheasant nodded. "She is a quirky one. I think you two will get along rather well. She studied under a monk at a young age and acquired some unique skills. She annoys many people in the palace, but she does things her own way. She is married now."

So this princess was not only overbearing, but also religious. I had no desire to spend my days chanting sutra with her or watching her strut around in the garden all day. "I told you, Pheasant. I am fine by myself."

He cocked his head, smiling.

"What?"

"When did you become so stubborn?"

I could never argue with him when he smiled at me like that. I sighed. "Fine, send the princess over."

"Let me arrange for her to visit next week. But meanwhile"—he walked over to his horse and swung his leg over—"stay out of trouble."

✦ ✦

Pheasant went to the Audience Hall early each morning for the next few days, trying to convince the Regent and the other ministers to summon the General back from exile and send him to fight the Tibetans. His request was immediately denied, but Pheasant persisted, and as the court continued to receive urgent horse-relayed messages of defeat, the Regent finally agreed to give the General a chance.

Overjoyed, Pheasant decided to meet the General in a border town, intending to encourage him and provide him with moral support. Pheasant promised he would return to the palace in four weeks, with a victorious General.

I was pleased to hear of our plan's success, and I hoped Pheasant's trip to the border would herald the beginning of his true reign of the kingdom.

Before he left, Pheasant gave me a gift he had promised years ago: a copy of Sun Tzu's *The Art of War*. I treasured it and hid the scroll under my pillow. I would need it someday. And I prayed Pheasant would return as soon as possible, for I was worried about the Empress, who would surely seize the opportunity to get rid of me.

7

LOUD NOISES ERUPTED AT THE GARDEN'S ENTRANCE.

The Empress had returned—not by herself, but with an army of palace guards. They were hammering and banging on the gates with something heavy.

I sat on the edge of the bed and listened. I would have liked to stand by the door and watch what they were doing, but my stomach was large, and I grew tired easily if I stood for too long. And I was nervous. What would the Empress do to me? She would not hold back, knowing Pheasant was not there to protect me.

The gates fell to the ground with a crash, and the guards' shouts became louder. Apricot raced into my chamber, her face white with fear.

I wanted to tell her not to be afraid, but I was too nervous to speak. Trying to stay calm, I put on my fur coat and tied a red scarf around my head. My hair had grown some over the past seven months, but it was still too short to style attractively.

With Apricot wringing her hands on my left and Hope trotting on my right, I walked to the entrance. The Empress, standing near the pavilion with a group of men and women, was gesturing at something. At my approach, she spun around and stomped toward me. Her body was wide like a giant kite spreading its wings in the sky. Her hair was pulled tightly behind her ears, and perched on her head was the same ceremonial phoenix crown, which she seemed to be obsessed with. I wondered if she went to sleep wearing it too.

Four ladies trailed behind her. From the way they carried

themselves, I could tell they were the new Four Ladies, the second-degree women, lower only than the Empress. The one on the left wore a white gown woven with golden threads, and the other three wore identical rose-pink brocade gowns. The three ladies had their arms intertwined, and their hair, all long and sleek, was twisted neatly in a pile on top of their heads like a conch. Their cheeks red, their beauty marks perfect, they looked so coy and attractive, like three pretty partridges with pink feathers.

I envied their beauty. I wished I still had long hair, but I had only the red silk scarf, and the wind was blowing it across my face. I tucked it behind my ears, worried the knot would loosen and the scarf would fall. If the ladies saw my short hair, I would become the laughingstock of the entire palace.

"*Zao an*, Empress." Good morning. I stopped a few paces away from her and bowed, trying to keep calm. What was her plan? Humiliate me? Threaten me?

"I have decided to make this garden public," Empress Wang said, towering over the women and guards behind her. "This garden shall be open to all the ladies, regardless of their ranks. I shall also add a new wing and expand this place. The gardeners will come tomorrow, and the pond workers and the painters too. Now, I would like to clean up everything that does not belong here. That means you must leave."

I stood erect. "I am afraid I can't, Empress."

"Do you dare to defy me?"

Her large shadow slid across the ground, covering my feet and then my face.

"Empress." I kept my voice even. "I do not intend to defy anyone. It is the Emperor's order I stay in this garden."

"The Emperor? He does not give orders in the Inner Court."

I did not like her tone or the certainty of her words. "Perhaps you should speak to him."

There was a pause, and the Empress turned to face the ladies behind her. "Ladies, perhaps you have wondered why I brought you all here. Have you wondered who this woman is? Let me inform you. She is a harlot of the late Emperor. The Regent exiled her to a monastery to repent three years ago, but she snuck back to the palace and seduced the Emperor! And now, as the Empress of the kingdom, I must do my duty and expel her."

The ladies lowered their heads, pressing closer to one another, and the Empress continued, her voice higher. "Do you hear me? This woman has slept with the father, and now she's sleeping with the son! A harlot, she is! With no sense of moral decency and virtue."

The maids near the Four Ladies were covering their mouths, whispering among one another. The servants and guards stared at me, their mouths agape, and Apricot's head drooped so low it seemed she could have buried herself underground. I wanted to cover my face, run to my chamber, and lock myself inside. But I forced myself to stand erect. Ten years ago, she would have gotten her wish, but I was stronger now.

"Answer me, harlot. Are you not ashamed?"

I raised my head to look into her eyes. Yes, I had tried to share Pheasant's father's bed, but I had not succeeded. All the same, it was my past and my shame to bear. "Empress, allow me to clarify: I did not seduce your husband."

"You can't deny it, harlot!"

Her voice was so shrill that I wanted to cover my ears, and the baby kicked inside me, so hard I almost doubled over. She was frightened by the Empress's loud voice. "I shall not argue with you, Empress. If you have finished what you have come to say, then I bid you a good day. I would like to rest."

"Stop! You will not walk away from me." She walked closer to me, her steps unsteady. "I will leave you…" she started, then her voice unexpectedly dropped to a murmur, so low I could barely hear her. "I will leave you alone…if you promise not to bed the Emperor."

I did not know what to say. This was such a childish request; I never would have expected to hear it from her.

"Yes. You promise me…promise me you will give him back to me." Her voice quavered, and her lips trembled as though every word was agony to her. "If he favors me, if he gives me a son, I will leave you alone."

She looked tearful, and I felt sorry for her. But she was barren. How could I help her? "I'm sorry, Empress. I'm afraid I can't make any promises."

Her broad face reddened, and her candlestick-like nose thrust to the sky. "Then I order you to leave. Get out! Out of the garden. Now!"

She was possessed with a burst of frightening violence again. I took a step back. "I told you, Empress. I can't do that."

She laughed shrilly. "How dare you disobey me? No one disobeys me, harlot. No one. If I say you must get out of the garden, then you must get out of the garden. If I say you will be punished, then you will be punished. Guards!" The men behind her answered, and she pointed at me. "Strike her!"

I could not believe what she just ordered, but the men lunged toward me, wielding thick rods. My throat tightening, I looked around. The women dropped their heads quickly and stepped back. Beside me, Apricot whimpered, her hands flying to her mouth. The guards Pheasant had ordered to protect me were nowhere to be seen.

Fear crept down my spine. But it would be futile to flee. I would not be able to outrun them.

A familiar growl rose beside me, and Hope leaped, baring his sharp teeth. I had yet to breathe out in relief when one of the guards struck at him with his club. But my brave Hope jumped aside and attacked the man's leg. The man fell, shouting in pain, and Hope spun around to face five more men before him. Circling them, he lunged and bit a guard's shoulder, pushing him to the ground. The other four guards hesitated, and Hope circled back to my side. Before I could touch him, a guard dove toward him and clobbered his bad leg. Yelping, Hope fell on the ground as rods rained on him.

I cried out. "Stop! Stop it!"

They did not listen, and my poor Hope writhed on the ground.

"Stop it." I threw myself in front of Hope, my arms outstretched. "Do not touch him."

"Get her!" the Empress shouted.

The men loomed over me, and my heart pounded. Rising to my feet, I tried to keep calm. "You cannot harm me. I am bearing the Emperor's seed. If you harm me, if you dare lay a finger on me, I will have you all thrown in a dungeon."

They hesitated, heads turning to the Empress.

She laughed. "Too late, harlot. I already gave you a chance. Strike her!"

They inched closer, and Hope yelped furiously. Perspiration dampened my armpits. She intended to make me lose my child!

A blow fell on my back. I staggered forward, and a guard kicked my stomach. Desperate, I bent over, my arms around my belly, but another guard kicked my knee, and I dropped to the ground.

"No!" Apricot screamed, her voice filled with warning.

I raised my head, the scarf flying before me, blocking my vision, but still I could see it clearly—a rod, raised high above my head. So thick and hard, it could break my arm, beat me into unconsciousness, or, worst of all, make me lose my child. I could not move.

Suddenly, a wave of indigo swirled before me. It caught the rod and hurled it into the air. As though it had eyes and hands of its own, the indigo cloth struck at the man in front of me, who fell backward, and slapped another on my right, who cried out, and then it wound around another man on my left, wrapping him up and throwing him aside, until finally, all the guards who had stood before me rolled on the ground and groaned.

Then the indigo-colored cloth began to spin, fast at first, and then slowed down, unraveling like a cocoon spooling, revealing a slim girl, one arm above her head, one arm near her hips, long sleeves draped beside her like curtains.

I tucked the scarf behind my ear, staring at her in shock. She had disarmed the guards with her long, indigo sleeves. She had saved me.

"Leave, Empress Wang," the girl said. She was even shorter than me and looked like a child in front of the tall Empress, but she stood straight and confident, as though she had done this many times before.

"How dare you come here?" the Empress said, her face hard like a stone.

The girl swept her sleeves behind her and raised her chin. "You do not ask me questions, Empress Wang. Now, leave. I do not like to repeat myself."

Slowly, the Empress moved aside. "I shall not forget this."

"I am counting on it," the girl said. Her voice was steady, and she stared at the Empress contemptuously, as if she was accustomed to having her words obeyed.

The Empress turned around and hurried out of the garden without a word. The Four Ladies glanced at me and turned to follow her, and the guards picked up their weapons and scurried away as well.

Apricot helped me stand. "Are you all right, my lady?" She brushed dirt off my shoulders.

She had been crying, and her hands were cold. Poor child. She was so young, not yet fifteen, and she must have been so frightened, seeing me beaten and yet unable to help. "I am fine," I said. "I am sorry the Empress has frightened you."

"No... My lady... I..." Apricot bit her lip. "I...I should have helped you. Please don't...punish me, my lady."

I shook my head. "Of course I won't punish you, Apricot. I'm just happy you are not hurt. They would have beaten you too if you tried to help." Apricot dabbed her eyes, looking relieved, and I turned to the girl in indigo. "You saved me. Now I owe you."

She was young, perhaps seventeen or eighteen, thin like a leaf, her shoulders small and her chest flat. With her long sleeves draping to the ground, she looked like a dancing sprite from the famous mural *Flying to Heaven*. Her hair, long and unadorned, was braided simply and fell in front of her chest, unlike the ladies in the Inner Court, who piled their hair high on their heads. She exuded a type of simple and soothing appeal that could never be found on the palace women, who were accustomed to powder and rouge.

"No. You owe Pheasant."

I stared at her. "You are Princess Gaoyang?"

Now I understood what Pheasant had said. She had learned skills from a monk...of course. There were many monks who practiced martial arts to strengthen their bodies.

"That's me," she said, grinning, showing two deep dimples, her eyes black like a pair of large onyx.

"I thought Pheasant said you were coming next week."

She raised her chin. "Do you think Pheasant can tell me what to do?"

There was a certain impish willfulness about her, but I liked it. I had never met a girl like her. "Of course not. That would be most outrageous."

She laughed, not bothering to cover her mouth, and her voice was clear and joyous, like a bell tinkling under a cloudless sky. "When

Pheasant told me about you, I did not believe him, but now I can see he was right after all."

"About what?"

She did not answer. Instead, she twirled around and flew toward the pavilion. When she reached it, she climbed onto the roof in the blink of an eye. "I'll be watching over you. From here."

"All right." I nodded, holding on to a stone bench to steady myself. No wonder Pheasant had said people in the palace were annoyed by her. No one liked to have a princess perched on their roofs, listening to their secret talks at night. But she was here to protect me, and I was glad.

Hope whimpered, and I went to him. "Come on, boy, good boy. Let me look at you." I picked up his paw. He lay there limply, and he was bleeding. Poor Hope.

"I will ask the physicians for some treatments, my lady," Apricot said. She was biting her lip again, but her face looked calmer, and her eyes were filled with concern.

"Yes. Do it, Apricot. Do it now."

I stroked Hope, soothing him while Apricot went to the physicians. When Hope quieted, I straightened. Something tugged the inside of my stomach, and a pain spread. I breathed hard, feeling dizzy. I hoped the beating had not harmed my baby. I hoped Pheasant would return soon.

The wind blew the end of the scarf across my face, covering my eyes. For a moment, everything in the garden—the trees with bare branches, the frost-covered pavilion, the black pond, even the stone lanterns—was shrouded in red.

The Third Year *of*

Emperor Gaozong's

Reign *of* Eternal Glory

LATE WINTER

FOUR DAYS LATER, A MESSAGE CAME FROM PHEASANT.
Everything was going well. He had met the General, who appeared to be
as strong as before, and now they were planning a surprise attack on the
Tibetans. Very soon, he said, he should return to the palace victorious.

I tucked the message into my girdle. I hoped he would return as
soon as possible, for I did not feel well these days, and the Empress had
sent her word again, asking me to give Pheasant back to her. When I
sighed and waved off her servant, she continued to harass me.

Every morning, I spotted furtive heads poking out above the
garden wall and figures flitting across the entrance, since the gates still
lay where they had fallen. They watched me as I meditated in the corridor, and near dusk, when I went out for a stroll in the garden, those
heads would withdraw, and I would hear the footfalls of the Empress's
spies, running around to report my activities.

Hope continued to guard me, warning me of intruders by barking
fiercely, as he was too injured to run after them. My new protector,
Princess Gaoyang, gave me a better sense of security. She collected
pebbles and threw them from the top of the pavilion when she spotted anyone lurking. Each time a pebble flew over the wall, a sharp
cry would follow. Her aim was impeccable, but still, at this rate, our
garden would soon need a replenishment of rocks.

"I owe you my life and my child's," I said to the princess that
morning after I received Pheasant's message. "How can I repay you,
gongzhu?" *Princess.* I addressed her formally.

"Don't call me that." She lay on the pavilion's rooftop, her legs crossed, her hands beneath her head, and her long sleeves draping down over the roof.

"Well, how else would you like me to address you?"

"Call me Gaoyang."

Only the Emperor and the princess's mother had the right to address her by her given name. I was surprised she honored me so. "I shall be happy to oblige, but only when we are alone." I paused. "It's a good name."

The High Sun. It fitted her, as she did seem to possess the quality of the sun at noon, brilliant and fierce. And, like her name, she was unique. She never sat still like the palace ladies; instead, she leaped and flew among the trees. She also had a penchant for the outdoor life, refusing to enter my chamber, even though the weather had grown cold. She dined only on bland grains and drank water, claiming she was already breaching the code of a true swordsman, who drank only the wind and fed on the sun.

She fascinated me, and I learned more about her. Her mother had been one of Emperor Taizong's third-degree Ladies-in-Waiting, whom I had remembered as a quiet lady of pale complexion. The lady was said to be a devout Buddhist who spent much time in a temple near the Altar House. Like the kind Noble Lady who had befriended me, Gaoyang's mother had died on the terrible night Taizi and Prince Yo revolted seven years before.

The princess was a peculiar child, whose acrobatic skill became known when she was very young. No one paid attention to her, being a child of a third-degree Lady-in-Waiting, and one day when she flipped off a roof to appear before Emperor Taizong, the Emperor almost fainted in fright. Angry, he sent her to live with a monk named Biji as punishment for her insolence. The monk Biji first taught her the movements of *taiji*, which she learned without difficulty, and then he taught her *qigong*, to both utilize the smooth movement of *taiji* and her excessive energy. She proved to be an excellent student who could leap to unusual heights and shatter a stack of bricks with the thin blade of her hand. When she turned fourteen, during the year Pheasant was named the heir of the kingdom, the Emperor married her to Secretary

Fang's son, who was named Fang Yi'ai. They had been married for four years, and she had no children.

I liked the princess. I liked her thin, sprite-like figure, her unconventional skills, her complete disregard of etiquette and protocols, and even her imperious attitude. Only a princess could get away with that. Above all, I was glad for her protection.

✦ ✦

It had been almost four weeks since Pheasant left the palace. One morning, I received another message from him.

"Gaoyang!" I shouted, running to the pavilion. "The General has defeated the Tibetans! They are coming home!"

The air was chilly but fresh in the garden. It had rained the night before. Some clear water drops were frozen, tucked between the tree's branches like translucent pearls, and there were icicles hanging under the eaves of the pavilion, standing still like strips of silver.

"When?" She was doing her regular exercise, which was a rather daunting routine to me. First she scurried up the large trunk of an old pine tree, then, her feet kicking against a thick branch, she somersaulted through the air before landing on the ground.

"He did not say. Perhaps he is already on the way back to the palace," I said, smiling. Because they had been victorious, the Regent could not object when Pheasant ordered the end of the General's exile, and once the General returned to the palace, he would be valuable support for Pheasant.

A shower of crystals spread in the air as the princess kicked a branch. "Good. Then I can leave. I need to visit my teacher."

"The monk?"

She vaulted over the top of the trees. "Yes."

I turned, my gaze following her slight figure. I was disappointed. I had hoped she would stay in the garden with me. "Will you come for visits when the baby is born?"

She landed lightly on the ground. She was not even panting, and I envied her agility. Now into my eighth month of pregnancy, I felt as limber as a yellow ox.

"Now you're asking too much," she said, but her dimples deepened in delight.

I smiled too. "Why are you helping me, Gaoyang?"

"Why not?" she answered in her imperious manner.

"Well, I can see you are not fond of the ladies in the court."

"Ah, but you're different from them. Less annoying."

I laughed. "Is that a compliment?"

"It is. But you need not worry." She somersaulted and landed on a stone lamp on one foot, her arms stretching out like the wings of a bird. "If you really do need me, I can stay here for a few more days." Then she folded her hands together above her head and closed her eyes.

She was meditating, while standing on a stone lamp. I was awed. "I meditate too. I learned it when I was in the monastery."

"Do you miss your nun's life?"

I shook my head. "I simply enjoy the silence of meditation."

An abrupt movement wrenched through my stomach. I groaned and sat on a stone bench to ease the pain. Ever since the Empress's men had beaten me, the infant had been quite active, and sometimes when she kicked, she gave me a sharp pain and dizzy spells that would stay with me for hours.

"You look pale. You should go inside." Gaoyang leaped off the lamp. She did not look like she was going to meditate after all.

"I'm fine." I wished the physicians could visit me, but the Empress had forbidden them to tend to me.

"You don't look fine."

"It's nothing." I inhaled and exhaled deeply until the spell subsided. "I've wanted to ask you, what happened between you and the Empress? She didn't seem to like you."

"Nothing, really. She simply dislikes me because Pheasant allows me to visit him freely. She says Pheasant spoils me." Gaoyang shrugged. "She is also insane."

"Do you mean she has an unpredictable temper?" I had asked Apricot about the Empress, and Apricot had gathered information from around the palace for me. The Empress was indeed hard to fathom, people said. Sometimes the Empress would scream, throwing things and beating her maids, frightening all those who served her—but at other times she would refuse to eat or get dressed, and with her hands around her knees, she would sit on the floor and rock back and forth, begging for people's forgiveness and weeping in her chamber all day. "They said she changes so swiftly, it is as though she is two different women. I wonder why."

"Isn't that obvious?" Gaoyang pulled her foot to her head from behind her back, her body arching gracefully. She was so limber. "She's barren. She's desperate. People mock her behind her back, saying she is a hen that can't lay an egg."

"I see." I nodded, remembering the Empress had asked me to help her conceive. She had surprised me too with her tearful look, and I wondered how she believed I could help her. "But don't you think it's odd that she'll behave so dramatically?"

"That's because there is a sick dog living inside her," Gaoyang said, releasing her foot.

That reminded me of Hope. I had not seen him this morning. "Where is Hope?"

I looked around the garden, searching for him. He had recovered splendidly under Apricot's care. Now he patrolled the garden for any possible intruders, and when he saw the Empress's spies, he growled and pounced, frightening them. I was very proud when he came to me, dragging one of the Empress's spies one day. "Gaoyang, have you seen Hope today?"

"Pheasant said to watch over you, not your dog." Gaoyang flipped in the air and landed on the ground.

"Where is Apricot? Perhaps she has seen him."

"She is getting us our meal." The Empress had forbidden the eunuchs to deliver food to my garden, so Apricot had to go to the kitchen to fetch us meals. "Hope might have gone with her. Where are you going, Mei? Wait! Watch out for the ice."

I stopped, took her hand, and crossed the ice-covered path. The surface was quite slippery, and I had to be careful where I stepped. "I'm going to find Hope. Perhaps he is on the other side of the pond."

We searched the flower beds, around the pond, and even in the woods behind it, but we could not find him.

When Apricot returned, she did not know Hope's whereabouts either. "I thought he was here."

For the whole afternoon, we searched the garden. There were no traces of Hope. We searched farther down the pond, the bushes, and the corners near the bamboo grove. Princess Gaoyang even leaped onto the roof and scanned the whole garden. My dog was nowhere in sight.

I thought of how cruelly the Empress's guards had beaten Hope, and I felt sick. She had stolen him, I was sure of it. When Apricot urged me to sit at the table, I stared at the trays that contained my favorite foods: chilled mushrooms, chunks of fried bean curd, and sweet red beans. I had no appetite, and I could not lift my hand.

"Hope is probably just lost in the woods, my lady," Apricot said, standing beside me. "He'll come back, right? Princess?"

Gaoyang, who had followed us inside, nodded.

I shook my head. "I do not think he is lost."

Apricot pushed the trays closer to me. "But it's almost supper, my lady. You haven't eaten anything today. The baby needs food. Please try something. Would you like to have some soup?"

"Leave it here, Apricot. I will eat later." Pain rose from my abdomen again. I closed my eyes and waited for it to pass.

"Here. Eat this." Gaoyang placed a large soup pot with a lid in front of me. "It's your favorite soup, isn't it? Eat some, and then you can get some rest."

I raised my head. "She is angry with me, Gaoyang. She wanted to punish me, so she took Hope. She is going to chain him up, beat him, and hurt him. Oh, my poor dog—"

"We'll get him back, you and I," Princess Gaoyang said. Before I could say another word, she continued, "We will go to her chamber and ask for your dog."

"She will not just hand Hope over to us." I remembered, a long time ago, I had gone to Jewel's chamber asking her to return some crowns she had stolen in order to blackmail me, and I had learned that you could not reason with women hungry for power.

"I shall ask kindly."

"She will not listen."

Gaoyang spread her long sleeves to the floor, reminding me of how she had disarmed the guards so easily. "Then I shall see what I can do."

Her face grew sober, and my heart was filled with hope. Gaoyang would help me. If she could subdue a group of guards, certainly she could make Empress Wang return my dog.

"Let's go now, Gaoyang."

"First, you should eat. Apricot is right," she said, and put a spoon in my hand. "You must take care of your baby. Once you have energy and are ready to fight, then we will go."

I sighed. It sounded like a reasonable plan. When I felt stronger, I would go to the Empress. There would be another battle with her. But I was not alone. With Gaoyang's help, the Empress would lose. She would have no choice but to give back my Hope.

I lifted the soup pot's lid, and a delicious aroma filled my nose. The broth was clear, and I could see the bamboo shoots, mushrooms, wood ears, and the yellow yolks of two hardboiled eggs. I was suddenly ravenous. I dipped the spoon into the pot and scooped a spoonful of broth. It tasted delicious. I took another spoonful. Near the eggs, a chunk of meat appeared.

I paused. "Apricot." I frowned. "I thought you knew I do not eat meat. Why did you put meat in my soup?"

"Meat? What meat?"

Gaoyang leaned over and peered at the soup. "It looks like meat to me. You don't know your lady is a vegetarian, Apricot?"

"I know, I know, Princess." Apricot's face turned red. "But I told the cooks in the kitchen. They know our lady's diet, and they always have special people prepare the food..."

"Did you watch them cook? Who gave you the soup?" I asked.

She swallowed. "The Empress's maid... She gave it to me, and the Empress was there too. I thought it was odd...and I didn't want to take it from her at first. I was worried... What if... I went to the food provosts and had them test it three times, just in case..."

The Empress would not poison me, I was sure of it, but then why would she bother to go to the kitchen, a low place where most titled ladies would refuse to be seen? I stared at the reddish chunk of meat in the pot. A shiver ran down my spine, and I dropped the spoon.

"What is it? What is it, Mei?" Gaoyang's voice echoed in the large chamber. "Are you all right?"

"It's... It's..." Sourness sprang from my stomach and surged to my throat. I retched. And retched again.

How could she do this? But I could not think clearly, see, or hear, for the chamber was filled with chaotic movements and high-pitched voices. Apricot was gasping, panting, out of breath, and Gaoyang cried out furiously. I blinked, trying to say something or see better, but I could not. There was heavy, rough rumbling drumming in my ears.

The chamber spun. The two figures swayed before me. I stretched out my hand, but they were shrinking, growing fuzzy, swelling, and darting out of reach.

The hard floor struck my side, and a pang, sharper than any I had experienced before, shot through my stomach. I groaned.

"What's wrong, what's wrong?" Gaoyang was holding me. I could feel her but could not see her, and the pain was everywhere, inside my stomach, my legs, my chest, and my bones. It hurt so much I could not breathe, but I tried to think, tried to hold still. This could not be happening. I must stay strong. I still had one more month to go. The baby was not ready. It must stay...

But it was too late.

I felt wetness between my legs. It flowed down my thighs and clung to me. I felt cold, my limbs turned soft, and my teeth chattered.

"She's bleeding... My heavens..."

Tripitaka's image appeared before me, his gaze helpless and steeped with premonition. I shook my head. No, no, no. It must not be. He was wrong. He was wrong! My heart wrenching, I held my stomach, trying to make the pain stop, trying to put my baby back where she should be. But my body would not listen. My abdomen grew heavier, larger, harder, like a frozen boulder, and it was rolling, rolling, threatening to drop, threatening to erupt.

"Apricot! Get the physicians!"

"But, Princess, the Empress won't let them come."

"Then watch your lady! I'll go get them!"

A torrent of power, fierce and unstoppable, pounded against my insides, and a ball of fire, merciless and brutal, raged through me. The chamber darkened before me. Fear, agony, pain pierced me and shook me to the core. I screamed.

I was broken. I was going to die. And my baby—my baby was going to die too.

✦ ✦

Someone gripped my shoulder, a face, round and pale like a pot of ashes, loomed before me, and many voices roared, urging me to listen, to push. I did not want to. I did not like being pinned there. I did not like seeing those strange faces. I only wanted Hope. Oh, Hope. He was such a good dog…

But those arms would not let me go. They touched me, their fingers sticky like the long legs of a spider. I wanted them to go away. I could not let them touch me or my baby. What if the Empress had sent them?

Then the arms disappeared. The voices dissolved. It was all dark again, so dark I could not see a flicker of the candlelight or a speckle of the moonlight. Where was I? Where did everyone go?

I felt tired, so tired. I wanted to sleep a little. But a voice, faint and painful, echoed in my ears. I tried to listen, but it vanished. Everything was quiet again, and then I realized it was my own groan I was hearing.

The pain seized me again, tearing me apart. I cried. I begged. I could not do this. *Let me die.*

"…agitated…the baby…can't save both…"

Who was saying that? I could not see. Too dark. And blurry.

"Pheasant… You decide… This is going on for too long… She is in so much pain…" Gaoyang's voice.

So he had returned. I was glad. I wanted to hold his hand. I wanted him to hold me.

"I lost her once…"

"But the baby—"

"Save her!"

Oh, he was angry. *Pheasant. Do not be angry. It's only pain. It's nothing…*

His face appeared before me, his eyes glittering like twin stars in the distance, bright and persistent. I wanted to touch him. There once had been a time, when I stared at those stars, I would see the reflections of the moon beside them. I would imagine the luminescent palace. I would dream. I would smile. I would forget the past and the future. I would long for hope and wish for more... Oh, these stars, these sparks, luring me, so close to the moon...

"Sweet face. Listen. Be strong. You will make it. You hear me? I'm here."

He was here. He had come back for me. His sweet voice was calling me. But he was wrong, and I did not think I could make it. It was impossible. The pain was impossible. I could not even hold back my tears...

"Listen, Mei. Hope... He would always protect you... You will beat her. We will beat her." Pheasant's voice.

I did not believe it. The Empress would crush me. She would. Had she not killed my Hope?

"Hold my hand, sweet face." His hand was large, dry, and warm. Covering me, like a fur cape. "For our son's sake..."

Our son...

Pheasant was right. It had to be. I did not need a submissive girl with a lowered head. I could not live quietly in the corner of the palace anymore. I needed strength, the strength of a son who would help me stand before my enemy. I would raise my voice to the Empress. I would stop her. I would fight her.

The pain returned again, surging through me. I screamed louder, my head bursting, and every part of my body seemed to scream with me. Yet it was different this time. I could see the darkness fleeing and the brightness of the light, emitting from a round pearl, shining a few steps away.

Relief came unexpectedly, and I lay back, spent. Many voices gasped and murmured around me. They did not say if my child was a boy or a girl, but I knew.

"You did it." Pheasant's smiling face appeared beside me. Oh, how beautiful he was. "Look."

He handed a bundle to me. The baby was a crinkled little thing with a head shaped like a gourd, his face a ghoulish shade of purple. His hands curled near his chest, and he had swollen eyelids and a flat nose, his mouth pinched tightly as though he were tortured and unhappy with this world. He felt almost boneless, too soft and too slippery.

But he was crying, his chest heaving, his lips flattening. And that cry was the most beautiful music I had ever heard.

I pressed my face to his and wrapped my arms around him. I listened to his urgent breathing, I felt his heart next to mine, and I wept in joy. "My son."

✦ ✦

I stayed in bed for days, my son in my arms. He was small, soft, and delicate. When he cried, his voice was faint, his breathing shallow. But for an infant who had come nearly six weeks early, he appeared to be healthy.

He spent a great deal of time sleeping. When he was awake, he gazed at the ceiling with the look of an old poet, contemplative and placid. A whole world seemed to be locked behind his eyes, and he was reluctant to share any inspirations with me. Sometimes he stared at me with a knowing look, as though he understood what I had gone through, but other times, it seemed he was not sure whether he liked me or his new home.

My son was a treasure to me, and I did not let him out of my sight. I slept when he slept, and I nursed him when he awoke. I watched him as he hugged himself tight inside a blanket, frowning and squinting. He made slow gestures, turning his head, raising his fists, like a careful dancer practicing every move. I took his curled fingers and kissed each of them. I breathed in his milky scent, I smoothed his wisps of hair, and I cradled him close. I knew I would give my life for this little infant.

Two physicians, under Pheasant's order, tended to me. They told me to bind my head with a thick cloth and warm my feet with fur slippers. They told me to drink hot water steeped with ginger and sugar. Bathing was forbidden. "Your body has not recovered from labor. Water will invade your organs and make you weak," they said. Walking was not allowed either. "Movement steals strength. Without strength, your inner *qi* debilitates." Going near the chamber's door, where the fresh wind blew, was also discouraged. "The wind is most detrimental to your weak body. It invades your brain and causes headaches that will haunt you for the rest of your life."

They also told me to feed on stews made of river fish and eat bean curd fried with the fat of a wild boar to increase my milk production. This was not the diet I was accustomed to, but I did not argue. This was not my war. My battle lay somewhere else.

I wrote to Mother and told her she was now a grandmother, and I was well. She replied with a letter overflowing with joy and delight. She was eager to meet her new grandson, and I hoped she would have her wish soon.

Perhaps very soon, for the General, who had defeated the Tibetans and saved the border towns, was finally allowed to return to the court. On the day of his arrival, he received a warm welcome, where ministers greeted him on the streets and the commoners of the city shouted in gratitude. Pheasant proposed restoring the General to his old position, minister of war, and allowing him to resume his duty of commanding all ninety-nine legions of the Gold Bird Guards. The Regent initially resisted but had to give in due to strong approval from the other ministers.

So to my delight, the General assumed his position in the court and devoted himself to Pheasant. Everywhere Pheasant went, the General went with him, and upon Pheasant's suggestion, the General sent ten of his men to guard my garden.

I was no longer alone in the Inner Court, no longer a pitiful exiled concubine who feared being banished again. Because of my son's birth, everyone knew that I, the mother of an imperial son, was to stay in the palace. And I was also officially named Most Adored, and Pheasant showered warm fur coats, precious jewelry, and his love on me.

Gaoyang found poor Hope's coat behind the kitchen, and we buried it in an empty lot near a bamboo grove in my garden. In tears, I stood beside my pet's grave, remembering how he had comforted me during my exile. I would never forgive what the Empress had done to him, and every day without hearing his bark, every glimpse of the empty corner where he used to sleep, would remind me of the danger that lurked around me.

Near Hope's grave ran a brook. I instructed my guards to build a bridge over it. I named it Hope's Bridge, for it was my hope that the bridge would cross over the realm of fire and thunder and take me to the land of safety and joy, where I would have no fear.

I would never forget Hope, for his companionship, for his protection, and for what his death had helped me understand.

I would overcome.

I would multiply.

I would thrive.

O

AD 653

The Fourth Year *of*

Emperor Gaozong's

Reign *of* Eternal Glory

SPRING

THE EMPRESS CLAIMED HER INNOCENCE WHEN PHEASANT asked her if she had killed Hope. "People eat dogs. There is no need to fuss about it," she said. "I wished only to cook the soup to strengthen her body." But when Pheasant reminded her of my vegetarian diet, she twisted her head away in resentment.

And she cursed my child, unleashing harsh words that would make any new mother cringe in fear. "He will not live more than a month!" "He will die in his sleep." "He will fall sick with a fever."

I clenched my hands in anger. I swore I would do anything I could to protect my son if she dared lay a finger on him.

✦ ✦

"Come, I have a gift for you." Pheasant beckoned at me as I entered the feasting hall.

Several days before, my son had passed the thirty-day mark, an important milestone in his young life. Pheasant had ordered a feast to celebrate. All the high-ranking Ladies were invited, including the animal-killing Empress, but they had not arrived yet.

"What gift?" I asked. The hall was crowded with servants, maids, and concubines. In the corner, the musicians began to play their flutes, zithers, and *pipas*.

They were playing a familiar song—"The High Mountains and the Trickling Streams." I remembered listening to the same song when

Emperor Taizong held a feast many years ago. In fact, everything here seemed familiar. It was the same hall, with the same gold-gilded tables, the red-lacquered stools, the ruby-encrusted aloes-wood screen with black-and-white landscape paintings. For a moment, I thought I would see my friends waiting for me. But they were all gone, like last year's cherry blossoms, once bright and alluring, the shining attractions of the spring, now withered and lost in dust.

"It's a surprise." Pheasant raised his goblet to me.

"Better be a good one," I said, sitting on a stool next to him. I did not have the heart to tell him I did not care for gifts. The only thing I thought of these days was my son and how I could keep him safe. I turned to make sure Apricot, who was holding him, was behind me. Only a month old, my boy did not have a formal name yet—he would receive that on his first-year birthday.

"You will not be disappointed, sweet face. I will give it to you once all the ladies arrive," he said, and touched my face with his hand. "You look like the goddess of the Luo River."

I smiled. He certainly knew what to say to make me happy. I had put on a new gown he had given me, a scarlet robe decorated with pictures of pagodas and waves. It complemented my supple bosom and had a broad girdle tied around my waist. I had paired it with a long fur shawl and a blue skirt. I had even put on white face cream and rouge.

But I could not do anything about my hair. It was still short, and I had no choice but to keep it wrapped with a long scarf.

"And you, Your Majesty, have never looked this splendid," I said. Indeed, Pheasant was happier since he had won the General's support. He had attended the audiences, listened to some petitions, and made some decisions that came into effect. I hoped Pheasant would build his influence, rise above the Regent, and become the true emperor he deserved.

"I feel good. Everything will be good!" he said, his handsome face alight with happiness. "But you are still recovering. If you're tired, we can end this feast quickly."

I was touched by his thoughtfulness, for I was still bleeding and felt fatigued easily. But I jested, "Why, so you can go behind my back and play the famous Firefly Game?"

He had played the game with the concubines during my exile, but it was nothing like what the rumor said. It did not involve any naked girls, only the fireflies, which he had collected in a round gauze container. But most people did not know the truth and believed the game was a dirty pleasure sport.

Pheasant laughed. "Should I take this as encouragement to do so?"

I pretended to strike him. He always did have a knack for making me smile.

"You started it," he said, serious now. "Here, have some wine."

I took a sip. The wine tasted sweet, with a thick flavor of plum and honey. "When will the ladies arrive?"

"They should be here soon."

The servants near the gate bowed as four ladies walked in—all the ladies I had seen in the garden when the Empress came to beat me. "The Noble Lady, Lady Virtue, Lady Obedience, and the Pure Lady," the announcer shouted.

They were Pheasant's Four Ladies of the second degree, different from those who had served Emperor Taizong but bearing the same titles.

When they came closer to me, I could not believe how young they were. They must have been eighteen or nineteen, with bright eyes, luminous skin, and slim waists.

I felt old. I was twenty-seven.

I rose to greet them. Even though I was now Most Adored, I was still a concubine without a rank, and I needed to be courteous so I would have them as my friends.

The Pure Lady, dressed in a white gown embroidered with purple plum flowers, came ahead of the three ladies, so I bowed to her first. "I am so honored to meet you, Pure Lady."

"The honor is mine, Most Adored." Her eyes flashing intelligently, she folded her arms across her abdomen and bowed as well. She looked calm, and her manners were reserved.

I wished to know her better, for I remembered what Apricot had told me. The Pure Lady was popular in the palace because she was the only high-ranking Lady with a son, whose name was Sujie, who would surely become the heir in the future since the Empress was barren. Apricot also said the Pure Lady had a rare talent in mathematics. She was skillful with the abacus, and she could calculate numbers faster than a court recorder serving in the imperial treasury. Because of her extraordinary ability—most ladies in the palace could barely read—the Pure Lady was given the task of examining the records produced by the Imperial Silkworm Workshops, which were overseen by the Empress. But the Empress was jealous of the Pure Lady and did not get along with her.

The Pure Lady sat down, and I turned to the other three ladies. At first I could not tell them apart. They were about the same height, wearing the same peach-colored gowns, the same conch hairstyle, and painted near their mouths was the same beauty mark: a red rose. Lady Virtue was the lady on the right, with puffy eyes; the Noble Lady, in the middle, was very attractive, with an oval face and a small nose; and Lady Obedience, on the left, had a habit of covering her mouth, perhaps too cautious with etiquette or self-conscious about her teeth. I gave the Noble Lady an extra stare, remembering my friend the late Noble Lady. The two women shared the same title, but they were so different.

"It is a pleasure to meet you, ladies," I said, bowing. "My son and I are honored by your presence."

The three ladies looked ill at ease, uncertain how to respond. Trying to make them feel more comfortable, I showed them my son. Their eyes widened, and cooing, they stroked his cheeks, touched his small feet, and shrieked in delight when he opened his mouth and drooled. They had not had the fortune to bear children, and I could tell they wanted them desperately.

Another stream of ladies entered the hall. The Ladies-in-Waiting, the Beauties, and the Graces, all splendidly dressed, their hair carefully styled and decorated with jewels and hairpins, their faces powdered and rouged. I knew none of them.

They peered at me from behind their fans and handkerchiefs. When I nodded, they lowered their heads and looked away. All of them must have known I had served Emperor Taizong, and I was expecting taunting and sneers. But Pheasant's ladies were not malicious. They looked subdued and fearful. I wondered why. Was it because of their young age? Had I been like them, blessed with youth but plagued by fear?

"Where is she?" Pheasant asked. "I'm waiting for everyone to arrive so I can give you your gift." He held the goblet near his lips, glanced at me, and then set the goblet back down. Ever since my return to the palace, he had drunk less.

The hall darkened, and a tall figure appeared at the threshold. My heart tightened. I put a hand on Pheasant's arm. "She's here."

All the women rose to their feet and lowered their heads, and the Empress in her golden gown walked between the rows of tables, making the women look like children in comparison to her towering stature. She paused in front of the feasting table where I sat with Pheasant. I straightened on my stool. She could not have my seat, even if she wanted it. For I was Most Adored, and even without a title, I was the mother of the infant whose feast we were celebrating.

I did not bow to her or greet her. In fact, I could not bear to look at her without thinking of my Hope. If I got even one glimpse of that ruthless face, I would throw myself at her and claw her eyes.

Finally, she went to a different table on my right and sat. The hall was quiet. It occurred to me the ladies were fearful because they were afraid of the Empress.

Pheasant stood up and cleared his throat, and all the ladies fixed their eyes on him. "My ladies, it is my great pleasure to inform you that this child and the mother of this child have brought great joy to me, and hereby, I shall give the lady a gift. I would like to make an announcement."

I studied him. What could be the gift?

"I shall honor the mother of my son by bestowing on her the title of a second-degree Lady."

My heart leaped in joy. A Lady?

The Empress gasped. "Your Majesty, this cannot be done."

I tensed, unable to look in her direction.

"Why not?" Pheasant's voice was steady. "Isn't it part of my authority to honor the women in my court?"

"She was your father's concubine!" I was certain if I met the Empress's gaze, her stare would kill me. "Besides, you've forgotten, Your Majesty, we already have four ladies who carry this honor. If you give her the title, do you mean to demote one of these noble ladies?"

"No one will be demoted," Pheasant said, and I was relieved. I would not want to have my joy at the cost of anyone's sadness. I felt his hand on my shoulder. "I will create a new title."

"Five Ladies? That is ridiculous. The ranks of the palace ladies were created eight hundred years ago. If you add a random one, you will bring this kingdom to ridicule. I am certain the Regent will disapprove of it," she said quickly, her voice sharp.

Pheasant walked to the Empress's table and leaned over her. I could feel his anger rising. "I forgot to mention it to you, Wife. This is not a suggestion."

"You will never have the court's approval."

"I don't need it, and may I inform you, I have just changed my mind. This new title should not be among the second-degree Ladies."

There was a pause. "What title is it?"

"Luminous Lady."

Before she said anything else, Pheasant took my son from Apricot. "May I formally make this announcement," he said, facing the crowd and holding the baby up, "and let all of you bear witness on this grand celebration of my son, that I now bestow this new title, Luminous Lady, on the mother of this infant, the second daughter of the Wu family. We shall all rejoice!"

"Your Majesty!" the Empress exclaimed, standing up.

"But I am not finished yet." Pheasant walked toward me. "I forgot to mention that this title should be *above* the second degree."

The Empress heaved the table away from her, crushing it against a pillar. Throwing her golden sleeves behind her, she stormed out of the hall.

Pheasant waved his hand. "Let her leave and never come back," he said, his voice the only sound in the hall. "All of you, hear this. I give you Luminous Lady."

"Luminous Lady," the women murmured, glancing at me.

I held on to the table. For a moment the vibrant colors of the ladies' gowns blended before me like a rainbow, and their gold hairpins and necklaces glittered like the rays of sunlight sprinkling through clouds.

I had not expected this. Luminous Lady. What a title, and how beautiful it sounded. I had struggled for fifteen years. From one emperor to another. From a nobody to a Talent, from a Talent to a nobody, and now from a nobody to a Lady.

I had been a little girl when I entered the palace, and now I was Most Adored, the mother of a little boy, and Luminous Lady, above the second-degree Ladies, below only the Empress.

It meant my family name—and my father's name—would be recorded in the imperial family history, and his dream that I would bring my family glory would be fulfilled. It meant I would have power to bestow gifts and provide comfort for Mother, who still lived and prayed in a humble monastery on the outskirts of the city.

It also meant my son was elevated, and no one could look down on him and mock him because he was borne by a mother without a rank.

I should have been happy, but for some reason, my eyes moistened. I turned away, blinking away my tears.

Pheasant, smiling, turned to me. "Did you get wine in your eyes?"

For the first time, I could not find the right thing to say to him. "You didn't warn me about this."

"That title was yours years ago." There was tenderness in his eyes, and even though he did not say it, I knew he was thinking of the nights we spent in the garden, watching the moon—and of all those lonely nights too when we had sat under the same sky but were far apart. "I promised you, remember?"

I nodded. "It's a good title. I like it. Who helped you with it?"

"The moon lady," he replied, referring to the girl in the tale I used to tell him when we met secretly. Chang E had left her husband and flown to the celestial palace on the moon, choosing immortality over her husband, and Pheasant had said she was foolish.

"Ah, I should have known," I said, nodding.

"Good. Now drink your wine and let the others toast you, Luminous Lady."

"Toast, yes." I smiled and looked at the Ladies with their perfectly rouged cheeks and beauty marks, their eyes timid and their smiles nervous. I felt a need to do something. I rose and went to their tables. "Honorable Ladies, would you care to drink with me?" I dipped my head, my scarf falling before my eyes. I swept it aside.

They looked startled, glancing at me in surprise, but no one answered me. I smiled, remembering how, many years ago, my friend the Noble Lady had broken the boundary between her and me when she held my hand.

I took the hand of the young Noble Lady. "Come, sit here with me. We shall all drink together."

She looked hesitant.

"All right then. I shall take a seat next to you. I hope you won't mind." I sat down and filled a cup for the Noble Lady. "Wine?" All the Ladies' eyes widened. The protocol was that the lower-ranking ladies poured the wine for the higher-ranking. "Shall we have some music too?"

Pheasant clapped his hands to give his signal, and the light notes of flutes bounced in the air. The zither players and the *pipa* players followed.

"That's better." I helped myself to some roasted chestnuts. "What are they playing? I am not familiar with this tune."

"That's a new song," the Noble Lady said. "It's called 'The Cuckoos' Song in the Summer.'"

"I haven't heard it. I suppose I have been out of touch with the world for a long time." I smiled to ease the tension.

"The baby looks adorable and healthy, Luminous Lady." Lady Virtue blinked her puffy eyes. "Does he have a milk name?"

"I call him Lion," I replied. It was a reminder of my Hope, whose thick coat looked just like that of a lion. I missed my pet.

Lady Virtue nodded. "Indeed, he's a little lion."

"If Luminous Lady needs good nannies, I shall recommend some for you. I have a list of them," the Pure Lady said. Her face was still serene, but a thread of wariness had crept into her eyes.

I understood she must have felt threatened because my rank was higher than hers, but if she knew me well, she would understand she did not need to fear me. "That is so kind of you, Pure Lady," I said genuinely. "I do appreciate your help."

Lady Obedience cupped her hand over her mouth and whispered in the Noble Lady's ear. The Noble Lady turned to me and said, "Luminous Lady, Lady Obedience would like to ask your permission to knit some clothes for our newest family member. I hope you will indulge her. She is the best at doing women's work."

"Oh, that would give me tremendous honor," I said, wondering why Lady Obedience needed the Noble Lady's help to get her words across. "More wine?"

They nodded, more at ease now, and I filled their cups and asked them to sing the cuckoo song. They obliged, although none of them had a singer's voice. But they looked happy, drinking the wine I poured for them. Soon they talked about a new rouge produced by a type of lac insect from the south. The color was said to be vermilion and last longer than the regular rouge they used. I must try it, they said. I nodded, promising to try it someday, even though I could not have cared less about beauty products.

In the midst of our drinking, I turned toward Pheasant, who held Lion in his arms. He caught my gaze and smiled.

I smiled too, the soft scarf falling behind my shoulders, but for the first time, my short hair did not bother me, for I knew I did not need to worry about my looks. My cheeks warm with the wine, I raised my cup. I would drink for Pheasant, and for me too, because there was a good reason to celebrate. My life had turned out to be just like wine. The more it aged, the better flavor it produced.

But I understood, even though I tried not to think, that the most flavorful wine could turn sour on the wrong tongue.

10

RUMORS SWIRLED AROUND THE PALACE. THE EMPRESS WAS furious about my new title. She gathered her uncle, the Secretary, and her other family members who served in the court, for an urgent meeting. Together, her uncle and the others presented a petition to the court, declaring the immorality of permitting me to stay in the palace and honoring me so.

"As our great teacher Confucius says, a woman must not serve two men, and this woman has served two emperors!" said the petition I saw in Pheasant's hands. "Furthermore, their relationship is nothing but incestuous. It is most deplorable that a morally corrupt woman should keep a high-ranking title, living in our palace and staining our kingdom's name!"

After a few days, they won support from a group of ministers, and weeks later, the Regent's servant, the Chancellor, and two of the Regent's brothers-in-law urged Pheasant to revoke his bestowal or "the spiraling degradation of the kingdom shall be afoot."

The Regent was silent, but I knew what kind of a man he was, and his silence clearly was an approval of the ministers' vicious attack on me.

Pheasant shrugged those petitions off and told me not to worry. But each time after he returned from the Audience Hall, he was silent. And then one day he returned extremely agitated, his face crimson with anger. He had to gallop on his horse in the woods to calm down.

Standing in the corridor near my bedchamber, I watched his

golden robe flare as he dashed through the woods. I could feel his anger, and I was sorry I had become a burden to him. His newly earned position and respect in the Audience Hall could be challenged because of me.

But I could not give up the title. It was my protection, my child's protection, and my child's future. If the Empress and her supporters succeeded in stripping me of the title, she could continue to intimidate me until I was pushed back to the corner of fear and helplessness again.

Pheasant rode farther away, his angry cries fading, and his golden regalia dimming to a dot on the horizon. I stared at the sky, a sheet of light indigo, where the sun shone weakly. I could imagine the arrival of a storm, always unexpected in the spring, and how it could block the sky and lash the flowers.

When the clouds gathered to darken the sky, when a thunderbolt threatened to tear it apart, should I wait inside, sitting in quiet and hoping it would pass, or gather my strength and be prepared?

A whimper came from the chamber. Lion was awake. I dashed inside the chamber before Apricot and my other maids could respond to him. I could always hear him, no matter how far away I was. I could always feel him and understand his needs, even in my sleep. That, for sure, was a mother's instinct.

I went to the bed where Lion kicked, his eyes open. He was so sweet, pouting his mouth, frowning. He was two months old, looking more like a child than a newborn, and his face was not as swollen, his skin more natural. But he still had that deep, meaningful gaze, and oftentimes he sighed, holding out his hand, as though he were contemplating a good rhyme of couplets. Love poured out of me, and I picked him up, rocking him until he finally calmed down and began to suckle. I played with his soft hair, watching his lips moving, and I wanted to hold him forever. He was mine, and I would do anything I could to protect him and keep him safe.

Outside, the sky was darkening. I hoped Pheasant would return soon, and I knew I must get ready for the storm and danger. For the thunderbolt could strike with all its might, and the storm could catch every leaf and every branch, gather speed, and turn into a downpour.

✦ ✦

I summoned Princess Gaoyang to my chamber. Since I now had additional guards in front of my garden, she did not stay with me every day, but she always came when I called for her.

I was putting Lion down for a nap when she appeared in the corridor. I put a finger to my lips, telling her to remain quiet. Gently, I patted my son. When he wiggled his lips and flung his arms above his head, I knew it was a sign that he was sound asleep. I took my arm from underneath him, got up gingerly, and slipped out of bed. Apricot leaned over his sleeping form, keeping him company.

"Really? It takes you that long to put him to bed?" Princess Gaoyang asked as we walked into the garden. "I have finished my meditating. I thought the whole day had passed."

She looked imperious. I took no offense, even though I was a high-ranking Lady and Gaoyang ought to at least bow to me. "You won't understand until you have your own child."

Gaoyang shook her head. "Now you even talk like a mother."

"Well, I'm honored to hear that, and may I remind you, some women never have the honor to become one," I said.

"I see what you mean. So is this what you wished to tell me, little mother?" She leaped on a pear tree nearby. Sitting on a branch, she swayed her legs. She was wearing a simple indigo tunic and a yellow girdle, which flowed through the air and danced as she kicked. She was so thin; she looked as though she could have flown away in a gust of wind.

"No. I need to speak to you about something important. Perhaps you can come down?" I asked, standing near a stone lamp beside the tree. It was a warm spring afternoon, and the air smelled fragrant. Pink peonies bloomed, red roses swayed, and the water in the pond glistened brightly like a polished mirror.

A shower of white pear blossoms rained down, and Princess Gaoyang appeared beside me. "What is it?"

I did not reply at first, enjoying the warmth of the sunlight on my face. The garden was so quiet. I looked around for Hope before remembering he was gone. I sighed. I missed him.

"Is there a problem, Mei?"

"I suppose you can say that. Have you heard that Pheasant gave me a title, Gaoyang?" I gazed at the maids around me. I had eight maids now, and they were busy with their duties. Some were dusting the chamber, some were doing Lion's laundry, and some were weeding. I had chosen four among them to be my personal maids and had given them new names—Chunlu, Xiayu, Qiushuang, and Dongxue, meaning, respectively, Spring Dew, Summer Rain, Autumn Frost, and Winter Snow.

"Of course." She handed me something covered with a red cloth. "That's why I came bearing a gift."

"Oh." It was a beautiful wig topped by an ornate hairpiece. I was delighted. The hairpiece had many delicate twists and gold hairpins shaped like birds, each with gold wings, a ruby beak, and jade eyes. Best of all, the wig was long and sleek, and the hair almost reached the ground. "For me?"

She nodded, smiling, and her dimples deepened into twin whirlpools. "Congratulations, Luminous Lady."

"Thank you." I could not help it. I had to put it on. "How does it look on me? Quick, get me a mirror."

A breeze brushed me, Gaoyang disappeared, and then she was back, holding a bronze mirror.

I peered into the mirror, delighted to see the black loops and delicate twists of the wig. The gold birds glittered on the top of my head, and the long strands fell behind my back like dyed dark cloth. I liked how the wig softened my face and how it swayed behind me with a pleasant rhythm. I looked gentle and graceful. "Thank you, Gaoyang. This is such a splendid gift. I never would have expected it."

"So you like it." She grinned. "It was Apricot's suggestion. I didn't think you would favor it. It's so fancy but cumbersome, and I think it's quite heavy when you wear it. Is it heavy?"

I nodded. I felt as though a fat rooster were sitting on my head, but I did not mind. "Where did you get it?" I combed the long hair with my fingers. It felt good. The hair was smooth and fine.

"I paid ten wig makers to craft it," Gaoyang said. "It took them seven days and seven nights."

"Oh, I hope you rewarded them handsomely. They certainly did a beautiful job." I walked carefully, balancing the wig on my head. Now I did not need to feel like a spring sparrow standing among peacocks when I sat next to the ladies with long, sleek hair. I decided I would never leave my chamber without it. "This is the second precious gift I have received this month."

Gaoyang laughed. "Well, Luminous Lady, you deserve much more."

It was very kind of her to say that. I wanted to hug her. Steadying the wig on my head, I walked toward the flower beds near the stone bench. "But, Gaoyang, have you heard the petitions from the Empress and her uncle?"

"My husband told me." Gaoyang's husband was a fifth-degree minister and had been unhappy in the court, I had heard. Because the court was crowded with the Empress's men and the Regent's relatives, many young ministers like the princess's husband did not have a chance to advance or to demonstrate their skills. "But do not let the petitions bother you, Luminous Lady. They will not change anything."

"I'm not sure, Gaoyang."

"I wouldn't let them bother me, if I were you."

I admired her spirit, and I wished I could brush aside the opposition like she did. But she was a princess, and she did not need to fight for her title. I took a rake near the flower beds and began to gather the weeds scattered on the path. It was good to use my arms again after months of sitting around and doing nothing. I could feel the loose skin on my stomach shaking as I worked. That was the price of having a child.

"The Empress is a powerful woman, Gaoyang."

Princess Gaoyang shook her head. "Not everyone is on her side. Many ministers in the court do not like her. They mock her behind her back, saying she's an embarrassment because she has failed Confucius's cardinal rule of producing a son. They are losing patience in her after all these years."

"Who is losing patience?" I turned my head, and my wig slid. I held it and set it upright carefully on my head.

She shrugged. "Many ministers. I don't go to the Audience Hall, so I can't give you the names. But my husband said loyalty is shifting in the court."

I had not heard the news. "What do you mean?"

"When she became the Empress four years ago, the Regent gave many important court positions to her family members. She was very powerful, and many people flocked to her, believing that she would have a son to inherit the throne, and the Wang family's blood would bear the imperial blood. They swore their loyalty to her and listened to her uncle's every order. But now people are not so sure."

"I see." I nodded. Since the Empress could not conceive, the heir to the kingdom would be someone else. It was too early to speculate who would inherit the throne, since Pheasant was still in his prime, but the Empress's barrenness had become her weakness, and it did not matter that she was sitting next to Pheasant. As long as she did not produce a male heir, the phoenix crown she wore would become a crown of needles. "Will she lose her support soon?"

"My husband believes so. He said some ministers also dislike the Empress's family members. It is said they are incompetent. No one likes her uncle, the Secretary, either. So even if she threatens to strip you of the title, she will not succeed."

I was glad to hear the Empress was not as powerful as I believed, but I was not optimistic that I was safe from her. "She banded with the Chancellor. He wrote a petition for her. He is determined to drive me away."

"The Chancellor? He is nothing. He only follows the Regent."

I sighed. Of course, the Regent. He was, after all, the man whom I feared the most. "What is your opinion of the Regent, Gaoyang?"

"That weasel?" She waved her hand. "I hate him. He was unkind to my mother."

"He is unkind to all women." Especially Emperor Taizong's women, and especially if they had Pheasant's favor.

"He exiled my half brother Prince Ke. Said it was my father's will. We all know it's not true. He got rid of him because he was worried Prince Ke would challenge him."

I remembered the prince. The Regent had exiled him, other princes, and ministers after Emperor Taizong's death. The Regent also imprisoned all of the Emperor's daughters who had not yet reached the betrothal age in a building in the Yeting Court, claiming it was for their safety, and they would receive exclusive care there.

The married princesses, like Princess Gaoyang, had escaped the fate of being imprisoned.

Prince Ke was the late Noble Lady's son. He was still in exile, but Pheasant's other brother, Prince Wei, I heard, had contracted pneumonia and died. Pheasant had mentioned his brothers to me a few times. He missed them.

I leaned on the rake and sighed. "The Regent has the kingdom in his hands now, and no one will challenge him. If he says I am not worthy of my title, then it will be stripped away instantly."

Gaoyang nodded. "I can't argue with you about that. So what are you going to do, Luminous Lady?"

A shadow flew across the path. I raised my head. High in the sky a large shape fluttered. A falcon? Or perhaps a vulture?

I had to do something. Or it was possible that I would become the vulture's meal.

I took a deep breath, more resolved than ever. "I am going to the Audience Hall. I will not let them take away my title."

11

I WAITED NEAR THE STONE STAIRS THAT LED TO THE Audience Hall, my eight maids standing behind me. I needed their presence to show the Regent and the ministers that I was Luminous Lady, whether they liked it or not.

I had put on the wig Princess Gaoyang gave me. It was difficult to part with it now, and I was accustomed to its weight and the motion of the long strands swaying at my knees. I also wore the splendid red gown Pheasant had given me for my son's thirty-day celebration. I was determined to show myself in the most magnificent form so the Regent and the ministers could not deny my worthiness.

It had been almost four years since I had last come to the hall in the Outer Palace. I stared at the building, a wide edifice with a blue roof and flying eaves. I had come here many times while serving Emperor Taizong, and the building still looked majestic.

Pheasant would be surprised to see me. I had not told him I would be coming today. I did not need his help. I would handle the Regent and his men alone.

I wondered what the Regent would say to me when he saw me. Would he denounce me? Would he attempt to get rid of me? But I was not a girl of thirteen anymore. I could face him, and I could throw myself into the fray if necessary. But somehow, against my will, uneasiness crept into my mind, and I grew nervous. I was alone, and he had so many servants—the Chancellor, for instance, who had called me "a morally corrupted woman," and there was also the Secretary, the Empress's uncle. He might not be liked by the ministers, but he certainly hated me for taking Pheasant away from the Empress.

I glanced at the Gold Bird Guards standing at the corners of the vast yard paved with white stones. Wearing maroon capes and bronze breastplates, they held their swords and bows still and did not turn their heads to me. I wondered where the General was. He was the commander of the ninety-nine legions of the Gold Bird Guards, as well as serving as the minister of war.

When the court announcer appeared at the corridor outside the hall, I knew the audience was over. I watched the ministers descend from the stairs, but Pheasant was not among them. Perhaps he was changing his formal gown or talking with some ministers.

I spotted the Regent immediately, wearing a black hat and a long, purple robe with voluminous sleeves that draped to his knees. He had not seemed to age much over the past four years, and his steps were agile, his chest thrust toward the sky.

A minister whispered in the Regent's ear, and he raised his head in my direction. Rapidly, he descended the stairs, his eyes on me.

I stepped forward and bowed. "*Zao an*, esteemed Regent. I was taking a stroll in the palace and happen to pass by. How marvelous you look today. I'm so pleased to see you in good health."

He frowned, his eyes landing somewhere over my shoulder, refusing to meet my eyes. "Ah, Talent."

Of course he remembered me. "Esteemed Regent has an astounding memory for my history in the palace."

"And you are a woman who has an astounding lifespan."

So he had expected me to die in the monastery, as so many of the other Talents had.

"Much with your blessing, esteemed Regent," I fired back. Since he was closer to me, I saw he had aged after all. His face was spotted with black dots, his beard speckled with white, his teeth were rotten, and his breath could have made a weak woman faint. Only his eyes had not changed, still shrewd and dangerous.

"What are you doing here, Talent?"

I bowed again, the black hair falling from my shoulders to my arms, reminding me I must remain humble if possible. "Perhaps esteemed

Regent has not heard—" Of course he had heard of my son, but he had not said a word of acknowledgment or sent a note of good wishes. "The palace has recently celebrated a great addition to our imperial family. My son and I would be forever in your debt if his great uncle would honor us with a drink."

He threw his sleeves behind him. "I regret to tell you, Talent, I am too busy."

Again, not a word of my son. I straightened. "Perhaps, esteemed Regent, you have heard I am not a Talent anymore. Our Emperor has bestowed on me the title of Luminous Lady."

"You!" a voice shouted behind me. I turned around. An old minister with cloudy white eyes stood beside me. He was the Chancellor, Chu Suiliang. "You should be ashamed, woman. You have no moral standards or sense of decency. How dare you show your face here?"

A gaggle of ministers gathered around him. They snarled, baring their teeth. I knew these faces. Among them was the Secretary, the Empress's uncle, a stout man with a fat, round face and a thick black mustache, a man who looked like a butcher. I had met him only once, when he came to visit Emperor Taizong while he was ill. Princess Gaoyang had said the Empress's family's power was being questioned, but her uncle still looked formidable.

And beside him were the Regent's two brothers-in-law, Minister Han Yuan and Minster Lai Ji, and several other advisers.

For a moment I recalled how the ministers had besieged me many years before when they believed I had something to do with the assassination plot against Emperor Taizong. My knees grew weak.

The Chancellor jeered at me. "Shame on you, unscrupulous, debauched woman! You served Emperor Taizong, and now you will deceive his son and seduce him?"

He jabbed his finger in my face, and I stepped back, shocked by his ferocious hostility.

"You despicable, low-born, vile woman!" the Secretary, the Empress's uncle, shouted at me. "You defile the name of the palace that shelters you!"

He wielded his fists in my face. I staggered back more, my heart pounding. But I could manage them. I had gone through many ordeals in my life. I had survived the rebels' attack on the palace. I had lived with the silence of a monastery, suffered the loss of a faithful companion, and overcome the pain of childbirth.

I raised my sleeve to block them. "Ministers! May I have your attention—"

More colorful robes surged around me. "Serpent woman!" one man snarled.

"Harlot!"

"Thrash her!"

"Ministers… Ministers!" I looked from one to another as they loomed closer, their fingers jabbing in the air, their open mouths spewing venom. They were ruthless, and they would not stop. I wanted to cover my face, to run away and never see these people again.

I turned but stumbled, falling to the ground. My wig slid askew, covering my right eye. A roar of laughter burst around me. My cheeks burned with humiliation. I hurriedly put the wig back on my head, but my hands trembled, and the wig kept slipping. All the while the men around me roared with laughter.

I wanted to cry, but then I understood the men would be pleased to see me in tears. They would be delighted that they had defeated me. I straightened and set the wig on my head again—whether it was askew or not, I did not care. They would not tear me to shreds so easily. I stood up, and with my hand covering my mouth, I laughed too. Loudly.

They fell silent and gaped at me.

"Excellent," I said calmly. "Now that I have your attention, I would like to have some civil discussions please, ministers. Let me ask you. Why do you hate me so? Did I torture your parents? Did I poison your concubines? Did I cripple your children?"

They looked taken aback, and the Empress's uncle pointed at me again. I did not give him a chance to speak. "Secretary Liu Shi, you accused me of low birth. May I remind you, my father Wu Shihuo was the governor of Shanxi Prefecture, the one who funded Emperor Gaozu's war. He opened my family's gates to shelter Gaozu's army when he was betrayed and fleeing. Would you not say my father helped found this great dynasty? Would you not agree my birth is equally as noble as any *shi* class? Did you or your family offer such help when Gaozu was in need?"

He scowled, and I turned away from him. "Yes. I served our Emperor Taizong." I faced the other ministers, keeping my voice even. "It was a great honor, and I am not ashamed of it. Dutifully, I served him, and I have accomplished many things. I called for help when an assassin attacked him. I saved his life when no one was beside him. Where were you, Chancellor, when Emperor Taizong needed you?"

The Chancellor's cloudy eyeballs rolled, and he opened his mouth to speak. I did not give him the chance. "I served Emperor Taizong faithfully for eleven years and tended to him while he suffered great pain in his bed. I comforted him while he struggled against the demons of the otherworld. I feel no shame in my service. Besides..." Some middle-ranking ministers had gathered around, watching me. I turned to the Regent. "May I remind you, Regent, you served Emperor Taizong as well."

He scowled. "That is a vastly different matter."

"Why is that?"

"I am a man!"

"And a great friend of Emperor Taizong, so we know. Then I trust you must understand, I did not have the honor to win our late Emperor's favor." Now they knew the Emperor had not taken me. But after this day, I should never mention my service to Pheasant's father again.

"It does not matter, Talent."

The Secretary stepped closer and spat at me. "Your slippery tongue will not fool anyone, woman. You have seduced our emperor, Emperor Taizong's son! You've committed an unforgivable sin. You should be hanged!"

The sticky phlegm caught the strands of my wig, slid, and dropped to my shoulder, scorching me like a fiery stone. I was stunned. These were the type of men I had to deal with. When they lost their arguments with words, they tried to drown you with spittle!

"What is this commotion, ministers?" Pheasant's voice rang out. The men parted, and Pheasant, still in his court regalia, appeared before me. "Is there a problem? Luminous Lady? I did not know you were here. Uncle, what's going on?"

"Nothing serious, Nephew. We are ready to leave," the Regent said, his voice steady.

"Do I see this correctly?" Pheasant came beside me and brushed aside the hair that covered my eye. "Has the Luminous Lady been treated unkindly?"

The Regent did not reply, but the Chancellor snorted. "She gets what she deserves, Your Majesty. This wicked, lascivious woman is dooming our kingdom and corrupting all souls."

I felt Pheasant tense beside me, and I lay a hand on his arm. He had to be cautious, or he would bring trouble to himself as well.

"Luminous Lady will doom our kingdom? How?" Pheasant asked, his voice slow and measured but filled with anger.

"It is plain to see, Your Majesty. You have breached the code of propriety and fallen to a woman's witchery, and now how can we instruct our people to follow the moral codes?"

Pheasant breathed hard, the pearls of his mortarboard jingling, and I remembered that years ago, Emperor Taizong had ordered a priest's tongue to be cut off when the man inadvertently hinted at his mental state. The Chancellor had challenged Pheasant's reign. But Pheasant was not his father. He would not act ruthlessly. "I could have you beaten, Chancellor, for your utter disrespect to your emperor."

"Beat me as you will, Your Majesty. I shall not forget the duty and my responsibility that your father bestowed on me."

Pheasant frowned. "My father died four years ago."

"He still has my loyalty."

"You are my chancellor now, Chancellor." Pheasant's voice grew louder.

"Yet I am wary of a morally corrupted emperor. The ancestors of the Li family will not forgive you for sharing your bed with your father's woman."

Pheasant stepped closer to the minister. "Perhaps you should not serve in your position anymore." His face grew dark, and his chest rose and fell in anger.

Silence fell in the vast yard, and the brainless Chancellor appeared shocked and confused, as though he had never considered that Pheasant might threaten him. His cloudy eyes rolling hesitantly, he turned to the Regent.

The Regent coughed. "Nephew—"

Pheasant shouted, "General!"

A great wind swept from behind me. "Your Majesty!" The General appeared, his hand on the hilt of his saber. It had been almost four years since I last saw him. He looked savage, half of his face covered with a patch of purple birthmark, and I almost drew a breath of fear. But he would support Pheasant, and he would remind the Regent and the other ministers who was the true emperor. I was glad Pheasant had succeeded in recalling him.

"Take him, and get him out of my sight," Pheasant ordered.

The General lunged forward and twisted the Chancellor's arms behind his back.

"Regent!" the Chancellor shouted, and the Regent looked as though someone had struck his cheek. His thin lips pursed tight, and his freckle-covered face was mapped with anger and shock. He could countermand Pheasant's order, of course, but to openly confront the General would be too risky for him.

The other ministers' mouths fell open as the General began to drag the Chancellor away from Pheasant. Obviously, they had never thought Pheasant would dare to remove a high-ranking minister because of a mere concubine.

"Wait, Your Majesty," I said, turning to Pheasant. "May I beseech you to reconsider? I would rather no one lose his position on my behalf."

"You would speak for him, Luminous Lady?" Pheasant raised his eyebrows.

I nodded. "I beseech you, Your Majesty. Please give the Chancellor another chance."

Pheasant turned to the old man. "Chancellor, do you hear this? Luminous Lady is a much better person than you. You do not deserve her kindness. If you apologize to her, your insolence will be forgiven."

The Chancellor twisted his head away. The man was not only idiotic, but also ungrateful.

"There is no need for apology," I said quickly.

"No apology?"

"I insist, Your Majesty." The ministers looked at me with interest. I hoped they would remember how Pheasant protected me and how I forgave the Chancellor.

"Well then. I shall honor the will of Luminous Lady. Now, go, all of you. I believe you all have more important matters to attend to, rather than stand here, pointing your fingers at others."

"I shall gladly take my leave, Nephew," the Regent said. His face was inscrutable, like a molded clay statue. Then he turned to me. "I bid you a good day," he said, and then to my surprise, he bowed slightly. "Luminous Lady."

He had acknowledged me! Why? Was it because I requested that Pheasant forgive the Chancellor? Or was it because he saw Pheasant had the support of the General? It did not matter. In any case, I should be happy. Smiling, I dipped my head as well. "I wish you more splendid days to come, esteemed Regent."

The Chancellor's face turned purple, but the Regent shook his head and gestured to him to follow. They both turned and walked away. The Empress's uncle lowered his head and departed too, his followers trailing after him. The lower-ranking ministers glanced at me, bowed, and asked Pheasant's permission to leave as well.

"It's good to see you again, General." I bowed to him after all the ministers were gone and we were the only ones left in the vast yard.

He stood stiffly, his purple birthmark looking like a black eye patch sitting askew on his face. His exile did not seem to have changed him. He was nearing forty now, still large, bulky, masculine, and cold. But he looked good in the maroon cape, the shining bronze breastplate, and the red hat. Did he know it was my suggestion that gave him a second chance in the court, a second life with his family?

"Luminous Lady." He gave me a curt nod.

"I am most grateful for your help," I said.

"I shall be right here, Your Majesty, if you need me." The General turned and walked toward the carriage that would take Pheasant to the Inner Court.

"Why did you not tell me you were coming here?" Pheasant, frowning, asked me.

"I was wrong. I should have told you," I said. "But did you hear what the Regent said? He recognized me. Now those old men will not renounce me."

"I know. I heard that." Pheasant nodded, looking happier. "You dropped this." He picked up a hairpin from the ground and put it in my wig. "Here...let me see. Now this looks better. Did I tell you how exquisite you look with this wig? Yes. Most exquisite, Luminous Lady."

"I am most delighted to keep my title"—I smiled—"and my wig."

He laughed, walking toward the carriage. "Indeed, Luminous Lady, you shall have everything you wish. No one will stand in your way. Come, let's enjoy some imperial entertainments."

I followed him, passing the Gold Bird Guards who stood in the yard like pillars. They still did not turn their heads, but their eyes were following me. I smiled. I had a feeling I was going to see them more often from that day on. As Luminous Lady, I could come to the Outer Palace as often as I wished. "What kind of entertainments?"

"Ah. There are so many. Horse dancing is my favorite, and, of course, Pitching-a-Pot game and floats. Prepare to be amused. Perhaps I shall honor you with a carnival, a weeklong carnival."

A carnival was always a good indulgence, where people could forget their troubles and have some amusement. When Emperor Taizong lived, he had often ordered carnivals on a whim. Sometimes those carnivals lasted three days, sometimes two weeks. "I do not believe I would object to that, Your Majesty."

I was ready to climb into the carriage when something caught my attention out of the corner of my eye.

On the other side of the hall, a carriage had arrived, and from it stepped the huge frame of the Empress in her voluminous golden dress. The Secretary, followed by a group of ministers, went to greet her. They surrounded her, gathering their heads together. The ends of their black hats jutted out behind their backs, and their heads rose and fell as they nodded, like a flock of crows plotting their next meal.

Were they discussing my son? Or me? I paused at the carriage. But I did not worry, for I was officially Luminous Lady, and they could do nothing about it.

113

○

AD 653

The Fourth Year *of*

Emperor Gaozong's

Reign *of* Eternal Glory

SUMMER

12

I HAD BEEN REBORN. NO LONGER WAS I REFERRED TO AS Emperor Taizong's maid or concubine. Everywhere I went, people bowed to me, calling me "Luminous Lady," recognizing me as a rising, high-ranking Lady, the mother of the Emperor's son, the woman who almost compelled the Emperor to demote the Chancellor. All of them—the servants, the ministers, and the scribes—lowered their eyes and bowed to me deeply as I passed by.

More luxuries were showered on me: bolts of fine silk, golden jewelry, exotic fragrances, and more wigs—I collected eight of them, each with sleek, long hair that draped to my ankles.

On hot days, I received large cooling fans made of pure white swan feathers, chilled watermelons stored in ice buckets, coveted golden peaches from Samarkand, and rare lychees—unique fruit with transparent, jellylike flesh that grew only in the warm south. I handed them out to my maids, sharing my reward, for they were my people, and I would take care of them and share my good fortune with them.

Pheasant decided to make improvements to my garden. He ordered a new hall with ten rooms to be built near my bedchamber, each room graced with golden screens, latticed windows made of fragrant sandalwood, and long, wide corridors. The garden was also expanded, and an enormous pond was to be constructed and filled with many exotic fish and blue lotus. Near the pond, a small replica mountain that bore the peaks and valleys of Tai Mountain, one of the Five Great Mountains in our kingdom, was built. And after the astrologers' careful inspections and consultations, a pavilion with a blue roof and a winding bridge that twisted and turned nine times were also added. With all the five features present—the pond, mountain, pavilion, bridge, and corridors—the garden was in perfect harmony with the standards of beauty and feng shui.

I did not need to move to the Quarters of the Pure Lotus, the residences for the Four Ladies, Pheasant said. He moved into the garden instead, and we lived there together like husband and wife.

Pheasant soon made a formal announcement that he would no longer summon any of his concubines or the high-ranking Ladies to his chamber, utterly discarding the bedding protocol. He would have only me, Most Adored and his Luminous Lady, as his companion.

The news shocked the whole palace. The ministers, who had heard of Pheasant's disinterest in the bedding protocol but had not considered it seriously, were astounded. "What about the Confucian cardinal rule of producing as many male progeny as possible?" they protested. "It is against the tradition and unheard of for an emperor to choose only a single bedmate."

"And one must not forget, Your Majesty," the Chancellor shouted, "the greatest ruler, your father, ever the most dutiful son of Emperor Gaozu, fathered ten sons and twenty-one daughters!"

Pheasant, so far, had only three sons—one by me, one by the Pure Lady, and one by Rain—and two daughters. With a calm look, Pheasant held up his hand to silence the Chancellor. "Do not forget this either, Chancellor: I am not my father."

The Empress was enraged, Apricot told me, and she blamed me for her inability to conceive. But as it turned out, no one believed what she said, and people began to treat her differently. When she passed by the halls in the Outer Palace, the ministers either looked at her askance or whispered behind her back, and some ministers even voiced criticisms of her other family members who served in the court; one minister even quarreled with her uncle, the Secretary.

The Empress vented her anger on her maids, punishing them and beating them, I heard. After that, she would pace in her bedchamber, gritting her teeth and cursing me.

But I did not care, and every night in our garden, I lay under the brilliant moon with Pheasant, bathed in its silver light. "I shall give you whatever you wish for," he whispered, his fingers tracing my naked skin. "Whatever you wish for, it will be yours."

His voice was most intoxicating. "Even the moon?" I asked.

He kissed my neck. A sweet sensation rose within me, and I leaned over, kissing him back.

"Yes, even the moon." He stroked my breasts, my stomach, and my lower abdomen. Gently, he bit me, tempting me, rousing me, urging me to want him and desire more. "For you, Luminous Lady, my sweet face, the mother of my child... One day, all your dreams will come true."

My heart swelled, my skin kindled with pleasure, and my body ached with an intensity I had never imagined before. Every touch of his hand, every echo of his words, was a memory of the past but also a reminder of the future—I was safe, I was protected, and my life in the palace too was protected.

Yes, I would dream again, and now, I would have my first dream. I would see my mother.

✦ ✦

Mother arrived at the palace on a breezy, pleasant summer day.

Wearing my best red gown and splendid wig, I waited in my garden, holding Lion, who was six months old, in my lap. I tried to remain calm, for it had been almost nine years since I had last seen her, but when her gray stole appeared at the garden's entrance, and when I saw her familiar features, her stooped back, her face marred by frost and wind, I could no longer sit. I gave Lion to Apricot and ran to her.

"Mother!" I gripped her arm. I was so happy I wanted to cry. "It's so wonderful to see you."

She gazed at me, her face the most enthralling picture I had ever seen. "My child, look at you. Look how beautiful you have become. So beautiful, so graceful. I never thought this would happen."

"I know, I know." I nodded, happiness swelling in my heart. She wore a stole patched with pieces of black and gray cloth and a pair of cloth shoes that looked thin and worn. She was shorter, skinnier, and smaller—a result of the simple life in a temple, I knew, but her eyes were clear, and her movements were agile. I was so relieved. As long as my mother was in good health, I could always see her.

"Is this my grandson?" She leaned over and took Lion from Apricot's arms. Happiness blossomed on her face, and her adoration radiated like a summer sun. "Look at him. Heavens! He is so small. He is so precious!"

She could not keep her hands from him. She cradled him in her arms, her fingers sweeping his hair, stroking his cheeks, caressing his toes. Lion did not pull away or cry as he often did with strangers, as though he felt her affection. When she tickled him, he even grinned a little. It might have been the first time I saw him smile.

Later, Mother and I sat near the pond, drinking chrysanthemum tea. I sat close to her, feeling the warmth of her arms, basking in her smile. When I was a child, I loved moments like this—leaning against her, feeling the affection in her soft voice and gentle touch. As a child, I had depended on it, thrived on it, and never gave a second thought to it. Now sitting next to her, I could feel her love continue to spring and nourish me like an eternal fountain, but there was something more in it. Because I was a mother myself, I felt more acutely the depth of the fountain and the strength in every droplet of love, and that gave me a new appreciation and a sense of gratefulness.

I went behind her and massaged her shoulders. She groaned in pleasure, and I could tell her backache had worsened over the years. Once upon a time, touching her and feeling her skin had given me strength and resolution. It still did, but it also offered me satisfaction and happiness. I told Mother she must come here and visit me again, and if she wished, she did not need to remain in the temple. I could purchase a house for her in the city, so she could live in comfort and good care.

I told her I could also recover our family house in Wenshui and our family's treasure, if she would like, and she could live there—but I would prefer for her to stay in Chang'an with me, rather than alone in our faraway family home.

She nodded. "All in due time."

"This is the time," I reminded her.

"I have been living in the monastery for so many years. I am accustomed to the simple life there. You must not worry about me."

I stood in front of her. "You do not wish for me to take care of you?"

She smiled, the lines around her eyes deepening. "Of course I do. But it is not that simple. You are a high-ranking Lady, but it does not mean you can do whatever you wish."

I did not know what to say. Mother was still worried about me. She was a cousin of a late empress and understood that a title would not keep me safe from the shadowy menace in the palace. She was also concerned my caring for her would be used against me, even though the Empress herself had showered numerous bestowals on her own family. The Empress was being criticized at the moment, but she could still find an excuse to harm me.

But I could not just let Mother live in poverty while I had all the indulgences. I traced the stitches on Mother's patched stole and the frayed edges of the sleeves. Perhaps there was another way I could take care of her. "I could request that the Emperor provide a donation to the monastery. Perhaps the abbess will accept that?"

"Donation?"

When I had visited the monastery years ago, the building was on the verge of collapsing. It must have been in a dire situation now. "Yes, for maintenance. Would you like to carry this message to her, Mother?"

"I shall be glad to do so."

I squeezed her hand in relief.

Mother held my face in her hands. Her eyes twinkling, she gazed at me. "I am happy for you, my child. I never dared to dream of this day. I wish I could tell you how happy I am."

"I know, Mother. I know." I embraced her.

"Your father would be so proud of you."

Father. Yes. He would have been. I was Luminous Lady. No one in my ancestral line had ever honored the Wu family so. And I was his daughter. I was part of him; I was his vision. Now that I had risen, he would rise with me. He must have felt that, the joy of the honor and the glow of my happiness. With my rank, I could pay proper tribute to him on his death anniversary. I could give extravagant gifts in his name and ask the monks to sing prayers for him to please his soul.

But was it possible, truly possible, that I could bring him the ultimate honor—that I would become a legend?

I sighed.

Mother patted my hand. "Will you promise me something, my child?"

"Yes, Mother."

"Be careful."

That was how much she loved me—always thinking of my safety. I hugged her. "I will, Mother."

We talked more and played with my son for the entire afternoon. When it was time for her to leave, I hugged her, wishing I did not have to let her go again.

The day after Mother left, I took out a portion of my allowances and sent them to Mother's monastery. I hoped the abbess would use the sum for maintenance and to improve the nuns' living conditions.

The abbess sent me a message to thank me for the donation and indicated that necessary repairs had been made on the monastery to accommodate the many women who had been abused and abandoned by their families and had gone to seek shelter there. What was more, the abbess said, many farmers, driven homeless by a recent sandstorm, had begged food from the temple as well. Knowing it was my donation that fed their stomachs and their children's, they were grateful for my help and prayed for me, the Luminous Lady in the palace.

I was happy to hear that my donation had helped the disadvantaged women and the poor. And I knew that in Chang'an, while there were dozens of Taoist abbeys, there were only a handful of Buddhist temples and monasteries, scattered around the far corners near the city walls. Because Buddhists did not receive any support from the court, the monks and nuns relied on their own hands and handouts from their penurious patrons. But I knew it was Buddhist temples, not Taoist abbeys, that provided relief to the poor who were struck by misfortune; for the Taoists, lofty in their thoughts, considered themselves to be superior and accused the poor of thievery and of being disease carriers. It became clear to me that Buddhist temples and monasteries had become boats to people on the verge of drowning, especially women, young and old.

I pondered the situation. I had not given any serious thoughts to religious beliefs before, even as I was incarcerated in the monastery, where I struggled to survive. To me, religion was like a flower in the fog. It was often vague, blurry, and I could not see a clear picture of it. But now I wondered if I should take part in the Buddhist belief, for if I spread my name among the believers, making an impact on their lives by caring for them, they would remember me, and they would think of me as a woman whom they could trust.

Did not the master Sun Tzu mention that the commander of an army must insert moral influence that could determine the outcome of a war?

I thought of my years in the monastery and the emaciated monks in Tripitaka's pagoda. I decided to provide donations to all the Buddhist temples and monasteries in the city.

I gathered my allowances, the gifts I received from Pheasant, and some extravagant gowns and jewelry I did not use, and declared them as alms to be allocated to the temples and monasteries.

I also gave each temple a water-powered mill that farmers used to hull and grist grains, for I remembered when I was home in Wenshui, many people had come to rent the five mills Father owned. The mills belonged to the temples, I told them, and they were free to lease them to millers and keep the income.

I did not stop there. I asked for help from Pheasant, who supported me with gold from the imperial treasure, which I used to improve roads around the monasteries and temples.

Gaoyang's husband, Fang Yi'ai, who served in the Ministry of Works, helped me with the construction of the roads. He was a serious young man with a tanned face, a loud voice, and an anxious expression. He hired artisans and laborers, purchased tools and material, arranged transportation, and personally inspected the progress of the projects. Soon, many muddy roads to the temples were replaced with new, solid earth paths covered with planks that would withstand the ravages of flood and mudslides.

I received grateful letters from the heads of the monasteries and temples. The living conditions of the monks and nuns were greatly improved, they said, and the monks had clean water, rice, and warm stoles. Also, the income from mills had ensured stability for the monks, and they were able to devote their time to deciphering sutras written in Sanskrit. The improvement of the roads had also brought more travelers, who, unable to afford the hostels and inns, used the temples as lodgings.

I also received a message from Tripitaka. He told me he had written parts of his journey, temporarily titled *The Great Journey to the West*, at his leisure, and he also thanked me for my help and donations. He said, "Even a great thinker like Buddha, who believes virtue fills the hall like incense's fragrance, needs the great wind to help spread it."

I smiled. I would be the wind. I would send the scent of benevolence and compassion to the people close and afar, and help fill their hearts with the divine fragrance of incense, and one day, perhaps, just perhaps, they would come to listen to me.

ₐₚₚₗₒₜ APRICOT, HER CHEEKS PINK WITH EXCITEMENT, BROUGHT me surprising news.

Two of the Empress's cousins who served in the Ministry of Rites were found guilty of bribery and relieved of their duties. And the Chancellor, the very man who had joined the Empress's petitions to attack me, had complained to the Regent that the Secretary, the Empress's uncle, was negligent in reporting to the court the counterfeited coppers that appeared on the market, and he had petitioned to investigate the matter. Consequently, the Secretary's duty in the court was suspended until further notice.

I was surprised. Bribery could hardly be defined as a crime, because it was a common practice in the court, and if one was determined to get to the bottom of it, then none of the ministers in the court were innocent. And the decision to suspend the Secretary's duty, merely because of negligence, was rather harsh.

It was a sign, I sensed acutely, that the Empress and her family were losing the power in the palace.

I wondered who wished to kick aside the Empress's men. It was difficult to tell. It could be some ministers who were displeased with the Empress and her family's influence in the court. It could even be the Pure Lady's family members—three of them held middle ranks in the court, I knew. But then it could also be the Regent's men, who coveted the important positions the Empress's family occupied.

The Empress was called home at once by her mother and her uncle, rumors said, and they chastised her for failing to protect her family. They warned her that all her connections, all her power, would be stripped away, and she would soon be alone in the palace. When the Empress returned to the palace, she was trembling, her eyes swollen from crying.

I began to hear some curious stories about her. She had grown rather pathetic, people said. Often, she stayed inside her bedchamber, biting her nails and murmuring to herself, looking anxious. She rarely ate her meals, and she suffered intense stomach pain. At night, she had nightmares and woke up in a cold sweat, and then she paced in her chamber, weeping and pounding her chest. When she was meeting her uncle in a building near the Chengxiang Hall, she broke down in tears and nearly choked herself. She lost her voice for days and was afraid of seeing anyone, even her maids. And she had lost more weight.

✦ ✦

I invited the Four Ladies to my newly renovated garden for some sweet chestnuts and dried, sugarcoated persimmons. It was, of course, the time to make allies—while the Empress was weak.

The Pure Lady sent her regards. She was ill and could not come. I was sorry to hear that. I was not certain if she was really ill or just trying to avoid me. With the Empress falling, people would certainly pay more attention to her and me, and I would have liked us to be on good terms. I sent the Pure Lady baskets of fruit and gifts and wished her to get well soon so she could continue her duty in the Imperial Silkworm Workshops.

The three Ladies came, looking splendid in their matching orange gowns adorned with kingfisher feathers. I complimented them, showering them with affection.

"I am delighted Luminous Lady likes our dresses," the Noble Lady said. As usual, they walked with their arms linked together, like inseparable triplets. From the way they smiled and whispered, I could tell they were close friends.

I walked down the winding bridge over the pond while Princess Gaoyang, the three ladies, their maids, and Apricot, who was holding Lion, trailed behind me.

"I wish to let you know, ladies"—I nodded at each of them—
"that I have talked to our Emperor about his decision to live here."
I had been happy when Pheasant announced he was disregarding the
bedding protocol, but I also understood the ladies would not have a
chance to conceive if he refused to see them again. I felt sorry for them.

The Noble Lady glanced at me, her pretty eyes looking excited.
"What did the Emperor say? Will he summon us?"

I continued to walk. "He said he would summon you very soon."

I did not have the heart to tell them the truth. When I had told
Pheasant to summon the ladies, reminding him that the bedding protocol was a tradition in the palace, he had shrugged and said, "I didn't
know you cared about traditions."

The Ladies smiled at one another, looking relieved. I decided to
work harder on Pheasant so he would take them to bed. I was not
jealous of them, for I knew Pheasant loved only me.

"Come, I will show you the water lilies." I waved at them. "Most
water lilies are blue, but that one with a white flower"—I pointed
at the plant floating in the center of the pond as I walked down the
zigzagging bridge—"is the most precious."

They did not seem to be interested in the plants or the newly
refurbished buildings, but they nodded politely.

"Have you heard that in the south"—I paused at the corner
of the bridge, breathing in the scent of the blossoms—"there is a
special water lily that droops its head under the water at night and
stands up again in the morning? It has large, snowy petals and a
strong, pleasant fragrance that none of the other types of lotus can
compete with. The locals call it 'sleeping lotus.'" I wanted to have
it in my garden someday.

The three Ladies nodded again, but soon they lost interest in the
plants and turned to play with my son, who was in Apricot's arms.

"How do you like the new garden, Gaoyang?" I asked, looking
around me. The bridge's red lacquer shone brightly in the sun, the tip
of the new house's eaves curved elegantly like a soaring phoenix's tail,
and the freshly painted mural looked beautiful on the pavilion's wall.
I was happy. This was my home and my garden, where I could plant
the trees of any fruit that I chose.

"The new garden is splendid," Princess Gaoyang said beside me. "And I also like the water lilies and the new pond."

"But?" I turned to her, studying her.

"I think you need to change one thing." Princess Gaoyang flicked a pebble to the pond, which bounced on the surface of the water.

"What, Gaoyang?" I patted my wig to assure it was centered, although I was not worried about the ladies mocking my hair. It was just my habit now, for being Luminous Lady, I needed to make certain my appearance was always appropriate.

"Your title. It doesn't fit you."

I was surprised. "What do you mean?"

"You deserve better than being a Lady, Mei. You should be the Empress."

My heart jumped. I was alarmed. Glancing around to make sure no one was listening to us, I said, "You shouldn't say that, Gaoyang."

"I say whatever I wish. You're almost her equal now. Maybe even more. She is barren, and you have a son. Don't you want to be an empress?"

Of course I did. I had not forgotten my father's dream. If I became the Empress, I would make his spirit proud, and I would honor my family greatly. But it was dangerous to think of this dream, and I would not do anything to challenge Empress Wang. Her power was weakening in the palace, but she was still the Empress.

"She curses me and my son." I gazed at the white lotus. "Have you heard that?"

Princess Gaoyang shrugged and tossed another pebble into the pond. "They're only curses. You have nothing to fear."

Only Princess Gaoyang would say something like that. "I don't know."

I had not forgotten how cruelly Empress Wang had beaten me and how she had slaughtered my Hope and cooked him. As long as I lived in the palace, I would need to watch out for her, and I needed to do anything I could to shield my son from her wrath.

Princess Gaoyang would not understand that, but she did remind me how precarious my position—and indeed, Pheasant's position—truly was. The support from the General was not enough. If Pheasant wished to become a true emperor, he needed more supporters, and I needed more supporters too, those who would surround my son and me like a protective net. But it was dangerous to ask for allies in the court. I was relatively new there. Few people knew me. If I did not prepare properly, I would only put my son in danger, and Pheasant would lose his newly won position.

"Do you miss Prince Ke?" I asked Gaoyang. When she looked at me in surprise, I said, "I remember you mentioned him to me. Pheasant misses him."

Pheasant missed all his brothers, I knew, even though he did not talk about them often. He especially missed Taizi and his brother Prince Wei, who had died years ago.

Princess Gaoyang smiled, two dimples deepening on her cheeks. "I do. We were very close when we grew up. We played many games together. He was kind to me. He is a good man and a good brother. Loyal and kind."

I nodded. Perhaps Pheasant could recall him from exile. The prince was the former Noble Lady's son, and I had liked him. He would also be a steadfast supporter if he returned to the palace, and being the son of the late Emperor, he could be a powerful ally.

That night, I talked to Pheasant about the idea of recalling Prince Ke.

"My uncle won't agree to that." He hesitated, even as delight flitted across his eyes. "But how splendid it would be if he could return. I would enjoy his company in the court. I haven't seen him for four years."

"So will you do your best to recall him?" I asked.

He put his hands together, intertwining his fingers. He had that calm look I often saw these days. There was firmness and determination in his eyes that I found intoxicating. Pheasant was looking more and more like a powerful ruler every day.

"I will do my best, and I will not give up until I succeed," he said. "And with the General by my side, I believe we might have our wish."

There was an uproar when Pheasant broached the subject of Prince Ke's return, I heard, the idiotic Chancellor being most outspoken. But Pheasant insisted. He wished only to spend more time with his brother, whom he had missed gravely all these years, he said.

In the end, Pheasant succeeded, and that autumn, when the maple leaves turned golden yellow in the palace, Prince Ke returned from exile with his two sons. Pheasant restored the land and houses that had belonged to the prince and reinstated his allowance.

The Regent was not pleased at the prince's return. He forbade his ministers to speak to the prince and his two sons. And when Pheasant held a private meeting, asking the Regent if the prince could be Pheasant's counselor—Pheasant was always courteous and respectful to the old man, even though he took the power from him—the Regent looked pensive. Pheasant pressed on, reminiscing about the years when he used to hunt and play polo with his father, Prince Ke, and his other brothers, and eventually the Regent sighed. "Certainly, brotherhood matters greatly in a man's life," he said, "and if you do not mind me saying this, I shall not forget how much your father's love meant to me. He indeed was like a brother to me." And then he nodded reluctantly to give his consent.

Pheasant was elated. He promoted Prince Ke to high-ranking counselor, giving him the right to accompany him at all times and to provide Pheasant with advice, and later, inspired by his success, Pheasant also recalled a number of people who had served him, among them his previous tutor, Minister Xu Jingzong.

I was so glad. Now with the General, Prince Ke, and Princess Gaoyang's husband, Fang Yi'ai, Pheasant had formed his own support group. Suddenly, his words rang loud in the Audience Hall, drowning the voices of the idiot Chancellor and the others.

I proposed a feast, using the approaching Mid-Autumn Festival as an excuse. It was time to celebrate their return and the wall of support Pheasant had built, but of course, it was also time to gather them around me.

14

ON THE NIGHT OF THE FESTIVAL, THE GARDEN NEAR THE imperial library, where the celebration was to be held, was transformed into a grand feasting place. Red lanterns, strung in fives, hung from the eaves of the pavilions. Lacquered tables, holding jugs of fragrant wine and trays of peaches and grapes, were set neatly on top. And there, in the smoke-hued sky, a round, silver moon peered at me.

Many ministers came to the feast. Most of them were middle-ranking ministers dressed in green or red. One by one, I greeted them, my head dipping low. They bowed back, and to my surprise, some mentioned that they were grateful for the improved roads near the temples. I was pleased they had heard of my donations.

Prince Ke greeted me. He had settled in his home outside the palace and helped review some petitions presented to Pheasant. But the prince did not look like he had recovered from exile. His waist was thinner than a dancer's, his skin looked pale, and his lips cracked. Smiling mildly, he still had kind eyes that reminded me of his mother. He remembered me, to my delight, and thanked me for receiving him.

"Luminous Lady," Pheasant said, his arm hooked around the prince's shoulders. He was truly happy tonight, laughing loudly, and he had drunk too much. "Perhaps you may honor us by composing a poem later."

I liked to see him in good spirits. With his recent victory of recalling the prince and the ministers, Pheasant was beginning to look like a real ruler. He was also gaining more confidence, since the Regent had become surprisingly agreeable over the past few weeks. When Pheasant had reinstated the positions of his previous tutor and several other ministers he had recalled, the Regent had made no objections.

Then to our great surprise, the Regent confessed that his health had been declining lately, his eyesight was failing him, and he dreaded he would soon lose the energy that was needed to attend to state affairs. He said it was time for him to step aside and asked to be free of daily duties in the court. He would come to the Audience Hall only for important matters if Pheasant summoned him.

Pheasant, of course, immediately agreed.

I took a goblet from the table and raised it to Pheasant. "It would be my greatest pleasure to amuse you, Your Majesty."

Pheasant's previous tutor, Minister Xu Jingzong, came and introduced himself to me. We had met before, he said. He was the old minister who had asked me about the answer to the riddle I had composed as a gift for Emperor Taizong nearly fifteen years before. I was surprised he still remembered.

He carried a confident and bold demeanor that intrigued me. Many who had returned from exile looked jaded and subdued, but he was not one of them. I found him worth noting. Only a man of extraordinary strength and insight would survive and rise above the adversity of banishment.

The Pure Lady, wearing her usual white gown, appeared near the entrance to the garden. Holding a little boy's hand, she stopped at a cinnamon tree, hesitant. I was delighted. At least she had come.

I went to greet her. "I am so pleased to see you're feeling better, Pure Lady."

She gave me a deep bow. "I'm coming to offer my gratitude, Luminous Lady. I would like to thank you in person for your gifts. You're most kind and generous." Her voice was soft, and her etiquette was impeccable.

"Oh, you must not mention them," I said. Her manner was somehow distant, but that was to be expected, and she was also wary of me, and that had to be respected. "I do hope you will not tire yourself with your duty. How is this year's silk harvest?"

A massive mudslide in spring had demolished many mulberry farms in the north of Chang'an, I had heard, and the leaf supply to the Imperial Silkworm Workshops was somewhat affected, but I did not know the details.

"Oh, it is worrisome," the Lady replied, but she did not elaborate. It was part of her duty to guard the secret of the silkworms in the workshops, I knew, and also a privilege. "I would be honored if you would like to meet my son," she said, and nodded at the boy beside her.

I smiled. That was certainly a gesture to make peace with me. "The honor is mine, Pure Lady. I am most delighted to meet your son." I lowered myself to look into the boy's eyes. I had heard so much about him. He possessed extraordinary literary talent, Apricot had said. "So you are the prodigy Sujie? Will you honor me by reciting a poem?"

He threw his sleeves behind him with a dramatic flare. And then to my astonishment, he recited the entire "The Preface to the Orchid Pavilion."

"Indeed, a prodigy!" I exclaimed, shocked by his talent. He was only four years old! His mother had raised him well, and I hoped my child would be as talented as him when he grew up. "Have you learned how to compose a poem yourself?"

"I have," he said in his childish but solemn voice. "I composed a poem about the Empress."

"Will you recite it to me?"

The Pure Lady coughed and pulled the boy's sleeve. She looked uneasy, glancing at the ministers behind me.

The poem must not speak of the Empress favorably. I liked the boy even more. "Perhaps you will recite it to me another day," I said, smiling.

Pheasant called me.

"Come, Sujie, you must meet your brother." I took the mother and the son to my table. Coolly, Sujie nodded his head at Lion in Apricot's arms, and Lion responded by drooling. We all laughed.

When the full moon revealed itself behind the clouds, it was the moment to compose a poem.

I began first.

Looking at all the guests around me, I raised my goblet and said:

"Misty lanes,
Inky doors,
A garden of wines, fragrances, and much more.

"Golden ceilings,
Rainbow floors,
Bright, fluffy, silky dreams galore.

"What are you waiting for,
My friends,
It's time
To climb the stairs of the moonlight,
And sing a new song."

Thunderous applause rose around me, and I bowed deeply to show my appreciation. I wondered how the Empress would react when she heard this poem. Would she have another fiery outburst?

Pheasant, laughing, raised his goblet and composed his poem. He was followed by Prince Ke, Minister Xu Jingzong, and the other ministers.

The night breeze sweeping my face, I sipped my wine. I enjoyed celebrating the moment with all the people who came to support me, and now that the Empress's power was waning in the court, I hoped there would be many more moments like that in the future.

✦ ✦

A few days later, I received a request from the Regent, who asked to meet Sujie, my son, the Pure Lady, and me in a building near the Taiji Hall. I was surprised and also excited. Since my son's birth, the Regent had never made an effort to meet him. Could this meeting have something to do with the Empress's barrenness?

When the Pure Lady and I arrived, Pheasant was sitting on a stool in the center of the building; near him was the Empress, wearing her golden gown and the phoenix crown. Her head dropped low, and her crown tipped precariously.

Sitting on the right side of the hall, the Regent nodded at the Pure Lady, the children, and me as we greeted him. He was squinting, and I was reminded that he had said he was getting old and his eyesight was failing him. Indeed, he looked frail. His back was stooped, his face was covered with many age spots, his hawkish nose appeared thinner, and he had a tendency to open his mouth and pause, as though his mind was addled and he had trouble remembering his words.

He had not attended audiences since Pheasant recalled Prince Ke and the other ministers, and he came to the palace only when Pheasant needed to consult with him about important matters. I wondered what he wished to discuss today.

"These are fine, fine children." The Regent wiped his mouth with a handkerchief, watching the two children: Sujie pacing in front of him like a learned scholar and Lion biting a hand drum, his favorite toy, in my lap. "It is my greatest pleasure to see the imperial progeny of the Li Family. I am greatly pleased, Nephew. I am certain your father would be proud."

He did not acknowledge the Empress or even look at her, as though she did not exist.

"I'm pleased to hear that from you too, Uncle. They are only children, and they need much tutoring," Pheasant said courteously. He was always respectful to his uncle, careful not to say anything to upset him.

"Certainly, Nephew, I cannot agree more. Tutoring children is an important matter, as we must decide what they will learn and who they will grow to be. I shall be glad to offer my suggestion if Nephew wishes. However"—he coughed to clear his throat—"I would like to bring a few important issues to your attention today."

"What may be of your concern, Uncle?"

"Your Majesty." The Regent sighed. "I would rather not bother you, but I'm most perturbed by recent reports of corruption and negligence in the palace. The matters have been dealt with. I know you have been aware of that. But some ministers, to my dismay, have come to me and spoken of another matter that concerns them. They expressed that they were worried about our kingdom's future and stated that it was a shame our dynasty, the great dynasty your father and grandfather had founded, would be subject to such a humiliation."

"Humiliation?" Pheasant asked.

The Regent blinked his eyes slowly, as though he could not remember what he had just said. "As you know, Nephew, we are all aware that it is a man's first and foremost duty to have a son who will carry the family's bloodline, as our sage teacher Confucius has instructed us for hundreds of years, and it has been the principle all nobles and honored men have followed, but now, regrettably, our Empress, the mother of the kingdom," he said without turning his head in the Empress's direction, "has failed us. Eight years, and she is unable to give us a male heir, and many are concerned that she is unable to conceive."

The Empress jerked. "I'm not barren!"

The Regent glanced at her, and I could see he was displeased that she had interrupted him. "If the Empress is fertile, as she claims, then perhaps she should conceive a male heir as soon as possible."

The Empress turned her head toward the wall. She was biting her lips hard.

I caught the gaze of the Pure Lady, who sat next to me. She was smiling. She too enjoyed seeing the Empress in disgrace.

"But, Nephew, I did not come here today just to ask our Empress to fulfill a woman's duty, as clearly, may I state this frankly, she has failed another duty as well."

"What duty are you speaking of, Uncle?"

The Regent sighed again. "I do believe you are aware of this. Nephew, the silk production by the Imperial Silkworm Workshops has been alarmingly low this year, and it is many people's belief that this is due to our Empress and her ill effect on the silkworms. As you know, silkworms are most delicate creatures."

The poor production of the silk actually had much to do with the mudslide that had damaged many mulberry tree farms. But I could see this was the Regent's, and the ministers', excuse to kick the Empress aside. I held Lion tightly in my arms, listening with concentration.

Pheasant nodded. "Silk. I see, Uncle. I was going to talk to you about this."

The Regent wiped his mouth with his handkerchief and put it in his pocket. "Our kingdom's prosperity depends on the silk trade, Nephew. I cannot stress how important silk is to our kingdom. Thus

I urge you, Nephew, for the sake of our kingdom's welfare, to take a proper measure, a drastic measure, if necessary, to ensure our kingdom's prosperity."

"Drastic measure?"

I felt my heart race faster in excitement. I had never dared to dream of this moment. But it was true. He was proposing to strip the Empress of her power in the workshops.

"You...you..." The Empress was shaking—her hands, her body, and even her crown.

The Regent sighed. He did not look in my direction, but I knew the old man's attitude toward me had changed considerably. Even though he was not yet warm to me, his old hostility and coldness had thawed a great deal. "I am afraid so, Nephew, and this is, after all, your decision to make. I trust you will choose whoever you see fit to oversee the most important venture in our kingdom."

Pheasant glanced at me, and I knew he would appoint me if I nodded. This was a perfect opportunity for me to rise in the palace. I was Most Adored, ranked only lower than the Empress, and if I took the most important position of supervising the workshops, my status in the court would be solidified, and many ministers would flock to me and support me.

But I turned toward the Pure Lady instead. I had never worked in the workshops, and she had been reviewing the records every year. If anyone was ready to take the control of the silkworms, it was the Pure Lady, and I could not fight against her simply because of my own selfish reasons.

Pheasant, reading my thoughts, smiled and turned toward the Pure Lady. "Pure Lady, would you consider taking over the duty of overseeing the workshops?"

The Pure Lady glanced at me, her eyes lit with happiness and gratitude. "I shall be greatly honored, Your Majesty."

"So it is settled." Pheasant turned to the Regent. "Are you pleased, Uncle?"

The old man nodded. "Of course, Nephew."

I smiled to congratulate the Pure Lady, truly happy for her, and I was not worried about the Empress anymore, for I knew her power in the court would soon come to an end. Some of her family members had lost their posts in the court, her uncle was suspended, and now she had lost the most important position in the Inner Court.

The Empress's golden gown swept beside me as she rushed out of the hall. And even though she raised her sleeve to shield her face and covered her mouth, I could hear her sobs, loud and furious, escaping from her throat.

O

AD 653

The Fourth Year *of*
Emperor Gaozong's Reign
of Eternal Glory

AUTUMN

15

THE EMPRESS'S ORDER CAME TO ME WITH A GRAVE WARNING.
All the titled ladies must gather in the Chengxiang Hall immediately.
Anyone who failed to appear on time would be punished.

I left my son to Apricot and my maids and went to the hall without
delay. What was so important that the Empress must see all of us so
urgently? It was not time for fruit or silk distribution, and most items
I needed were delivered to my garden directly.

I wondered whether the Empress, having lost control of the
workshops, had found some excuse to clamp her hands on me and the
other ladies.

Gaoyang, who happened to visit me, decided to come with me.
"That mad cow cannot be trusted," she said.

With Gaoyang by my side, I walked as fast as I could. When we
arrived at the courtyard, it was crowded with servants and some
ministers holding scrolls and calligraphy brushes. So whatever the
Empress wished to let us know must have been worthy of making a
court record.

No guards. A good sign. She would not resort to violence.

I stood in the corridor, waiting for the eunuch to announce my
arrival. Princess Gaoyang turned her head left and right, watching
everyone who passed. A moment later, the Four Ladies and the other
titled ladies entered the courtyard.

"Did we do something wrong?" the Noble Lady said to me in her
faint voice. Today the three Ladies were wearing purple gowns with

round medallions and black fur shawls with golden trim. Despite the cold, they looked slim and warm. "Is she going to punish us?"

The other ladies all bore the same expression of fear on their faces, except the Pure Lady, who looked thoughtful.

"Not while I am here," Princess Gaoyang said.

I put a hand on the princess's arm to quiet her and said to the Noble Lady, "Don't worry. If she wished to harm us, she would not need to gather us all together and bring the ministers."

The Pure Lady nodded. "I think so too."

"All ladies enter!" a eunuch announced at the entrance of the hall.

I hurried up the stone stairs to step inside the building. Princess Gaoyang followed me, and the other ladies entered behind us, according to their ranks.

Inside, more ministers had lined up against the wall. In the center of the hall were two stools set on a raised platform, where the Empress and a scrawny youngster sat. The youth slumped a little in his seat. His skin was pale, his nose red, and his eyes narrow and slanted. He reminded me of someone… Rain. He had to be Rain's son, Zhong. I had seen him only once during a feast Emperor Taizong held to celebrate his birth, and Zhong had been only a few months old. He had been living outside the palace with Pheasant when Emperor Taizong punished Pheasant and ordered him to leave the palace. When Pheasant became the heir, Zhong had moved to the Eastern Palace with Rain, but after Pheasant became the Emperor, Empress Wang had kicked Zhong back to the house in the city, claiming her future son would be the heir, thus the Eastern Palace was his residence. And I had also heard that the barren Empress, worried Zhong would become the heir, had forced him to live in isolation, forbidding him to come to the palace or meet the ministers.

He was about ten years old, and he should have been living in his house outside the palace. What was he doing sitting next to the Empress?

"All kneel," the Empress ordered, blinking her closely set eyes slowly. She was wearing her usual phoenix crown and the voluminous yellow regalia that draped on her shoulders like a shapeless bag. Her broad forehead bore more wrinkles than I remembered, and her flat face, covered with too much white powder, spread out like a snow-dusted graveyard.

She looked pathetic, weak, and old, but she was still dangerous. I stepped forward and knelt as ordered. I was so close to her, I could see the golden threads on her embroidered shoes and smell the pungent herb odor from her sachet. "Greetings, Empress."

I was not sure how to address the boy. Although he was Pheasant's son, his position was low because of his mother's low rank, and according to the hierarchy, I was of a higher rank than him.

The Empress raised her head. "I'm certain you all have heard that the Regent was concerned about the kingdom's future. I assure you, such a concern is not needed, for today I have summoned all of you to make an important announcement," she said, her voice loud. "I have decided to adopt this child."

Adopt Rain's child?

"And why not?" her voice rose, louder now, as though she had sensed my objection. "This child bears imperial blood, and his mother was an honorable woman, a good friend of mine. And for that reason I have decided to accept him as my own and raise him as my son."

But she was not just raising him as her own. She was using him to secure her power. She must have been desperate after losing her position of overseeing the workshops, and her family must have helped her find the solution.

"I shall make this adoption legal, and by law, he shall become the heir of our kingdom." She nodded at the ministers near the wall. "I now order this to be written in our imperial family's record."

My back stiffened. The Regent had said she must produce a male heir, and we had thought she would conceive one, not adopt. She was very cunning indeed. But the adoption could not happen. The child could not become her son.

"Does our emperor know of this?" I asked, frowning.

"The Emperor has been consulted, of course, and he has agreed."

"The Emperor has agreed?" I did not believe her. If Pheasant knew of the adoption, he would have told me, but he would never agree to it. Oftentimes he had told me he was concerned about Zhong. He was so young, and alone without his mother's protection. For his own safety, he had to stay away from the palace, Pheasant had said.

"I don't believe you," Princess Gaoyang said. "Pheasant would never agree to this."

"*Gongzhu.*" The Empress's voice was cold. "You must watch your words. This is not your place to speak. I will decide when the Emperor will know of this adoption."

So she was lying! I raised my head.

She stared at me triumphantly, a cold smile on her face. "And I must remind you," she continued. "Zhong bears the imperial blood, and this is the reason why he will be my child. I have summoned the Secretary, who has agreed to come to the Outer Palace to draft the adoption papers as we speak, and when we finish this formal adoption ceremony, I shall inform the Regent of my decision, and he will see to it that Zhong will become my son. Now, ministers, prepare to conduct the ceremony."

I wanted to walk out, yet I was unable to move. An empress adopting a child of a concubine and using him to secure her own crown was not common, but it had been done a few dynasties back.

I lowered my head. Empress Wang had made a vital move to secure her own position. With the adoption, the ministers who doubted her would stay with her again, and those who were not with her would be inclined to come to her side as well. She had solidified her crown and gained even stronger support in the court.

A court recorder stepped up and cleared his throat, unfurling a scroll. "With the presence of all the titled ladies in the Inner Court and the court recorders, I do now announce that the court commence the ceremony of the imperial adoption as so ordered by Empress Wang, the mother of our kingdom."

"Come, Zhong." The Empress beckoned to the boy. She looked proud, her broad shoulders square, her back erect. "Come to your mother."

"Mother." The boy pulled up the front of his robe and knelt before her.

"The wife of Emperor Gaozong, Empress Wang, has officiated the adoption of the son of Emperor Gaozong and his deceased concubine, Rain of the Chang family. The child, who was given the name of Li Zhong, shall be known and honored as the firstborn of the Empress and Emperor Gaozong, the grandson of Emperor Taizong, the great grandson of Emperor Gaozu, the founder of the Tang Dynasty. Now the court commences the recital of the lineage of the imperial Li family and that of the Empress's."

The list went on and on, and finally, the court recorder finished his reading. "Now the court commences the ceremony of mother and son. Li Zhong, pay respect to your mother."

I watched in distaste. The boy must have been grateful to the Empress for his new status. For years he had lived in obscurity, and now with the adoption, he would come to fame. He would bow to the Empress, do her bidding to please her, and he would be rewarded.

Zhong touched his head on the ground. Once, twice, three times. "Empress Mother, Empress Mother, Empress Mother."

"My son." That woman extended her hand. She smiled, but her face was rigid and her voice was dry. She seemed to be addressing a dog blocking her way or a servant whose name she did not know. Then she turned to a red lacquered tray to pick up a gold necklace intertwined with dragons. "This is my gift to you."

She put it around his neck, and Zhong bowed again, three times. Then together they stood, with her giant stature and his lean figure, his back slightly stooped, like a pair of poorly matched clowns.

"I am pleased. I am greatly pleased." She put her hand on his shoulder, but her hand was large, and it must have come down heavier than she intended, because the boy cringed, hunched his back, and straightened again.

She was not a mother. She would never be. Some women could never be mothers—no matter how hard they tried—and Empress Wang was one of them. I remembered once my friend the Noble Lady had said a mother was a tree whose branches would grow to shelter the nest for her birds, but the woman in front of me was a rock that provided no shelter or warmth, from which no life could breed.

Princess Gaoyang nudged me, and I sighed, preparing to rise.

"Ladies, I now command you to listen to my son's order." She was not finished with us yet. "Zhong. Tell them."

I frowned. It was rude that a newly adopted son would command us, the ladies of his father, but I could see why the Empress was doing this. She wanted to use him to intimidate us.

The boy's face brightened, and he grinned, too widely. He went back to the stool where he had sat earlier and cleared his throat. "Ladies of the Inner Court, by the order of my Empress Mother, I now command your loyalty to me, the son of Empress Wang and Emperor Gaozong, the new Crown Prince of the Eastern Palace, the future heir of Great China."

A wave of murmurs, mixed with surprise and disbelief, came from the ladies behind me, and I could feel Princess Gaoyang shaking her head beside me. And I wanted to sigh. He already considered himself to be the heir. That was extremely bold of him, and that he would order us to give him an oath was even more shameless.

"You heard him." The Empress's voice came again, impatient. "Recite the verses of oath."

For a moment, I could not recall the words I had learned from the Code of Courtly Conduct many years ago, but the others around me began to speak, and I remembered. "May the Crown Prince of the kingdom guide us with the teaching of the woman's way, govern us with the light of his wisdom and righteousness, and punish us when we forget the principle of compliance. I beseech the heir of the kingdom to accept my pledge. I shall serve you, I shall obey you, I shall revere you, with my soul, my heart, and those of my progeny."

A cage of words. I felt trapped, shut inside its thick bars and stifling air. And the Empress was watching me, like a prowling beast ready to pounce on its prey.

16

PHEASANT WAS FURIOUS. HE HAD NOT BEEN CONSULTED about the matter, and he would not consent to the adoption, he announced in the Audience Hall. But after Pheasant retired from the audience, Prince Ke, who had been advising him on some matters, pulled him aside and spoke with him. A man of mild disposition, the prince did not think it was wise to oppose the Empress, since the adoption had already been made public.

Unsure of what to do, Pheasant summoned the Regent and asked his opinion.

"It is unacceptable that the Empress would adopt the child without your consent," the Regent said with a frown. "She has crossed the code of obedience and propriety, and she should be reminded that a woman must not override her husband and make her own decisions!"

But he shook his head when Pheasant expressed his desire to denounce the adoption. "This is your domestic affair, Nephew. I understand I must not interfere, but the Empress is barren. She will never conceive. Adopting a son, even the one born by a low concubine, is better than being without any son. We shall hope that with the adoption, she will find peace, and our kingdom will find peace and cease gossiping."

Still unwilling to accept the adoption, Pheasant asked me as we lay in bed that night. He was deeply concerned about Zhong, I could tell. The boy had lived in the palace only a few years, and he had yet to understand the treacherous web spinning around him. "I had planned

for him to live in quiet outside the palace, and now it is too late."
Pheasant gave a heavy sigh.

I was tormented. For days I had been angry, sickened by the
Empress's scheme, and I was inclined to urge Pheasant to denounce
the adoption. But the Regent did not seem to like to hear any more discussions on the subject, and in my heart I also understood Prince Ke's
concern. Pheasant's position was still delicate in the court. He had just
gained his support, and if he openly waged a war against the Empress,
it would cause an uproar in the kingdom.

I sighed, stroking Pheasant's back. Near us, Lion was sleeping
soundly, his breathing a soothing melody.

I had to be patient. Pheasant had to be patient too.

✦ ✦

The next day, Pheasant reluctantly announced that he would accept
the adoption and recognize Zhong as the future heir. That afternoon,
Zhong moved into the Eastern Palace, joining his adopted mother,
and began his new life.

Zhong settled in comfortably, Apricot reported to me. A group of
tutors were assigned to him, to teach him law, classics, rites, and the
prefectures in the kingdom. They were either the Empress's relatives
or the Secretary's close allies, handpicked by the Empress. Zhong also
proved to have quite a talent for governing, quickly learning the rituals, protocols, and the duties of the government. Given time, he would
become a capable candidate for the throne.

The Empress took her newly adopted son everywhere in the Outer
Palace. Her head held high, she introduced Zhong to the ministers and
asked them for recommendations of noble maidens of betrothal age. It
was time for the heir to wed, she said. He was only ten!

The ministers bowed to her, promising they would make inquiries
into any suitable maidens. No one mentioned the Empress's barrenness again, and the Empress asked for her uncle's return as Secretary.
As it happened, the Chancellor found someone else who had failed
to report the counterfeited coppers and deemed the Empress's uncle
innocent. He was reinstated the next day.

The Empress also demanded that she take back her duty in the workshops, which Pheasant refused. But the Pure Lady fell sick again and was unable to provide care for the workshops. Pheasant had no choice but to turn to the Empress.

With her power restored, the Empress was triumphant, and she ordered Sujie and Lion to pay respect to the new heir at dawn each morning. This was a new protocol, she asserted, and for hours, the two poor children knelt in the dawn light, yawning, shivering in the cold, waiting for the heir to rise from bed. Lion, who had just started to crawl, cried and fell asleep on the ground. Little Sujie was late one day. The Empress chastised him and ordered him to crawl around the courtyard for ten rounds. Poor Sujie was in tears.

I was worried. She was tormenting the children to punish me and the Pure Lady.

Prince Ke told me of another incident that concerned me. He was reviewing tax documents with some ministers when the Empress burst in with the new heir and her uncle. She grabbed the scroll from a minister's hand. "There!" she cried out, pointing at a word that, when spoken, bore the same sound as "zhong." "He has defiled the heir's name!"

The poor minister was lashed before everyone's eyes, and from then on, few ministers dared to join the meeting with Prince Ke.

The Empress, armed with her new son, had started to retaliate. She was cutting us out, eliminating us, like a gardener trimming the unwanted branches of a tree.

✦ ✦

"Why do you want to visit the Pure Lady?" Princess Gaoyang asked me as we walked down a path that led us to the Quarters of the Pure Lotus, the residences for the Four Ladies. Behind us, my four maids Chunlu, Xiayu, Qiushuang, and Dongxue followed.

It was a pleasant day. The wind blew on my face without its usual sharpness, and the sun had a warm touch.

"I haven't seen her for many days. I heard she is sick again," I said. I had brought gifts for the Pure Lady, some precious ginseng roots and other herbs that were said to warm a woman's blood. I also wanted to talk to her about the Empress's new rule that our children must visit the heir every day. We must do something to stop the Empress from torturing our children. The Pure Lady would agree with me, I believed, since we were on the same side. "I heard Sujie is sick too." He had not come to wish the heir good morning for at least ten days.

"Sujie is sick?"

"Yes." I nodded. "He composed a ballad before he was sick. Have you heard it, Gaoyang?"

I sang:

"Once there was a young fellow,
Lean as a lynx, swift like a swallow.
He drinks the jade liquid and dines on the emerald grapes,
He struts in his golden robes and sleeps in his damask capes.
In awe, people watch and gape
At his vermilion hat and exquisite shape,
But beneath all, everyone knows he is only an ordinary ape."

It was clear to whom Sujie was referring, and I wanted to smile. I was sure the Empress would have another outburst if she heard it.

"Oh, that little imp!" Gaoyang said fondly. "I love that ballad. I laughed out loud when Apricot told me. 'An ordinary ape.' Is there any ape that's not ordinary? I think he's being rather kind to Zhong, actually. Speaking of your maids, how is Apricot doing?"

Gaoyang walked like a child, skipping and twirling along the zigzagging path, unable to stand still. I had long ago abandoned the thought of reminding her to walk like a lady. Princess Gaoyang simply could not be tamed, for better or worse.

"Apricot?" When Apricot first came to serve me, she had been young and bashful, but over the past two years, she had grown more confident. She brought news from the eunuchs and gathered messages from around the palace for me, and I had grown fond of her. She was also wonderful with Lion. "She's trustworthy. Why did you ask?"

"I saw her with the Secretary. They were in a corridor near the Chengxiang Hall."

I frowned. The man with a fat, round face like a butcher? He had resumed his position. He usually worked in a building near the Taiji Hall in the Outer Palace, but the Empress often summoned him to the Inner Court, so he had many chances to encounter Apricot. "What were they doing?"

Gaoyang shrugged.

I waved my hand. Apricot would not betray me. "She's trustworthy," I said again.

"Of course she is. I have no doubt about that."

I nodded. Through the thinning autumn foliage, I could see the corners of the flying eaves and the red wall of the Quarters of the Pure Lotus. "Have you met the Pure Lady, Gaoyang?"

"I saw her during the Empress's adoption ceremony, but I never spoke to her. I don't know her very well."

I patted the wig on my head, my fingers touching the gold hairpin on the side, and I arranged the strands of black hair in front of my chest and let it fall near my waist. "You'll like her. She has a mathematical mind; she is good at using the abacus and adding numbers and subtracting them. Very rare for her age."

Soon, we arrived at the Quarters. The moment I entered the compound, old memories rushed to me. The beautiful but conniving Jewel. The benevolent Noble Lady. The other vengeful Pure Lady who plotted to overthrow Emperor Taizong. The obsessive Lady Virtue who would not part with her mirror, and the great dancer, Lady Obedience. Now the former three were dead, and the latter two were imprisoned in the Yeting Court.

I shook off the memories and stepped into the courtyard. Everything looked the same—the small mountain—a replica of the sacred Mount Hua—the pond, and even the birdcage under the eaves of the house where Jewel had lived. It was still there but empty. Gone was Jewel's yellow oriole.

Several maids dashed away to notify their ladies of visitors, and soon a woman rushed out of the chamber on my left. "Luminous Lady!"

I could not tell which lady she was until I saw her puffy eyes. Then the other two ladies, the Noble Lady and Lady Obedience, appeared behind her.

"Ladies." I bowed to each one.

"I am most pleased to see you here, Luminous Lady. What a surprise. Would you like to have some chrysanthemum tea with us?" the Noble Lady said, dismissing the maids who gathered to greet us.

"I would be honored," I said. "Perhaps another day? I came to visit the Pure Lady. I hope she won't be surprised. I did not give her notice. Which house is hers, may I ask?"

The Noble Lady nodded to the house on my right. "But, Luminous Lady," she said, her pretty eyes blinking quickly. She looked uneasy. "I wish to tell you something important. I think something might have happened…"

The Pure Lady lived in Jewel's old house. The door was shut, and no maids came out to greet me. I was surprised. As a second-degree Lady, she ought to have had eight maids. I walked up the stone staircase to the Lady's chamber. "Come, Noble Lady. We shall visit her together. What do you think has happened?"

Princess Gaoyang had already pushed the door open, and I stopped at the threshold. A screen stood in the center of the chamber. Near it were two stools with fur cushions and a table that held a black lacquered jewelry box, a dozen small powder boxes, and a bronze mirror. In the right corner of the chamber stood a tripod brazier, which was covered with a thin layer of dust, as if it had not been lit for some time. The room was cold and empty; the Pure Lady and Sujie were nowhere to be seen. "Where is the Pure Lady?"

Lady Obedience, who talked with her hand over her mouth, whispered into the Noble Lady's ear, and the lady coughed, her pretty eyes lowering. "Luminous Lady, that is what I wished to speak to you about. The Pure Lady has been missing for a few days."

"Missing?" I frowned. Princess Gaoyang went behind the screen to check the bed. When she came back, she shook her head. The Pure Lady was not in her room.

"She was sick. Then she went out for a stroll near the lake and disappeared."

"Disappeared?" I stared at her in disbelief. "Did something happen to her?"

She hesitated. "That's what we thought."

"Have you searched the area near the lake?"

"We have, Luminous Lady." The Noble Lady squeezed closer to the other two Ladies, grasping their hands.

"And you didn't find her? Where is Sujie?"

"He is gone too."

"Sujie is gone?" I was shocked. "Not sick? Why didn't you tell me sooner? We must find them!"

The Noble Lady hesitated. "We told the Empress, Luminous Lady, since she is the head of the Inner Court. She said…"

An ominous feeling seized me. "What did she say?"

"She said she would find them, and she warned us not to mention this to anyone: you, the Emperor, or the Pure Lady's family. We dared not disobey her, but it has been nine days since they disappeared."

The room felt stuffy, choking me. I stepped out into the corridor. Somehow it was colder on this side of the courtyard. The sun was weak, printing streaks of timid rays on the replica mountain's jagged surface. It was the late autumn, but there had been no snow yet.

I went to sit on a stone bench. Did the Empress have something to do with the Pure Lady's and her son's disappearances? Could it be possible the Empress resented the Lady for taking over the duty in the Imperial Silkworm Workshops and she wanted to punish her and her son? "Do you know anything about Sujie's ballad, Noble Lady?" I asked.

"Yes, Luminous Lady. The maids were talking about it days before the Pure Lady's disappearance, and the Empress…she forbade us mentioning it. She said if she heard anyone repeat it, she would throw them in a dungeon filled with snakes."

"I see." I cringed at the cruelty in her words. "I'm grateful you told me, Noble Lady. I understand this is an important matter, and for your safety, I promise I will not mention anything you told me today—"

"She's taken them," Gaoyang said, interrupting me. "She hates the Pure Lady, so she decides to punish her and Sujie."

"We should go back to my garden now, Gaoyang." I gave her a stare to silence her and then bid the Ladies my leave.

Gaoyang, however, was not appeased as we walked down the trail outside the Quarters. She slashed at the trees and bushes with her sleeves. "You know she took them. You know I'm right."

"Perhaps." I nodded, passing a pond on my right.

"Then what are you going to do? Are you going to help the Lady and her son?"

"I don't know," I said quietly.

"What do you mean, you don't know? Are you going to tell Pheasant?"

"I could." But then the Empress would know I had discovered the Lady's disappearance and told Pheasant.

We came to a pavilion where the ladies often hosted picnics, and I lowered myself onto a garden rock. From here, I could see the corner of the walls at the back of the Quarters, the swaying willow branches, the white birch trees next to a large lake, and the bridge with latticed frames.

I turned to face the other direction. Through the thin tree branches, I could see a red wall in the distance—the Empress's house, which had been constructed solely for her four years ago. I had never set foot there.

Did she have the Lady and her son? I wanted to know what happened to them. I hoped they were safe. But did I wish to provoke the Empress? If she found out I was looking for them, if she believed I was trying to help them, she would fix her venomous closely set eyes on me, and perhaps my son as well. The image of my Hope appeared in my mind, and my hands grew chilled.

✦ ✦

I had never been more worried about my son. As soon as I returned to my garden, I called for Apricot and held him in my arms. At ten months old, Lion had grown one tooth, but he had not learned to speak. Most of the time, he stayed in Apricot's arms, biting his toy hand drum.

He looked up at me, waving his hand drum and drooling. I wiped his chin with my handkerchief and smiled at him. But I thought of the Pure Lady and Sujie again. He was only four. Such a talented boy too. Could I pretend I did not know anything while he was missing?

I decided to look for the Lady and Sujie in secret. Princess Gaoyang would volunteer to help, but I would rather leave her out of this. I remembered my old trick of receiving information through eunuchs and servants, but with my high rank, I could not go to them in person. I let Apricot help me, and through her I sent inquiries to the eunuchs who served in the Empress's quarters. Did they know of the Pure Lady and Sujie? They did not. I invited the Empress's maids to come for sweets in my garden. They sent their regrets. The Empress would not allow them to visit.

I did not give up. I sent bribes—I had many valuables and silver trinkets now, thanks to Pheasant—to the eunuchs and some maids who knew the Empress's maids. But there was no news of the Lady's and Sujie's whereabouts.

Where were they? Had the Empress harmed them? Had something terrible happened to them?

✦ ✦

I was napping in the chamber when Apricot announced that a eunuch wished to see me. He had news of the Pure Lady and Sujie, he said. He had found them.

I took in a sharp breath as he told me what the Empress did to the Lady and her son. When he finished, I rewarded him with two silver ingots and waved him away. But I was so shocked at his report that I had to pace in the chamber to calm down.

I had to help the Pure Lady and her son; in fact, I would do anything I could to save them. Even if that meant I would enrage the Empress.

17

"MISSING?" PHEASANT ASKED AS HE SPOONED SOME mutton from the soup pot. He had just returned from the morning audience and was hungry. According to tradition, an emperor should dine alone in a hall separate from everyone else, but he preferred my company during meals. "I heard she was sick."

"She was, and now we cannot find her," I said, rocking Lion in my arms. He was fussy, but I did not know what was wrong with him. "Sujie is missing too. I have asked around and found out they are inside the Empress's house."

"So they are not missing, then."

"Not precisely. They are in the Empress's house and"—I paused—"they are kept in a secret building." The eunuch had told me some details about the secret building, but I did not wish to spoil Pheasant's appetite.

"Tell the Pure Lady to go back to her own chamber." He took another bite of mutton. Pheasant was a picky eater. On the table lay many dishes—flavored pork with sweet glutinous rice, roasted snow pheasants basted with savory garlic sauce, broiled camel hump seasoned with zesty red pepper, and sliced bear meat glazed in yellow fermented soybean paste—but he had eyes only for mutton.

"It's not up to her, Pheasant."

Pheasant put down the spoon. "Do you mean the Empress keeps them as prisoners?"

"I cannot say." I decided to tell him all I knew. "But I am worried.

The place is locked. No one is allowed to enter except two eunuchs who deliver food." Lion began to cry and hiccup and could not be consoled. I patted him, not knowing what to do. Apricot asked me if I wished to give him to her, but I did not have the heart to let him go.

Princess Gaoyang approached the table. "Pheasant. You know what the Empress is capable of. She is most ruthless. You must save the Lady and Sujie." She took Lion from my arms and threw him in the air. As he fell, she spun around, leaped, and caught him in her arms. Lion giggled, his sobs forgotten. I did not know whether I should sigh or feel relieved. Throwing him in the air was an extreme remedy for his fussiness. Only Princess Gaoyang had the skill, and the stomach, to execute it.

"You said Sujie is there too?" Pheasant frowned. "I haven't seen him for a while. The Empress told me he was petulant and mistreated his tutor and had to be disciplined. He was ordered to study *The Book of Odes* and write poems ten times a day."

"I think," I said carefully, "you should pay the Empress a visit."

Pheasant wiped his mouth and stood. "I will do that now."

I rose too. "I will go with you. Gaoyang," I said before she could object, "would you stay here and watch Lion for me?"

"No. Let Apricot take care of him. I will go with you."

"Please? He will be happier with you." I gave her Lion's toy hand drum. "Give this to him if he complains."

"You want me to step aside while you rescue the Lady?"

"Yes," I said firmly. I trusted Apricot, but it gave me reassurance when Gaoyang was there to protect my child.

She sighed. "Fine. I would do this only for you, Luminous Lady."

Pheasant was already at the garden's entrance. I hurried to catch up with him. Behind me, my maids followed.

It was early afternoon, the sun high in the sky. The court was quiet. Dozens of servants strode past, carrying trays of food and water jugs. I tried to keep pace with Pheasant, but I was easily exhausted these days, and I could not walk too fast.

"Is the Empress mistreating the Pure Lady and Sujie?" Pheasant asked. He looked troubled, his voice hoarse, and the sunlight shone brightly on his face, giving his skin a youthful sheen.

A few eunuchs, bowing, stepped aside to the edge of the path as we passed. "I don't know."

"I will never forgive her if she is." He snapped a low-hung branch from a pear tree. "First she cooked your dog, and now this."

His face was dark, his eyes determined. I remembered seeing that same look back when he had decided to persuade his brother Taizi to abandon his plan to rebel against the Emperor years ago, and I knew not to say anything. I reached out and put my hand on his arm. "Please, just get the Lady and Sujie back safely. Do not threaten the Empress and make the matter worse."

She would not forgive me if she saw me bring Pheasant to her house. But I did not care. I had to save the Pure Lady and Sujie.

We soon reached the Empress's residence. It was not a single building like the other Ladies' chambers, but a large compound with high walls. From the length of the wall, I could tell her house was as enormous as my newly renovated garden.

The Empress's maids told us that she was visiting her uncle outside the palace. I was relieved. At least I did not need to confront her face-to-face.

"Take me to the Pure Lady and Sujie." Pheasant scowled. "And do not tell me you do not know where they are."

The maids glanced at each other, looking panicky, but they dared not reject a request from the Emperor. Their heads lowered, they led us behind a sand garden, passing a pavilion and a few houses.

They stopped as we approached a low building surrounded by walls. It looked like it could have been a stable, and there were chains on the gates, just as the eunuch had told me.

A foul stench wafted through the air, and a wave of nausea rose from my stomach. I covered my nose with my shawl, wishing I had brought a handkerchief. Was it true that the Pure Lady and her son were imprisoned there?

"What are you waiting for? Open the door!" Pheasant shouted at the two maids. As soon as they unlocked the chains, he kicked the doors open. "Sujie? Pure Lady? Are you here?"

Angry barks rose from a shed in the small courtyard. Hesitating, Pheasant walked to the shed and pushed open the closed door, and I followed behind.

The stink! It was overpowering! I pressed the shawl harder to my face and peered inside. It was dimly lit, but I could tell the shed was divided into two parts by a fence. On the left growled some dogs, chained to the fence. On the right, the ground was a morass of mud and feces, and there were two animals there, chained as well, crouched at the far end of the corner.

I blinked and froze in shock as I realized what I was looking at.

The crouched figures on the right were not animals. They were the Pure Lady and Sujie, their faces caked with mud and feces.

And the beasts on the left were not dogs. They were wolves—their yellow eyes blazing, their white teeth sharp.

Fear seized my throat. I tried to stay still, but my legs grew weak, and I could hardly stand. "Pure Lady? Sujie?" I called out. The stench shot into my nose, and I wanted to vomit.

Sujie's slight figure did not move, but the Pure Lady raised her head. She crawled to get closer to me, but the chains stopped her. Twisting her head, she growled. Her voice was hoarse and painful, and something crawled from her long mottled hair to her shoulder. I could see clearly with the light coming from outside—maggots.

Pheasant stretched to hold on to the fence, nearly losing his balance. "Pure Lady?"

I held on to Pheasant to steady him and myself. That woman with maggots crawling on her hair and her neck was the calm Pure Lady? "Heavens, Pheasant. Unchain her. Get her out. Get Sujie out."

"I…I can't do it. Where is the key? Give me the key!" He doubled over and vomited. Poor Pheasant. He wiped his mouth and grabbed a cluster of keys from the maid behind us. His hands trembled as he leaned over the fence to unlock the chain tied to the Lady.

A shadow leaped at the corner of my eye, and Pheasant fell back, crying out in surprise. Another shadow lunged from my left, its sharp claws tearing my shawl. The wolves! They were so close. If they had not been chained, they would have torn me apart.

"Quick, quick," I urged Pheasant, and when he finally unlocked the chains, I gave my hand to the Lady and pulled her out. "Unlock Sujie," I urged Pheasant again. "Get him out. Get him out now."

But the slight figure at the far side of the corner still did not move, and Pheasant could not reach him.

A sour wave surged in my stomach, and I gagged. I turned to my maids behind me. Two were helping the Pure Lady, but the others were standing there, holding their noses. "Come here, Chunlu, Xiayu! Get him out, do you hear me?"

They held their hands over their noses, shaking their heads.

"Let me." Pheasant stepped into the morass and stretched out his hand. But each time he tried to grab Sujie, the wolves pounced, barking fiercely. Once, a wolf almost latched on to Pheasant's shoulder, missing him only by a hand's length.

I cried out in fright. "Watch out, watch out, Pheasant!"

The deafening barking drowned my voice. They were so loud I felt my head was going to burst, but I could see the chains on the animals were tied to be long enough for the wolves to reach the edge of the fence, but short enough so they would not tear Sujie apart. It sickened me to think how frightened the boy must have been when the wolves sprang toward him each time he tried to escape.

Finally, his feet sinking in the feces, Pheasant reached out for Sujie. "Come, come to me!" he urged. His hands were now covered with shit too, but he did not seem to care.

I wished he could hurry up. I felt like fainting with the earsplitting howling and growling of the wolves. And they just would not stop! I felt dizzy. My heart shook, and I wanted to scream in frustration. I could not imagine how the Pure Lady and Sujie had survived in the foul mixture with the wolves constantly clawing at them. I would have gone insane in one day.

"Try again, try again, Pheasant. Almost, almost! Sujie, good boy, give the Emperor your hand," I shouted, frantic.

Pheasant grabbed his hand. "Good boy. Good boy! Now. Let's go. Now!"

But his hand slipped out of Pheasant's, and Sujie fell back again.

I was going to pass out. I could not breathe. My head pounded. And the wolves swam before me, while the morass of the feces seemed to surge like an angry sea, its foul waves splashing at my feet.

My maid, Chunlu, came to her senses. She ducked to the other side of the pen and pulled Sujie out. As soon as he was safe, we fled.

The kennel door shut behind me, and the barking ceased. I gasped for breath, grateful for the fresh air and some quiet.

"Tell the servants to come here and bring water to wash their faces. Some warm water. Yes, warm water. Go, Chunlu, go now. You too, Xiayu. Go. Go get water." I ordered my maids, and they ran off. The air out here smelled like Heaven, and I breathed in greedily.

Once I felt better, I went to the Pure Lady, who was hunched against a wall near the gate.

"Pure Lady." I knelt beside her. Two maggots rolled from her head and fell on my foot. I shrank away. "I'm so sorry for what you have suffered."

She was shivering, her arms wrapping around her knees, staring at the ground. I called her again, but she did not raise her head. I did not think she heard me or knew who I was. She smelled like excrement, and there was no trace of the intelligent woman whom I had met months ago.

I straightened, biting my lips in fury. The Pure Lady was of the second degree, only lower than the Empress and me. No one was supposed to punish her except the Emperor. But the Empress had imprisoned her and tormented her. The Empress had committed a crime.

Pheasant was talking to Sujie. Poor boy. He kept shaking his head but would not speak a word.

The maids returned, buckets of water in hand. A dozen eunuchs, carrying basins, followed behind them. When they entered the building, they doubled over, their sleeves flying to their faces.

I directed them to the Pure Lady and Sujie and ordered the eunuchs to clean them. They poured water on top of them, and foul yellow shit spread on the ground, sending white, writhing maggots to my feet. I stepped aside, but it could not be helped—I was wet from the knees down. And Pheasant was worse; his whole robe was soaked with the foul mixture. He stood unmoved, however, and his eyes, filled with pain, watched Sujie as the water poured down his head and he gulped and groaned.

Finally, the Pure Lady was cleaner, and I could see her face—a sheet of gray. Her lips were pale and cracked, her eyes red rimmed. Sujie was clean too. His lips were purple, and he would not raise his head. I ordered the eunuchs to take them to the Lady's chamber so they could get some rest.

The Pure Lady wept when she was carried away, and her voice, so pitiful, pierced my heart. This was, after all, the worst part of the torture: it did not simply kill you—it changed you forever.

Pheasant turned to the Empress's maids. "Where is the Empress? Where is she? Tell her to come to me! Tell her to come now!"

They lowered their heads. She was still not home.

If she had been there, Pheasant would have struck her. I put my hand on his arm. "Let's go home, Pheasant."

He pushed me away and headed toward the entrance, yelling at anyone who got in his way. He was fuming, his face red with anger as we walked back to my garden. I walked beside him. My heart was taut like a pressed springboard.

"What happened?" Princess Gaoyang was shocked to see our shit-covered gowns. She gagged, covering her nose with her sleeve.

"I shall tell you later," I said as Apricot removed my stained gown and shoes.

After I was clean, I sat down on a stool and poured myself a cup of wine. It tasted foul, like the feces whose putrid odor still lingered on my tongue. I forced myself to swallow and poured another cup. I told Apricot to get my bath ready and to light incense to expel the odor, and then I told the princess where we found the Pure Lady and Sujie.

"In a kennel?" she repeated, astounded. "With wolves!"

"Yes." There were so many things I wished to tell her. The revolting squalor in the kennel, the shocking sight of the wolves, the torments of the Pure Lady and Sujie, and the heartbreaking fear in their eyes. But all I could say was, "Go home now, Gaoyang. I need a bath."

Gaoyang looked like she wanted to say more, but I was too tired to listen. Shaking her head, she left the chamber.

Apricot brought in the wooden tub, followed by Chunlu and Xiayu, who came in with buckets of hot water.

I took off my underrobe and loose trousers and stepped into the tub. Pheasant followed me and got into the tub too. His brows knotted and his lips pursed, he leaned against the tub, looking strange and intense, like someone whom I had known a long time ago. Taizi. He looked like Taizi. I remembered his face, taut, dark, full of agony when Emperor Taizong ordered him to end his lover's life.

I moved to Pheasant and put my arms around him. He was hot. His back, wet with beads of steam, was red, as though a fire was burning within. There was a fire burning inside me too, and the heat, the steam, and the scented water only fed its flame.

I wanted to tell him I felt sorry for the Pure Lady and Sujie. I wanted to tell him he must punish the Empress, for I would not tolerate this kind of atrocity, and I would never allow her to harm me and my child so.

He thrust his head under the water.

I waited.

When he raised his head, he wiped his face and turned around to lean against the tub. "My mother used to tell me: 'Love those who serve you, and those who serve you will love you.' I have always believed that."

"Your mother was wise," I said, wiping off the beads of water on his chin.

"But then why would I have a wife like that woman?" He closed his eyes.

I sighed. "She punished the Pure Lady because she took her position in the workshops. She wants revenge." And Sujie had to suffer because of his ballad and, perhaps, simply for being Pheasant's son.

"I cannot bring myself to look at her, Mei. I cannot even look at her."

"She was not your choice." His father had chosen her, and Pheasant could not have known what kind of a woman she was.

He pulled me toward him, and then, roughly, he took me.

I could feel the muscles on his legs tighten and his skin burn under me. I held on to his shoulders as the hot steam rose and swelled before me. "What are you going to do, Pheasant?"

He had to hold the Empress accountable; he had no choice. Or the court would have no peace and the Empress would terrorize everyone, including me.

He gripped me tightly. "I am going to divorce her." He thrusted, panting, his breath hot and thick.

I stopped, looking into his eyes. An empress did not get divorced. She lived with the crown or died with it. "It will not be easy."

"I cannot stand her anymore. I want to divorce her. I must divorce her." He turned me around. Fast and recklessly, he moved against me.

I could feel him; I could feel his anger and his determination. All at once, my own need, my desperation, my fear, and my hope, erupted like the hot steam. I clutched the rim of the basin, the water lapping against my stomach, splattering my face.

We collapsed together, the hot water splashing into my mouth. For a moment, we held on to each other in silence. Then, gazing at me, he brushed the stretched skin on my soft stomach, his eyes filled with determination. "You have to help me. You have to be on my side. The court must learn what kind of woman she is. She must be punished."

I nodded. I would start a war against the Empress then. I would expose her cruelty so she would never hurt anyone again. She would consider me her evil enemy after this day, but there would be no looking back. "I will help you," I said.

"Good. I shall divorce her."

I shook my head. We could not rush into this. The Empress had regained her power, and we had to tread carefully. I held his hand. "We need to have a strategy."

Pheasant leaned back. "I'm listening."

The Empress would be furious. She would do anything she could to destroy me. And there would be an upheaval, a violent one, if we decided to do this. We would turn the whole palace, and perhaps even the kingdom, upside down.

But she had beaten me, she had killed my Hope, and she had tortured the Pure Lady and her son. It was the only way, the just way, to fight the unjust.

I turned to Pheasant. "We will impeach her."

18

PHEASANT AND I TALKED FOR A LONG TIME. THREE EXTRA aromatic candles had burnt down to the wick, filling the room with clouds of aroma. It was too late to wake Apricot and ask her to light another one, so we lay in the dark and discussed what actions we must take.

Pheasant did not think it was necessary to have an open trial. He wanted to issue an edict to denounce the Empress immediately, stating how she had mistreated the Pure Lady and her son. But I thought Pheasant's position in the court was not strong, and if he issued such an edict, the Empress would accuse Pheasant and me of framing her, and Pheasant and I would become the target of all the hateful arrows unleashed by the Empress and her aids. It would be too dangerous.

An open trial would tell people that Pheasant and I had not framed the Empress. The witnesses and victims—poor Pure Lady and Sujie—would come to the court and expose the Empress's crime, and she would not be able to deny it. It would also give people in the palace an opportunity to see what an atrocity the Empress had committed. Her supporters in the court would not be able to protect her, even if they tried.

Pheasant decided to speak to Prince Ke as well as Fang Yi'ai, who had also become a reliable consultant. Perhaps they would offer some suggestions.

"Come and see me tomorrow at the polo field, and I will tell you what I decide," he said.

I nodded. I would go visit the Pure Lady tomorrow to make sure she was in good care. I would also need to speak to the three Ladies and see if I could gain their support.

The Empress would be impeached, and soon all the people in the palace would know her cruelty. Then Pheasant's plan to divorce her would succeed.

✦ ✦

The next morning, I rose before dawn, finished my morning routine of meditation, and fed Lion. After I saw Pheasant off to the Audience Hall, I instructed Apricot to take good care of my son and then left the garden with my four maids.

When I arrived at the Quarters of the Pure Lotus, the sun had not risen yet, no one was walking in the compound, and the buildings were cloaked in a quiet, hazy veil. Several maids, their heads drooping, were asleep near the replica of Mount Hua. I shook my head when my maids attempted to wake them.

I turned to the stone stairs in the courtyard and walked toward the Pure Lady's chamber.

Faint cries, like those of a cat, drifted through the air. They filled the open space in the courtyard, resonating in the morning fog and clinging to my skin. I turned around, searching.

I did not see any cats. Confused, I walked toward the sound. A maid cleared her throat behind me, but I put up my finger to stop her, for the cries were changing, turning into a wave of layered, rich groans, and I could tell that they were not cats, and the noises were coming from the Noble Lady's house.

I walked down the corridor near the Lady's house. The doors were shut, and the silk windowpane was thick. I stopped there, listening.

I felt my cheeks flush. The groans had changed into a chorus of higher sounds, steady, pulsating, filled with vigor and pleasure. And there was no mistake. They were the sounds of the Noble Lady, Lady Virtue, and Lady Obedience. Together.

I turned around and walked away as fast as I could. I wondered why I had never thought of it before. They were always together, the same outfits, the same makeup, and above all, the intimate closeness among them when they held arms... I should have suspected that. When I reviewed the scroll of *The Dreams of Spring* many years ago, it had contained pictures of women comforting each other. I did not believe them then, but after living in the palace for so many years, I knew it was only natural that this might happen.

Fear could rope people into a tightening ring, bonding them like a cocoon, blinding them, reducing them to something they never intended to be—but loneliness...loneliness was more lethal and insidious. Like a wheel, it turned and turned as days went by, changing you, forcing you to find a footing somewhere, anywhere, and continued to spin even if you wished to stop.

The maid cleared her throat behind me again. I wondered if they all knew the Ladies' secret. Maybe Apricot knew it too but thought it would be inappropriate for her to tell me.

I thought of Taizi and his affair with a male flutist, which led to his disgrace. When Emperor Taizong discovered them, the shamed Emperor had ordered Taizi to kill his lover. The scandal had cost Taizi his crown and his life. Pheasant would not be so cruel to his women, but all the same, this information could be used against the Ladies if someone else, especially the Empress, found out.

I should tell Princess Gaoyang. She could warn them to be cautious.

"You heard nothing," I said to my maids. "Do not tell anyone about this."

"Yes, Luminous Lady." They lowered their heads. I was glad they did not glance up to meet my gaze, for certainly they would see something on my face that I did not wish them to know.

"You swear it. And now go knock on the Pure Lady's door." I paused in the corridor, calming myself.

The Pure Lady's maid answered the door and led me behind the screen that shielded the lady's canopied bed, which she shared with Sujie. She was jabbering something with her eyes closed. Sujie seemed sound asleep, his face pressed against her back.

This must have been the first time in days they had had a restful night. I did not have the heart to wake them.

When I turned around to leave, the three Ladies, in red sleeping tunics, loose trousers, and slippers, burst in. Their young faces looked dewy, fresh, and their long hair was undone.

I hoped they did not know I was aware of their secret. I would not judge them, and I would not mention it either. But I would look out for them and protect them when they needed it.

"Ladies." I beckoned them to sit. *"Zao an."* Good morning. "I hope I did not wake you."

"Zao an, Luminous Lady." They bowed. "We came as fast as we could."

"I am grateful you came. I am certain that now you all know what happened to the Pure Lady and Sujie," I said. "I would like to ask you all to help her, take care of her and her child."

"It is our privilege, Luminous Lady," the Noble Lady said.

"Did she eat anything last night?"

The Noble Lady shook her head. "Nothing. She hasn't spoken a word either. The same with Sujie. But we shall feed the Pure Lady some chicken broth with dumplings later. It's her favorite food. Sujie will like that too."

"Good. I am pleased to hear that, Noble Lady. Now, sit down, Noble Lady, Lady Virtue, and Lady Obedience. I wish to tell you that the Emperor is very concerned about what the Empress has done to the Pure Lady and Sujie. I promise you she will be held accountable for her actions. Can I count on your help when you are needed?"

When Pheasant agreed to the trial, they could testify. But for now, the trial must remain a secret, for if the Empress got wind of it, she would tear me apart.

"Most certainly, Luminous Lady." The Noble Lady held my hands. "I cannot tell you how grateful we are. We have been worried these past days. The Empress has been most…harsh with us. The court is not like what it was. I hope you can help us so the court will have peace again." She pulled the other two's hands, and together they stood and bowed to me, deeply. "You shall have our gratitude and any help you need."

Joy bloomed in my heart. They trusted me. "Of course, we shall have peace in the court. Soon. Very soon."

✦ ✦

After I left the Quarters, I went to the polo field.

It was unusually empty today. Pheasant was playing with the General, Prince Ke, and Princess Gaoyang's husband. At the far end of the field, there were only a few grooms and guards sauntering about. I hoped Pheasant had talked to his men and decided on the trial.

Pheasant, in his yellow polo outfit, galloped to me when he saw me. His sleeves flying behind him, he swung off the horse with the easy grace that had dazzled me many years ago. He had lost all the weight he had gained during my exile, and he had been practicing mounted archery with Prince Ke, an excellent archer, for the past few months. Pheasant was a fast learner. After only a few months of training, he was able to shoot the target from five hundred paces while riding a horse, an impressive skill that had won even the General's praise. "If my enemies dare to harass our border again," Pheasant once told me, his face beaming with pride and confidence, "I shall lead my own army and kill them myself."

I smiled as he strode toward me. His yellow outfit shining in the sun, he looked strong and muscular, a powerful presence. His shoulders broad, his face resolute, Pheasant walked with strength that could not be defied. He looked more and more like his father, but unlike his father, who never smiled, Pheasant was beaming with kindness.

"*Zao an*, Luminous Lady. I was waiting for you." He grinned at me, handing off the reins to Prince Ke, who had dismounted with the others.

"*Zao an*, Your Majesty. I hope I didn't interrupt your game." I smiled, bowing to him. He looked in a good mood.

I greeted Prince Ke and Fang Yi'ai—ever a serious man, he looked grave—and then the General. He did not speak, only glanced at me and went to speak to some guards on the other side.

"Luminous Lady, I'm pleased to tell you my brother and I had a good discussion," Pheasant said. "It turns out he has a high regard for your proposal. And I have decided to follow your plan." I smiled, pleased at Pheasant's decision, and he continued. "Brother?"

"My lady." Prince Ke bowed to me. He looked healthier, but his figure was still as slim as a maiden's. Since the Regent had withdrawn from the court, the prince had taken over the Regent's duty of review-ing petitions these months. He had done well in the court, and many ministers liked his quiet manner and praised his ability. "Good day. I'm most honored the Emperor has decided to discuss such an important matter with us."

"Brother, no need for courtesy." Pheasant waved his hand. "Why don't you tell Luminous Lady what we have discussed?"

"Yes, Your Majesty. Luminous Lady." Prince Ke's face reddened for a moment. Ever a humble man, he still had a tendency to grow nervous when Pheasant showered attention on him before a crowd. "I find the revelation of the Empress's atrocity most stunning. I am appalled. It is unimaginable that she would chain a high-ranking Lady and the prince in a kennel with wolves. And I do agree that a trial is a just way for the Empress. I shall do my best to set it up, and I do believe I share the same opinion with Minister Fang." He turned to the princess's husband, who nodded seriously.

"Good." I was relieved. "When do you plan to draft the impeachment?"

"I shall have the statement ready tomorrow, if Luminous Lady wishes."

"And the date of the trial?"

"As soon as possible." He hesitated. "Whenever Luminous Lady desires."

"The matter is most urgent, but it must not be hurried either—"

"In two days. Let's have the trial in two days. I don't see why we must delay this." Pheasant waved his hand. "I shall order the Pure Lady and Sujie to come to the Audience Hall. I shall also order the Empress to be present at the hall, where she will listen to their testi-mony. She can't deny that."

"The three Ladies may wish to give their accounts as well," I added.

"Very good. They shall be summoned."

"There is only one thing, and I beg Luminous Lady's attention," Prince Ke said, looking apprehensive, his hand supporting his chin.

"What is it?" Pheasant asked.

"This trial of the Empress is a grave matter that has seen no prece-dence in our kingdom. I fear we may need to speak to the Regent and ask his opinion. It is part of protocol, after all."

"Ah." I nodded. Prince Ke was right about the protocol, but I wondered what the Regent would think of the Empress's trial. He did not like the Empress. Would he be glad to see her impeached?

"As you know, the Regent must be notified about the important matters that happen in the court." Prince Ke grimaced. He had never liked the Regent, who had banished him, but the prince never spoke anything ill of the Regent or slighted him in any way.

"I shall speak to him," Pheasant said. "He is most reasonable. He will certainly agree with us. I have no doubt about that." He patted my shoulder.

"Will you arrange a meeting with him tomorrow?" I asked.

"Brother, will you see to that?" When the prince nodded, Pheasant smiled. "Now, would anyone care to play some polo before my brother goes to his writing table?"

"I would!" a clear voice called out, and the sound of hooves beating on the ground rang behind me.

I wanted to smile. Of course. Princess Gaoyang. "Come here, Gaoyang." I beckoned at her. I had not seen her yet today, and I missed her. I wanted to tell her what Pheasant and I had discussed last night. She would be delighted to hear we had decided to impeach the Empress. "I wish to speak to you."

"What?" Her horse reared up, and she rose upright, pulling the reins. She was so slim. I envied her. "I went to your chamber, Luminous Lady. You were not there. Your maids said you went to the Quarters of the Pure Lotus. Why did you go there without me?"

"Well—"

"You were supposed to wait for me. After what happened to the Pure Lady and Sujie, you should know the mad cow will not leave you alone."

Her face was moist, and her long, braided hair stuck to her neck. She looked as though she had run all the way here. "Oh, Gaoyang," I said happily, "were you worried about me?"

"Worried? Of course not."

Liar. "Well. You found me here, didn't you?"

She shrugged, ready to kick the horse and gallop off.

"Come here. You cannot play with the men. Pheasant won't let you."

"Pheasant cannot stop me." She tilted her head, looking petulant again.

I sighed. "Anyway, it's too dangerous. Those men—come back, come back, Gaoyang!"

She had already galloped across the field. Holding her mallet high above her head, she struck at Prince Ke's mallet, knocking it to the side, and stole the scarlet ball just before Pheasant hit it.

I gasped. A woman should never play so aggressively. And among the men! But Princess Gaoyang was not an ordinary woman, and she would not be bound by rules. I envied her. I wished I could play polo; I wished I could play polo like her. Perhaps I should join her.

But I could not do that now. Perhaps next spring.

I stroked my stomach. I was with child again. It was only three months and too early to tell anyone. Only a few people knew: Pheasant, Princess Gaoyang, and Apricot, who helped me dress every morning.

I would have a daughter this time. Our son was for Pheasant, but our daughter was for me, and I wanted her to be just like my dear Princess Gaoyang, to have no fear or care for conventions and take part in life's many games and enjoy life's boundless joy. Perhaps I could even name her after Gaoyang, although that would be a breach of etiquette. The custom allowed mothers to name an infant after someone only when that person was deceased.

For a long moment I stood watching her chasing the ball with Pheasant, Prince Ke, and the General. It was one of the most wonderful sights I had ever seen, and I decided I would form a team of female polo players in the palace in the future, so all the women could have fun.

Then I turned around. I had to get ready. The cruel Empress, the animal killer, would soon be tried.

✦ ✦

I stepped out of the carriage, alarmed. Many people were crammed in front of my garden's entrance. There seemed to be a standoff, with some unfamiliar guards in black robes shouting, and my own guards were pushed to a corner near the tangerine grove.

"What's the matter?" I shouted, walking fast toward them. They quieted, turning toward me, and I stopped sharply. My blood turned to ice.

The Empress.

Standing among the guards, she was wearing her usual golden gown and the phoenix crown. Her back facing me, she stooped over, her hands outstretched toward something I could not see.

What was she doing here? The words died in my throat as I caught sight of a familiar red tunic.

Lion.

He was sitting at her feet. He had not started to walk yet, and, with one hand holding his favorite hand drum, he tried to push himself up.

"Stay away from him," I shouted, running. "Do not touch him."

Where were my maids? Then I saw Apricot, racing out of the garden, her hands flying to her mouth, her face ashen.

The Empress straightened and turned toward me. Her face, powdered white, looked plain and broad as ever, and her closely set eyes were daggers. All her sickness, her pathetic look I saw when the Regent asked to relieve her of the duty in the workshops were gone. "How dare you break into my house?" Her voice was deep and thick like smoke, filled with anger and threat.

"I didn't break into your house." I stopped, panting. Oh, my child. He was not trying to stand up anymore, and there were tears in his eyes, and the hand drum was rattling as his hand shook. What did she say to him? What did she do to him?

"You brought the Emperor to my house. The Emperor! While I was away!"

"You imprisoned the Pure Lady and Sujie. They did nothing wrong."

"They mocked me! That insolent woman intended to replace me. Me! She said I was barren! And her impudent monkey mocked my son—my son, the heir!"

Everyone knew she was barren. "They did not deserve to be tortured like that."

"They deserved worse than what they got! And how dare you challenge me." Her voice was shrill. "You? You challenge me? You set them free while I was away!"

Lion stretched his hand out to me, his lips trembling. My heart ached. He did not like loud noises. She was frightening him. "The Emperor shall be here momentarily," I said. "I ask you to leave, Empress Wang."

"Be careful, harlot, of what you say." She gritted her teeth. "This is my court, my palace, and you are nothing. You are no one. You do not tell me to leave." She gripped Lion's arms and lifted him in the air. Lion shrieked, thrashing his legs.

She was hurting him. She was hurting him! Fear clenched my throat. I stumbled forward despite myself. "Put him down. Put him down!"

But she lifted him higher, above her shoulder, as though he were nothing more than a toy. "You see, you are nothing to me. Nothing. Like this little thing. Nothing!"

Lion screamed, tears raining down his cheeks. I could not bear it. All the strength drained out of me. I staggered toward the woman who held my child in her hands. "Please put him down, Empress. Please. He's crying. He's frightened. Please put him down."

"Frightened?" She raised her face to my child, her chilly voice stabbing my heart. "Are you frightened, little devil? I only wish to play with you. Look, you are small, so small. Do you know how small you are, little devil? Do not fight me. I cannot hold you like this. I shall drop you." She shook my son, and his hand drum fell from his hands. "Then you shall fall, yes, fall, like this toy. You shall break your legs or arms. Do you hear me? Do not fight me."

I shuddered, choked with fear. She would make me pay for saving the Pure Lady. She was going to hurt my son. "No, don't drop him. Don't drop him. No!" Tears blurred my vision. I wanted to kneel before her, to beg, to plead, if only she would let my son go. "Please, please, do not harm him."

She raised her head and laughed, her voice loud and disturbing, like a murder of cackling crows. "Look at you, look at yourself. You fat sow! You are nothing without your son, do you understand that? Nothing. You're nothing—"

A swirl of indigo spun before me. Gaoyang! The Empress cried out, stepped back, and then magically, her hands were empty.

"Leave, Empress." Gaoyang's beautiful voice rose beside me, and in her arms was my Lion, hiccupping, swallowing his tears. I dove toward him and wrapped him in my arms. Relief, euphoria, and gratitude washed over me. I rocked him. I kissed him. I held him tight.

"I shall not forget this, you little clown," that despicable woman said.

"Neither shall I, Empress." Gaoyang's voice was firm. "Neither shall I."

I could feel the Empress's venomous stare, and I held my son tighter. Finally, her enormous shape began to move, and when she passed me, she kicked at something on the ground.

The hand drum flew in the air and crashed against the wall. I jolted, searching. Near the wall were the shards of the drum's wooden band and the toy's broken handle, still bearing the teeth marks of my son, and the crashing sound, although long disappeared, rang in my ears and pounded at my heart.

✦ ✦

I did not sleep well that night. I dreamed of the Empress, her arms spread like the claws of a beast, stretching to seize my son from me. I awoke bathed in a cold sweat.

Lion could not sleep either. He missed his hand drum and was irritated when he could not have it. Apricot offered him another toy, but he would not take it. For the whole night, he cried, agitated, his eyes red and ringed with shadows.

I kept him close to me. I would not let him out of my sight, and when my hands failed to find him at night, I grew frantic, afraid he had been taken away from me. In the bright sunlight, when Princess Gaoyang played with him near the pond, I could see the shadows under the trees, the shadows of the Empress's wrath, creeping close to me and my child.

If she learned of my plan to impeach her, she would never forgive me. Was I ready to face her wrath? Could I protect my son from her?

I told Pheasant not to start the trial of the Empress.

"Perhaps we should reconsider the matter of impeachment," I pleaded to him. "It might be too risky."

He was hesitant. I had nothing to fear, he told me, his eyes filled with concern. Then he put his arms around me to let me know that he would protect me. But I was not convinced.

He was not a mother, and he could not understand a mother's anxiety.

I closed my eyes. "I have made up my mind," I said to Pheasant. "We must not impeach the Empress."

AD 653

The Fourth Year *of*
Emperor Gaozong's Reign
of Eternal Glory

WINTER

THE EMPRESS ISSUED NEW RULES FOR EVERYONE IN THE
Inner Court. No one was allowed to mention a word about the
kennel, wolves, or the Pure Lady. Anyone who defied the rule would
receive ten lashes by thick rods. Gatherings of groups more than three
were forbidden in the Inner Court. And all titled Ladies must stay
in their compounds and request permission if they needed to leave.
If they left their compounds without the Empress's permission, they
would be subject to ten lashes and other severe punishments.

So, like all the other ladies forced to stay in their chambers, I was
confined in my own garden.

✦ ✦

Two months passed. I quietly celebrated my son's one-year birthday,
followed by his naming ritual. Only Princess Gaoyang and a group
of imperial astrologists were invited, by Pheasant—not me, since I
must follow the Empress's new rule. During the ritual, the imperial astrologists named my son, the third son of Pheasant, Li Hong.
Pheasant was pleased. After the ritual was over, he gave Hong a set
of twelve wooden horses, all in various sizes and breeds, and taught
him how to ride on a toy horse, even though he had yet to learn
how to walk.

Sitting on a stone bench near a bare cinnamon tree, I watched them
play. I felt calm, basking in the warm winter sun, and I tried not to

think of the danger and the unease that haunted me. I was five months pregnant. Four more months, and I would have another child, and I hoped she would provide me with enough distractions so I could forget about the Empress and her threat.

"I heard about her order." Gaoyang came to stand by my side. She was wearing a light indigo tunic with patterns of bamboo stalks stitched around the hem. Around her waist was a green girdle with a similar pattern. It wound so tightly around her, it seemed her thin waist could snap easily.

I nodded. I knew she would bring this up.

"This is most outrageous. I would not accept that. Is this why you changed your mind, Luminous Lady?"

"It's for the best."

"Best?" She frowned.

I sighed. She was too young. She could not understand my fears.

Apricot covered my shoulders with a sable coat. Kneeling before me, she tied the strings carefully under my chin. She had grown taller, and her chest had filled out. When she had come to serve me two years before, she had been only a girl, and now she looked like a grown woman. Even her manner had changed. She was no longer timid or bashful, and she spoke fluently without pausing or whispering.

I patted her hand to show my gratitude. Gaoyang had seen her with the Secretary, but I did not think she would betray me. It was not her fault either that my son fell into the Empress's hands the other day. Hong was curious about the surroundings these days and was crawling everywhere. Apricot was doing her best to keep him from the pond, not the entrance. She was serving me well, I had to say, and whenever I needed information, she would find it. I had promoted her to be the chief maid. In a few months, I would give her another handsome reward.

"Thank you, Apricot." I waved her away. "Gaoyang, I am afraid you will not understand."

"But you know the Empress will not leave you alone, Luminous Lady," Gaoyang said, her eyes following Apricot as she rose to leave. Apricot gave her a deep bow, and the princess nodded.

The two women were only two years apart, Gaoyang being older,

I realized. But how different they looked. Apricot was round and curvy with womanly charm, while Gaoyang was thin and flat. Both, however, were graceful. "I know, Gaoyang. Of course she won't."

"Then what will you do, Luminous Lady?"

I wondered if the master Sun Tzu had any good advice to help me out. Perhaps he did, but I could not fish it out of my mind right now. So I said, "Look." I pointed at a brown hare dashing in the woods on the other side of the pond. It stood still, crouching near a stone lamp, watching us. "You see, we have hares, trees, rosebushes in the garden, frogs, and goldfish in the pond. When spring comes, we'll see cicadas, orioles, and hawks, and many insects and animals."

She folded her arms. "What do you mean by that?"

"There is a place for all creatures in the garden, my princess."

"But would you rather be the mantis behind the cicada, or the oriole behind the mantis?"

She was referring to the old saying: "The mantis stalks the cicada, unaware of the oriole behind."

I gazed at her. I did not know what to say.

"Let me tell you something." Gaoyang waved her arms. A breeze swept my face, and she was gone. "Fear," she said from the pavilion, "is a roof. If you do not break it, you shall not see the sky. My mentor's words."

I looked up, shading my eyes with my hand. The sky bore a shade of unimpressive gray, but the white clouds, round and small, were pretty and pleasant, floating around like silkworm cocoons. "Your mentor has interesting observations."

He reminded me of Tripitaka, the monk who was also wise and enigmatic.

The color of indigo swirled from the pavilion, and Gaoyang stood beside me again. "You cannot live in a pavilion built with fear, Luminous Lady. It gets smaller and smaller, hotter and hotter inside, until you cannot breathe."

I considered her words. "I don't know." I sighed. "Perhaps, Gaoyang, you will understand me better when you are older."

"Perhaps you ought to get out of your garden," she said. "Do you want to go visit the Ladies?"

I shook my head. "You know I can't, Gaoyang." Since the Empress's new order, I had not set my foot outside the garden; I had not heard anything about the Pure Lady or seen any of the Ladies.

"Well, you do wish to see them, don't you?" She pulled my hand. "Let's go now. I'll go with you. If that mad cow dares to stop me, I'll throw her over the roof."

Gaoyang was serious about this, and I knew she would scoff at me if I said anything about obedience. "Now?"

"Yes." She would not let me sit.

I glanced at Hong. He was climbing on the wooden horse, and Pheasant was laughing beside him. He would be safe with Pheasant. "All right," I said to Gaoyang. "Let's go."

◆ ◆

The Pure Lady looked almost her former self. The color on her face had returned, and her hair was done carefully in the Cloudy Chignon style. Leaning against the engraved headboard of her bed, she stared at something on the quilt while biting her nails.

"Pure Lady, I am relieved you are feeling better." I stopped near the bed, breathing in the strong aroma of cassia wafting through the chamber. Behind me, Princess Gaoyang was batting at the air. She did not like fragrances, I realized, and if it were not for me, she may have refused even to enter the chamber. The three Ladies stood beside her and watched the Pure Lady sympathetically.

"Yes…yes…" the Pure Lady said. Her voice was barely audible, and she was trembling.

I wished she would look at me, but her eyes darted here and there, never resting anywhere for long. I wondered if she remembered how I had rescued her and her son. "Pure Lady, if you need anything, please inform me and the other three Ladies. We are here to help if you need us."

She did not reply, nor did it appear that she had heard me. I hesitated and stretched out a hand to pat her shoulder.

She raised her head sharply. I froze, shocked at the look in her eyes. It was not kindness, not gratitude—but hatred.

I frowned. I could not understand.

"Luminous Lady." The Noble Lady tugged at my sleeve. "Don't touch her. She does not like to be touched."

"Well then. We shall let her rest." I beckoned to the women around me and went to the other side of the screen. Near it, a maid was feeding Sujie some broth from a bowl. He glanced at me, looking surprised, and pushed the maid. With a loud crash, the bowl shattered on the ground.

"Wolves! Wolves! Where? Where?" Shrieks rose from the bed behind me, startling me.

I turned around. The Pure Lady staggered toward me. Her lips trembling, her eyes wild, she came face-to-face with me and stopped dead. It seemed she was thinking, as though trying to remember who I was, but then fear shot through her eyes, and they widened in terror.

"Pure Lady," I said gently, trying to calm her. "It's me—"

She lunged at me, and frantically she began to strike me, her arms flailing, her legs kicking, knocking my carefully placed wig to the floor.

"What are you doing, Pure Lady?" the Noble Lady shouted.

Gaoyang's voice rose. "Stop it, Pure Lady!"

"You!" The Pure Lady did not seem to hear them. Her breath was hot and moist in my ears. "You and the wolves! You and the wolves! I curse you. I curse your family. I curse your parents! I curse your families of five generations!"

"Stop! Stop! This is Luminous Lady!" the women shouted.

The Pure Lady jumped and slapped my head. Staggering back, I raised my arm to block her. "Gaoyang…Gaoyang…"

"She tortured me. She tortured me! She and the wolves, she and the wolves," the Pure Lady shrieked. "I will never forgive you, Empress Wang. Never forgive you, Empress Wang!"

"Enough, Pure Lady," Gaoyang shouted, and I fell gratefully into her arms. "Get her away, Noble Lady. Take her to her bed. Are you all right, Luminous Lady?"

"Yes…yes…I think so…" I dabbed at my face. "Did you…hear…" I turned to the Pure Lady, and I could not finish my words.

She had stopped screaming. Pulling away from the other women, she scrambled backward to the bed. Holding on to the bedpost, she trembled, tears pouring down her cheeks. "Let me out… Please… Let my son out… Don't hurt him… Please…"

The three Ladies put their hands on their mouths, looking stunned, and Princess Gaoyang held me tighter, her black eyes flashing brightly. Without a word, she picked up my wig, handed it to me, and helped me rise.

"Has she been like this since we rescued her, Noble Lady?" I asked softly, shocked by the Pure Lady's change.

She hesitated. "She does not like to talk or to be touched, that we know, but attacking…" She shook her head.

"I see." I stared at the Pure Lady in utter sympathy. Her torture in the kennel might have been over, but her memory of the torture would never end. "How is Sujie?"

He was hiding under the table, his arms covering his head.

"It has been two months since he was rescued, and he has not said a word," the Noble Lady said, her pretty eyes looking sad.

I sighed. I had hoped the little prodigy would recover more quickly than his mother. "Clean up the shards," I said to the maids near the door. "And now, someone get the court physicians. Tell them the Pure Lady needs them."

Meng Shen, the disciple of the great physician Sun Simiao, came promptly. After an extensive examination, he gave a diagnosis. The Lady's pulse was erratic, he said in a halting voice. It was a polite term for a mind that had gone insane.

My heart was heavy when I walked out of the Quarters. I thought of what Gaoyang had told me earlier. There was some truth in what she said, that the pavilion built with fear would shrink. I could see there were only two ways that could happen next: either you let the roof crush you, or you destroy the roof.

I understood what I had to do. Raising my head to the sky, I greedily breathed in the crisp winter air.

"Come, Gaoyang," I said, beckoning to her and my maids behind me. "We must speak to the Emperor. Now."

✦ ✦

Pheasant had already left when I reached the garden. Hong was napping. I instructed all my maids to stay by my son's side, made sure the garden's gate would remain closed, and then went to the Outer Palace with Princess Gaoyang.

I found Pheasant in the clearing in front of the Archery Hall, where many ministers and servants were gathered. Pheasant was playing Pitching-a-Pot with the General; Prince Ke; Fang Yi'ai; Pheasant's former tutor, Minister Xu Jingzong; and several other ministers.

While the servants ran to inform Pheasant of my arrival, I sat on a stool near an oak tree with Gaoyang.

"I do hope the Pure Lady will recover," I said and wiped my face. I was perspiring, even though this was a cold winter.

"What happened to her is an injustice." Gaoyang tossed her braid behind her back. "The court is a dark place, Luminous Lady. You should know that by now."

"I promise you the Pure Lady will have her justice, Gaoyang. That's why we're here."

"That is not what I'm talking about."

Pheasant strode toward me with his consultants before I could ask what she meant.

"Here you are, Luminous Lady," he said. Wearing a golden robe with a medallion of coiled dragons embroidered in the front, he looked handsome, confident, and agile.

"Your Majesty." I rose to bow to him.

"Sit, sit." He gestured to me with the arrows he used to play the Pitching-a-Pot game. "My lady. You're getting big."

I smiled happily despite the gloominess sitting in my heart. It was true my stomach was growing round fast with my second pregnancy. "Princess Gaoyang and I have something important to tell you, Your Majesty." I waved away the maids and the servants around me and told him what the physician had said about the Pure Lady.

"Insane?" Pheasant frowned. "Are you certain?"

"Yes. Princess Gaoyang heard it too."

Gaoyang nodded. "She struck Luminous Lady, and she also believed Luminous Lady was Empress Wang."

Around Pheasant, Prince Ke and Fang Yi'ai frowned.

"The Empress has driven the Pure Lady insane." Pheasant's chest heaved in anger. "I will not let her get away with this. What do you say, Brother?"

Prince Ke nodded. "Now, Your Majesty, perhaps you may wish to revisit our plan."

"I'm afraid you're right, Prince Ke. This is why I came here," I said.

"I thought you changed your mind." Pheasant looked surprised, but he was grinning, the lines around his eyes deepening. He was no longer young, and his eyes were darker than they used to be, but that smile was more beautiful than anything I had ever seen.

"I know…" I looked around me. The ministers, Pheasant's attendants, my maids, and other eunuch servants had wandered to the edge of the clearing. I did not want them to know we were discussing something important. I took Pheasant's arm. "Come, let's talk and play."

Pheasant nodded and led me to the center of the field where many brass pots stood in rows. There were only five of us—Pheasant, Gaoyang, Prince Ke, Fang Yi'ai, and me—and we were safely out of earshot. "We can talk here. Do you want to try?" He handed me two arrows.

"Well, I shall be honored." I took the arrows from his hand and stepped in front of the row of brass pots. Each pot was identical, with two rings around the opening. The goal was to toss arrows into the openings, each indicating different scores. I positioned myself ten paces away from it. I had never played this game, and it certainly was harder than I had thought. But I needed to do something so the people at the far end would not get suspicious about us.

"Prince Ke." I called him over, and even though I was certain none of the servants could hear me, I lowered my voice. "I do hope you still have the statement ready."

"Why, of course, Luminous Lady." The prince took a few arrows from a quiver too.

"What are you thinking, Luminous Lady?" Pheasant asked, pacing in front of the brass pots.

"We will hold the trial," I said. "The Pure Lady must have justice."

Pheasant nodded. "When?"

"As soon as possible," I said.

"Tomorrow." Pheasant nodded again.

"There is just one more thing." I gazed at the pot's opening, holding the arrow tight in my hand. "Have you seen the Regent recently?"

"No. I haven't seen him for a month. I heard he caught a chill. He was bedridden for weeks."

"I heard he scolded the heir a few weeks ago," I said. The Empress, intending to win the Regent's support for her new son, had invited the Regent for a feast. It had gone well, and the Regent appeared pleasant, but when they were leaving the feast, the heir passed ahead of the Regent, showing great disrespect to the elderly.

"Ah. I heard that too. My uncle said the heir needs to learn some manners, and he also unleashed a tirade of how young people these days fail to observe ancient etiquette and grow to be boorish." Pheasant threw an arrow at a brass pot. The arrow missed the pot and fell on the grass. Princess Gaoyang snickered, and Pheasant frowned at her.

"My turn," Princess Gaoyang said, and a dozen arrows flew out of her hands. They dropped into the pot's small opening as though they had eyes to see where they were going.

Pheasant groaned. I tried hard not to smile. "Well, I do hope the Regent will be in a better mood," I said, positioning myself in front of the brass pot in the center. "For we're going to visit him."

"I thought you didn't like the Regent," Princess Gaoyang said.

I shrugged. "Prince Ke is right. We must follow the protocol. If we try the Empress without the Regent's knowledge, he might be offended, and we may face some difficulties. But if the Regent decides to help us, he will be a powerful ally." Then the Empress would have no chance to fight back, even with her uncle and her newly found support.

If he refused, well, then we would face unknown challenges at the trial.

"I agree with Luminous Lady, and I think it is very possible the Regent will be on our side," Prince Ke said.

"There's no doubt about that. My uncle is wise." Pheasant waved his hand.

"Then we will visit him tonight," I said to Pheasant. We would bring gifts. The imperial vault, an enormous two-story building, stored countless precious tributes presented by many ambassadors, khans, foreign merchants, and vassals over the years. I would choose something valuable to bring. "And, Gaoyang, would you come to my garden tomorrow and help me with the Pure Lady? I'm afraid with her mental condition she might resist if we force her to leave her chamber."

"As you wish, Luminous Lady." She raised her hand, aiming at the brass pot again.

"So it's settled." Pheasant nodded. "We'll speak to my uncle, and then tomorrow we will give her a trial."

"We shall have everything ready for you by then, Your Majesty," Prince Ke said.

"Luminous Lady, forgive me to speak this at the moment," Fang Yi'ai, his face solemn, said. "But I wish to warn you that if we start the trial, we're also inviting an onslaught of the Empress and her family."

"Who's afraid of her?" Princess Gaoyang waved her hand. "As long as I am here, she will not touch Luminous Lady."

I smiled, grateful for Princess Gaoyang and her protection. Indeed, I was very fortunate to have her friendship.

"I'm pleased to hear it," I said and held a hand out to Gaoyang. "Wait for a moment. It's my turn." I tossed my arrow into the pot in front of me. With a swift motion, it fell into the opening with a clear click. The men chuckled around me, and Princess Gaoyang looked at me, her eyebrows arched in surprise.

I shrugged happily. She had skills, but I had luck, and with that, I should win the Regent's support.

But when I looked at the edge of the field again, I froze. The ministers and the servants were either walking idly or whispering among themselves, but behind them, near a tree, a lank figure with a slightly stooped back appeared. His hand supporting his chin, he was watching us. It was too far to see the expression on his face, but there was no mistaking who he was.

The heir.

He was indeed a useful son to his mother. Only a few months into his new position, and he had learned many skills and helped consolidate his mother's power. Why had he come to the field? Was he eavesdropping on us?

He turned around and walked away.

20

WHEN THE NIGHT DESCENDED, PHEASANT AND I PUT ON plain clothes—he a purple tunic, and I a black gown—and went to the back of the orchard, where a small carriage was hidden. Our gifts were already loaded inside, and the General and one of his guards were waiting for us. "The General will protect us when we travel in the city," Pheasant had told me. "The curfew is after dusk. He will help us reenter the palace." I had brought only Apricot with me, and quietly, we left the palace.

I sat on the carriage's silk-cushioned seat and leaned back. How would the Regent react to the news of the trial? Would he be angry at us and accuse us of making a scandal? Or would he be relieved the Empress would be impeached? He did not like her. He was displeased with the Empress's barrenness, and he had proposed to relieve her of the duty in the workshops.

He did not like me either, and he had exiled me. But he had also recognized my Luminous Lady title, and recently, his attitude toward me had softened a great deal.

I had a good feeling about this. We would win the Regent's support.

The Regent lived in a ward south of the palace. It required an hour's walk with two horses. If we hurried, we could reach it much more quickly, but I did not wish to attract attention, so we trotted slowly. When we arrived at his house, the watchman had just rung the gong seven times to inform the residents of the hour of the night, and everywhere the lanterns hung low from the eaves.

The Regent's house looked majestic, even in the dark. It had two thick vermilion gates, with a string of red lanterns on both sides. From a distance, it looked like one of the halls in the palace.

The General sent his guard to inform the old man of our arrival, and moments later, wearing a black hat, a purple silk robe, and black leather boots, the Regent came to greet us. Behind him were his family members: two sons, nine daughters, eight grandchildren, one wife, ten concubines, and many servants.

"Your Majesty, on behalf of the Changsun family, I hereby extend my warmest welcome to you and Luminous Lady to my humble dwelling. Your visit has given me and my family great honor, and we shall be eternally grateful."

He looked submissive, kneeling by the carriage, observing the custom of paying respect to a ruler. I wondered what really was in his mind. He certainly had not expected our visit, but he did not say anything about it, and I was also surprised to see how agile he appeared. When I saw him in the hall last time, he had looked rather frail. But tonight he appeared spry and energetic.

"There is no need for such courtesy." Pheasant helped him rise. "This is an informal visit."

But the Regent insisted, and all his family members dipped their heads, prostrating, chanting the lines of how grateful they were to receive the ruler of the kingdom. When finally they finished, Pheasant stepped inside the house, and I followed, trailed by Apricot and Pheasant's two attendants. The General guarded the outside of the house.

The reception hall was spacious. A sign displaying the characters *Zhi Hui Tang*, the Hall of Wisdom, was set in the center of the room. The walls were painted with murals of eight immortals and the famous Penglai Islands. Lined against the walls were several shelves that held many gold and silver statues. In the left corner of the hall were twelve panels of screens made of aloeswood encrusted with gold, and in the right corner of the hall stood a human-height jade statue of a phoenix.

The Regent's wealth was evident, and the layout of the hall reminded me of my family's large home in Wenshui.

"Sit, sit." The Regent ushered us to a row of low-rising tables. The womenfolk retired, as custom forbade them socializing with us. But they would not miss any of our conversation. I could see their shadows lurking behind the screens.

An awkward silence hung in the reception hall as we took our places at a table near the screens. The Regent studied us wordlessly. He knew we had come for a reason. After all, it was unusual for an emperor to pay a visit to someone's house, even if the person was his uncle.

"Esteemed Regent, how gracious of you to accept us into your home." I sat next to Pheasant. I was uncomfortable sitting on the cushion on the floor, for I could feel my swelling stomach sitting on my thighs, but I smiled pleasantly, to show him and his sons my friendliness. "And look, what a fine residence you have."

"Praise our Emperor Taizong," the Regent said and sat across from us with his sons. His back stooping, he groaned as though his bones were hurting, but his eyes darted quickly, and he did not seem to have trouble remembering his words like he did last time I had seen him. "He gave my family this dwelling when my sister became the Empress. My family and my ancestors shall take eternal pride in this honor."

I did not like that he mentioned the late Emperor, but I continued to smile. After all, I had not come here to elicit war.

"That was very thoughtful of Father," Pheasant said, nodding.

"Your father was a great man, most loyal and most benevolent. I confess, when he ordered me to assist Your Majesty, I was fearful of this challenge. I questioned myself whether I was worthy, but now I can speak with confidence that I have fulfilled your father's wish and I do not fail him."

"Of course, Uncle. We are grateful for your meritorious contribution to our kingdom," Pheasant said sincerely.

I did not like the direction of the conversation. I tugged at Pheasant's sleeve under the table.

"I almost forgot." Pheasant waved his hand, and his attendants stepped forward, carrying a chest, placed it in front of the Regent, and then carried in another. Inside the chests were two hundred bolts of silk, many precious fragrances, spices, seasonings, and gold and silver, gifts fit for a khan. I wished we could have opened them and shown the Regent the extravagance, but that would have been poor manners.

His sons glanced at each other, their eyes filled with excitement, but the Regent's face remained blank, like a snowy field. "I cannot accept these, Your Majesty. This is too extravagant," he said. We insisted, and he declined again. In this manner we continued one more time—as was the protocol—and finally, he accepted the gifts. "I thank you, Nephew and Luminous Lady, for your generous bestowals. Now, please do us an enormous honor and accept some refreshments."

"Do not trouble yourself, Uncle," Pheasant said. But the servants already hurried to bring us trays of fruit, wine, and meats. The hall grew noisy with footsteps and servants' voices.

"I shall be grateful for your hospitality, esteemed Regent," I said, feeling relaxed. Food was a good distraction.

He gave me a look that was filled with meaning. "Luminous Lady, it is a pleasure to see you again. I heard you have become a great patron to Buddhist temples and monasteries. This is utterly heart-warming," he said, his tone flat, and I could not tell whether he was truly complimenting me or not. Like many nobles, he did not agree with Buddhism, and he was a devout Taoist, like Emperor Taizong.

"I'm surprised this has come to your attention," I said, although I knew nothing would escape his sharp eyes. "Of course, it cannot compare to what you have contributed to the Taoist abbeys, esteemed Regent."

A great champion of Taoism, the Regent had continued to support the official religion of the kingdom after Emperor Taizong's death. He had designated an astounding number of cattle to the abbeys as an annual fund, fattening the priests and their followers, as Taoists did not have restrictions on diet. Furthermore, all the Taoist priests, regardless of their ranks and services to the kingdom, were given the privilege of receiving monthly allowances, including clothes, incense fees, and food compensations, the amount far exceeding that of a Talent in the palace.

"Buddhism is a superficial religion," the Regent said, waving his hand dismissively. "Its emphasis on hell and salvation is rather outland-ish and sensational. It appeals mostly to butchers, burglars, and beg-gars. Any sensible scholars will see that. Are you a Buddhist yourself, Luminous Lady?"

I felt my face heat up, and even though I could not claim myself to be a devout believer of Buddhism, I made up my mind that as long as I was Luminous Lady, I should never allow anyone to speak so poorly of the religion to my face again. "I have yet to be recognized as such, esteemed Regent, but I strive to follow the disciplines described in the scriptures. Although"—I paused—"I do beg to ask, is immortality really achievable through ingestion of elixir, as so claimed by Taoists?"

It was an essential part of Taoism to pursue immortality. Thus many Taoist priests, claiming to be alchemists, had been mixing minerals— mercury, cinnabar, and even gold—since the First Emperor of the Qin Dynasty. Yet the Emperor, a zealot of such elixirs, had died at half of the Regent's age. But of course, the Taoist priests never gave up, and they always used immortality as a bait to lure the gullible.

The Regent snorted slightly, that arrogant goat. "Taoism itself, like the elixir, is not to be comprehended by a commoner."

Now I wished to argue with him about Taoism. For sure, this one-thousand-year-old religion demonstrated philosophical inspirations, but the language it used to express such beliefs was often cryptic, and as a result, the meaning was muddy and esoteric.

But I remembered my mission. "Of course," I said mildly, and decided to please him by quoting the famous line from the *Tao Te Jing*, the central scripture of Taoism, which I had learned since I was a child. "*Dao ke dao, fei chang dao. Ming ke ming, fei chang ming.*"

The Dao that can be explained is not the real Dao. The Name that can be named is not the true Name.

He tilted his head toward me. "What a surprise, Luminous Lady, that a woman would be interested in this lofty philosophy. Would you like a piece of honeydew, Nephew? I preserved it in an ice pit. Honeydew is your favorite, I remember." He turned to a servant holding a basket of fruit.

"I like honeydew, Uncle. I would love to have a piece…" Pheasant glanced at me. I knew what was in his mind. He was thinking how to tell his uncle the purpose of our visit. Yet this was not the time. We must wait for the old man himself to bring up the topic.

The Regent picked up a honeydew and pressed to check the

firmness. "You used to eat many of them when you came for visits with your mother, you remember?"

"Uncle has a good memory."

"Your mother, may she rest in peace, was a most noble and virtuous woman." Sighing, he put a melon on the table and gestured to the servants for a fruit knife. "So, Nephew, forgive me if I am being uncouth, but to what do I owe the honor of your visiting?"

I could feel Pheasant straighten beside me. "A grave matter, Uncle." He cleared his throat. "I would not trouble you if I wasn't concerned. Are you aware of the misdeed the Empress has committed in the Inner Court, Uncle?"

I was too nervous to drink, and the servants' footsteps seemed quieter too. No one was talking anymore. I could hear the Regent's sons slurping the wine.

"Misdeed?"

"It regards the Pure Lady and Sujie. You do remember the Lady, do you not? She took over the duty in the workshops for a while, and Sujie, the little poet, had composed a ballad, which is said to deliver an unfavorable opinion of Zhong. Empress Wang was most displeased."

I remained stiff. Would the Regent feign ignorance? To my surprise, he sighed.

"Nephew, I was going to consult with you on this matter."

"Indeed?"

"Empress Wang," the Regent said, "I have heard, has taken some improper measures to punish her foes. She imprisoned the Pure Lady and her child in a kennel with wolves. I found this behavior rather unthinkable."

"The Pure Lady, who is of most delicate nature, has now gone insane," Pheasant told him.

"This is most deplorable, Nephew." The Regent shook his head. "Most deplorable. I regret to hear this has happened in your household. I can see the Empress is a willful woman. I only wished I had known that. When she adopted Zhong, I had thought this was over." He sighed. "You must not give women too much freedom. They know not right from wrong. They are like dogs. They must be trained and chained. If you let them loose, they go wild."

I was not sure how to respond. I was happy the Regent disliked the Empress, yet I took no satisfaction in his reasoning. He seemed to bear ill will against all women. Pheasant was quiet now.

The movements in the hall slowed. The servants hunched their shoulders, glancing at Pheasant and me, and the Regent's sons sat there stiffly, their faces tightening.

"So what do you have in mind, Nephew?"

Pheasant coughed and glanced at the servants around us.

"Of course." The Regent dismissed the servants and ordered them to close the hall's door behind them. Now there were only him, his two sons, Pheasant, and me. I felt better with fewer ears about.

"I appreciate your caution, Uncle," Pheasant said, "and I am most pleased you agree with me regarding the Empress. This is why I wish to tell you, Uncle, I intend to bring her to the hall and ask her to state the matter. Tomorrow."

"A trial?" The Regent's voice was sharp, too sharp.

"I have decided." Pheasant sounded resolute. "She must be punished for her behavior, or the palace will have no peace."

The Regent did not speak. I peered at him, trying to see if I could find any sign that would reveal his thoughts. "That will be unprecedented, impeaching an empress," he said finally and stood up to pace in the hall.

"I am aware of that, Uncle."

I wished the Regent would sit in front of me so I could discern the undercurrent of his thoughts hidden behind his hooded eyes, but he walked away from me, his face averted from mine, his hawkish nose looking sharp like a thin blade.

Finally, he sat down. "The kingdom will be shocked. You will face an upheaval." He picked up the fruit knife the servant left on the table and began to slice the honeydew. The tone of his voice changed, becoming measured and even. "She comes from a noble family, after all. She was chosen by your father to be your chief wife and the mother of the kingdom. And now she has a male heir, and she is backed by all her family and many ministers in the court."

"Yet, Uncle, I cannot let it pass and close my eyes. As the Emperor, I have responsibilities to all the women serving me in the Inner Court."

The Regent sighed, slicing the melon with one quick stroke, and clear juice flowed from its rind to the tray. "You mentioned the Pure Lady has gone insane?"

"Indeed, she has. That's why I came here to ask your opinion."

The Regent knew, though, that we came not to ask for his opinion, but for his support. "I see." He pulled up his long sleeves and arranged the melon slices on the tray. "Nephew, have you discussed this matter with anyone else?"

"Only with my brother."

"Ah, Prince Ke. You get along with him, do you? I heard you played Pitching-a-Pot with him today. Was it a good game?"

"It was, Uncle."

"Prince Ke…" The Regent looked thoughtful now. "He is indeed a fine fellow, like your father. I am pleased he has returned."

That was a lie. He had exiled the prince and feared he would be a threat. Since the prince's return, the Regent had never spoken a word to him.

"Oh, you know he is trustworthy, Uncle. Father used to adore him too. Do you remember?"

"You do not worry about him?"

"Worry? Why?"

"Young fellow, always headstrong. That's all." The Regent presented the tray before us and gestured to us to eat. "I hope you like the melon, Your Majesty."

Pheasant took a bite. "Sweet melon. So, we trust to see you tomorrow at the hall, Uncle?"

Our plan depended on this moment. If the Regent agreed to join us at the hall, it would be his promise to support us during the trial. If not, it meant his disapproval, and that would pose many challenges tomorrow. I watched him, my heart tightening.

His head lowering, the old man poured himself some wine. "Have you made any offerings to your mother these days, Nephew? Bless her. May she rest in peace."

"Of course, Uncle."

He nodded. "And how is our Princess Gaoyang? Still her usual old self?"

"You know her, Uncle. Gaoyang will never change."

"I hear, Luminous Lady, she is a good friend of yours?"

"Indeed, she is," I said, watching him. Why was he changing the subject?

The Regent cleared his throat, drumming on the table with two fingers. "And may I ask, Nephew, what will be the Empress's punishment for her crime?"

Pheasant leaned forward, ready to speak, but I put my hand on his arm. "You know, Regent, our emperor is most lenient, and he has not decided on this matter yet. Perhaps, esteemed Regent will care to give us some advice."

He gave me a long look, and I smiled to please him. I was not being truthful perhaps, but a little deception, like oil on a rusty wheel, was needed to keep the carriage moving. Did the master Sun Tzu not believe it as well?

"I see." The Regent nodded. He did not speak again, and the hall fell quiet. Pheasant pushed away the tray of melon, sat upright, staring at the trail of juice on the table. Feeling his nervousness, I held his hand and waited.

The Regent cleared his throat. "Nephew and Luminous Lady, I am compelled to offer you my service. I shall be glad to come to the hall tomorrow. However, I must advise prudence in dealing with this matter. Would it be agreeable to you, Nephew, if I select a small number of ministers, say four or five of my trusted men, to oversee the trial?"

"Why, may I ask?" Pheasant asked.

"Only to ensure it proceeds smoothly."

Pheasant hesitated.

"I have only the kingdom's welfare in my heart, Nephew, and I hope that with my men's presence, they can give their opinion in deciding the judgment of the Empress. After all, this is a matter of utter importance."

"Uncle—"

"That sounds splendid." I squeezed Pheasant's hand to quiet him. It seemed the Regent had his own punishment in mind for the Empress, and that should cause no problem for us, as long as the Empress was tried and dishonored. "I am grateful for your support, Regent."

He sighed, as though this was indeed a great burden for him. "And I must remind you again, Luminous Lady and Nephew, I have only the kingdom's welfare in mind. I do hope you understand. It is my firm belief that even as we try the Empress, we must avoid chaos in the kingdom at all costs."

"Of course, Regent. I should expect nothing less from you," I said and breathed out.

The air in the reception hall suddenly grew lively. The Regent's sons poured us wine, and the Regent called back his servants to bring more fruit to our table. Chuckling, the old man made a toast to Pheasant and talked about horses. The war against Tibet had depleted our horse reserve, he said, and now the five Imperial Stables were hoping to receive rare steeds from the Eastern Turks.

"That should increase the number of the steeds in our Imperial Stables, and next spring, we shall see some good breeds," he said.

I felt a weight lifting off my shoulders. We had won the Regent's support, and I was happy, but he was indeed a formidable man.

When it was time for us to leave, we bid good night to the Regent and his family, who knelt at the gate to see us off, and walked toward our carriage.

The night's darkness had masked the trees and all the buildings near the Regent's house. Only our horses and carriage were visible in the pool of light from the lanterns.

"General Li," Pheasant said, "you missed good wine and good company."

"Yes, Your Majesty." He opened the carriage door for us.

I paused to face the General. In the dim light, his purple birthmark looked like a vicious tattoo. "I thank you for waiting so long, General. Would you like to have some wine?"

He shook his head. "Luminous Lady, I only drink alone."

"Is it so?" I gave him a long look. The General, like the Regent, could be hard to read sometimes.

When I sat down, I let out a sigh, rubbing my shoulders. I had been so tense, I could feel the strain from my neck and my lower back, and my swelling stomach was sitting on my thighs like a heavy basin. "Are you pleased, Pheasant?"

Finally. Tomorrow the Empress would be tried. How would she react when she knew she would be dishonored, the daughter of the renowned Wang family, the legal wife of the Emperor, the Empress of the kingdom?

Pheasant nodded, grinning widely. "Yes. I cannot wait for tomorrow." He looked happy, and I remembered how enraged and shocked he had been in the kennel and how determined he was to punish the Empress.

"Now, let's go to the palace." He waved, and Apricot came to the carriage to close the door.

I stopped her. Through the open door, I glimpsed a round, red light, the size of a polo ball, glowing, as it slid in the dark in the distance. It looked shining, urgent, and sinister.

A lantern.

Who was carrying it? A night watcher? A horse-rally carrier? "Pheasant. Look."

"What is it?" he asked, leaning over.

I pointed at the light, but it was gone, and in the place where it had been were only shades of darkness.

"It's fine. Don't worry." Pheasant patted my back. "Let's go home and rest."

The carriage rolled forward, and I leaned back.

Tomorrow would be a long day, a crucial day for Pheasant and me, and I had to hone the edge of my words, sharpen my vision, and strike with force and precision. But for some reason I could not explain, the ball of red light lingered in my mind.

21

I ROSE BEFORE DAWN THE NEXT MORNING. AS USUAL, I SAT and meditated, letting my mind drift and setting my spirit at ease. The room was warm from the fire in the brazier and fragrant with the rich scent emitted from scented candles. When the dawn's first pale light illuminated our chamber, I finished meditating and put on a scarlet skirt, a padded robe, and a silk shawl embroidered with thrushes and finches, for good luck. We would need it today.

Pheasant's attendants entered the chamber, holding golden regalia lined with fur, a pair of embroidered silk trousers, a bejeweled belt, a sparkling mortarboard, a pair of shoes, and a silk pouch holding his jade seal.

"Let me." I waved away the attendants and helped Pheasant dress.

"Will you wait for my summons?" Pheasant asked. He had not slept well, but he looked exhilarated, his eyes gleaming and his footsteps forceful.

"I will." I nodded, tying the strings of his mortarboard under his chin. Pheasant would attend the audience in the morning, listening to the regular petitions so as not to arouse suspicion. Both Prince Ke and Fang Yi'ai would join the early audience as well, together with the Regent and his ministers. Then, during the rest hour, Pheasant would summon the Pure Lady, the Empress, and me to the hall, where the Empress would face the trial as we stood by.

"Where's my sister?" Pheasant asked.

"She will arrive soon." Princess Gaoyang would help me escort the Pure Lady to the hall at Pheasant's summons, so she could testify on her own behalf.

"That's good." The skin on Pheasant's face looked luminescent, giving off a sheen of youthfulness. He looked very attractive, and the maids were not paying attention to us. I stood on tiptoe to kiss him. He caught me and put his arms around my waist. "Later."

I smiled happily. "Are you nervous?"

He squeezed my cheek. "Of course not. I know what I am doing, Luminous Lady. And by the way, I have added extra men outside the garden, in case the tiger sends her dogs here to bother you."

I did not argue. The Empress would not let me breathe easily once she was punished, and I had to make certain she would never come near my son again. "I shall wait for your summons."

He gave me a firm nod and strode to the garden's entrance, the wide sleeves of the golden regalia swaying near his knees. His attendants and the General, already waiting, stepped aside as he climbed into the carriage.

I watched them until they disappeared behind the grove of tangerine trees, and my heart beat faster. When those attendants returned, they would carry the order of the summons, but also the drumming sound of battle.

I was nervous. I could only imagine how ugly the scene might become at the Empress's trial. I wished Princess Gaoyang were here. She would help calm my nerves.

"I'm going to take a walk, Apricot." I needed to exercise and also to keep calm. "When the princess comes, tell her I am in the back of the garden."

"Yes, Luminous Lady," Apricot said. She was feeding Hong near the bed. Here, it was a battle too. Apricot cooed, coaxing my boy to open his mouth, but Hong twisted his head away. Apricot pushed the spoon near his mouth, but he batted it away. He was often like this, refusing to eat.

I walked down the path near the bamboo grove. It was still early in the morning. The garden looked sleepy in the dawn's milky shade. My stomach was growing large every day, and it was getting difficult for me to hike up the hill. I turned around and crossed over a bridge.

When I found my way back to my chamber, the morning's golden light shone in my eyes. The garden was noisy with birds twittering, and I was sweaty. But Princess Gaoyang had not yet arrived.

"Has she sent a message?" I asked Apricot while searching for Hong. He was stabbing something in the flower bed with a stick. Now that he was finally walking, he had become fascinated with anything that crawled. He would dig in the flower beds, finding beetles and ladybugs, and put them in his mouth. I was worried he would get a stomach ulcer, but Gaoyang had laughed it off. "That's nature. Nature won't hurt boys," she said.

"No." Apricot shook her head. Chunlu brought a handkerchief for me to wipe my face while Xiayu came with boxes of tincture and rouge, ready to apply them on my cheeks.

"Nothing?" I sat on a stool in front of a bronze mirror. It was not like her. Princess Gaoyang was never late, and she always showed up when I expected her to. Even when she went to meet her mentor on the mountain, she would tell me days ahead of time so I would not worry.

Apricot shook her head again.

I should get the Pure Lady myself, and perhaps by the time I returned, the princess would have arrived.

"Come." I gestured to Xiayu to apply the cream to my face. "I must get ready now, and then we'll go to the Quarters of the Pure Lotus together."

"The Quarters?" Apricot poured some water into a cup and handed it to me. I was always thirsty after a walk. "I need to tell you something, my lady…"

"Yes. What is it?"

"Luminous Lady, some maids in the Quarters were gossiping. They said something strange is going on in the Empress's quarters," she said. "The Empress received a message and left the court. She was very angry. She said something about you."

Alarmed, I turned to her. "What did she say?"

Apricot bit her lip. "Well…"

They must be hard words. I frowned. "Who sent the message?"

Apricot shook her head.

"When did she leave the court?"

"Before dawn broke."

I frowned. Did the Empress suspect something? Had the Regent changed his mind and betrayed us? But it could not be possible. He hated the Empress, and he had agreed to the trial.

But what if the Empress, sensing a plot forming against her, had offered the Regent something in return? Something irresistible?

I rose and paced across the chamber, but a sick feeling sat in my stomach, expanding like a spoiled meal.

I went to the door. "Come with me, Apricot. Let's go to the Quarters." Whatever the Empress was up to, I must do as we planned.

We had just reached the garden's entrance when Pheasant stumbled in, his mortarboard askew. He looked as though he had run all the way from the Audience Hall to my garden. Out of breath, he leaned against the cinnamon tree. He was alone, without his attendants or the General.

My hands turned cold. Something terrible was happening. "Pheasant! What's wrong?"

He kept swallowing, as though a rock had gotten stuck in his throat.

I held him. "Come, sit down, and tell me."

His hands on his knees, he bent, breathing hard. His mortarboard dropped on the ground. "The Audience Hall...is...empty," he said, his voice hoarse. "All the high-ranking ministers—the Secretary, the Chancellor—are absent."

My heart sank. "Where did they go? Where is the Regent?"

"He is not in the hall."

"Why? Where is he?"

"At a trial."

"What trial?" I picked up Pheasant's mortarboard and handed it to him. "Are they trying the Empress?" I asked, allowing myself to hope.

"No." He stared at me, his face ashen. "It's a trial against Prince Ke and Fang Yi'ai."

"What? Why?" Those two men had committed no crime. "On what grounds?"

"Treason."

"What?" I could not believe my ears. "Where is the trial being held? Take me there. We must stop them."

"I asked the ministers in the hall, but they did not know. I have sent the General to find out. He'll report to me as soon as he learns the location." Pheasant raised his head to look at me. He was swaying, as though he had lost the strength to stand. "I had to come here. I had to let you know."

My heart thumped. I could see the shock and pain in his eyes, and I could feel his desperation and helplessness. "Who is judging the trial?"

"It's her…" Pheasant squeezed his eyes shut and balled his fists. "I trusted him, Mei. I trusted him…"

The Regent.

He had betrayed us.

The lantern I had seen after we left the Regent's house must have been a messenger he sent to warn the Empress, who, outraged and furious, must have offered him a deal. Together they had decided to eliminate Prince Ke and Fang Yi'ai, the two people Pheasant and I trusted and relied on.

I realized now how cunning the Regent was. He had felt threatened by Pheasant's growing power as he recalled Prince Ke and the other ministers, but instead of voicing his objection, he took a step back and feigned weakness, hiding behind a show of old age. But all these months, he had been waiting for a chance to strike back. By siding with the Empress, the Regent had much to gain. He would win the support from all of the Empress's people, and he would have full control of the court again. But Pheasant, my poor Pheasant, would be alone, his support cut off and his efforts in the past months wasted.

"Your Majesty!" The General strode through the entrance. "They are in the *Zhengshi Tang*."

The Hall of State Matters. It was located east of the Audience Hall, and it would take one hour on foot to reach it from the garden. "Get in the carriage, Pheasant. General, take us to the hall."

"Yes, yes!" Pheasant put on his mortarboard and leaped toward the carriage. "Let's go now. Let's stop them. We must save my brother!"

I quickly entered the carriage after Pheasant. I felt angry at the Regent's betrayal, but I was also nervous about the impending fate of Prince Ke and Fang Yi'ai. Clearly, they were targeted because they supported Pheasant and me. But what would the Empress and the Regent do to them?

Once the carriage started to move, Pheasant told me more of the alleged treason the Regent and the Empress had accused our friends of. They claimed Prince Ke, his two sons, Fang Yi'ai, and a few others had gathered at a tavern in the capital a month before. They had been drinking, discussing the failed revolt Taizi and Prince Yo had led years ago. Those men were idiots, they said, and if they had been given a chance, the outcome of the revolt would have been completely different. They would have succeeded. They went on lamenting how their talents had been wasted in the court. When the opportunity came, they would overthrow Pheasant's rule and give the kingdom a new start.

The story was so ridiculous that I wanted to laugh. It was sheer slander that bore no truth. But the prince and Fang Yi'ai would not have a chance to speak for themselves. If we did not arrive on time, the Empress and the Regent might find them guilty and throw them into a dungeon. All of Pheasant's efforts at recalling ministers and building his support group would come to nothing, and Pheasant would return to being nothing but an ineffective ruler.

When the carriage slowed, I leaped out, nearly falling over. Pheasant caught me and pulled me up. "Are you all right?"

I pulled away and rushed through the courtyard, climbed the stairs, three at once, my hands holding my swelling stomach, and burst into the hall. My jaw dropped.

The hall was empty.

"Where is everyone?" Pheasant shouted. His voice echoed in the great hall. The sunlight lingered at the door, refusing to enter the enormous room. "General? I thought you said they were here."

"They were an hour ago." The General turned around, frowning.

"Your Majesty, General Li, Luminous Lady." A minister in a green robe hurried to greet us. He performed a full court courtesy, his head lowered to his waist, and then dropped to his knees. "Kneeling before you is your humble servant Li Yifu, the assistant minister of justice." His head went up and down. "May Heaven continue to bless Your Majesty with eternal good health, and our Luminous Lady with eternal beauty and courage. How may I be of service today?"

There was no time for etiquette. "Was a trial being held here?" I asked. "Where is everyone?"

"Luminous Lady, it's the Regent's order. I am afraid—"

Pheasant seized the minister by his robe and pulled him toward him. "One word of shit, and I will send you and your family to the farthest corner of the kingdom for the rest of your lives, Minister."

"Your Majesty! I will speak the truth...yes. They were here. But the trial..."

Pheasant let him go, and the minister fell back to the ground. "Where is the trial?"

The minister swallowed. "Yes... Your Majesty, the trial... Allow me to give you the details. The procedure was not followed properly. Several ministers were not present—Minister Yu Zhiwen, for example. It was conducted rather hastily, as well. First, the Empress stated the crime of each criminal, and the Regent confirmed it. No witnesses were called, which I thought was quite out of ordinary, and then the Regent announced the sentences. The convicted prince and the others did not have a chance to speak or deny. It was the queerest trial, if I might be allowed to say so," the minister said in a maddeningly slow manner. "And—"

"Just tell me." I could not bear to listen to him blather on anymore. "Where are the prince and the princess's husband?"

"Luminous Lady, it is an honor to answer your question," he said. "But I regret to tell you they are on the way to the Western Market."

"The Western Market?" The execution grounds where Emperor Taizong had executed his uncle and many conspirators of the revolt? "He sentenced them to death? To be executed now?"

"Again, Luminous Lady, the shock you have expressed is equally shared by many of us—"

"They want to kill my brother! How dare they!" Pheasant strode out the hall, sizzling with anger. "Go to the market, General. Now!"

I ran after him. "We don't have time." The execution grounds were located in the center of the Western Market, the busy area in the city, and the Regent must have left the palace half an hour ago. It would take us another half hour at least to reach the market. I wiped the perspiration off my forehead. It was so hot. "Send an edict, Pheasant. State that you have conveyed mercy on them and spare their lives. Ask the General to carry it on horseback. Ask him to go to the market now. He will be faster than us."

Pheasant agreed, and immediately, he drafted a letter on a sheet of paper Minister Li Yifu offered and pressed his jade seal on the edict. The General took the edict and raced off on horseback.

"We will follow him." I walked toward the carriage. Two of

the General's guards were standing there. I gestured to one to drive the carriage.

"You don't look very well, Mei." Pheasant stopped me. "You need to rest."

"I'm fine. Let's go. I must see them." I climbed inside the carriage. But Pheasant was right. I did not feel well. "We must get to the market as fast as we can."

"Sit, then. Captain Pei! To the market!"

The carriage lurched, throwing me forward. Suddenly, the carriage felt so small, and the air, a mixture of stale sweat and sour odor, choked me. I gagged. My toes bent, and a spasm seized me.

"What's wrong?"

"I have a cramp in my leg." I breathed hard.

Pheasant rubbed it. "Here? Here? Better? No? Let's go back. Let's go find a physician. Captain Pei!"

"No, no." We had to keep moving. We had to go to the market. Desperately, I kicked my legs to ease the cramp and shouted at the top of my lungs. "Go, go now. Take us to the market!"

The carriage sped up, throwing me to the side. Pheasant held my shoulders to steady me. I buried my head in his arms as the pain eased. I wanted to cry.

Prince Ke. He was a good man, a good brother to Pheasant, and a trusted friend. He held no grudge against Pheasant or even the Regent, and he wished only to start anew after his return to the court. He had brought much happiness to Pheasant and good memories to me too. Now he was facing his death because of us. And Fang Yi'ai had certainly done nothing wrong.

And my poor Princess Gaoyang. All morning I had wondered why she had not come to my garden. She must have been going through the horror of having her husband arrested, tried, and sent to the execution grounds. She would be shocked and devastated. So alone she was, surrounded by the Empress and the treacherous Regent, and now she was probably at the execution grounds, shouting in anger and despair while no one listened.

I clenched my hands and pounded on the carriage door. "Faster! Faster!"

22

A THICK ODOR OF CHARRED FOOD, SWEAT, AND BURNED hide wafted to my nose, and a wave of rumbling noises, mixed with curses, shrieks, and shouts of selling noodles and firewood rose around me. We had left the palace and arrived somewhere near the market.

I opened the carriage window. Many bodies jostled around the carriage. Many people, wearing straw hats, black hats, and leather caps, flooded the street, blocking our way. A gray wall—the wall of the market—stood in the distance, cloaked in a cloud of coppery dust. We were still far from the execution grounds.

The carriage slowed down.

"Aside, aside!" the driver, Captain Pei, shouted.

But the carriage slowed more.

I could not sit still. A moment stopped here was a moment wasted. "Tell them to get out of the way," I shouted at the Captain.

"There are too many of them, Luminous Lady," he replied. "They won't step aside."

I stared down at the people blocking the path, a thought dawning on me. They were here to watch the executions. Rage rushed through me. I knew the commoners of the city liked them, idling around with nothing to do. They watched executions with a feverish fascination as though they were at circus shows, and afterward, the blood of those spilled would become drinks of their amusement. The kingdom was filled with people of that sort, and the rise and fall of the dynasties before us had fed their fascination and fired their morbid appetite for more. It was a disease, a deep-rooted pandemic that paralyzed people's brains and devoured the basic nature of human sympathy.

"Would you like us to wait here, Your Majesty?" Captain Pei asked.

"No," I answered for Pheasant, and closed the window. I would run all the way to the market if necessary and confront the Regent and the Empress face-to-face. I must stop them, question their baseless trial, before they had a chance to murder my friends. "We must get to the execution grounds."

"It's not safe, Luminous Lady," the Captain replied. "We have only twenty guards with us."

I did not understand at first, but then I heard a faint clamor rise outside the carriage. I pushed the window open again. People on the street were turning to me. Some whispered, and I could see anger simmering in the eyes of those close to me. Some shouted, waving their fists, spittle flying through the air. My heart constricted. Spectators of executions were nothing more than senseless ants, but spectators filled with anger could be a dangerous mob. And they looked dangerous now.

"The prince is innocent! He would never conspire to revolt," one man shouted.

Another raised his head. "Fang Yi'ai only built roads for us. Is that a crime?"

"Your Majesty, spare the prince!"

I was wrong. The people had come to speak. I turned to Pheasant.

"Do I hear them correctly?" Pheasant frowned. "They think I ordered the executions?"

I nodded. "I think so. You must order them to disperse. We must get through."

We might be able to force our horses through the crowd. The four steeds were powerful enough, but people in the crowd would be hurt.

Pheasant straightened. "Captain Pei, order them to disperse."

The Captain shouted, "Aside, aside! By the imperial order!"

A thunderous roar erupted to answer him. Fists flung in the air, and waves of voices rocked the sky. The carriage began to shake as the crowd swarmed forward. I lost my balance and slid sideways into Pheasant's arms.

He steadied me and held me tightly. "Don't worry. I shall take care of it."

I was about to speak when a rattling came from above my head. Something pounded on the roof of the carriage. Rocks.

We would not make it to the market on time. Where was the General? I hoped he had reached the execution grounds safely. I hoped he had delivered the edict before it was too late. Outside, the roar of the crowd was deafening, and the carriage shook violently. I swallowed hard. I was so nervous I could hardly breathe.

The Captain shouted something, but his voice was drowned out in the din, and we could not hear him.

Pheasant raised his voice. "What did you say, Captain Pei?"

"We have a riot, Your Majesty!"

The carriage rocked, and Pheasant grabbed me as I slipped to the floor. "Hold on here. How many of them, Captain Pei?" Pheasant's voice, to my amazement, was calm.

"At least two thousand. They are…out of control." The carriage shook again.

From behind the carriage came the frightened shouts of the ministers who had followed us from the palace.

Pheasant opened the carriage door. "You stay here," he said, and before I could ask him what he was going to do, he stepped outside. "Good people of my kingdom!" he shouted, and for a moment the noise quieted. "I ask you, everyone and each of you, to move back two hundred paces, and cease throwing the rocks in your hands. I have come here to investigate the executions that you are concerned with, and I promise you, I, the son of Emperor Taizong, your Emperor, is here to give you justice."

"Don't listen to him!"

"He ordered the executions!"

"The Empress came to deliver his message!"

Another uproar erupted, louder than before, and through the half-open carriage door, I could see the bodies of the maddening mob surge to break through the wall of the few guards who shielded Pheasant. A rock flew through the air.

It was too dangerous. He must come back to the carriage.

"Arrest that man!" Captain Pei shouted. "Attacking the Emperor is a capital crime!"

"Hold it." Pheasant raised his hand. "Arrest no one. Let them speak. I wish to hear."

I did not know what to say. Pheasant was such a benevolent man. His people were threatening him, but he still cared about them.

"Your Majesty…"

His voice was drowned out as another wave of shouts broke out. I shuddered. Pheasant needed help. I needed to help him.

Please. Let the General announce the edict before my friends are dragged to the ax.

Taking a deep breath, I patted my wig and stepped out of the carriage. The clamor grew louder for an instant, and then the crowd turned their eyes to me.

I knew what they saw: a court lady with a magnificent red gown and long, black hair adored with gold hairpins and pearls. I was certain they had never before seen a woman in such a glory and splendor. Did they think I was the Empress? They should know that I could not be, because of my protruding stomach.

"People of Chang'an." I bowed, my heart tightening in my chest. When I straightened, I took a good look at the crowd. They were not tattered-clothed beggars or tattoo-faced bandits. They wore stained tunics, felt hats, and cloth shoes—ordinary Chang'an civilians. My fear of being cornered by a mob subsided. "I am Luminous Lady, and I beseech you to follow our emperor's order. He is a just emperor, a kind emperor. He protects you, your sons, and your family. He has opened the markets for trade, put meat in your bowls, and punished the thieves who stole your sheep. Go home, forget this, eat your wheat buns, serve your parents a cup of drink, play with your children, talk with your wives. They are waiting for you. Let there be no bloodshed today."

There was silence around me. The commoners looked stunned, and the ministers behind the carriage gaped at me. Their gowns were torn and their faces were smudged with yellow dirt and horse dung.

I knew what they were thinking. Ordinary women did not speak in public, and a court lady would never deign to lower herself to bow to the commoners or show her face before them. But this was not an ordinary situation. I could not bear to see my Pheasant get hurt; I could not bear to see anyone get hurt today. And we had to hurry. We needed to save our friends.

"Luminous Lady? This is Luminous Lady?" The angry faces near me turned, whispering to each other.

"She is the Buddhist lady, is she not?"

"She built roads and gave alms. Is this the one?"

They knew I had helped them.

I bowed again. "Please—"

"You're putting yourself in danger," Pheasant said in a low voice, pushing me to the carriage. "Let's go inside, now."

"But—"

"Look, the General!"

Near the market's gate, the General darted toward us, his maroon cape flying in the air. Behind him was a group of imperial Gold Bird Guards. They shouted, wielding their swords.

The crowd gasped. They might have heard of my title and my donations, but they certainly had learned of the General's name and his prowess. The crowd moved back, and a circle of space cleared around our carriage.

"Arrest them!" The General's voice rose sharply as his men dove toward the crowd. Their arms raised high, the guards struck those who were slow on their feet. "Arrest them all! How dare they attack the Emperor!"

"Hold! General!" Pheasant shouted beside me. "Leave them! Leave them be!"

"Your Majesty!" The General turned toward us, his whole face crimson with anger. "I came as fast as I could. Mobs! How dare they! I'll not let them get away with it!"

"No arrests. It is my order. Now, General. Tell me." Pheasant made sure I had climbed back into the carriage and turned to the General. "Did you see my brother?"

"I…did."

"He's not too upset, I hope?" Pheasant sat down next to me and wiped perspiration off his face. I dabbed at my forehead too, watching the General intently. "Come on. Let's go get him. He'll be safe with me. I'll speak to my uncle. He'll listen and get his sense back. Now, go, General, drive the carriage. Why are you just standing there?"

He cleared his throat, and slowly, he spoke, his voice cold as usual. "Your Majesty, I don't believe it's necessary."

"What do you mean? You said you saw my brother, didn't you?"

The General nodded and said something, but his voice was lower and I could not hear him from inside the carriage. I leaned forward. He had seen the prince and the others, the General said, but they were already on the ground. I could not understand at first, and then I saw dark liquid splashed across the sleeves of the General's cape. The front of his black trousers also looked damp and dark.

The strength drained out of me. We were too late. The prince had died, and poor Princess Gaoyang would be a widow. I had ruined her life. "Oh heavens. Oh heavens."

"You didn't deliver the edict?" Pheasant's voice cracked.

"I gave it to the Regent, Your Majesty. It was too late," the General said, his face bearing no emotion. "The prince put up a fierce fight, they said."

The prince, who had never raised his voice, shouted for his life and delivered a touching speech that moved the crowd, the General said, and after him followed the prince's two sons, the Princess's husband, and the others.

"My brother…" Pheasant's shoulders sagged. Breathing hard, he turned his face away from the General, his anguish filling the carriage. "How many died today?"

"Eight."

"Eight men had committed treason, you said?"

"Eight were executed, but not all were guilty of treason." The General coughed. "One was convicted of adultery. He was the princess's lover."

"What? What lover?" I stared at him. "What are you talking about?"

"The Empress found the princess guilty of adultery with a monk named Biji. He was executed here, pulled apart by five horses." The General paused. "It was quite a spectacle. The commoners were shocked."

A shiver ran down my spine. "The monk Biji? He was her mentor. He raised her! What are you talking about?"

The General folded his arms across his chest. "According to what

I have learned, Your Majesty, Luminous Lady, the Empress indicated that the princess gave the monk a jade pillow as her love token, and her maid confessed that the princess met him regularly in a scripture house in secret."

"Liar! All liars! Do not believe her. The Empress hates the princess because of me. She will not get away with this!" I panted, anger shooting from my stomach.

The General glanced at me. Oh, that indifferent look. In that moment, I hated him. He was powerful with his sword, it was true, but like the sword, he was made of steel and untouched by human empathy. "Luminous Lady, there's something else. With the evidence and the witness, the Empress announced the princess was also guilty of adultery, and she was sentenced to death."

"What? That wicked woman! She cannot do this! She cannot simply declare the princess guilty. She wants to get rid of the princess! She hates the princess because she's my friend. She cannot do this! Where is the princess? Where is the princess? I must see her now. Pheasant, take me to her house." I struggled to catch my breath. "The Empress cannot touch her! She is a swordswoman. She will not sit there and accept the sentence. Take me! Take me to her house."

The carriage did not move, and the General fell silent.

"Did you hear me? Take me to her! I want to see my princess!"

The General glanced at me again. Something I had never seen before—something like pity—flitted across his eyes, and his purple birthmark twitched. But he turned away from me and leaned over to Pheasant, whispering in his ear.

I wanted to grab the General and make him face me and speak to me. He had told me years before that he was my father's friend, and I thought he would be kind to me. He had tried to help me once, offering to sever my foot when he believed bad blood had clogged me, but he had been wrong. And he had given me the message from my mother. But that was all he had done to help me. Since he returned from exile, he had never even bothered to give me an extra glance. The men with swords and the men with words. They were all alike. They stabbed you all the same with the dagger of treachery and heartlessness. I should not have trusted him.

"What is it? Why are you not telling me?" I demanded.

The General drew back, and Pheasant looked as though he had been struck by a club, his eyes dazed and his shoulders stiff.

"What are you waiting for, Pheasant? We must go to the princess's house! Pheasant?" He did not move, and I shook him. "Say something!"

He swallowed, leaned back, and closed his eyes. Tears ran down his cheeks, flowing over his chin and wetting the front of his yellow robe. I shuddered. Suddenly, I wished I had never asked. Suddenly, I hoped he would never answer me.

He said, "Let's go home."

I howled.

✦ ✦

Later, I learned what happened.

The night Pheasant and I returned to our garden from the Regent's house, the Empress met with her uncle, who went to see the Regent and planned their betrayal. In the morning, while I was tying the mortarboard strings under Pheasant's chin, a group of two hundred Gold Bird Guards took the Regent's order and burst into the princess's house, ambushing the sleeping household. Arrows rained from the sky and pierced the windows of the sprawling building Fang Yi'ai had inherited from his father. The cries of the servants were cut short, and some ran out of the house, screaming. The princess put up a fierce fight but was finally caught after six arrows pierced her legs and chest.

By the time I finished my morning walk and returned to the chamber, expecting to see her, asking Apricot whether any message had been delivered from her, two guards had placed a noose around her neck, one standing on her right, one standing on her left, twisting the rope that wound around her throat, and strangled her.

AD 654

The Fifth Year *of*
Emperor Gaozong's Reign
of Eternal Glory

EARLY SPRING

23

A MONTH HAD PASSED SINCE PRINCESS GAOYANG'S DEATH.

Winter lingered. The water lilies wilted in the pond, leaving piles of brown leaves floating on the surface like shattered birds' nests. The peonies were long dead, and so were the roses. Their branches, once strong and prickly, had been either trimmed or removed, and on the bare flower beds, once a rich playground for insects, spread a thin coat of frost like a layer of ashes.

Every day I sat on the stone bench in the garden. The wind swept across my face, ruffling my unstyled hair. I did not wear my wigs anymore, or apply whitening cream or bright rouge to my face.

Wiping the tears off my face, I searched the pavilion's sloped roof—Gaoyang's favorite perch—the pavilion's windowsills, and the skeletal trees nearby. They were quiet and empty.

I folded my arms on my swelling stomach. My baby kicked inside me, as though reminding me to think of her, and indeed, in two months, I would meet my child, but I felt no joy. In utter anguish and gloom, I stared at the pond. I could see my own reflection, a plump lady with short hair falling limply on her shoulders. There, my shining red gown had turned black, my arms became a mere dark cloud, and my head, a shadowy, pathetic globe, floated on the surface of wavy water like a cracked tortoise shell.

In the pond, I had no face; in the pond, I looked like a mess of rootless grass; in the pond, I was nothing.

When the sunlight warmed the top of my head, I looked up at

the sky. The sun's rays were mild but bright, stinging my eyes, and I thought of my friend again. The high sun. But the sun above me would come and go, while the sun in my heart would never rise again.

Rage burned inside me. I wanted to shout. I wanted to curse. And the sun was hurting me now, blinding me, leaving mountains of shadows standing in front of me. In those shadows, thick and formidable, I saw my friend and the last moment of her life when the air failed to reach her chest. I heard the wicked grunts of those executioners beside her, I heard the scream build in her lungs but choke at her throat, and I could feel her fierce spirit waning, struggling, fluttering, and finally flying away.

I had to look away. I could not bear the sunlight in my eyes, I could not bear to see her die before me, and yet the mountains of shadows did not disappear. They swayed, expanded, growing rugged, dominant, and turned into a jagged cliff threatening to thrust into my eyes.

Tears ran down my cheeks. I had led her to the edge of the cliff. I had thrown her into the dark abyss. It was my fault.

If she could have spoken to me, would she have blamed me? Would she have hated me? She should have. She had protected me with her life, provided me with safety and laughter, and I had brought her the noose.

Gaoyang was buried with her mother, who had died during the rebellion against Emperor Taizong. Their family tomb, a small mound already infested with centipedes and snakes, was located far away from the late Emperor's mausoleum, and her funeral was unceremonious. Few imperial family members attended for fear of being branded as sympathetic toward an unscrupulous woman.

But her husband and Prince Ke suffered a worse fate. Their bodies were left in the market for days, until Pheasant, defying the Regent, ordered the General to bury them. But that was after the blood from the execution grounds had flowed to the alleys of the market, soaking the hard ground, and become glued to the bottoms of many people's shoes with dirt and horse dung. A few days later, a sand storm assailed our city from the north, carpeting everything with coppery loess. Once again the ground was muddy, and once again the streets of Chang'an turned into their usual morass of dirt and dust.

But as long as the sun was above my head, I would remember my friend, and I would strike back. I would seek every opportunity to destroy my enemies, even if it meant the execution grounds would be stained with blood again.

✦ ✦

Pheasant vowed to restore his brother's name. He questioned the Regent about the prince's trial, but the Regent was his usual cunning self, coating the explanation of the murders with his sense of duty and his concerns for the kingdom's safety.

What else was he supposed to do? the Regent asked, throwing his arms out. All the evidence was in front of him. Prince Ke's mother, the late Noble Lady, was the daughter of Emperor Yang, the ruler of the perished Sui Dynasty. Prince Ke certainly had the motive to avenge his grandfather's death, and it was probable that he would scheme to overthrow the dynasty Emperor Taizong had built. Even if the prince had not actually gathered his army, any evidence of discontent was a budding sign of treason. And Fang Yi'ai, the son of Secretary Fang, had always hated the Regent. Surely, he had his reason to revolt too.

Pheasant laughed bitterly. "Of course, if you wanted to make a predator out of a sheep, you would accuse the sheep for possessing the teeth to chew." His face crimson with anger, Pheasant demanded to speak to the people who overheard the prince's treasonous conversation in the tavern. The Regent turned a deaf ear to the request, the Chancellor chided Pheasant for neglecting state affairs, and the Secretary snickered behind his sleeve.

None of the middle-ranking ministers attempted to support Pheasant. Quietly, they stepped aside, and the lower-ranking ministers, the potential allies who were unable to fit in the Regent's or the Empress's circles, were afraid to speak to Pheasant too, fearing they would lose their positions, or worse, become the target of the Empress.

Every day, Pheasant went to the Audience Hall with his fists clenched, and every day he returned home with his spirit broken.

The General, the only one who still stood by Pheasant's side, came to see him in the garden. His whole face taut with tension, he threw his cape behind him and knelt in front of Pheasant. Without mentioning the Regent or what he had done, the General laid his sword, the sword he had never parted with, on the ground and said simply, "Say the name, Your Majesty."

He would chop off any man's head if Pheasant wished, I could see, and he did not care what the Regent or the Empress would do to retaliate. I was touched. Even though the General did not care for me, he was loyal to Pheasant from the bottom of his heart.

Pheasant twisted his head away, his hands clenched. He was struggling; he was tempted, I could see, to let the General avenge his siblings' deaths. But Pheasant faced the General again, and his eyes glittering with tears, he asked, "Do you think I am my father? Do you, General? Do you?"

"They have defied you, Your Majesty," the General said. "Defiance means death."

Pheasant wiped his eyes furiously. "They deserve to die, yes. They do. But I will not have blood on my hands. I will not! Pick up your sword. Pick up your sword now. As long as you serve me, you will kill no one. It's an order, General."

His face bearing the usual mask of impassiveness again, the General lowered his head and picked up the sword. "Yes, Your Majesty."

Pheasant patted the General's shoulder, turned around, and slowly walked back to our chamber.

✦ ✦

The Empress celebrated her victory by appointing the Regent's sons to the court. No doubt this move strengthened her newly forged tie with the Regent, and his sons, grateful for the promotion, would serve her faithfully.

She also rewarded her uncle, the Secretary, who played an efficient part in my friends' trials, and a number of his servants with lavish presents. She thanked the Regent with a one-hundred-year-old Koguryo ginseng, which was said to prolong youth and bring vitality to the person who ingested it.

Not only that, she also made sure no one in the court would mention a word of the trial we had planned for her, or the Pure Lady's condition. Even the Noble Lady's request to have the Pure Lady's family visit her was turned down, and if anyone happened to mention a kennel or wolves, that person would receive ten lashes by thick rods. Soon, not a single maid dared to gossip about the Pure Lady's insanity or the evil that had befallen her and Sujie.

The Empress enjoyed herself, inviting a music troupe to the palace to entertain her. With her adopted son sitting next to her, she clapped and laughed, asking for more songs. The celebration went on for days, and the palace was filled with the notes of flutes and zithers.

✦ ✦

Meanwhile, the Regent, claiming the impending threat of a revolt that would throw the kingdom into turmoil, declared he would return to the court as before. His health had been restored, and he would resume full duty as the Regent. He ordered all matters, large and small, to be reported to him, and any edicts to be reviewed and approved by him before they were passed on to the related ministries.

To ensure he would have an iron grip on the kingdom, the Regent suspended the Keju exams, the system the court used to select talented men to serve the kingdom. He named all his nephews, related by both blood and marriage, to governor's positions in various prefectures. He gave the major posts, such as tax collectors and judges in *yamen*, to his and the Empress's relatives, and these men then distributed other important civil positions to their relatives. Very soon, all the important positions in the kingdom were occupied by the families and servants of the Regent and the Empress.

✦ ✦

My poor Pheasant. He was not himself these days. He would not give the General the order to retaliate, but he was tormented by his uncle's betrayal and the deaths of his siblings. His skin was pale, and dark spots appeared on his face. His jawline was sharper, his eyes sank deep into their sockets, and his voice grew husky, as though his throat had been burned and his heart was smoldering from the smoke of guilt and grief.

He was not yet thirty, but he looked twenty years older. And he reminded me of his father. Both men were haunted by the past, although Emperor Taizong was consumed by the crimes he had committed, while Pheasant suffered with guilt over those he had failed.

He spent hours riding through the woods alone. Impatiently, he kicked the stirrups, jerking the reins, and veered the horse forcefully. He rode past the hills, reaching the walls at the back, turned around, flying through the garden's entrance, heedless of the servants standing in his way, and galloped again, rocking the garden with the deafening sound of the hooves.

Sometimes he went to the lot where he had practiced mounted archery with Prince Ke. But he did not ride his horse or shoot any arrows. He only stood there, staring at the empty lot and the wooden target board, his face pierced with pain.

At night, he came to sit with me on the bench in the garden. He ordered servants to bring jugs of wine and drank them before a bonfire. He did not speak, only drank one jug after another. When he finished, he waved for more. A long time ago, I would have stopped him, worried about his health, but now, my hand on my round stomach, I drank with him. I let the strong liquid race down my throat and simmer in my stomach, and let my head sway in blissful dizziness.

The night was long, the sky dark. The moon hung in the distance, covered with a wan, yellow hue. It looked sick, helpless, like the eye of a dying man. Forlornly, it stood above us until the surging clouds drifted over and swallowed it.

Before us the bonfire hissed, black smoke surged and thinned, the pond was silent, and the water was black like poison. The wind, like a shameless thief, blew at our faces, stealing our warmth, our voices, and our hopes.

24

I GAVE BIRTH AT THE END OF SPRING. A PRINCESS, AS I had expected. She was beautiful, with black eyes like a pair of shining prunes, her eyelashes lush like a black swan's feathers, and her skin pink, delicate, and smooth. When she squinted, two dimples appeared in her cheeks.

"My princess, my treasure, my precious heart, my little oriole," I whispered in her ear. Could Gaoyang hear me?

My daughter was strong and healthy, unlike Hong, who had been sickly when he was born. She cried loudly enough to make the guards outside the garden turn their heads. When she was hungry, she suckled with vigor and concentration, placing her little hand protectively on my chest, as though ordering me not to move. When I held her, she grabbed my hand and kicked with force, the bed board shaking underneath her. She grew fast, her face quickly rounding, her arms thickening.

It was clear to me she had arrived in the world with a purpose. She had come to fight. She was a warrior.

I played with her little fingers as she lay beside me. They were plump and soft. In a few months' time, she would grin her toothless smile, and very soon, she would begin to crawl on her strong legs. By this time next year, she would toddle and explore the garden and palace, and as the years went by, she would grow, she would call for me sweetly, climb into my lap, asking for presents and making demands, and I would give them to her. I would give her everything she asked for. I would fulfill every wish she made upon the moon, and

I swore I would do anything I could to keep her safe, to make her happy, and never see a drop of her tears.

For she was not only my sweet daughter; she was more. She was an oriole that stood proud and tall, a bird that flew on her own wishes. She could laugh without covering her mouth, she could fly instead of walk, she could play polo, and she would own her own destiny.

And she would be my friend. She would be my companion, bring me an eternal spring of happiness, encouraging me with her sweet smile and comforting me with her soothing voice. She would walk down a path unknown to me and find a future I had longed for. She would be everything I hoped for and more.

If only Gaoyang had been here. She would have understood how I felt. She would have shared my joy. She would have seen her spirit in this child.

And Pheasant was gentle and tender with my Oriole. He gave her a gift, a splendid doll wearing a red silk gown and a gold headdress. When she smiled, showing two dimples, Pheasant stared at her, his eyes filled with grief, and then without a word, he picked her up and pressed her to his heart.

I wrapped my arms around them. "My little oriole." I kissed her fingers.

✦ ✦

The three Ladies sent me gifts in baskets decorated with golden flowers. Inside were soft fur hats, feather-padded shoes, thick gowns, and many pairs of small trousers, each adorned with intricate designs of flowers, rabbits, trees, and fish.

"Why didn't they come themselves?" I asked Apricot, who brought the baskets to my chamber. Then I remembered the Empress's restrictions on leaving the compounds. She must have denied the Ladies' request. But it was part of court protocol, and a tradition, for them to visit me after I gave birth, and I knew they adored children and would like to see my daughter. They wished to have their own children too, and I hoped they would succeed. Pheasant had agreed to summon them when I urged him repeatedly last winter, but since the deaths of

Prince Ke and Princess Gaoyang, he had been too distraught. Bedding the ladies was perhaps the last thing on his mind.

Outside, Chunlu and Xiayu were playing hide-and-seek with Hong. The two maids were laughing, but Hong's face was solemn. He had become more serious since his sister's arrival, and grumpy too sometimes.

"Oh, they did wish to come," Apricot said. "I could see that. They kept me there for a long time, asking many questions about the baby. What was the baby's weight? How did she look? Had she smiled yet? Did she like to sleep? They wanted to know everything about her. They did not want me to leave."

"I see." I pulled a thread from a skein of yarn sitting in a basket. I had begun to knit when I started my confinement in the chamber after my daughter's birth. At first I had tried to knit a glove, but it looked like a bag with uneven stitches. Now I was knitting a blanket for my Oriole. Gaoyang would have laughed at me if she had seen me knitting.

"And they asked about you, Luminous Lady."

"Tell them I am doing well." Apricot nodded, and I added, "Are they still looking after the Pure Lady and Sujie at least? How are they doing?"

"They are fine. The lady is under the physicians' care. She is taking her herbal medicine, but she is...unpredictable at times. Sujie plays *weiqi* a lot. He will not speak to anyone other than his two maids." Apricot cleared her throat, and her voice dropped lower. "And the three Ladies also said..."

"What?"

"They said they were sorry about the princess."

My heart pained. I pulled the thread harder. "Send them gifts and tell them I am grateful they were thinking of me and my child. After I finish my one-month confinement, I shall go to their quarters and visit them. You may take this message to them now."

"Yes, Luminous Lady."

She did not move. I glanced at her. "What is it?"

"I...I..." Apricot covered her mouth. Tears spilled out of her eyes. "I do not wish to say this, but the princess..."

I put down my knitting sticks. I wanted to comfort her, but I refrained myself. "Do not cry because you are frightened, Apricot. I will not allow it."

"Yes, Luminous Lady." She nodded, wiping her eyes. "But...but... the princess saved me. Luminous Lady, I was afraid to tell you..."

"What do you mean?"

She dropped her head, and her voice was so low I had to strain to hear. "The Secretary followed me when I was fetching your clothing from the laundry women. I...I was frightened. I did not say anything. I only wished for him to go away...but he did not...and once I was crying when the princess saw me. She stopped him."

I remembered Gaoyang had mentioned seeing them together. "Was he bothering you?"

Apricot's hands were trembling. "It doesn't matter now, Luminous Lady...please...do not be angry with me."

"No. I am not angry at you." I pushed the knitting sticks aside. "What did he do? Did he touch you?"

Apricot lowered her head.

Anger rose inside me. Apricot was mine, and that shameless man had molested my maid! I reached out and put my hand on hers. "Why didn't you tell me before?"

"I was frightened, Luminous Lady."

"When did this happen?" Apricot was my spy. She went to many corners of the palace, and that meant she was vulnerable every day.

She swallowed hard. "A few times when I went to fetch your clothes from the laundry women, and when I was using the privy chamber. I don't know how he always found me... I tried to fight him off, but...but..."

I took a deep breath to keep calm. "Does anyone else know?"

Panic crossed her face. "No! Please, Luminous Lady, do not tell anyone. I should not have told you. It was just...I miss the princess, and now with her being gone..."

"Do not fear." I leaned back, my heart burning with anger. That evil Empress had cooked my pet and murdered my most cherished friend, and now her uncle had forced himself on my maid. "He will not get his hands on you again, Apricot, I promise. And if he dares to approach you, you come to me, understand?"

"I will, I will. Luminous Lady, please do not tell the Emperor. I beg you. He doesn't know anything. I don't want him to hear that. He'll be very upset. He'll—"

"I will not tell him. Trust me." Pheasant had left for the audience this morning, looking grim. Chang'an was suffering from a drought, and the court was discussing some emergency measures to deal with it. "Has the Emperor come back yet?"

"I...I will go see."

"Good." I nodded. "Inform me when he arrives."

Apricot hesitated for a moment, then she bowed and left the chamber. Her footsteps were light, and soon, I heard her asking Chunlu whether supper had been prepared.

I turned to my daughter beside me. She was sleeping, her plump cheeks pink and her lips full. And I thought of what Apricot told me. What should I do?

I was not the Empress's match. I had lost Princess Gaoyang; I had lost my guardian. If I resisted the Empress, I would not be able to protect myself.

Yet I must fight back.

I rose.

I asked Qiushuang to bring me *The Art of War* scroll that I had kept in my dresser. When she carried it over, I got out of bed and sat at the lacquered table. With the sunlight shining outside, with Hong's voice echoing in the garden, with my daughter beside me, I read and reread the master's words. *When in battle*, he said, *be swift as the wind; when resting, majestic as the forest; when raiding, like fire; when in vigil, firm as the mountains.*

Firm as the mountains.

✦ ✦

A few days later, a sandstorm swept through Chang'an and destroyed many mulberry tree farms in the city, and the drought persisted. Many farmers became homeless, and people in the north near the Steppes, as well as those in Chang'an city, faced the threat of famine. Many families abandoned their homes, begging on the streets or fleeing to temples for meals. Hundreds of mulberry tree farms were left unattended. During one month, the Imperial Silkworm Workshops suffered a short supply of mulberry leaves again.

The Taoist abbeys, as usual, turned away the homeless, and it was the Buddhist temples and monasteries that opened their gates and provided the homeless with shelter. I was glad. At least something I had done bore fruit.

I began to collect information on the ministers in the palace. The court had one hundred and eighteen of them, and about twenty of them were unrelated to the Regent or the Empress. I asked Apricot to find more details about them. How long had they served in the court? What were their hobbies? What did they like to eat? What were their strengths? What were their weaknesses?

Apricot soon told me something interesting about Minister Xu Jingzong, Pheasant's former tutor. He had held the position of the Secretary during Emperor Taizong's reign, but he was too talented and too efficient, and Chancellor Chu Suiliang got jealous, accusing him of breaching Confucian morality when he accepted gifts from his Turkic son-in-law. So Minister Xu was censored and banished.

But the minister did not change his ways after his return from exile. He still enjoyed luxurious gifts, indulging in silk and rare jade. Now in his sixties, he was still bold, his voice loud. I thanked Apricot for finding out the minister's history, and I knew I needed such a man, a man with a purpose, who was eager to pursue it and who also disliked the Regent.

When I finished my one-month confinement, I took Apricot with me and walked toward the library in the Eastern Palace, where the minister worked. I wanted to familiarize myself with Minister Xu Jingzong.

The Empress would know I had left my garden and defied her rule, but I did not care. She could stop me.

With my maids holding parasols beside me and Apricot following behind, I passed the arched bridges, the stone statues, the elaborately carved gates, and the towering pillars of many majestic halls in the Outer Palace. The path reminded me of the days when I had served Emperor Taizong as he went to the Audience Hall. But I blinked away the memory. The sun stood high in the sky by the time I arrived at the imperial library in the Eastern Palace. I had taken a long route to reach it, but it felt good to walk again. I dabbed at my forehead, patted the side of my wig to assure it was in place, and stepped into the vast yard in front of the library.

The palace had three libraries: one for Pheasant, one for the ministers, located in the Eastern Palace, and a pitiful one in the Inner Court, which I had frequented when I was trained as a Talent. I had been to Pheasant's library, back when it was still Emperor Taizong's, and visited it many times. But I had never gone to the ministers' library.

It was a magnificent five-bay building, sitting on a high platform. It had the usual blue flying eaves, gray tiles, red latticed windows, and a large bell in the corridor, which was used to summon the scribes. In the center of the building sat a horizontal board inscribed with three characters: *Hong Wen Guan*. The Great Literature Building. Beside the board were two couplets written in grass script.

I ascended the stairs and found a group of ministers gathered in the corridor. They glanced at me curiously. Some frowned, and some looked away. They were afraid to be associated with me and potentially become a target of the Empress's revenge.

I ignored them and entered the building. Inside, I glimpsed Minister Li Yifu, who stood among a group of other ministers.

"*Zao an*, Minister Li," I called out in a pleasant voice.

He turned toward me, a calligraphy brush in hand, and his face reddened, and then he bowed reluctantly. Courtesy was, of course, the best action to give when you could not decide what to do. "*Zao an*, Luminous Lady."

I saw Minister Xu Jingzong, the fifth-degree minister who had once recorded the explanation of my riddle, standing near a pile of scrolls.

"*Zao an*, Minister Xu." I wanted to speak more to him, but there were too many ears around me.

"*Zao an*, Luminous Lady," the minister replied.

He did not approach me, like the others, but he did not look away either. Then, he gave me a nod, and that was enough to make me feel better.

Minister Li Yifu cleared his throat. Obviously he was the highest-ranking among them, and he had no choice but to speak to me. "Luminous Lady, may I, on behalf of the imperial library, offer you my sincere welcome. Your arrival has honored me and everyone here. With your permission, may I ask how I can assist you with your reading pleasure?"

His manners were courtly, as usual. I went to a writing table as Apricot cleaned the space for me. "I do hope my appearance will not interrupt your important work. If you do not mind, may I have a look at Lao Tzu's *Tao Te Jing,* or Zhuang Tzu's *Zhuang Zhou Zhuang?*" Those were two central scriptures of Taoism.

He looked surprised. If I wanted to read any classics, I could always order my maids to bring them to my chamber.

"I shall be more than happy to oblige," he said, turning to the ministers around him.

A minister in a green robe whispered in his ear, and Minister Li grimaced, his eyes avoiding me. They must have been debating whether they should inform the Chancellor, the Secretary, or even the Regent of my request to read the classics, although I believed Minister Li, the highest-ranking minister in the imperial library, should have had the power to grant my access.

Finally, Minister Li ordered a younger man to fetch the scrolls from a shelf and spread one before me. I read carefully, although I had read the scrolls countless times when I was a child. As usual, I found the sentences filled with confounding mystery, especially the story of Zhuang Tzu's "The Butterfly Dream." It said one day a man named Zhou dreamed he had turned into a butterfly, and when he awoke, remembering the image of the butterfly so vividly, he asked himself, "Was it a man named Zhou dreaming of a butterfly? Or was it a butterfly dreaming of a man called Zhou?"

This story was only helpless musing that produced nothing useful, yet the Taoists treasured it. I could say it was the essence of Taoism: it was fond of spinning a conundrum that led to no clarification or enlightenment. What was the use of philosophy if it failed to unmask mysteries that offered solace to a wounded soul? Life was complicated enough, and Taoism, rather than provide a vision and an inspirational destination, took pleasure in muddling people's minds, firing up a pot of doubt and skepticism, and obscuring the picture of possible happiness that should be the ultimate reward.

I read the stories anyway, and when the other ministers were no longer paying attention to me, I said casually to Minister Xu, "Minister Xu, what is your interpretation of Lao Tzu's words?"

"Luminous Lady, I regret to tell you I have better things to do than read Lao Tzu's words." He stood beside me, his hands crossed behind his back.

"Why?" I was surprised and interested. "You do not like his philosophical inspirations?"

"Not at all," he said. "Yin and yang, light and darkness, five elements, five directions, and the truth of Dao, they are all good if they make sense."

I wanted to smile. "Well, Minister Xu, if they don't make sense to you, then what is your philosophy in life?"

"To live in glory, Luminous Lady." He watched me intently. "What is yours?"

Minister Li Yifu was frowning at us. It was time to stop. I rose. But before I turned to leave, I answered the minister, "Patience, Minister Xu, patience."

When I left the library, I took a deep breath. It was a good trip, after all. But I could not smile yet, for I had not felt like smiling since Gaoyang's death, but perhaps, I would have the pleasure of feeling joy very soon.

AD 654

The Fifth Year *of*
Emperor Gaozong's Reign
of Eternal Glory

AUTUMN

25

PHEASANT LOOKED LONELY, SITTING ON THE BENCH facing the pond. The light from the bonfire lit up the front of his robe, where the embroidered dragon seemed ready to take off and soar, but the night stood at his back, leaving its possessive, dark fingers on his hair and shoulders.

I put a fur cape on his shoulders. "It's cold here."

He was drinking again, and empty jugs of wine stood beside his feet like dwarf soldiers without a conviction.

He shook his head. "It doesn't bother me."

I sat down beside him. There was no moon tonight, and the sky was shrouded by layers of clouds. The pavilion was barely visible, and the trees blended into the darkness, forming a thick, inky wall.

Pheasant was frustrated. I could feel the defeat, and his deep hurt spread around him like a sticky cobweb.

For months, in an attempt to clear his brother's name, Pheasant had searched for the witnesses of the conversation that had brought doom to Prince Ke. Pheasant finally located them and summoned them for an investigation. But the process had been fruitless. One moment the witnesses argued they had heard no seditious talk of the prince, and the next they would weep and say they could not remember anything.

"Did you play polo today?" I asked him, pulling my fur cape around me.

"No."

"What about archery? I bet your skills have become even more improved."

He snorted, waving his hand.

I waited for a moment. "I heard the imperial stables received some fine horses."

He did not speak.

I sighed. "Well, it's late. Are you tired? Perhaps you should go to bed, Pheasant."

"You go to bed. I won't stay here for long." He took a swig of his wine.

I nodded, but I did not rise.

"I heard you went to the imperial library again today."

I believed everyone in the palace should have learned I had gone to the library by now, and of course that evil Empress would be the first to know. But she had not attempted to imprison me or whip me. Perhaps she was sure all my efforts would be fruitless; perhaps she was simply watching.

"I did." I waited for him to ask more questions, but he did not. So I added, "I talked to your former tutor again. He is an interesting man. He's a Buddhist, do you know that? Minister Li Yifu was there, of course, and many others."

"If you wish to read, you may order the scrolls to be brought to you."

I shook my head. "I wish to make myself visible among the ministers, Pheasant. That's why I went there, so they would know me better. You never know. We may need them someday."

"It's useless. It can't be helped." Pheasant waved his hand.

"I know it's a long-term goal, but—"

"Can't you see? Nothing is going to make a difference. The Regent supports her. He protects her. There is nothing we can do to get rid of her."

I was silent.

"She can't be touched, and whatever she wants to do, he will do it for her. Whoever comes to us will be cut down; whoever is close to us will be executed. He killed my brother and my sister! He's ruthless. No matter how many ministers you win over, he will execute them all. You can't fight a cruel man with words!"

His voice was loud. I cringed, turning my head toward the bed-chamber. He was going to wake up Hong and Oriole.

"As long as she lives in the palace, as long as she is the Empress, nothing you do will help. So don't bother, Mei. Don't bother." He put his hands on his knees, gritting his teeth. "Nothing we do can change it. Nothing. Nothing."

I felt his pain. It had to be distressing and hurtful for him to go to the hall each day, watching the Empress's men laugh and the Regent give orders. "You're not alone, Pheasant. You have the General."

He did not speak for a moment, staring at the fire. "I will say it now, Mei. If I did not have the General's support, my uncle would have deposed me."

I swallowed with some difficulty. The statement was frightening, but perhaps Pheasant was speaking the truth. The Regent could do that easily, since he had control of almost everyone in the court, including the heir.

"You know that, of course; everybody knows that. But I didn't know. I didn't." Pheasant's voice was sad. "Until now."

I could not bear to see him like this. "He cannot depose you, Pheasant," I said firmly. "The General follows your orders. He is on your side. Whatever you tell him to do, he will do it. He put his sword in front of you, remember? You refused. He would give his life to you if you wished. He's loyal to you, not the Regent."

Pheasant turned to me, and I reached for him. "Now tell me, did anything happen today in the Audience Hall? What made you say that? What made you so angry?"

Pheasant looked away. "The Regent instructed me not to attend to the audiences from now on. There is no need, he said. His men would take care of all matters. But I am the Emperor! I! What am I if I am not allowed to attend the audiences?"

I frowned, anger rising in my chest. "What did you say to him?"

"Nothing. What could I say?" He laughed bitterly. "I'm a weak man. I'm a coward. I'm useless! I should have refused. I should have told him to go home instead." He swallowed more wine. "But I asked him to restore Prince Ke's name. He was the son of a Lady! You know what my uncle told me? He told me to forget about my brother, that

I must summon more maidens. He said I need to pay more attention to my domestic affairs so I can have more sons and daughters like my father." His voice was louder, and his anger was stretching long and dangerous, like the tongues of the fire.

I bit my lips, staring at the bonfire. I wanted to shout too. The Regent was too greedy. What would he do next if Pheasant refused? Dethrone him by force?

"He is always telling me of the obligation as a son. You know what? He can't fool me now. They're all lies. He was using me so he could have the kingdom in his hands. And he always uses my father to tame me, always admonishing me. 'A good emperor listens to his counsel,' so he says. 'Remember your father's words!' Of course I remember my father's words!"

I remembered too the words by the late emperor:

With bronze as a mirror, one can correct one's appearance;
with history as a mirror, one can understand the rise and fall
*   of a kingdom;*
with honest men as a mirror, one can distinguish right from wrong.

Pheasant laughed. "But my father made a good show, that's all. He stitched up an astrologer's lips! No one said anything about that, did they? A show of humility. A show of kindness." He shook his head. "He wasn't a kind man, Mei. My mother knew it, my older brother knew it too, and I knew it. But I never said it. Now I'm saying it."

The memories flooded back to me. How the late emperor butchered his brothers and his nephews and nieces and forced his father to abdicate. How he kept Jewel for himself and then brutally discarded her. I shook my head. "You're different, Pheasant. You're not like him."

"You're right. I am not."

I put my hand on his. He felt hard as stone, but hot, as though the fire were burning on his skin. "You are a good man, Pheasant."

"That's the problem."

For the first time, I could see how Pheasant saw himself: he was a man with a good heart, and that was his strength and his weakness. "Let's go to bed. You're tired."

"You go. Oriole is crying."

I heard her soft whining too, followed by Hong's grunts, but I could not leave Pheasant alone. I sat back. "Apricot will get her. I'll sit with you. Can I have some wine?"

He handed me the jug. "I was twenty-two when I became Emperor, Mei, and the kingdom has been mine for six years now, but I'm telling you, I can't say I am an emperor."

I drank some wine. It tasted bitter, like Pheasant's words, like the air, like everything around me.

"But I don't want to live like a useless emperor anymore. I'm going to change that. My brother will not have died in vain." He took a deep breath. "I'm going to the hall tomorrow, whether he likes it or not. I'm going to do what I want." He raised his fist at the bonfire. "He's not going to stop me. No one is going to stop me."

Surprised, I turned to him. "What are you going to do?"

"I want her to be gone. I want the Regent to be gone too, and all his men, gone." Pheasant's eyes glittered like the tips of twin blades, blades that were forged in pain and whetted by the fire of determination. "I'm going to be a true emperor. I'm going to take back my hall."

"But how? You need supporters."

He gave me a crooked smile. "No. I don't. Now finish up your wine, Mei. Then we'll go to bed." He stood up. "Come to the Audience Hall with me tomorrow, and wait for me in the antechamber."

"Why?"

He walked toward the bedchamber. "Just come."

26

THE NEXT MORNING I LEFT MY CHILDREN TO APRICOT AND went to the Audience Hall with only two maids in attendance. I did not know what Pheasant would do, but since he asked me to come, I would be there for him. The antechamber was quiet when I stepped in, and all of Pheasant's personal attendants were sleeping in the corner. I did not disturb them. Quietly, I went to sit on a painted stool and watched the hall from behind a screen.

It was Pheasant's kingdom all right, but it was the Regent's hall.

All the Empress's men were there—her uncle, the Chancellor, the Regent, his two brothers-in-law, and many other ministers. They lined up on the two sides of the hall, each holding an ivory tablet that inscribed their positions. In the center of the hall, on a raised dais, the Regent sat on a golden stool, and next to him was Pheasant on his throne.

The ministers all addressed the Regent. "Esteemed Regent, this" and "Esteemed Regent, that." Anger brewed in my stomach as I listened. But I remained still as they came forward to give their reports. One announced the taxes they had received this month. Another minister reminded the Regent that the current land distribution according to the Equal Land System had reached the three-year expiration, and it was time to redistribute the land again. Then another minister stated that counterfeited coppers were now out of control, and they were inundating the market.

No one turned his head to Pheasant, and he had no chance to question or investigate before the Regent put forth his opinion.

Pheasant looked sick sitting there. His face was pallid, his mortar-board askew. The pearl curtain draped in front of his face, shielding his eyes, but I could tell he was suffering from a headache because of the wine last night.

I frowned. How was Pheasant planning to drive away the Regent and his men? How did he plan to take over the hall?

I hoped the audience would end quickly. I needed to return to my garden soon to feed my Oriole. I was nursing, and my breasts would become engorged if Oriole did not suckle after a few hours.

The General's large figure appeared in the corridor, his long shadow reaching the foot of my stool. He paused in my direction, his eyes briefly resting on my face, and continued to patrol.

"Esteemed Regent," the Secretary, the man who molested my maid, said. I sat up stiffly as I saw his fat, round face oily with grease. "It is my pleasure to inform you that our Crown Prince has shown superb judgment and wisdom in administering state matters. Since his eleventh birthday is approaching, I recommend an opportunity for the Crown Prince to learn more administrative skills by attending the audiences from now on."

"Ah, has our heir expressed such a desire?" the Regent asked. He was sitting on the left side of Pheasant, and I could not see his face.

"He has, esteemed Regent. Our heir is most eager to learn."

"Then we shall be delighted to have his presence."

The heir was young, and according to the protocol, he would not need to attend the audience until he was fourteen. The ministers were already planning on replacing Pheasant. I bit my lip in anger.

"May I add, esteemed Regent, our Empress, may her virtue be praised, has also planned a grand occasion to celebrate the heir's birthday. A boat race is arranged, where all the ranked ministers can sit and have a feast. This will be a perfect moment to introduce our Crown Prince to the kingdom." The Chancellor smacked his lips in satisfaction.

"I concur," the Empress's uncle said. "Furthermore, after a careful review of a list of families with daughters at the age of betrothal, the Empress has made a decision. She wishes to inform our esteemed Regent that our Chancellor, who happens to have a granddaughter with extraordinary beauty, has agreed to—"

"Wait." Pheasant put up his hand.

I leaned over and watched intently. I prayed Pheasant would be careful.

There was a moment of silence in the hall.

"Nephew," the Regent said. "These are the matters of the state—"

"Where is the Empress?" Pheasant asked. "Is she in her chamber? I need to speak to her about a most important matter. Summon her over to the Audience Hall."

No one answered.

"She won't come? Well then. I shall announce it myself." He turned around to face the ministers again, a jug of wine in his hand. Was he inviting a torrent of accusations? Drinking in the Audience Hall was the utmost disrespect to the court.

But what he did next astonished me more.

He burped. Loudly.

The Secretary's eyes bulged, and the Chancellor gasped, his face red.

"The Emperor is drunk. Take him away. He needs rest." The Regent waved his hand.

"No one moves! That is an order," Pheasant shouted.

"Your Majesty!" The Chancellor's loud voice rose like thunder. "This is the Audience Hall, may I remind you. And the esteemed Regent has spoken—"

"I have spoken! I! The Emperor!"

"Nephew." The Regent's voice was dark and filled with warning. "If you have something to say, now is your moment."

"Well, Uncle, this is so kind of you. Indeed, so very kind of you! I shall be eternally grateful that you give me this permission. Well then, I shall speak now. Regent, ministers, all the men who offer your services to this great kingdom, I would like to inform you that I have made a decision. As of today, Empress Wang, the daughter of the Wang Family, is no longer the Empress of our kingdom. I am divorcing her."

A thick, uncomfortable silence descended in the hall.

I froze. That was it? He just announced it? This was too risky! Dethroning the Empress was not merely a matter of words. He should have thought more carefully. He should have planned better!

"I shall order a written statement to be drafted after the audience. All the proper procedures of divorce shall follow, and the divorce will be formalized. Tomorrow, all the people in the kingdom will know of the news, and Lady Wang will leave the palace and go home. Go on. Tell your family—"

"Your Majesty!" The Chancellor's voice rang out. "The Empress is the most virtuous, most judicious woman of the kingdom. She is the mother of the Crown Prince, mother of the kingdom. You can't divorce her."

"And I refuse to draft an edict that lacks the consensus of the wise counsel," the Empress's uncle, the Secretary, added.

Pheasant turned to him. "I did not order you to draft the edict, Minister Liu Shi. You're no longer my Secretary."

Voices exploded.

"You must not do this, Your Majesty!" Lai Ji, a brother-in-law of the Regent, protested.

"Relieve the Secretary of his duty, for what?" Han Yuan, another brother-in-law of the Regent, shouted.

"This is unlawful!" The Chancellor's face was turning purple.

My heart pounded. I started to sweat. It was like watching a horse fighting a pack of wolves, and it was most agonizing because I loved this horse and knew how ruthless the wolves were. They would tear Pheasant to pieces, they would cripple him, and he would never gallop again.

But Pheasant raised his hand and hurled the jug on the ground. A thunderous crash erupted in the hall. "I am the law!" he roared. "I, the third son of Emperor Taizong and Empress Wende, hold the mandate of Heaven. Have you forgotten? Do you dare defy me?"

Silence descended on the hall again.

I wrung my hands, shocked at how determined Pheasant was. But I was also afraid. Pheasant was playing with fire. He was going to be burned. He was going to suffer from the Regent's wrath, and the Empress's, for the rest of his life.

"But divorcing the Empress! This is impossible!" the Chancellor said. "It is unseen in our history. What has she done? This divorce will be not granted. Your Majesty, you know it will not be granted!

A wise emperor would not even propose such an outrageous idea in the first place!"

Pheasant stepped down from the dais, kicked aside the broken shards of the jug, and walked toward the Chancellor, moving out of my sight. I stood up, and my knees bumped against the stool. I groaned in pain.

My maids hurried to help me. I waved them away. But the Regent turned toward the antechamber. He knew I was there.

"Watch your words, Chancellor." Pheasant's voice came from the hall. "My tolerance is not limitless."

The brainless servant turned his head away. "I will not hold back my tongue at this most ridiculous moment of the kingdom. Your Majesty is bewitched! You have let that harlot whisper too many wicked words in your ears. Can you see? That woman is poisoning you. She wants to be the Empress herself!"

I held myself still, though my nails dug deep into the frame of the screen. Just like that, he had spread his vicious lies. From now on, I would be known as the harlot who whispered wicked messages to my emperor. I would be the seducer who lured him to my bed and plotted to depose the Empress so I could replace her. And the most ridiculous part was no one would know what an evil woman the Empress really was. She had tortured the Pure Lady and murdered Princess Gaoyang, Pheasant's sister, my most trusted friend!

Pheasant leaned over. "I have been kind to you, Chancellor. I took no offense of your stupidity. But this is enough. I will tolerate no more. Kowtow thirty times and repent, or I will chop off your head."

"Nephew—" The Regent's voice, loud with warning.

"I do not need your counsel, Uncle." Pheasant's voice was steady. "Now, decide, Chancellor. Kowtow or face my punishment."

The Chancellor's lips trembled, out of fear or anger, I could not tell. But conceited as he was, I doubted he would apologize.

And just as I imagined, he said, "I owe my duty to your father."

"General!" Pheasant shouted. "Bring me your saber."

"Yes, Your Majesty." The General strode into the hall. Standing next to Pheasant, he unsheathed his saber and handed it to him. He had offered Pheasant his sword before, but Pheasant had refused, and now he took the sword with two hands, raised it above his head. His hands steady, his face solemn, he positioned himself in front of the Chancellor.

I could not breathe. He really was going to do it! He would shed blood in the Audience Hall! With his own hands!

"Kneel!" Pheasant ordered, his voice sharp and hard.

The Chancellor trembled. He turned toward the Regent, but before the Regent could say anything, Pheasant kicked the Chancellor, and the brainless man fell. "Kneel!"

"I will resign," he cried out.

Pheasant did not move.

"I will resign," the man said again and laid his ivory tablet on the ground.

"That was easy, wasn't it? My dear former Chancellor. I shall gladly accept your resignation." Pheasant kicked the ivory tablet aside. "But this is not the choice I offered."

Chu Suiliang's eyes, those cloudy eyeballs resembling cooked cocoons of silkworms that would never yield a metamorphosis, darted here and there in desperation. Then in an astounding moment, he looked down at his empty hands, and his face crumpled. Slowly, he knelt and hit his head on the ground. One after another. Thirty times. By the time he finished, he was hatless, and blood trickled down his forehead.

The ministers standing near him looked stunned, their eyes round, their mouths agape, but those near the back of the hall, who were unrelated to the Regent, shifted their feet and nodded toward one another. It occurred to me that these ministers, who must have suffered from the Chancellor's domination all these years, might have been pleased to see him punished.

"That is better, old man." Pheasant lowered his sword. The tension in his voice eased, and just as I thought he was finished, he pointed the sword at the Secretary. "Now, your turn, Minister Liu Shi."

"Nephew!" The Regent stood up on the dais.

Pheasant turned around sharply. Throwing his long sleeves behind him, he strode toward the Regent, each step loud, steady, and heavy, echoing in the spacious hall. Then he stopped in front of him, leaned over, and said slowly, "Sit down, Uncle. There is no hurry. I shall take care of everyone." His voice was calm, strong, filled with meaning and power.

The hall was as quiet as though all the men had stopped breathing.

My heart clenched in utter shock. I never would have dreamed Pheasant, the filial son, the man who loved and respected his elders, would dare to threaten his uncle like that.

"Nephew!"

"I will not say it again, Uncle." Raising the sword, Pheasant tapped at the stool where the Regent had sat. The hard metal struck the stool. A deep, bold echo rang out. Once. Twice. Three times. And when he stopped, the sound still lingered, sharp, clear, and unyielding.

The Regent stood stiffly, as though pierced by the sword itself. Gritting his teeth, he said, "He is the Empress's uncle."

"No." Pheasant shook his head. "I have made it clear. That woman is no longer the Empress."

"You will not act so recklessly!"

Pheasant turned away, ignoring him. "General! Hold the Secretary. I will chop off his head if he refuses to kowtow!"

The General answered and dove toward the Secretary, who cried out, turned to run, but tripped, his hands scrabbling on the ground. The General seized his robe and threw him against a pillar. The Regent looked outraged. He threw his sleeves behind him and stormed toward the hall's entrance.

I was shaking. I could not speak. I could not breathe. That was it? Pheasant had succeeded in intimidating the ministers? He would reclaim the hall?

But it was not over, I could see, for the Regent had approached the threshold. His hawkish nose looking sharper than ever, he nodded to someone in the corridor. A guard ran to him, and he whispered something into his ear. The guard nodded, sidled behind the pillars, and disappeared through the gate.

Before I could move, thunderous footsteps pounded from outside, and figures in maroon capes poured into the hall. They pushed aside the ministers near the entrance and raced in. The Regent's guards. I stood up, my heart pounding.

"Pheasant!" I shouted to warn him.

"All of you! Stay away fifty paces! Fifty paces!" The General lunged toward Pheasant to shield him, took the sword from his hands, and pointed it at the approaching guards.

"I command you. Out! Now!" Pheasant ordered. "All of you!"

But they did not listen, and one spun forward, a sword lashing out. The General pivoted, knocked it off with his elbow, and sank his saber into that man's chest. Another man leaped forward. The General twisted around and kicked him with his foot. All of a sudden, the figures of men filled the hall, and the ministers shrieked, running to the corners.

I wrung my hands nervously. The General would not be able to fight off those guards alone. Where were his men?

"Luminous Lady!" A voice came from behind me. A woman stood there—one of Pheasant's attendants, the pretty one with a round face. "Some guards are coming."

"Toward us?"

She nodded, trembling. "What should we do, Luminous Lady? It's frightening out there. What should we do?"

They knew I was here. My head spun, but I could see fear on her face and the others'. I stood up, trying to remain calm. "Bolt the doors. Make sure no one enters this antechamber. Do it. Do it now!"

The moment the attendants bolted the door, heavy pounding came from the other side. My heart raced in fear. The antechamber had two entrances: one to the corridor and the other to the Audience Hall, where Pheasant and the General were standing. We had bolted the entrance to the corridor, and as long as the guards did not get through the General, they could not get to me. If they did, however, everything would be over.

The cries from the hall grew louder. Another group of Gold Bird Guards had leaped across the threshold, pushing the intruders to the left side of the hall. They were the General's men, I could see. And the intruders, outnumbered, shouted, slowly receded to the corridor, and ran off.

The General ordered a pursuit, and all his men rushed out of the hall. Heavy footsteps rose in the corridor, and someone cried out in pain. After a moment, to my great relief, all the footsteps faded away, the pounding on the door of the antechamber ceased, and the corridor was quiet.

I went to the other side of the screen, my legs shaking. Inside the hall, Pheasant slumped on the throne. The hall was quiet too. Many of the Regent's ministers had vanished, including the Chancellor and the Secretary. Those unrelated to the Regent and the Empress stood quietly, their faces grave. They turned toward Pheasant, waiting.

Pheasant straightened and raised his head to look at the ministers in front of him. "You may go home, if you wish."

They hesitated and walked closer to the throne. Although they were trembling, they stared at Pheasant with awe and respect.

"Your Majesty." Pheasant's former tutor, the bold Minister Xu Jingzong, prostrated himself, and his voice throaty, he shouted again, "Your Majesty!"

More ministers came around him. "Your Majesty!" They bowed before him, shouting, "Your Majesty!"

Pheasant looked stunned. For a moment he did not speak, his hands gripping the throne tightly. And the shouts grew louder, filling the hall with a unanimous, fresh wave of awe and wonder.

"Your Majesty!"

Pheasant raised his hand, and in that supreme gesture, with his palm facing Heaven, he said, "Rise, my ministers."

I felt dizzy. My eyes were misty, and my robe was drenched with sweat. But I was happy for Pheasant. I had never expected he would discard his love and respect for his uncle and threaten him. It was very dangerous, but Pheasant had succeeded, and with his relentless charge and anger, he had done the unthinkable—announcing his intention to divorce the Empress—and even better, he had found his power in the hall.

✦ ✦

Later, after the ministers left the hall, I went to Pheasant.

"Pheasant?"

He turned to me. The corners of his mouth curled up, and his eyes were strangely bright. "Did you see that?"

His voice was gentle, so I understood how much effort it had taken him to raise his voice to his uncle and wield that sword. "I was so worried about you."

"It was the only way." He stared at the bloodstained hall. There were pools of blood on the ground and splashes of red on the pillars. "All these months, I struggled, angry at what they did to my brother and sister. I thought about what to do, how to drive her away, how to drive my uncle away and take back my place in the court without bloodshed. I was so tempted to give the General my order and end everything with his sword."

"But you didn't." I touched his arm. His robe was stained with blood too, and soaked with sweat. "I'm proud of you. And your father and Prince Ke would be proud of you too."

Now the prince's death was avenged, as was that of Princess Gaoyang. For the first time since her death, I felt like a cloud of gloom had been lifted and I could see everything in full splendor again.

He sighed. "This is not over."

"What is your plan?"

He turned to an attendant beside him, took two goblets, and handed one to me. "I shall follow my announcement of the divorce with formal procedures. Then she will leave the palace, and I will have nothing to do with her. And I shall also announce my uncle's retirement. He's an old man, after all. In fact, I shall draft the edict myself and send it to him."

He looked confident, as though he had become young again.

"Will he accept that?"

"Oh, after today, I think he will accept it gracefully. He can no longer use me." He waved his hand. "Did you see the faces of the ministers? They want him to be gone too."

"Yes." And they would be overjoyed at the Regent's retirement, judging from their reaction at the Chancellor's resignation. And once the Regent retired, with the demotion of the Secretary and the exit of the Chancellor, all the powerful threads that held the Empress's cobweb would be severed. She would be alone. Even if she resisted the divorce, she could not stop it.

Pheasant raised his goblet. "To tomorrow. It will be a new day.

251

I shall have my ministers' support, and I shall rule my kingdom as a true emperor."

His voice was solid and powerful, the most beautiful sound I had heard in a long time. I drained the wine. I felt light-headed. I could see a soft, golden sheen glowing in the hall, enveloping the pillars, the standards, the stools, and the attendants like a colorful mural. A fountain of poetry bloomed within me, poetry that sang of victory and dreams.

When it was time for Pheasant and me to leave the hall, we came into the corridor, where the General stood like a pillar, his eyes watching the vast space before him. Near the bridge in the distance, the General's men were still fighting against two of the Regent's men. And as I watched, the General's men thrust their blades into the Regent's men's hearts, and they dropped to the ground.

But a thought came into my mind. The Regent had many followers among the Gold Bird Guards, and those men below me were only a handful of his followers. Would he obediently retire?

And the Empress. She must have heard of her denunciation by now. She would not give up. She would bite, and she would bite hard.

Would the fountain of poetry that had bloomed within me spout tears, tears that would inundate us all?

My hands turned cold.

27

IT WAS NEARLY NOON WHEN WE REACHED THE GARDEN.
Through the open carriage door, I glimpsed a large vulture standing on
the wall of the garden, its wings outstretched and its black head turning
to watch me, and then as though it had seen enough, as though it had
completed its mission, it soared into the gray sky.

I blinked nervously. It was only a vulture, but why did I feel as
though I had looked straight into the bulbous eyes of the tiger that had
killed my father so many years before?

One guard, Guard Cao, knelt on the ground and helped me get
out of the carriage. The other guards lowered their heads and bowed
as I passed them. I was not certain if they had heard of the Empress's
denunciation. My face hot with the wine, I steadied myself and followed Pheasant into my garden.

It was empty and quiet.

"Where is everyone?" I asked, looking around. I had twelve
maids and nannies now. Some of them should have noticed my
arrival.

"Perhaps they are playing behind the pond." Pheasant strode to our
bedchamber, his steps unsteady. He had drunk too much. We both
had. "I shall go lie down for a moment."

I nodded. I wanted to join him, but I missed my Oriole; she should
be with the maids. I had never left her for so long before, and I was so
accustomed to holding her, my arms felt empty without her. "I hope
the maids fed Oriole."

Just then I heard Hong's shriek behind the woods. My heart jumped. He sounded frightened.

"Don't worry, sweet face. He probably just saw a frog." Pheasant pushed the chamber's door open.

"Let me take a look. I shall come right back." I turned.

Pheasant waved and disappeared inside the bedchamber.

"Hong! Apricot!" I went down the trail that led to the grove behind the pond. I had to pause now and then, holding onto the pear trees, for my head was dizzy from the wine. But I was worried.

Hong shrieked again. I pulled up my skirt and clambered up the hill as fast as I could. What happened? Had someone hurt him? Had the Empress come to hurt him?

I was panting by the time I reached the top of the hill. There, I saw Hong, dressed in a shining red tunic, standing near a creek with Apricot and the other maids. That despicable Empress, of course, was not in sight. "Hong!" I called out in relief.

"Luminous Lady!" Apricot turned to face me. "You are here!" She looked delighted.

"There you are. What are you doing?" I breathed hard, glad to see my boy safe with my maids. "Why was Hong shrieking? Where is little Oriole?"

"Oh, she's sleeping in the bedchamber."

"Ah." I nodded and picked up Hong. "What's in your hands? Is this why you were screaming?"

He showed me. A baby turtle. He had always been fascinated with turtles. Once he had told me a turtle talked to him and it sounded like Princess Gaoyang. It pained me to hear that. Hong had adored the princess and asked about her constantly during the early days after her death.

"I see. Such an adorable turtle. No wonder you were so excited," I said. "Did you feed Oriole, Apricot?"

"Chunlu did," Apricot said. "I took Hong to see the physicians."

"What was wrong?" I felt my boy's hands.

"He had a fever earlier, Luminous Lady."

"Fever?" I was sorry I had not been there when he had needed me. But Hong was laughing and squealing with pleasure as the turtle flipped over in his hand. "What did the physicians say?"

"They said it was the weather. We must keep the doors shut when he naps."

"Did he nap?"

"In my arms."

I was glad. At least he got some sleep.

Pheasant called out for me. I gave Hong to Apricot. "Bring him to me when he finishes with the turtle." I felt my chest tighten. I was leaking milk. Time to feed Oriole.

"Yes, Luminous Lady." Apricot swallowed, and her face turned red. She still had the tendency to blush when she grew nervous. "There is something I need to tell you, Luminous Lady... It's not important, I think."

I waved. "Then tell me later, Apricot. Watch Hong and make sure he doesn't fall in the creek and hurt himself."

"But...Luminous Lady...it's just..."

Pheasant's voice rang out again, sounding frantic.

"Later, Apricot." I hurried down the trail. "I must go now."

Quickly, I reached my bedchamber and pushed the door open. It was warm inside, and the fire was burning in the brazier. I was glad, for Oriole could catch a cold easily if we were not careful.

"You were right, Pheasant, it was only a turtle. I was so worried," I said. My feet kicked at one of Hong's lacquered wooden horses on the ground, and I bent over to pick it up. "So what is it? Why did you call me like that? I ran all the way here to the bedchamber. Is Oriole awake? Did she throw up on you?"

"Wh...what?" Pheasant was standing by the bed where Oriole was sleeping. "No... I mean throwing up... And yes... She is..."

"Then pick her up. Don't just stand there." He adored Oriole, but if she soiled herself or wet his hand, he would act in such a way one would think the barbarians had encroached our Great Wall. "I thought you saw a ghost, calling me like that."

Lying on the ground near Hong's horses was Oriole's favorite doll, dressed in a yellow gown. She had round cheeks and hair shaped like bunny ears. Another present from Pheasant. Girls needed dolls, he had said repeatedly. I picked it up too and put the toys on the dresser. My maids should have taken better care of the toys rather than leave them on the floor, but I could not blame them. Tidying up the room, with two little children, required constant effort. Even a maid needed a break.

"I...I..."

There was something strange about him. I turned to him. "Are you all right?"

"Yes." He jolted, as though he had fallen asleep and I had awoken him. "I'm fine... But Oriole... I don't know... I think... I...don't know... Mei... You have to... She is..."

Something unspeakable, something frightening, wormed its way inside me. "What do you mean?" I pushed him aside and looked down at the bed. The room was dim with the smoke from the brazier, but I could see Oriole was lying below the embroidered pillow, her head tilted to the wall, her cheek touching the blanket I had knitted. "She is fine, you see, Pheasant? Let me get her."

I bent over and put my hand underneath her. I had told Pheasant many times to support Oriole's head when she was younger, and now that she was almost six months old, I was still accustomed to supporting her neck.

"Don't pick her up." Pheasant sounded desperate. "Don't—"

"Why not?" I picked up my daughter. I could see her face now. Her black eyes, wide open, were staring at me. "When did you wake up, baby girl? Are you hungry, sweet Oriole? Come..." My breath caught in my throat.

Usually, she would turn her head the moment she heard my voice. She would kick her legs, fling her arms out, or even smack her lips and babble, excited about suckling. Not today. She did not turn to face me, did not kick her legs. She did not babble. Her head was still turned to the wall, her arms at her sides. She did not do anything.

I turned her head toward me. She felt different. She was heavier somehow and harder. Her skin was pale like a pool of white candle wax, as though my maid had powdered her, and there was something wrong with her eyes. She was staring at me strangely... Those eyes... They were looking at me, but not seeing me... Those eyes... They were hers but did not look like they belonged to her. I blinked, then blinked again.

Someone caught my arm. "Mei…" There were tears in Pheasant's eyes.

"What's this? Pheasant? What's going on? What is this, Pheasant?"

"Mei…"

"I don't understand." I felt her hand, which had slipped out of the robe's sleeve. Cold. I felt her feet. Cold. I held her tight to my heart. She did not move. I shivered, then shivered again. "I don't understand…"

They had fed her, they told me. And she had suckled this morning. She had burped loudly, flinging her arms and kicking her legs, those strong legs, striking against the bed. She had grabbed Hong's toy. And…the fire was blazing! The room was warm. She should be warm!

Pheasant was weeping, pulling his hair, shouting something, but I could not understand a word. My head felt as though it were splitting. A wall of darkness cloaked me, and the ground was rising and dipping like an imbalanced scale. The bed slid beside me, and Pheasant blurred.

Something hot ran into my eyes. I wiped it away furiously and held my baby tight. I rocked her. I rocked her back and forth. Back and forth. She always liked it when I rocked her. She always opened her mouth, giggling with pleasure.

"Put her down, Mei. Put her down…" A hand covered Oriole's face.

"No, no, no! Don't touch her! Don't touch her!" I slapped the hand and held my child tighter. "Smile, smile, Oriole, my little girl, my treasure, my precious heart…smile…"

But she remained still. She remained frozen.

I buried my face in her chest. My throat was burning, my eyes were burning, my head was burning. But this could not be happening. This must be a dream. I was drunk. I was stupid. I was crazy. I should not have drunk so much wine. I should not have drunk at all…

I just wanted her to look at me. I just wanted her to kick her legs. I just wanted her to say something, to cry or throw a tantrum. But around me rose all sorts of groans, weeps, and frantic cries, and none of them belonged to my Oriole.

"Luminous Lady… Luminous Lady…"

Chunlu's voice. Then Apricot's. Suddenly my arms were empty. I jumped, frantic. "My baby. My baby. Give her back to me. Give her to me!"

"I'm sorry… I'm sorry… I was trying to tell you… Luminous Lady… She had come to visit…"

What was she talking about? I tried to ask, but the hot air plunged into my throat like a spear, cutting my lips and tongue, and I could not think. "Oriole! My baby! Where is she? Give her to me! Give her to me!"

"What are you talking about, Apricot?" Pheasant's voice.

The figure before me dropped to the floor, and all the others fell too. They seemed to tremble, like a huge wind chime struck by a powerful club. Their black hair swelled, and their white gowns piled on the floor, looking like funeral tents fluttering in a gust. "She… The Empress was here… She…she said she wished to see Oriole…"

Nothing was making sense. Why would that evil woman come to see my infant? She had cursed my Hong when he was born, and she had cursed Oriole too when she was born. She had forbidden the three Ladies to visit me, and there was no reason why she would come here to see my child herself.

"Why did she wish to see Oriole?" Pheasant asked.

"We don't know, Your Majesty."

"When did she come?"

"Before noon, Your Majesty."

"What did she say? What did she do?"

"I do not know, Your Majesty… She asked to be alone with Oriole… When she left, she was in a hurry."

It still did not make sense. The Empress feared no one. She had no reason to run away. She would not run. That woman was without fear and had too much hate.

Pheasant howled, his voice filled with pain and fury, and the figures before me sobbed, trembling violently. But I still could not understand what all these meant. My mind was not working. It was heavy, frozen, dark, and unable to function. Then suddenly, a thought, sharp and flinty, penetrated me like an arrow. My eyes burned, and a surge of fire, catching my thoughts, turning them into raging flames, burst in my abdomen.

The Empress killed my child! The Empress killed my child! The Empress killed my child!

28

I SHOVED PHEASANT ASIDE AND RAN OUT OF THE CHAMBER, out of the courtyard, out of the garden. I wanted to set the sky on fire. I wanted to split the ground in half. I wanted to pound the walls into ashes. I wanted to tear that woman apart and devour her. Alive.

"Where is she? Where is she?" That heartless woman! That devil! That plague! Death to her! Death to her family of five generations! How could she hurt my child? She was only six months old! She was capable only of suckling and kicking. How dare she have the heart to choke that little innocent life?

The path ahead of me twisted, treacherous, like the child murderer. Now and then it wound around, testing me, blocking me, stopping me. Skeletal branches whipped my shoulders, thorny bushes cut my knees, chilly wind slashed my face, and hard dirt stabbed my eyes. I flung my arms out. Hateful trees! Loathsome wind! Out of my way. Out! Out!

The ground slammed into my face. Something salty poured on my lips. I swallowed it, struggling to rise. Behind me, people were chasing me, crying out for me, and their footfalls rolled like thunder.

"Mei! Mei! Come back!"

"Luminous Lady, Luminous Lady, wait, wait!"

What did they want? To stop me? They should know better. They could not stop me. Nothing could stop me.

I pulled myself up and ran. My skirt was slowing me down. With one yank, I tore it off and kept running. One corner, another, and another. One pavilion, another, and another. One pond, another... I was closer. I could see the red walls in the distance, and the corner of the blue flying eaves of that woman's nest.

I sped up. And then suddenly, I fell, and water...water was everywhere, up to my knees, into my mouth, and into my eyes...

I screamed. A taste, silky, stale, salty, like moss, poured down my throat and thrust into my eyes. I could not breathe or see. I shook my head, and I could sense a cave of water, sinister and oozing, pale and glistening, gliding to swallow me. It was whispering, an oily sound, a wicked sound. *Die...die...die...* I punched, I flung, I spun, but it began to touch me with a thousand fat feet of a monster, sticky and slimy, reaching into my mouth and squeezing my heart. Oh, that wicked woman!

Something strong gripped my arms and pulled me out. I gulped, feeling the fresh, open air. Oh, what a relief to lose the grip of those fat feet, to lose that taste of moss, and to escape the prison of the stealthy, slimy water.

But it was not fair.

Why must she die and not me?

"You're safe. You're safe. It's all right. It's all right." Pheasant's voice, but he looked so far away, and even this sound that had been the rope of my life had lost its appeal.

I swatted him away. It was not all right. It would never be all right. "Let me go, let me go!"

I would not be stopped. I had to get my hands on the Empress, but someone was holding me tight, someone else was dabbing my face, and yet another was wringing my sleeves. I wanted them to stop all the nonsense. I was alive, but what was the good of being alive if I could not avenge my child?

"I've sent men to arrest her." Pheasant's face appeared before me. "Fifty armed men are bringing her to us as we speak. I swear to my ancestors, Mei. We will get her."

His voice was hoarse, and his promise should have been comforting, but I was not satisfied. "I must get her now. I must get her myself." I stood but swayed and splashed back into the pond.

He put his arms around me. "You nearly drowned, Mei. Let me take you back."

"No, no!" He was lifting me up. "Let me go!"

But he did not listen to me.

No one did.

Nothing did.

Not even my legs or my arms.

And from Pheasant's shoulder, the world looked demented. The trees were uprooted, people were dropping like dead birds, and the sky was sinking.

✦ ✦

My teeth chattered, and my eyes were burning. Since I had no choice but to wait, I had to wait here, at the entrance of the garden, where I could catch the first glimpse of the child killer and stare into the hateful eyes of the murderer, the last person whom my daughter had gazed at.

The sky dimmed to a sickening gray. The wind howled, and it began to snow. Large flakes tumbled from the sky like dead moths, covering the pebbled path and sticking to the branches. I hated snow. So deceptive it was. It struck you in silence and swallowed you up just as you thought everything was fine again.

A creature was circling above the treetops. Was it the vulture that had stared at me when I arrived at the garden? Had that been today? It seemed it had been an eon ago. Was the vulture sent by my enemy to watch me? Did it smell the odor of death that was spilled by my enemy? Did it crave my child's blood?

The guards recounted what had happened. The Empress had come to my garden before the sun moved to the treetops; by then, she must have heard of Pheasant's announcement to divorce her. But the guards did not know. She had carried a basket of apples. Gifts for the children, she had said. The guards had hesitated, but she had come without her personal guards, and she was smiling, so they let her in.

She also brought some gifts for my maids and nannies: two vests trimmed with silk, two scarves made of fox fur, two pairs of boots made of deer leather, two pairs of jade earrings, two sachets filled with dried mint leaves and cloves, and two bottles of jasmine oil. A pair of everything, for the sake of auspiciousness, she said. While her maids were distributing the gifts, showing the presents to my maids, the Empress went into the chamber and asked to be alone. It was a short visit. When she came out, my maids were still trying on the leather boots.

Hong had been sick, so Apricot took him to see the imperial physicians before the Empress had arrived. It was fortunate, perhaps. If he had been here... But perhaps things would have been different if Apricot had been in the garden. Apricot would not have been distracted by the presents. She would have been cautious. She would have watched the Empress, and she would not have left the Empress alone. And Oriole would still be alive.

But perhaps I should never have gone to the Audience Hall... I should never have left my garden... I should have taken my daughter with me...

That child killer was still not here. Why was it taking so long?

Xiayu, holding an umbrella, came to stand beside me, and Apricot dabbed at something on my face. My lips were swollen, and my face was cut, she said. Would I let her clean me?

I did not answer.

Qiushuang put a fur coat over my shoulders. My gown was soaked with water, and she asked me to go inside and get changed.

I did not respond. Did she not understand? Nothing could keep me warm. No. I would not change my clothes. No. I would not go anywhere. My daughter's killer was going to arrive any minute.

They tugged at me again.

"Leave me alone!" I said, my voice a low growl. They lowered their heads and looked down at their toes. They were frightened. They should be. How could they leave the Empress alone? Did they not know how evil she was? And Apricot, why did it take her so long to see the physicians? She was the chief maid. She should have returned as soon as possible.

"It's cold here. Come inside, Mei," Pheasant said. He had stood with me for a long time. He had tried to hold me, but I shook his hands off. I did not look at him or speak to him either. There was nothing to say. He had tried to make a difference, and this was the difference he had given us. If he had not declared his intention to divorce the Empress so tactlessly, she would not have been so angry, and my child would still be alive.

I should not blame him. He did not know that woman was capable of murder, and he was only doing what he thought best. But our daughter was dead. What could we say now? He thought he could assert his will, he thought he could take back his hall by force and control his fate, but really, could he ever control anyone? Even himself?

And was I any better? I had never been in command of anything, but why did I always believe I could be? Why did I believe I could fight against the Regent and the Empress? Where did that belief come from? They had taken away my most cherished friend, and they had taken away my child.

I was a fool.

We were fools.

We would never be the same, think the same, or feel the same again, and there was nothing we could do about it.

I heard the sound of crunching gravel and jerked my head. Nothing. Only the empty path painted by the night's dark hand. Only flurries of snow.

I hated waiting and doing nothing. Why must I wait? Why could I not give an order like a man and go kill her like a man?

The fur cape felt heavy on my shoulders. I wanted to shake it off, but I could not move my arms. They did not feel like they were part of my body; they felt like two dried branches of a dying tree, and like the tree, I did not feel hot or cold, I could not cry or bleed, I could not swallow or breathe, and like the tree, I was hollow inside.

My daughter…my daughter… She was part of me, the hope of me, the future of me, and she had been smothered. I would never see her again. I would never have the pleasure of feeling her fingers gripping mine, her hand touching my chest, or her legs kicking in my arms again. She had been mine, but now she was gone. What should I do?

"Don't cry, my dear, don't cry," a voice whispered to me. A familiar voice, coming through the flying flakes. "You must be calm."

Gaoyang? I seized her hand. *Is that you? Oh, thank heavens you are here. Help me, Gaoyang. Help me. Yes. I will be calm. Yes. I will not cry. But tell me, my friend, and help me, please, my princess. I do not know what to do.*

She did not reply but, with a tender touch, dabbed at my eyes, where finally all my tears came free.

"Let's go inside, Luminous Lady. Dawn is coming."

❖ ❖

Pale light shone in the distance. What was it? Dawn, already? No. It was a lantern, glimmering in the shower of snow, and with it followed a group of figures trailing behind like strips of black cloth. The murderer! I lurched forward.

The General stopped before me. Two piles of snow sat on his shoulders like two conspiring white cats, and the lantern swayed near his knee. Behind him stood a few guards. No Empress.

"Speak," Pheasant ordered. "Where is she? Why didn't you bring her?"

"Your Majesty," the General said. "We searched everywhere: the stable, the groves, every corner of her house. We cannot find the Empress."

How could he not find her? How could fifty men fail to find one woman?

The General was lying. He was protecting her! I pointed at him, but again I could not hear my voice.

"What do you mean?" Pheasant asked.

The General glanced at me. The wind swept his cape around, and he looked as though he were soaring like a vulture. "She has fled," he answered. "Her maids said she has left the palace."

I shrieked, pounding the snow-covered ground. Was there justice in the world? Why did Heaven let her get away?

The next day, Pheasant ordered the guards to search every hall, every pavilion, every corner of the palace. They could not find her. The search expanded to the Empress's maternal house and that of her uncle's. Two thousand Gold Bird Guards swept through the courtyards and scanned every beam, every bed, every well.

They could not find her.

AD 654

The Fifth Year *of*
Emperor Gaozong's Reign
of Eternal Glory

WINTER

29

It was time.

Bells tinkled, brass clappers clinked, and the monks near the grave began to chant. I swept my hand across from the coffin's lacquered wood. A glossy trail appeared behind my hand, but as soon as my hand left the wood, a thin layer of snow clouded the surface. I wiped it off again, more carefully, and then on a second thought, I took off the cape I was wearing and covered the box. It would not keep her warm, but at least she would not be bothered by the snow.

Someone put a hand on my elbow as I straightened, and unsteadily, I stood, watching the eunuchs carrying the box containing my child's body to the mound where Hope was buried. Next to it, a new hole had been dug. My Oriole would rest there. She was too young, her soul having yet to be formed, they told me, so she could not share the Li family's ancestral tomb. She would be alone in the place, separated from her ancestors. But she would not be lonely. Hope would keep her company. At least I could take comfort in that.

No earthen chamber was built to house her young body, and no name was chiseled on the tombstone either. Because, again, she was too young, without a name and without a soul. So, quietly, without a trace, like the wind, my child would leave this world.

The three Ladies in white silk gowns came to my side. Snowflakes were piling on their elaborate Cloudy Chignons like cobwebs, and their faces were masks of anguish. Behind them stood my maids, servants, and the Ladies' maids.

"I am so sorry, Luminous Lady. So sorry," the Noble Lady murmured, her head shaking in sadness. Lady Obedience was dabbing at her eyes, and Lady Virtue covered her mouth, her eyes red.

The snow was numbing my lips and my face, and my neck was stiff. I could not nod or speak. I understood their grief and their genuineness, but they could not understand me. For them, grief was like a sting by a mosquito. They felt the bite and the lingering itch inflicted on their skin, they scratched it and moaned, but when the redness of the bite subsided, when the sting eased, and when the bump disappeared, they would forget the ache, forget the pain. They would not remember anything.

For me, it was different. For me, grief was a sickness that was never expected to heal. It sat inside me like an unwanted beast, taking root, making a home, and each time when I saw my own Hong, other girls, other children, it would whisper in my ear, it would remind me of my Oriole, and as the sun rose and the moon appeared, it would awaken, it would bloom, it would swell, and I would grow sicker and sicker.

Should I envy the ladies? If you never gave birth to a child, you would never suffer the pain of losing one.

The eunuchs, trudging slowly through the snow, were near the hole now. The monks stepped aside to let them pass. I glimpsed Pheasant standing near the monks, and the General behind him. Only the General, no one else.

The coffin stopped before Pheasant. He dropped his head, and his hand shaded his eyes as though he could not stand watching the coffin. What was he thinking? Blaming himself? He should. It was his fault. If it had not been for his thoughtless actions, our daughter would have lived. She would not have been harmed. He was responsible, even though he was not the one to smother Oriole.

Pheasant had come to my chamber every night, telling me the progress—or rather, the ineffectiveness—of the search for the Empress. I could not bear seeing him. I could not bear listening to his voice. I could not even bear him breathing next to me. I turned my back on him, rolling to the other side of the bed, gritting my teeth. I did not say anything, but I wanted him to get out. Out!

And now, seeing him standing so close to the grave where my

child would lie, I could feel the anger I had bottled inside racing to my throat. Why was he there? Why was he not searching for the murderer? Did he even care for Oriole? Did he even love her?

I lurched forward to tell him to leave, but the sky dimmed and the snow darkened before me. Someone held me again, asking me if I was all right. I pushed her away and fixed my gaze on Pheasant. He put his head in his hands, crouching, his shoulders quivering. He was weeping.

I took a step back. I did not believe it. I did not believe his pain or his tears. He had not cared about Oriole the same way I did. I knew why she cried, when she would cry, or what she wanted from the way she cried, the tone of her cry, the pitch of her cry. I had felt her, as though the cord that linked her with me had never been severed, as though she were a kite and I the holder of the string that tied her. I felt every dip and every rise of her emotion, while Pheasant was only an onlooker. How could he feel the loss of the kite the same way I did?

Hong was crying, clear mucus flowing down his lips, his little nose pink in the snow. I took him from Apricot's arms, wiped his face with my sleeve, and hooked him onto my hip, the comfortable position he liked. I had a hard time keeping my balance, but I had to calm him. For he needed me. Only me. Not Pheasant. Not Apricot. So I swung him. Left and right. Left and right.

The eunuchs standing near the grave straightened and stepped aside, and then before me was nothing but flurries of snow. My Oriole was gone. My heart wrenched. I cried out and fell. Many hands reached for me and Hong, but I held him tight and stood up again.

Music rose into the air, followed by a wave of chanting, and the monks started to circle around the hole. With all the strength I could muster, I went to them and followed them, Hong in my arms, one step at a time, one round at a time.

I remembered a similar moment that had happened many years before, when another coffin slid into an earthen chamber before my eyes. I was twelve then, and now I was twenty-eight. I had buried my father, my beloved pet, my best friend, and now my daughter.

How had this happened? How had I come to lose them all? Had I sinned? Why must I endure all these losses?

But my daughter. She was innocent. She should have lived; she should not have perished for my sin. How could I tell my mother what had happened? I had notified her of Oriole's birth, and Mother was planning on visiting me.

"My child, I am sorry for your loss," a monk in a black stole said beside me.

I raised my head. I would never forget his voice, the deep voice with a warm echo, the sound of a bell calling the arrival of dawn. It still sounded the same, although it gave me a different feeling, and somehow it was damp like snow.

Tripitaka.

"You…" I stumbled, and Hong complained. Apricot hurried over and took him from my arms. "What are you doing here?"

Then I realized he had come to conduct the burial service for my child. I should have been honored, I supposed, for a monk of his stature to see my child off. But… Oh, that gaze. The same gaze that had haunted me when I was five years old. I could not stand it.

I lurched forward and stumbled again. Someone tried to hold me, but I pushed her away. Trying to stand straight, I swept the snow off my face and hair. "Why didn't you tell me?"

He knew. He had known from the very beginning, and that was why he had spoken about the fire of grief when I had met him in the pagoda.

Tripitaka's back was straight as an oak, and his eyes were bright and sober. "My child"—his voice melting into the freezing air—"it's your destiny, can't you see it?"

"You mean this? This is my destiny?"

And now he looked sad, and his eyes were swelling with the light of compassion. But I did not need compassion.

"This and more."

I balled my fists, rage rising from my chest. "I do not care about my destiny, Tripitaka. You should know that by now. I do not want anything to do with your prophecy. You should never have said that to my father."

Had he kept the prophecy to himself, I never would have come to the palace. I never would have lost my father. I never would have lost my child.

"Heaven chooses its own stars and moons. I am only the eye," he said.

I turned away. "Go, Tripitaka, get out of here. I do not wish to see you again."

"I shall be glad to obey, Luminous Lady." He sighed. "But I will tell you this before I leave. The fire of grief shall set ablaze a thousand trees, but only virtue will bear the fruit of your trees."

The same line again. I knew what he meant now, and I hated it even more. "What virtue? Who cares about virtue?"

The snow was drifting like fog, separating him from me, but his voice came, unbidden. "Forgiveness, my child."

I laughed. I laughed so hard tears burst from my eyes. Forgive? Forgive the woman who smothered my child? What was he talking about? What kind of mother did he think I was? "You are crazy, Tripitaka. You have seen the edge of the world, but you have yet to explore the inside of a human, of a mother! You don't understand. You will never understand. You are not a mother, Tripitaka."

He could not understand what it was like when you made a life inside you. He could not understand that when you held a child, her face became the sun, the moon of your whole sky. He could not understand how the touch of my child, her hands, her feet, and her skin, became my joy, my need, and my obsession.

She was my light, and I was her incense. I existed so she could shine. I burned for her, but my enemy had blown out my light and turned my heart into ashes, and he wished me to forgive her?

"I shall never claim to understand a mother's pain, Luminous Lady. Your grief is your mountain to climb, and I only offer you a path."

I tasted bitterness. "Tell this to someone else. Someone who believes in you, Tripitaka."

For I would believe what I wanted to believe, not what I was told to believe. Not now. Not ever. And I would seek my own path, my own destiny, no matter how many trees would burn along the way.

Tripitaka did not speak for a moment. "And yet, Luminous Lady, soon you shall understand. The light of kindness, of compassion, is dim, like the light coming from a candle's small wick, but when it is kindled, it will illuminate the whole hall. And virtue, like the prick of light, needs only a spark of flame. Once it is lit, the flame shall light up the path that benefits many—the weak, the sick, and the poor—and that, my child, is the path for peace, the path for all."

His words sounded smooth, like a stream flowing over rocks. They flew across from me, approaching me, surrounding me, attempting to touch me and feel me. I could bend down, lean over, and scoop up the drops of wisdom, then let them lap against my face and wash my skin, but I could not do it. I refused to do it.

"No." I shook my head. "There is only one path."

I would not forgive. I would avenge. I would thrust the spear of grief into the Empress's heart, just as she had done to me.

Tripitaka folded his hands together and lowered his head. When he looked up again, the light in his eyes had vanished, and his taut, tan skin slackened. He looked as though he had aged in a swift moment.

I walked away.

WHEN I RETURNED TO MY BEDCHAMBER, I ORDERED A BATH to be drawn. Leaning against the wooden tub, I let Apricot and Chunlu bathe me. They massaged me gently, their hands soft and silky. I did not like it. "Scrub harder," I told them. I needed some pressure, some roughness to feed my mind.

They obeyed and rubbed me with all their might. I bent over and lowered myself into the steamy water. Hot. My face felt scorched, my breath was steamy, and the scent of peach petals plunged down my throat and burned my chest. But I did not care. I smelled only the acrid odor of revenge.

Where was the child killer? They still had not found her. After all these weeks! How long would the search take? What if they could never find her?

I had to do something. I had to take the matter into my own hands. I could arrest Zhong, her adopted son, the ignorant boy with a stooped back and a red nose, and use him as a weapon. Once I had him in my hands, I could lure that child killer and force her to come out of her hiding. If she refused to come, I would torture him. I would crack his skin with a whip and burn his hands in fire so he would suffer. If she still remained hidden, I would send her his hand, then his leg, and then I would smother him, just as she had done to my Oriole.

"What's the heir doing now?" I asked Apricot while she rubbed my back. He had not come to my child's funeral. He would not dare.

"The heir"—she slowed down some—"is the same…"

"What is he doing these days? Is he still going to his tutors?"

"He did not go to his calligraphy class."

He was hiding, then. But I should have him. "Does he have any guards with him?"

"I do not know."

Apricot was not helpful, but anyway, I knew what I should do. "And the Regent, did he come to the Audience Hall?"

He had not sent flowers or a message to express words of consolation. To think my daughter, an imperial descendant of the Emperor, his own niece, had been murdered, and yet the Regent did nothing. That was not a simple lapse of courtesy. That was the sound of a battle horn.

Perhaps he had played a role in my daughter's death.

"I don't know, Luminous Lady," Apricot said, her face flushed.

"You are not hiding something from me, are you?"

"Oh, no, Luminous Lady. I would not dare."

And Chunlu lowered her head, looking frightened.

What else could they do other than look frightened? They were my people, and they should have been stronger. They were disappointing me. I waved my hand impatiently. "Hurry up. I have much to do."

When they finished washing me, I sat down to apply white cream to my face, which I had not done for weeks. Then I put on a white mourning gown, a white skirt, and tucked a white silk flower near my right ear. I let my hair down. It was still short, only reaching my shoulder blades. But I did not care. I did not need a wig.

Then I sat at the table and ate some porridge with sliced eggs and ginger. That was the only solid food I could swallow these days. I had no appetite, but I had to eat something so I would be strong.

Afterward, I told my maids to come with me to Pheasant's private library, where he had spent much time lately. He would be surprised to see me there, and perhaps pleased. But I had not come to please him.

The forecourt of his library looked just as I remembered. Many eunuchs, scribes, and ministers on duty scuttled around, their faces taut and their backs bent. Red lanterns swayed under the eaves, but the lights inside the bamboo frame were not lit, since it was still twilight. I had come here many times, accompanying Emperor Taizong before he fell ill, but this was the first time I had set foot there since Pheasant became the Emperor.

There were many ministers waiting in the forecourt. Gathered in groups, they discussed something eagerly, and some even threw back their heads, laughing. That was a rare sight. When the Regent was in the court, I never saw them this spirited.

They turned toward me as I crossed the yard and quieted, their faces suddenly sobering. When I passed them, they bowed to me. Some even murmured to express their sympathy. I did not speak or bow, walking as calmly as I could. I knew every man in the palace would have learned of my child's murder by now.

I walked to the building set on a high platform. Through the open door, I could see the Regent's two brothers-in-law, Han Yuan and Lai Ji, and a few other ministers, kneeling in the hall. Han Yuan was speaking rather vehemently, his fingers stabbing the air, his spittle flying. The Regent was not there.

"Luminous Lady." The General's large frame appeared in front of me, blocking me. "What is the purpose of your visiting here?"

Revenge. But I did not need to explain to him. "None of your concern, General."

"Do you have the Emperor's permission to come here?"

I looked up to stare into his eyes. He had protected Pheasant and me from the Regent's guards in the Audience Hall. I should have been grateful to him, but I did not care. It felt like such a long time ago. "No."

"The Emperor is meeting with the ministers. It's a formal meeting. You may not enter."

"Then stop me. If you dare."

He raised his eyebrows, giving me a long look, and then he turned to the guards lined at the wall. "Take Luminous Lady away."

"I will not be taken away."

"I am only doing my duty, Luminous Lady."

Duty? I had saved his life by summoning him back to the palace, but he had never acknowledged me, and now he would pay me back with a stale excuse and try to stop me from speaking to Pheasant. I pointed my forefinger at him. "I should never have told Pheasant to summon you back. I should have let you rot at the border, you ungrateful, low soldier."

He looked frozen, and his good eye that was not covered by the purple birthmark fixated on me. It occurred to me he had not known it was due to me that he had had a second chance in the court. I growled at his ungratefulness, looking hard at him.

The guards came to my side, but the General raised his hand, waving them away. Then he stepped aside.

Holding my head high, I passed the General and ascended the stairs, where a eunuch announcer readied to announce my arrival. I stopped him. I wished to listen to what the ministers had to say without them knowing I was around.

I stopped at the hall's entrance, pricking my ears. There were dozens of ministers in the hall, with their backs to me. Pheasant, sitting at the center of the hall, was facing me, but he did not notice me. His gaze was on the ministers.

The Regent was ill, Minister Han Yuan and Minister Lai Ji, said, but he had sent a letter to Pheasant. Minister Lai Ji took out a scroll, unfurled it, and read in his loud voice: "Your Majesty, nephew of mine, I am told you have continued to summon the ministers to the Audience Hall during my absence. I must remind you, as indicated by your father's will, all these gatherings are considered unlawful. For any urgent matter, I request all documents to be delivered and reviewed by my subjects as my health improves. Furthermore—"

Pheasant put up his hand. "Unlawful? How could he say that? Did he not receive my proposal? What is his reply to my request that he retire?"

Minister Lai Ji exchanged a look with Han Yuan. "I'm afraid, Your Majesty, the Regent is too ill to review the proposal."

"He is too ill to review my proposal but not too ill to write this letter?" Pheasant frowned. "What else did he say?"

The man cleared his throat. "Nephew of mine, I am also gravely concerned about your recent behavior. It is atrocious that you should intimidate your most dutiful and capable minister. I find your reckless-ness inexcusable, and I declare such a tyrannical action should not be tolerated. Had your father still lived, he would have disowned you, and it is with a strong sense of obligation that I urge you, Nephew, to repent and take proper actions to examine yourself. Do not be fooled by a devious woman with a pretty face. Our kingdom is truly on the verge of great danger now that our Chancellor lies in bed in injury and our Secretary fears for his life. Do take my advice, Nephew, and make amends now and put our kingdom on the right path again."

Fooled by a devious woman with a pretty face? Fury shot through my chest. I wanted to rush forward and tear the letter into pieces.

Pheasant leaned back behind the large lacquered table. "Is that it? Is that all he has to say to me?"

"The esteemed Regent also requests all ministers to present their petitions to him personally."

"Tell my uncle that he must request this to my face."

The two men did not speak but turned away in defiance.

"Minister Han Yuan," Minister Xu Jingzong in a red robe interrupted. "What is the Regent's opinion of the recent tragedy in the Inner Court? It is rather concerning, is it not, that our Empress would commit such a crime, and it is most sorrowful that an innocent child would become a victim."

"Our great Regent has some advice on this matter, Minister Xu," Minister Han Yuan, the man in a purple gown with a jade belt, said. "And these are his words." He took out another letter from his pocket. "I am most saddened, Nephew, by the recent development in your Inner Court. Empress Wang, the daughter of the noble Wang family, the rightful wife of the Emperor of our kingdom, is the most benevolent and virtuous woman of our kingdom. It is most unfortunate that an innocent woman like her—"

"Innocent woman?" I strode over the threshold. "She killed my child!"

Everyone turned to me, and Han Yuan and Lai Ji frowned. They could protest all they wished, but I would not stand by and listen to a lie.

Pheasant raised his head. "Luminous Lady—"

"Your Majesty." I bowed. "May I request your kindness in granting me this privilege to speak to the ministers? It would bring me peace if I hear their opinions."

He nodded. "It is granted."

"Minister Lai Ji, Minister Han Yuan, may I have this liberty to ask you what punishment the Regent has in mind regarding the Empress, the woman who murdered my child?"

"Punishment?"

"Surely, ministers, the court has heard of the case and taken steps to assure a necessary trial regarding the murder of my daughter?"

The two men glanced at each other, and Minister Han Yuan blinked so slowly, I could see the mole on his right eyelid, and then his eyes appeared, and the mole was hidden in the folds of skin. "Luminous Lady," the dog of the Regent said. "I regret to inform you there is no trial arranged regarding this matter."

"No trial?"

"I beg you to understand, Luminous Lady, and this is what the great Regent wished me to inform everyone as well," Minister Lai Ji said, and his tone was full of contempt even though his words were courteous. "The Empress is the highest-ranking woman of our kingdom. She is not responsible for a crime. She cannot be involved in a case as nefarious as this. A trial is out of the question."

Anger simmered in my chest. They would let her get away with her crime. She would be sleeping on her cushioned bed, drinking wine, and laughing while my daughter was buried underground! "Do explain, Minister Lai Ji. Why can't she be tried?"

"Luminous Lady, I am simply reiterating what the great Regent has told us."

"Is the Regent unaware of the murder?"

Those two were eyeing at each other again, and the dog replied, "As it appears, Luminous Lady, many people believe the Empress is innocent."

"So you have repeatedly said! Then who murdered my child?"

"Luminous Lady." The man bowed, but his body, his limbs, the turning of his head were nothing but gestures of combativeness. "I'm only—"

"How do you explain her visit?" I was screaming, but I could not help it, and Heaven help me, I would explode in fury if I did not let my words out. "Explain her visit!"

"Luminous Lady, I fear I cannot answer that question. However, if I may be allowed to express my opinion. Is it not so that a chief wife and the head of the Inner Court owes her duty to visit a newborn? Is it not part of tradition?"

"She never cared about visiting my daughter! And she asked to be alone with her! Is this part of the tradition too? My child was sleeping when she came, and she was…she was…" I trembled, and my breath was so hot, it burned my throat. "How does she explain that?"

"Luminous Lady, you must forgive me. Only the Empress herself could give you an answer." He bowed again, but his shoulders were stiff, and when he straightened, his face was that of a hog ready to charge.

I wanted to strike him. "Then bring her here. Ask her to come here! Ask her to face me!"

"Luminous Lady, I am merely a minister. I do not know where she is."

But he did. And the Regent knew too. I was certain of it. "You're a liar. You, and you." I narrowed my eyes and walked closer to them. And I pointed at Minister Lai Ji and then Minister Han Yuan, and I made my voice loud and clear. "And the Regent. All of you. You are all unscrupulous liars, morons, and murderers."

The men's lips pursed, and anger and hatred flitted across their eyes. They would have said most vicious words to me, cursing me or striking me, if Pheasant were not here.

But I was not done with them yet. I leaned over, pointed at them, and put ice into my voice as I spoke. "I shall not forget this, ministers. I shall not forget every single word you said to me today, and I promise you, ministers, I shall catch that child killer. I shall have her in my hands. I shall take everything from her. I shall take her crown, I shall take her honor, and I shall take her life. I shall have you too—you and the Regent. I shall make you regret what you just said to me. I shall make you weep and cry for mercy. Remember this. Remember my words."

That did it. The two dogs turned abruptly to Pheasant, bowed, and hurried out of the library. I watched them. I could imagine the Regent's fury when he heard my words. He would consider what I said as a declaration of war, and he would be right. It was.

After a long moment, Pheasant spoke again.

"Go. All of you. Leave me alone with Luminous Lady." He waved the rest of the ministers away. He looked tired, staring at the table, where scrolls, brushes, ink stones, and his jade dragon seal were all strewn in a pile.

Minister Xu Jingzong raised his head to me. It seemed he wished to speak to me, and there was something glittering in his eyes, something like pity, but I did not need pity. I turned away. He hesitated and then left without a word. More footsteps rushed behind me as the other ministers left as well.

"You too, General," Pheasant said to the General who stood at the door. "Leave me alone."

"Your Majesty—"

"I'm fine. Leave us."

The General gave me a long look and left as well. The attendants followed him out, and then it was only Pheasant and me.

"I'm pleased to see you here, Luminous Lady. Come." He beckoned. It was dim where he sat, and I could see only half of his face. Behind him spread a vast, ornate jade screen that depicted a beautiful landscape decorated with gold, rubies, and many precious gems. I used to adore it, but now it did nothing to appease me. "Come sit with me."

I refused. Biting my knuckle, I paced in the hall. I wanted to shout, throw something, or scream. But above all, I wished those two liars had not left so I could strangle them with my bare hands.

"You heard what they said, didn't you? They won't punish the child killer. They think she's innocent. Are you going to do something? Are you going to punish them?"

"I will."

"Good." I walked to his table and leaned over. He was wearing a black fur hat with a map of shining gems embroidered on it. They shone brightly in the dimness, hurting my eyes. "Kill them, Pheasant. Kill them all. Kill those two dogs and that old goat, and then no one will dare to protect her."

He raised his head sharply. "All of them?"

"You heard them! The Regent refuses to retire. He is going to denounce you. Will you sit here and wait for him to throw you in prison?"

Pheasant stood up and began to pace in the hall. His face was dark, and the light in his eyes dimmed and sparked like the quivering candlelight. "He…he is so stubborn… Why? Why would he hate me so? He was not like this…"

I stood in front of him and gripped his arms. "Now you know what kind of man he truly is! He does not care about you, nephew or not. You must forget he is your uncle! And you must arrest Zhong too. You will arrest him and give him to me." Zhong was Pheasant's child too, and he would protect the boy. But I did not care.

Pheasant froze. "Zhong? He's innocent. He's only a child."

I threw up my hands in disgust. "I want her to suffer. She has to suffer! She has killed my child! And he's her pawn! He has to pay for her crime."

Pheasant sighed. "I know these days have been difficult, Mei. I wanted to talk to you. I'm glad you have come out of the garden."

I did not want him to change the subject. "I have thought it through, Pheasant. You must act. Act now. You must arrest Zhong, her adopted son. Cut him off from her. Without him, she is nothing."

"Calm down, now. We need to talk about this." He took my hands and held them. I realized I had been clenching my fists so hard that my fingernails had cut into my palms.

"Are you going to do it?" I asked. He was hesitating. "Are you afraid?"

"I'm not afraid."

"Then what are you waiting for?"

He lowered his head and slowly walked to his table.

He was weak! "She's with him! You know that. The Regent! You wanted him to be gone; you said that to me. Do you remember? Have you changed your mind? Do you still wish to be a true emperor?"

He slumped, and then he turned to face the pillars on the left side on the hall. It was dark there, and empty, but he stared at it for a long time, and I wanted to shake him to wake him up. "If we start this..." He swallowed. "More lives will be lost. More innocent lives..."

"You started this bloodshed."

"I know, Mei, and I wish I had not." His voice was hollow, drifting in the large, dark building. "And look what happened to us, our daughter... I was wrong. Revenge is not a remedy... Violence is not a remedy... Mei, it's not a way to rule."

"It is. Revenge is the only way to live."

"But the Regent is my uncle, and Zhong... He is my blood too."

"Do you think the Regent will ever let you sit on the throne? Do you think he will step aside peacefully and bow to you? He killed Prince Ke and Princess Gaoyang!" I gripped his arms to give him my strength, to make him stronger. "Wipe them out, Pheasant, wipe them out. All of them."

"That is a lot of lives, Mei."

"Think about your father, Pheasant. Do you remember what he did?" The ambush at the Xuanwu Gate, where he killed his two brothers and imprisoned his own father to seize the throne, and the hundreds of children, women, servants, and ministers he had slaughtered. He had been ruthless. He had been determined. And he had won.

Pheasant took a deep breath and held my face in his hands. I could feel his tenderness, and I watched him with hope. He loved me, and he had to side with me. After all, Oriole was his daughter too. But he said, "Listen, Mei. I understand how you feel. You want justice. Nothing else. I understand—"

He could not do it. He would never be his father. He had too much love in his heart, just like what his father had said a long time ago. I pushed him away. "You are a coward. Your father was right about you."

He winced and dropped his hand.

Pheasant was weak. Oh heavens! I was wrong. I had been delusional. I had been wrong about him all these years, and now my child was gone, the murderer was running free, and the father of my murdered child, the Emperor of the kingdom, had no spine for revenge!

I grabbed his arm. I smelled the scent of musk from his robe, felt the smooth silk with my fingers, his soft skin underneath the fabric, his hard bones, and I lowered my head and sank my teeth in his arm, savagely.

"What are you doing?" he cried out, but the sound only infuriated me, and I bit harder. "Stop, Mei!"

Footsteps came from the corridor, and the General was shouting, "What's going on? What's going on? Your Majesty, Your Majesty!" He burst in.

I stepped back, breathing hard.

"I'm all right. Nothing to worry about, General." Pheasant held his arm, looking ghostly pale.

He could order his guards to beat me to death for biting him, but I knew he would not do that. He was a coward. A coward!

I could not breathe. I could not stand. But I tried, very hard, to stand straight and pointed at him. "You killed her. You. You killed her, your own daughter."

31

THE GENERAL OFFERED TO ESCORT ME TO MY GARDEN AS the imperial physicians poured into the library to tend to Pheasant. I refused and stormed out. He followed me anyway. I spun around.

"What do you want?"

"The Emperor—"

"So you listen to his orders? Then go get that murderer's son. Get him, and kill him!"

He hesitated. I snorted in disgust and entered my carriage. I told my driver to drive as fast as he could, and when I reached my garden, I stormed through the gate.

"Apricot!" I yelled. I could not persuade Pheasant to act, so I must do it myself.

A figure in white appeared in the corridor. "Luminous Lady."

I stopped to catch my breath. "You have failed me, Apricot. You serve me, you are my chief maid, and you are supposed to protect my children. You failed me!"

"Yes, Luminous Lady." Apricot's voice was barely audible, and the old familiar quaver had crept in.

"Why were you not here when that child killer came? Why? Why?"

"I…I have told you… Hong…" She dropped her head lower.

"That's convenient. So convenient. I don't believe it!"

"It's true."

I pushed up her chin. "Look at me. Look at me! Did you betray me? Did you? Did you lie to me? Did you play with that fat butcher and tell that woman to come and kill my child? Answer me! Do not lie!"

Her lips trembling, she closed her eyes.

I pushed her away in fury and turned to the few people who had gathered around. "Everyone to the yard and kneel. Now!"

The maids came quickly and knelt before me, their heads lowered. They all wore splendid silk gowns and fragrant sachets, and their elaborate hair was adorned with silver and jade hairpins, gifts from me. If any of them walked out on the street, people would have mistaken them for high-ranking Ladies. Had I been too kind to them and spoiled them with jewelry and fine clothing? Had they become lazy and lax with all the riches?

"I ask you, who do you serve?" I demanded.

"You, Luminous Lady." They spoke as one.

"And yet what have you all been doing? You have failed your duty. You let my enemy kill my daughter!" Their heads bowed so low I could not see their faces. I fixed my eyes on Apricot. My chief maid. Anger shot up from my stomach again. "Apricot. What do you have to say before I punish you?"

"Luminous Lady, let me explain." She trembled. I remembered the first time I saw her, a bashful young girl who had a tendency to wring her hands when I asked her a question. The brief strength she had possessed these years had disappeared, and she was her old nervous self again. "I have told you, I was with Hong. I took him to see the physicians. They could tell you, I was not here when the Empress came. For that, I am truly sorry. Please forgive me."

I would not forgive her. It was her negligence that cost my daughter's life. I had to punish her, and I had to use her to set an example so the people who served me would remain loyal to me. I remembered the polo match many years ago when Emperor Taizong ordered a slave to be trampled by horses to frighten his vassals. I must do the same. "You have been derelict, Apricot, and you must be punished for that."

"Yes, Luminous Lady." She was weeping.

"Guards," I ordered, and several men ran to the courtyard, more quickly than I had expected. They must have been waiting close by, watching me. Some eunuchs were peering from behind the moon-shaped gate too, and as I raised my head toward them, they shrank back to hide.

"Ten lashes!" I ordered.

Apricot squealed in fright. But she did not resist as the guards took her arms and pushed her to the ground.

The rod fell. "One!"

Apricot shrieked. Her voice shot up to the sky and shook the garden. The maids around me trembled, their hands on their mouths.

"Two!"

I heard a crack, as though the rod had hit her hip bone, followed by Apricot's heart-wrenching scream.

"Three!"

A pool of redness bloomed on her white gown. I did not look away. I continued to stare at her twisted face, and I listened to her agonizing cries. I wanted to remember this moment, remember her pain, for this beating had to mean something. It had to be worthwhile. My maids perhaps did not understand this now, but one day, they would.

Finally, the rods ceased falling, my inner robe was drenched with perspiration, and Apricot's screams were reduced to whimpering. I stood beside her and waited. She did not rise, and I did not give her my hand.

AD 655

The Sixth Year *of*
Emperor Gaozong's Reign
of Eternal Glory

EARLY SPRING

32

AN URGENT MESSAGE REACHED MY EARS. MINISTER XU
Jingzong and other ministers had been ambushed by a group of armed
men after they left the palace. Two ministers were beaten to death,
others were seriously maimed, and Minister Xu Jingzong was badly
beaten. He was punished because he had mentioned the Empress's
murder, he was told. If he dared to speak on my behalf again and challenge the Empress's authority, the armed men threatened the minister,
he would face a worse fate, and his family would suffer a similar fate
as well.

Pheasant was disturbed. For days he did not speak, trying to think
of a solution. But a few days later, another alarming message shook
him up.

The Regent had secretively gathered some five hundred Gold Bird
Guards in his ward. Standing on a high platform, with torches burning
at his sides, he informed the crowd that the Emperor, bewitched by
me, had threatened to kill him, the ministers, the Empress, and all of
his trusted men. The threat was real, he warned them, for they must
not forget how reckless Pheasant had been in the Audience Hall and
how he had threatened to chop off everyone's head. The time had
come! He thrust his fist in the air. The guards must hold their swords
and nock their arrows, for the Emperor would have them killed next.

The heir, Zhong, was said to have been there. He had slipped out
of the palace soon after I had threatened the ministers, I heard, and was
now standing beside the Regent. He nodded in agreement and told

the crowd that I had attempted to poison him, and two of his personal attendants had consequently died.

Pheasant was shocked at the Regent's instigation. That was rebellion, he warned him in a letter, demanding him to disarm immediately. The Regent refused, claiming Pheasant had defied Emperor Taizong's will. "It is a shame," he said in the message that returned to Pheasant, "that the kingdom your father and grandfather have built would be ruined in your hands!"

I wanted to laugh when I heard that, but his words also reminded me of the prophecy that had haunted Emperor Taizong when he was alive. The Li family's reign had a foe who would end their rule, it said. Was it possible the Regent was the enemy described in the prophecy? After all, his given name was Wuji, and the enemy was described as being named Wu.

No one seemed to realize the connection, however, and if it were true, it would be ironic. Emperor Taizong would certain fly into a rage in his grave, knowing his most trusted friend was the foe he had tried to eliminate.

◆ ◆

What hurt me the most was not the potential arrows released from the Regent's army, rather the other invisible and dangerous arrow unleashed from the Empress's mouth. She spread these words all over the kingdom: "Luminous Lady has viciously accused me of a most pernicious crime that I would never have the heart to commit," she said. "It bears not a thread of truth, and it is most condemnable that she would vilify me so. I did not murder her child. As to who smothered the infant, Luminous Lady herself knows very well."

So the vicious rumor arose and circled throughout the city. I had murdered my own child and blamed it on the Empress, people said. The details were vivid. I had watched the Empress approach the bedchamber, and I had waited in a corner, and when the Empress left, I entered the bedchamber, dismissed all the maids, and smothered my Oriole. I then pretended nothing had happened and went about my chores, and when Pheasant came to the bedchamber, I pretended to know nothing. When Pheasant discovered Oriole was not breathing, I pretended to be shocked and screamed in grief. I had put on a good show, they said, a very good show.

People in every ward were outraged. When they went to the markets to sell firewood or fruits, they appeared red-faced in anger, repeating the morbid details of my child's death. What kind of woman was Luminous Lady, to murder her own blood? people asked. She was the most malicious woman who had ever lived. More people shook their heads. Very soon, everyone in the city learned that I, Luminous Lady, the heartless, ruthless woman from the Wu Clan, had smothered my own daughter in order to become the Empress.

I heard that some monks and nuns doubted the stories. But when they tried to speak for me, they were reminded that I, after all, was a court woman with a deep desire for indulgence and fame, and for devout men and women like them, it would be very hard to understand.

The Regent seized the opportunity to fan the people's hatred of me. That sort of woman was a shame to the kingdom and must be punished, he demanded. He then ordered his two dogs, Han Yuan and Lai Ji, and their men, to paste bulletin after bulletin on the markets' gates and the wards' walls. One day, the bulletin said such a vicious woman must be hunted down and stoned. The next day, the bulletin stated that two more dutiful ministers in the palace, who had questioned me, had been prosecuted under my order.

The kingdom was no longer safe, the Regent announced, and he even hired bands of ruffians and mercenaries to surround his ward, claiming he had to protect himself.

And finally, the Regent warned the kingdom to watch the skies. The heavenly signs, the signs that would give any man permission to rise against Pheasant, the signs that showed Heaven would rescind its mission to Pheasant, the signs that would affirm the Regent's desire to remove Pheasant, would soon come.

✦ ✦

I hardly slept at night anymore, and, like those days after Princess Gaoyang died, I spent much time on the bench in the garden.

Each time I thought of the Empress and the rumor she had spread, I felt powerless and angry. I imagined people in the city, those faces I had seen in the market, spitting my name in spite, and I shuddered with anger. How sly that woman was to spin vicious rumors to ruin me.

Could I fight against rumor? I did not think so, for rumor had no grave and only bore seeds. It germinated in the air, thrived in the sun, and ripened in the shadows. It would not die in the rain and fly only higher in the wind.

For the first time since my daughter's death, I was afraid, but I did not want to be afraid. The rumor would not harm me or change me—I would not allow it. But it would change the perceptions of me and, perhaps, even my future.

I did not know what to think. I did not know what to do. I had lost my child, and in the midst of revenge, I would lose my reputation, my name, and my father's good name. Father. He would have been so angry with me...

I began to drink more. Plum wine. Ginger wine. Wine produced from millet, rice, and barley. Wine made of rare black grapes. There were so many to choose from in the imperial cellars. But the wine made of millet, unadulterated with fruit or spice, became my favorite. It was bitter and strong. It lit up my head like a fire and knocked me out. I would sleep well for a night without feeling anger or fear.

I always drank alone. Pheasant had not come to the garden since I bit him. He had gone to visit the three Ladies, I heard. They were ecstatic, and they had put on their finest clothes, applied white powder and fragrances, and painted bright beauty marks. They spent the night playing lutes and zithers. I did not envy them. Let them have him. Let him have them.

He visited the Pure Lady too, whose mind was still caught in the web of terror woven by her imprisonment. She had lost a lot of weight and had a tendency to sleepwalk at night, muttering and weeping. When Pheasant visited, she appeared startled and threw vases at him. Somehow she stepped on the shards and cut herself. Unable to understand what was happening, she screamed and released a vitriol speech of how the Empress had imprisoned her. "Empress Wang, Empress Wang," she screamed, pointing at Pheasant. "I shall curse you until my death!"

Sujie seemed to have adjusted to his new, calm life, they said, but he had become reticent. He could not remember any poems, and he was interested only in his pet crickets and *weiqi*.

Pheasant watched him play for long hours, I heard, and when he left the Quarters, Pheasant was in tears.

I wanted to know why he cried. Was he worried about the boy's future? Was he worried about the Regent's attack? But I tried not to think of Pheasant. He had disappointed me, and I would not forgive him.

I thought of Mother. I had not told her of the murder of my daughter yet, but perhaps she had already heard it, and the rumor that I had killed her. She would be heartbroken, but she would not believe it. Any woman who was a mother, who had loved someone, would not believe I had strangled my child with my own hands. But the world was not made up of mothers; instead, it was manned and manipulated by vile, barren women and, worse, by men. Heartless men.

Someday, when I felt better, I would write to her, and it would be the day I asked for her strength, not her tears.

✦ ✦

In the dark, I heard guards whispering outside the garden, and I leaned close to listen.

A dozen Gold Bird Guards had abandoned their posts inside the palace, claiming they would not serve a woman who would kill her own child. They had turned rogue, following the Regent, Guard Cao said, his voice echoing in the night.

"That's because they hate our Luminous Lady," a young voice said. "Do you think she did it?"

"That's a rumor. Do not believe it." Guard Cao's voice was sharp. "I was here when the Empress came. Ask Old Chan. He was here too. We let that woman in, and she smothered the baby."

There was a pause. "But you didn't see her do it, did you? And now everyone in the city believes Luminous Lady killed the baby after the Empress left the garden. Smothering her own child." There was a morbid fascination in that young voice. I heard the sound of a slap.

"Ouch! What did you do that for? I'm just telling you what people are saying, that's all! Do you know people are throwing horse dung at the palace walls, and the front gates too, shouting how evil Luminous Lady is—ouch!"

"They are the Regent's ruffians, blockhead. Watch your mouth, or you'll be thrown out of the palace walls yourself!"

"Hey, don't shout at me, old man. You stay here all day; you don't know what's happening outside. Captain Pei said there was a skirmish last night, did you hear? He's not going to make it up."

"Captain Pei! That man would sell his wife for a jug of wine."

"All I want to say is people in the city are listening to the Regent, old man. Our Emperor is in trouble—ouch!"

I leaned against the wall. The Regent had succeeded. He had fanned people's hatred of me, taken advantage of their uncertainty, and used their fear to attack Pheasant. Now, like me, Pheasant was facing the sharpened edge of the people's wrath.

✦ ✦

From my bed, I looked out the window. The night was dark and mute. There was no wind, no birds chattering from the trees, no animals rustling in the garden.

It was dark in the chamber too. The candles had long burned out. I pressed my cheek to Hong's head, stroking his hair, fine as silkworms' filaments, and his skin was pale like Pheasant's. My right side, where little Oriole should have slept, remained empty, cold, and silent.

An ache, throbbing and persistent, pricked my skin and spread to my veins. I remembered this feeling, years ago, when I was confined in the monastery. It seemed that loneliness and pain, like migrating wild geese, had returned to land near me.

This time, however, the silence had more teeth to it, and I could feel its raw edge saw at my heart. I wanted to resist it, to drive it away, but I did not know how. I did not know what to do.

I could not remember the last time Pheasant had come to my garden. Perhaps he was spending the night with the three Ladies or some concubine who was lying with him now.

I kissed Hong's cheek, tucked the cover under his chin, and got out of the bed. Near the brazier, Chunlu, Xiayu, Qiushuang, and Dongxue snored softly, and Apricot, lying on her stomach, moaned in her sleep. I could see the muscles on her back contracting now and then. It had been at least a month since I'd beaten her. The bleeding on her back had stopped, but the scabs hurt her each time she turned, and she had a hard time falling asleep. Still, she insisted on tending to Hong at night with the other maids.

I stood beside her. It would take her at least another month to be able to sleep normally. I should not have lashed her and used her to set an example. She was a victim of my wrath.

What had I become? Had I been so blind in grief I had forgotten what I valued most? I had always been kind to my maids. I had always believed kindness was an essential attribute of being a human. But with the tragedy of my daughter's death, I had not seen clearly. I had not thought clearly, and I did not know if I could ever again think or see as clearly as I had before.

I turned around, took a fur blanket, carefully placed it on Apricot, and tucked it around her. She stirred, and I quickly withdrew.

I put on a fur coat and leather boots, unhooked a lantern hanging at the corner, and opened the door, closing it behind me.

Cold air plunged down my throat. I shivered. Heading down a trail, I walked slowly, my footsteps echoing in the garden like an old man's groans.

It was my nightly routine to take a stroll to the back of my garden. Sometimes I walked until the palace night watcher hit his gong three times—the hour of *chou*—or five times—the hour of *mao*—when the dawn's light began to creep at the edge of the darkness. I did not know how long I would walk tonight.

It had snowed all day, and a thick layer of snow had covered the path. The garden looked like the inside of a dark cave, which the lantern's light failed to illuminate. The trees, their branches thin and skeletal, stretched in the distance like black webs; the rocks, large and tall, stood silently like armless, weeping statues; and somewhere the animals cried, their sound sharp and desperate, floating on the top of the pavilion like a secret spell.

I reached the back of the garden where a creek snaked down a hill and turned around. I would walk through the bamboo grove and reach the front of my garden for another two rounds, and then I would cut through an arboretum, cross the wooden bridge—Hope's Bridge—and stop at my usual destination: my child's burial ground.

Near the bridge, I stopped dead.

Someone was already there. A lean figure, standing near the nameless tombstone covered by shards of light from a lantern. His back was lit by the lantern as well, and he bent over as though to cover his eyes. Pheasant.

I wanted to turn around. I did not want to see him or talk to him. But then I could not move, remembering a long time ago when we had stood on either side of a bridge. He had tried to talk to me, but I had turned my back on him.

Those memories, sweet and scented, had lingered in my mind like fragrant summer blossoms, but now they had withered. Was this life? How bitter it was. We spent our whole lives seeking the fruit of happiness, trying to feed our hearts' desire, and when we finally found the fruit and cupped it in our hands, it took us only a moment to savor its sweet taste, and then it turned sour.

I should leave. I could not be alone with him. Such a distance, even with a forest between us, was too close, too much. But he looked so lonely and forlorn, standing beside a red lantern.

He put one knee on the ground, and with one hand on the stone, he slowly swept the top of the rock. A cloud of snow drifted in the red light, and his hand seemed transparent and glowing, like a lamp of hope. Then he leaned over and brushed the side of the stone with two hands. The motion, so delicate, so tender, reminded me of how he used to brush his fingers over Oriole's cheeks. Something choked my throat.

Finally, he pushed against the ground and stood up with a grunt, like an old man, and then he fumbled in his pocket, fished out something, and placed it on top of the tombstone that he had cleaned. He turned around, picked up the lantern, and walked toward the trail near the grove.

I waited until he disappeared into the trees, and then I went to the grave. The tombstone did not look so lonely, and on the top stood a small figure, like a vigilant sentinel—a wooden doll dressed in a fine, red gown.

My eyes misted. I remembered the dozens of dolls he had given Oriole. He had always insisted girls needed dolls and boys needed horses, and he had held her so carefully, always with a tender look in his eyes.

I ran down the bridge and went after him. "Pheasant. Wait. Pheasant."

He turned, raising the lantern. "Mei? Is that you?"

I stopped in front of him. I did not know what to say. "Why did you come here? I thought you were with the Ladies."

"It feels good to come out. It's quiet. What are you doing here all by yourself? Where are your maids?"

"They are sleeping." With the lantern's light, I could see all the signs of grief on his face I had not noticed before. His eyes were smaller, bleary, rimmed with sadness. His skin was pallid even in the red light, and his face slackened. There were dark circles under his eyes, and his jaw was sharper. Yes. He had grieved. It was simply that I, drowning in my own grief, had failed to see it. "I could not sleep."

"Me either." He lowered the lantern, spreading a pool of red light between us. "You know I am still searching for her."

"I know."

"I'll find her."

I nodded.

We both fell silent.

Then to my surprise, he put down the lantern and pulled me into his arms. His chin resting on my head, his breath warming my hair, he held me tightly. "I thought…" He paused, then spoke again, his voice gentle. "I thought you would never speak to me again. I thought… I was so worried about you."

He still cared about me, after everything that had happened. Tears ran down my face. I should have known. We had shared our youth, loving each other in secret, and we had gone through so much— doubt, suspicion, isolation, rebellion, and separation. We should have been strong; we should have gotten through the trial of losing our beloved child. Together.

"I'm sorry. I'm sorry, Pheasant."

"Do not blame yourself."

I nodded. I would stop blaming myself. I would stop blaming him too, and I could not let anguish push us apart, for our deep love, our shared bond to our child, in life or in death, would never change. And even though the loss of our daughter would leave a hole in our hearts that could never be filled, we could not let the void swallow us. "You shouldn't either."

His hand flew to his eyes, and he turned away. His shoulders trembled, and I held him. A spasm burst through his body, shaking him and me. Then he howled, loudly, the voice of fury and frustration piercing the night's darkness. I held him tight, my heart close to his. I let him be. I would be here for him, as he had done for me.

And perhaps, even as death broke our hearts, in the dust of cruelty, our love would heal us both and make us whole again.

Finally, he buried his head in my hair, and his voice was all pain. "I could not do anything right. Why? Why? I tried. I tried. So hard..."

I shook my head, but it had just occurred to me how difficult these days had been for him. In silence, he shed the tears of his failure; in loneliness, he swallowed his grief. And at the same time, he stood tall and remained strong in front of the guards and ministers, searching for the child murderer and trying to fight against the Regent.

"And our daughter...our daughter... I found her first," he wailed. "My little girl...lying there before me..."

I could not hold back my tears. "I know, I know."

"And you were right. I killed her. Did I not kill her? I proposed to divorce the Empress. I should not have done that. I killed our daughter."

"No, it's not your fault. It's not yours. You had to..." I shook my head, showering his robe with my tears. But how strange. For the first time since my child's death, tears released me.

"But I'm sorry, sweet face. I can't kill them all. I simply can't. I'm not my father."

I wiped my face. "I know. You must do whatever you believe is right. You are the Emperor, after all, Pheasant."

He kissed my forehead. "Thank you. Thank you for saying that." For a moment, we stood there, not speaking, not moving, only embracing. Finally, he picked up the lantern on the ground. "It's cold here. Your hands are freezing. You want to go inside?"

I nodded, and with the light of the lantern illuminating our path, I walked down the trail toward our bedchamber. "Come. Let's go warm up. How's your arm?"

"Sore."

"Will you whip me for biting you?"

He shook his head. "The whip is only for my enemies."

I smiled, stepping over a pile of snow. "Now perhaps we will have a good night's sleep."

For I needed it, and I believed Pheasant needed it too.

But there was silence. I turned around. Pheasant was not following me. Standing near the bamboo grove, he held the lantern in one hand, his head raised toward the sky, frozen. I followed his gaze.

The sky was dark as usual, and the moon looked strange, with a white halo encircling its edge. It would storm soon, perhaps, or snow.

But Pheasant was not worried about the weather, I knew, for near the moon, in the distant dark fabric of the sky, a bright stream, like an arrow, shot downward. Another followed. Then another.

Shooting stars.

This was what the Regent had been waiting for, the sign of Heaven rescinding its approval of Pheasant's reign. With this heavenly sign, all the rebels in the kingdom could place a claim to the throne.

I put my hand on Pheasant's arm. I did not look at his face, but I could feel him and his fear standing next to him like a vengeful ghost. "We should go," I said gently.

We had not yet reached the pond when urgent footsteps and pounding erupted at the entrance to the garden. "Your Majesty, Your Majesty, emergency!"

"What is it?" Pheasant shouted, racing toward the entrance.

"You must go to the watchtower now, Your Majesty!"

33

VIOLENT SCREAMS RANG OUTSIDE THE CARRIAGE AS WE rode through the Outer Palace. The commotion grew louder as we approached the watchtower near the palace gates. As soon as the carriage stopped, Pheasant leaped off to greet the General, who strode toward us.

Dawn had not arrived, but near the watchtower, it was as busy as though it were the middle of the day. Groups of eunuch servants were racing around, banging on pots to frighten the evil spirit that caused a moon eclipse, even though we had seen only shooting stars. Near the wall stood rows of bowmen holding crossbows, the long, steel-headed arrows ready on the strings. Behind them were axmen, swordsmen bearing wide-bladed sabers, men holding torches, and guards carrying long spears. All suited in golden armor and scarlet leather boots, they looked strong and well fed, and I was glad.

But some were glancing at me with a questioning look that worried me. I recognized one of them, Captain Pei, who had escorted Pheasant and me to the market when I tried to save Prince Ke and the princess's husband. His bald head glowing white like a snowball and his two ears sticking out like two round fans, Captain Pei met my gaze and put his hands on his hips as though to challenge me.

I swallowed. I could explain, of course, but would he believe me?

"What is it, General?" Pheasant said to him.

"Your Majesty, Luminous Lady." He gave us a curt nod. "You may come up to the watchtower and take a look yourself."

Pheasant went ahead, taking three stairs at a time, and I followed.

The top of the watchtower was as wide as the Heavenly Street, and many torch holders and archers were standing near the brick rampart, their backs facing me. The wind was strong here, slashing my face, and my eyes started to tear up. I pulled my fur cape tighter and hunched my back to stop the chilly wind from entering the folds near my neck.

Then I looked down.

In the dark, the city looked like a dried mulberry leaf with lots of burning holes. And those holes, glowing red, were spreading. Some seemed to be bonfires, and some were men carrying torches, marching through dark alleys toward the palace. A group of palace guards below the watchtower, holding torches too, shouted and charged forward. The two clashed. Men's cries, muffled in the distance, drifted up to us, and sparks of fire burst, smoke billowing in the air.

It was all happening so fast. The shooting stars had just occurred, and the people were already responding. If I had not seen it with my own eyes, I would not have believed it. But it was true. The Regent's plan had succeeded, and soon, he would gather all the rebellious people and his hired mercenaries and attack the palace, since he could claim that Heaven had given him permission to revolt.

And all of that started because of the lie about me.

I stared at the glowing tents and the blazing fire in the distance. Where was the Empress? What was she doing? Had she seen the shooting stars? Was she celebrating the heavenly signs with Zhong? Was she glad the rumor she had spread was ruining me and Pheasant's reign?

I wished she were dead.

"Do you know who those rebels are, General?" Pheasant took a torch from a man near him. He held it in front of him to get a better look at the people below the watchtower. Some snowflakes drifted above his head, spreading white speckles on his fur hat. He let out his breath, and a cloud of white surged in the air and vanished.

"Some rascals, encouraged by the Regent, no doubt," the General said, facing the city. "Some could be the rogue guards who serve him."

"Rogue guards." Pheasant struck the brick rampart, a splash of snow bursting from his hand. "I should have arrested him when I had a chance."

The General, standing still, did not speak.

"Do we have enough men?" Pheasant gestured toward the palace guards below him.

"Enough to secure the front gates," the General said and turned around. "But, Your Majesty, it's time for you to leave the watchtower. It's too dangerous."

"I am fine." Pheasant shook his head. "General, do you think the Regent will truly attack the palace?"

The General was silent for a moment. "The question, Your Majesty, is rather when."

His words sent a chill down my spine. I pulled my cape tighter and walked behind the torch holders and the archers standing by the rampart. I could not imagine what would happen if the Regent were to break into the palace. Pheasant, Hong, and I would all be in danger. Many people, many innocent people, would be slaughtered.

The Regent was too strong, supported by those rogue guards, mercenaries, and the frightened people who were easily manipulated. He knew the palace's layout and was well versed in war strategy. He was a formidable enemy, more frightening and destructive than the Empress.

I thought of the night when Taizi and Prince Yo revolted. I could still see the kneeling women by the tree stump, their blood-smeared faces, and the severed heads rolling on the ground. I could hear the dirges the women sang and their screams, and I remembered seeing my friend Plum near the tree stump...

I shivered. This could not happen. The imperial palace would not suffer another rampage.

I had to stop this. After all, I had started it.

But how? How could I stop the bloodshed? How could I defeat the Regent and his army? I was only one woman. Unlike my friend Princess Gaoyang, I did not know the art of fighting or the art of wielding weapons. But even if she had been here, she would not have been able to stop the Regent's army.

I stopped at the top of the stairs, scanning the soldiers standing near the wall. There, I found Captain Pei.

"General." I turned around. "Do you believe the rumor?" I did not say what rumor, but he would know what I referred to.

He gave me a quick glance. The wind sent his red cape flying behind him, and his birthmark, which often looked dark, seemed to shine like gold in the torchlight. "It is only a rumor, Luminous Lady." His voice was softer than I expected.

I nodded. Ever since I told him I had given him a second chance in the palace, he had not seemed so cold to me. "I know, but will the guards and the people believe me? Will they believe their emperor's words?"

He held the hilt of his sword. "A good sword serves his lord; a good swordsman believes in his lord, Luminous Lady."

I could count on his faith in Pheasant. I supposed I should have been happy to hear that. But what about his men? Could he speak for them? "What will you do, Pheasant?" I asked him.

He turned around to scan the rows of bowmen, axmen, and swordsmen. "The palace must have peace, and my kingdom must have peace. I must do anything I can, Luminous Lady. Anything I can."

So must I, I said to myself silently. *So must I.*

✦ ✦

For the next few days, Pheasant rose early and went to the Audience Hall. I was not sure how many ministers would be present or how many petitions he would hear. Most of the ministers avoided the court, and the ones who came to the audience these days looked fearful and lacked energy. They often gossiped about the riots, and no one seemed to care about the taxes on grain, salt, or silk.

Pheasant spent his afternoons on the watchtower, scanning the city and meeting with the General. They had divided the guards into two large groups, one to safeguard the front gates and the other to guard every corner of the palace. Nearly a quarter of the Gold Bird Guards had turned rogue, and that meant we had not only lost a vital number of forces, but also needed to fight the very men whom our guards had trained with.

A few days later, someone broke into a weapon storage chamber and stole all the weapons. The General was incensed, furious that his men would now stand with only clubs in their hands. Soon everyone in the palace learned of the news, and people began to panic.

And Pheasant spoke fewer and fewer words.

I pondered what I could do to stop the bloodshed. I read and reread

The Art of War. Perhaps the ancient master Sun Tzu would offer me some advice. Perhaps he could help me stop the disaster. While I was reading, I thought about the Regent. What was his weakness? How could I defeat him before he attacked?

And the Empress. What could I do to defeat her?

Hong was ill again and cried constantly. The physicians believed he had a stomach ulcer and instructed me to feed him tonics mixed with rhubarb root each morning, and honey water with licorice before bedtime. I worried that someone had poisoned Hong, and I hoped that the Empress's evil hand had not reached my son.

One afternoon, I was reading *The Art of War* when I saw Apricot pick up Hong's clothes in a corner. She stood up, wincing. I put down the scroll.

"Come and sit with me, Apricot." I patted the side of the bed. "Let me see your back."

Her eyes widened in surprise, but she obediently untied her coat and pulled up the back of her robe. The scabs looked crimson in the red light, and I remembered how Pheasant's back had looked when he was once beaten by his father. I wanted to tell her I was sorry, but I could not. I should not admit my fault before the people who served me. "You were beaten badly."

She put down her robe. "I should have died for my mistake. I deserved to be beaten, Luminous Lady."

Her voice, to my surprise, was gentle and without bitterness. I did not know what to say.

"Luminous Lady was beaten too," she added.

"Yes," I said sadly, remembering how the Empress had ordered her guards to beat me when she discovered I had returned from my exile. "I had forgotten about that."

"The Empress is evil, Luminous Lady. I shall not forget that, and I will not forget that she took our precious princess's life." Apricot's eyes glittered. "And Princess Gaoyang's too."

I felt my eyes moisten. I had punished her, but she bore me no grudge. She was faithful to me. She would never betray me. I blinked quickly to make my tears go away. "You have grown, Apricot. How long have you served me now?"

"It'll be four years this year." She smiled proudly.

She would serve me many more years, and I would be proud of her and her devotion. I wanted to stroke her hair, but I stood up instead. "Come, gather Hong and the others. Let's go visit the Emperor."

✦ ✦

I wanted to know what his plan was. Perhaps he and the General had figured out something to stop the Regent before his attack. I could not find Pheasant on the watchtower and instead found him in his library, where he was studying a scroll laid out on the vast lacquered table.

I ordered my maids to wait in the yard in front of the hall, while Apricot carried Hong to the corridor and awaited me there. After I lost my Oriole, I kept Hong with me whenever I could.

"Excellent. You are here," Pheasant said and waved away the attendants lined against the wall. "Come and take a look at the scroll, sweet face, and read it to me."

"It would be my honor, Your Majesty," I said, moving closer to the scroll. The hall was dark, even with the candlelight, and I traced the characters, each in perfect lines and elegant form, with my finger. "On the sixth year of the Reign of Eternal Glory, I, Emperor Gaozong, the Emperor of our kingdom, the son of Emperor Taizong, do hereby denounce Li Zhong, the adopted son of Empress Wang, as my heir. He has no right to claim the throne in the time of my reign or after the time of my death."

I raised my head. I knew he had thought of denouncing the boy many times since the news of the Regent's rebellion reached us, and finally Pheasant had decided to do it. "I think this is the time."

If Zhong was denied the throne, then we would cut the root of the support on which the Regent and the Empress relied.

Pheasant sighed. "The boy is speaking like he is already the Emperor, have you heard? I must stop them. I ordered Minister Li Yifu to draft the edict this morning."

"You have no choice but to push him aside, but renouncing Zhong is risky too," I said. "Especially at this moment."

"I understand. But the imperial weaponry chambers are empty. We do not have enough weapons for every guard. When the attack comes, it will be a disaster. We need to take action now, before it's too late, and this is all I can do at this moment." He rubbed his eyes.

Pheasant looked tired. His face slackened, and his right eye looked askew, the eyelid drooping, like an inflated leather bag that had lost its elasticity. "Are you all right, Pheasant?"

"You will not believe this, but I am getting old." He shook his head and blinked hard. "I don't see very well anymore."

My heart sank. His father had lost his sight too. "You're tired. That's all." I patted his shoulders. I would have the physicians examine him later. "It must be the weather. You need a warm cape. It's spring, but it's still very cold these days. I can't leave my chamber without a fur cape. I'll tell your attendants to bring you one."

"Never mind the fur cape." He rubbed his temples. "I'm going to invite my uncle over for supper. I shall be courteous, and if he declines the invitation, I will order him brought to me, and then I shall corral all of his servants."

Of course the Regent would refuse to come. "Bring him to you? How?" Months ago, we could have taken the Regent's life quietly and successfully, but with him surrounded by his mercenary army, arresting him would be difficult.

Pheasant flexed his fingers. They seemed rigid. "I shall hire some skillful guards. They will go around the rogue guards who protect him."

I nodded. I had to think about the plan. I was not comfortable with it. It could go awry.

An announcement came. Minister Xu Jingzong requested to see Pheasant.

"Let him in."

The old minister limped into the hall. Holding his cane, he bowed to Pheasant three times and then lowered his head toward me. "Luminous Lady," he said.

I nodded to acknowledge him. "I hope Minister Xu has had a smooth recovery."

"These old bones don't break easily, Luminous Lady." He laughed.

I liked his spirit. "I'm certainly very pleased to hear that. But it is late, minister. Are you still on duty?" There was a dark ink smudge on his thumb.

"Your Majesty, Luminous Lady." He bowed again. "Indeed, I have been on duty at this late hour, for I have a most urgent matter I'm eager to discuss with you."

"What is it?" Pheasant asked, leaning back.

"It is my understanding that many people are confused with some rumor they have heard. Yet I question the nature of the rumor. I believe the Empress is responsible for throwing the palace into confusion, and her behavior has put many people's lives in danger. As a fifth-degree minister, I feel it is my duty to question this matter, and thus I propose a team be set up to conduct a formal inquiry into this rumor."

"Be more specific, Minister Xu." I could not fully understand the meaning of his words. "A team to inquire about this rumor. Does it mean you will set up a trial against the Empress?"

"Precisely, Luminous Lady, and, Your Majesty, I beg you to give me your permission to lead this investigation. It is my conviction that whoever is guilty must be impeached and brought to justice at all costs."

Pheasant nodded. "Yes, Minister Xu. You have my permission to lead the investigation."

"Why are you doing this, Minister Xu?" I asked. He was inviting another beating from the Regent's men. "Don't you fear the retaliations of the Empress? And the Regent?"

He straightened. "Luminous Lady, Your Majesty, of course I do. Last time they beat me, I lay in bed for a month. I could have died like the others." His voice, always loud and clear, filled the hall. "I have eight wives, fourteen children, six grandchildren, and two of my father's concubines to care for. What will they do if I die? But I am sixty-three years of age. I will not live forever. Sooner or later, I will go to the Yellow Rapids. But I'm sick of the Regent. He ruined my life, banishing me to the South, and he will never let me live in peace. As long as he's the Regent and I'm the minister, I will live like a worm in this palace and die like a worm. I do not wish to live like a worm or die like a worm, Luminous Lady. I want to die in glory, or better, to live in glory."

I recalled the same words he had said to me in the library. He was indeed the boldest minister I had seen in the court. "You said you will impeach her."

"Yes. And depose her, if she is guilty of murdering an innocent child."

"She is. I give you my word."

He sighed. "Luminous Lady, regrettably, your word is not enough. It has to be proven."

Proven? I stood, my heart racing fast. Suddenly, I had an idea of how to defeat the Empress and the Regent.

I had to expose her lie and reveal to the kingdom what had really happened and what kind of an empress she was. If I could do that, if I could show the people the truth, the Regent would lose his support, his army would dissolve, and the palace would be saved.

Minister Xu would try the Empress, and she would face justice. And my child's death would be avenged.

All I needed to do was to get her to confess.

I was so excited I could hardly contain myself. I went to the minister and bowed. "I thank you, Minister Xu. You have heard the Emperor's order. Please do form an impeachment party. Choose ministers you trust, and I'll prove to you she is guilty. I will get you the Empress's confession."

"I do not understand, Luminous Lady." He looked confused. "The Empress's confession?"

"Do what you need to do. Leave the rest to me."

"Of course, Luminous Lady. I shall not doubt you." The minister bowed and left the library.

If everything succeeded, I would promote this man. I would appoint him Chancellor and reward him beyond his wildest dreams.

"How will you get her confession?" Pheasant asked, looking confused. "She'll die rather than confess."

I went to the hall's entrance to make sure no one was around to overhear. Near the pillar in the corridor, in the pool of red lantern light, Apricot was rocking Hong, who had fallen asleep sucking his thumb.

Several eunuchs yawned at the far end of the forecourt, and near them, a few servants unhooked the lanterns under the eaves and changed the candles inside. Dozens of guards, their hands on the hilts of their swords, paced solemnly along the corridor.

I closed the door behind me. "We will capture her," I said in a low voice and told Pheasant of my plan. "It's from *The Art of War*," I added.

He shook his head. "Too dangerous. Anything can go wrong. What if someone warns her?"

Of course, the Empress had many spies hidden in the palace, who spun large, sticky webs in the dark. And those who did not yet work for her could be easily wheedled by her gold and influence. Anyone—a greedy eunuch, a vengeful servant, a cowardly minister, or even an ambitious guard—if any of them heard what I was intending to do, that person could become a loose hinge on the wheel of my plan.

But I could use the very nature of these lowly people and make them work for me.

"You must trust me," I said.

Pheasant sighed. "Sweet face, you know it's not that I do not trust you. But you have no idea what will happen."

"We have the General, Pheasant."

"I know, but…"

I put my hand on his arm. "Do you remember Taizi's rebellion? Do you remember how many died? This is our only chance to stop the war. If this plan succeeds, we will have her confession. The people will know she is a liar, and it will be all over for her, and for the Regent."

He walked to the table and put his hand near the candle's flame. "Do you know you are walking through the fire? And what could happen if you fail?"

I stared at the flame. It looked like a ruthless, orange heart, its smoke dark and ominous. I wondered what my friend Princess Gaoyang would have said to me if she had been here. "Are you afraid, Luminous Lady?" she would ask me.

Yes. I was. I was very afraid.

What had she said about fear? "Fear is a roof, Luminous Lady. Once you break it, you shall see the sky."

I thought I had understood what she meant, how a pavilion built with fear would get smaller and smaller and hotter and hotter inside. But now I understood more.

I nipped the flame with my thumb and forefinger. "What we fear is not the fire, Pheasant, but rather the fear itself."

He let out a heavy sigh, and then with his hands crossed behind his back, he paced in the hall. He reached the threshold of the hall and returned. After two more rounds, finally, he nodded. "I shall summon the General."

34

WHILE PHEASANT ORDERED HIS EUNUCH ANNOUNCER TO summon the General, I went outside to see Apricot. She was humming something, rocking Hong in her arms. Beside her, my four maids, Chunlu, Xiayu, Qiushuang, and Dongxue, were leaning against a pillar, sleeping. There was something sweet and comforting about seeing them safe and content, and my eyes wandered to search for my Oriole.

I caught myself.

"Luminous Lady." Apricot tugged at Chunlu and Xiayu beside her. They jerked awake, glancing up at me in fear. Ever since I had ordered Apricot to be beaten, they often looked at me this way. Apricot, however, stood straight, patting Hong in her arms.

"Apricot," I said softly. "Come. I need to speak to you."

"Yes, my lady." She gave Hong to Chunlu and followed behind me.

I led her to one of the buildings near the library, where the ministers and scribes reviewed petitions. I dismissed them. When the footsteps faded away in the corridor and we were alone in the chamber, I asked Apricot to sit on a stool.

"I have a favor to ask, Apricot. It's very important, and only you can help me," I said.

"Of course, Luminous Lady. Anything, anything you wish me to do. I shall be happy to oblige."

"I need you to betray me."

She raised her head, looking confused. "Luminous Lady?"

I put up my hand to stop her before she could speak more. "I trust you. You would never truly betray me. But I need you to do this for me." I paused. "You will spread the word that I am planning on capturing the Empress. You will tell her how I curse her, and you will incense her." Carefully, I told her what I would like her to do. "And you will also make her believe I am vulnerable. You will expose me to her."

"Why?" Apricot's mouth fell open in horror.

"This is a secret plan. It's very important, and my life depends on you," I said. The Empress's men would trust Apricot's every word, believing she was betraying me for revenge because I had beaten her. "Will you do it?"

She was thinking, biting her lip, wringing her hands, and when she raised her head again, she looked somber. "Yes, Luminous Lady, if this is your wish. I will follow your order. I will do everything you told me. I'll go to the Empress's uncle."

I was surprised to hear how quickly her mind worked, and I was proud of her. "I am grateful that you have made a proper decision, Apricot, and meanwhile"—I wanted to stroke her hair again but refrained—"you must be careful."

"Yes, Luminous Lady."

"Now go." I watched her open the chamber's door and leave.

When I stepped out of the building, the ministers and servants in the corridor were eyeing me. I straightened, pulled my cape around me, and passed them.

Apricot was the first arrow I let loose, and I prayed it would fly well in the air.

✦ ✦

The General was waiting in Pheasant's library.

"You returned at a good time, Mei." Pheasant raised his head. "Would you like to tell the General yourself?"

I nodded. "General Li." I gave him a bow. He returned another but looked cautious. He was not cold toward me anymore, but I could tell he was not accustomed to listening to my orders. "Perhaps you already knew this: the Emperor and I have been thinking about how to stop the war."

He nodded. "How?"

"We will force the Empress to confess her crime. When the people know the truth, when they understand she has murdered my daughter and instigated the rebellion, they will back off. They will not support her, or the Regent."

"She will not confess."

"We have a plan."

The General folded his arms across his chest, frowning. I could not afford to have him doubt me, or worse, betray me. He was loyal to Pheasant. Would he be loyal to me? "Do you have a family, General Li?"

"A son."

I folded my sleeves across my lap. "The Regent is not a kind man, General Li. You know him better than I do."

The General waved his hand. "Luminous Lady, if you don't mind, let me hear what you have to say. What is the plan?"

"We will capture her."

He looked up to the ceiling. "We would have done that days ago if it were that simple. We do not know where she's hiding, Luminous Lady."

Pheasant spoke sharply. "General, I command you to listen to Luminous Lady. That is an order."

He dipped his head. "Yes, Your Majesty."

"Here is what you are going to do," I said, trying to sound calm and assured. "The Emperor has ordered the edicts drafted. He has renounced the heir. You will order your men to post the bulletins of the heir's denunciation in the city the moment you leave this hall. Make certain you watch how the crowd responds to the message. Have your men follow anyone whom you suspect may be her spies."

The Empress's own men would lead us right to her.

The General shifted his feet, the hem of his cape swinging in the candlelight. I could not see his face, hidden in the dark, but I could sense his surprise. "Renounce the heir? This will cause an uproar."

"Are you afraid?" I challenged him.

He snorted, waving his hand.

I breathed out in relief and explained the second part of my plan.

The General would send a messenger bearing Pheasant's invitation to the Regent's house, and meanwhile, he would secretly order another group of his trusted men to leave the palace quietly and wait outside the Regent's heavily guarded ward. As the messenger delivered the invitation to the Regent, the masked guards would seek an opportunity to break into the ward and bring the Regent to the palace.

These two plans, to borrow the master Sun Tzu's words, used the strategy of striking the west by making noise in the east. There was also a chance that one of them would fail, but if one succeeded, we would have either the Regent or the Empress in our hands.

The General gave me a long look.

"Of course, much depends on the General's service," I said calmly.

The man's face thawed. "I shall give the orders to my men right away."

I shook my head. I was not finished yet. I went into the most important part of the plan, in which I commanded his service and loyalty. I looked straight into his eyes. "Are you a good swordsman, General?"

I reminded him of what he had told me on the watchtower, "A good sword serves his lord; a good swordsman believes in his lord."

"Of course, Luminous Lady."

"I want you to believe in me."

The General held my gaze. He looked surprised, and I waited for him to digest the message—so far he had always obeyed Pheasant, and I wanted him to obey me. "You must serve me. You must follow my orders. Our kingdom's future depends on you. There is no mistake about this. Do we understand each other?"

He did not answer, and I was worried that he would refuse. Then he turned around and headed toward the hall's entrance, where he paused. "You must be careful, Your Majesty and Luminous Lady," he said. "The Empress is not in the palace, but her spies are everywhere."

I relaxed. He did understand. "Thank you for your warning, General. You may go now."

With a curt nod, the General pushed the doors open and left the hall. His heavy footsteps pounded in the courtyard, echoing in the thick curtain of the night. Both Pheasant and I sat down with a sigh.

"Now we wait," he said. But he was too nervous to sit. Instead, he steadied his hat, crossed his arms behind his back, and walked all the way to the threshold and back to the large table. Back and forth, he paced in the library.

I went to the corner of the hall and sat down. Then I closed my eyes and began to meditate.

Breathe. Breathe the scent of the night. And listen. Listen to the silence of the air, for when I opened my eyes again, I would feel as calm as the mountain pine, and I would stand high, steadfast, and victorious, like the rising moon.

✦ ✦

An hour later, a guard sent by the General informed Pheasant and me that the announcement of the heir's dethronement had been posted on city gates and market walls across the city. They were now on the watch for any suspicious men who might inform the Empress.

Later, another Gold Bird Guard, running straight from the watch-tower, told us of a sudden burst of light coming from the Regent's ward. It seemed there was a great commotion inside the Regent's house. The General's men were now waiting for their opportunity.

Everything was going smoothly.

✦ ✦

Someone tapped lightly on the door. I rose to my feet, startled. There had been no announcement from the eunuch announcer of anyone arriving. Who could it be? The General?

Another tap. More urgently.

"Who is it?" Pheasant spun around.

A minister garbed in a purple gown stumbled into the hall and knelt before us. Minister Li Yifu. The assistant minister of the Ministry of Justice, who had a penchant to bow deeply and was fond of elaborate speeches. I went before him, remembering I had spoken to him last time in the library. He had let me read Zhuang Tzu's books.

He gave a litany of gratitude of being received at this late hour, and finally, Pheasant cut him off and asked him about his business.

"A petition," he said and presented a scroll with two trembling

hands. He was so nervous he was unable to speak clearly. "A petition...to remove our Empress and appoint our Luminous Lady, may
her beauty and courage remain to be our inspiration, to be the mother
of the kingdom."

Pheasant turned to me, his eyebrows raised. I studied the man in
front of me carefully. "I am grateful for your support, Minister Li," I
said. "But may I ask why I have your loyalty?"

His sleeve flew to his face, and he started to weep. When he calmed
down, he spoke rapidly, shuddering and stuttering. It took me a moment
to understand that early tonight, he had received a letter from a minister
by mistake. The letter stated the Regent had ordered to exile him, and the
order would be effective at dawn. Fearful for his future, he had decided
to come to me and offer his support in hopes of keeping his position.

"Why did he exile you? What did you do?" I asked.

"Luminous Lady, I have done nothing wrong," the minister
protested. "I acted only out of duty, drafted the letter of the heir's
repudiation as the Emperor ordered. The great Regent must have
heard of it and become angry. He was angry at me before, for helping
you at the library, and now that I drafted the repudiation of the heir,
he said it was an act of betrayal."

I could always tell if a man lied out of convenience or if he spoke
the truth in desperation. He was speaking the truth.

"I see," Pheasant said. "You will not be exiled."

Minister Li Yifu wiped his forehead in relief. "I am most grateful
for your kindness, Your Majesty. This is not all, Your Majesty. I come
here bearing another message."

"What message?"

"When I received the order of my exile by mistake, I heard some
scribes whispering. The Regent has chosen a time to attack the palace."

I jerked, and Pheasant took in a sharp breath. "When?"

"Today. Before dawn, Your Majesty."

My heart hung in the air. It was only hours before dawn. "Are you
certain, Minister Li?"

"Most certain, Luminous Lady. He has instigated the commoners,
sending them to protest in front of the palace, and brought together
an army of his hired men."

"The Gold Bird Guards can take care of my uncle's men, but the commoners…" Pheasant stood. "I must go to the watchtower now. I will not see any bloodshed tonight."

"I will go with you." I rose.

"You stay here." He rushed to the hall's door.

"Pheasant! Wait." I followed him.

He had just reached the door when it suddenly flew open. He stopped abruptly, frozen. I took quick steps and rushed to Pheasant's side. One glimpse into the dim yard, and I felt my heart stop.

Through the entrance of the compound, people burst in, waving their hands and shouting. In a moment, the empty yard became crowded with many shadows.

Were they the Regent's men? Pheasant tensed beside me, and he stretched out his arms, pushing me behind him to protect me. But already I saw the faces in the dim light. They were ministers and scribes who worked the night shift, eunuch servants, and some palace guards. Some were weeping, some were shouting to one another, and others were running toward us.

"The Regent has attacked!"

"Heaven help us!"

"We have no weapons! The guards have no weapons!"

"Let us out, Your Majesty! Let us out before it's too late!"

Cowards! The palace had not yet been breached, and they wished to flee! But we had to calm them.

"Keep them back," I ordered the guards who had rushed to stand before Pheasant and me to protect us from the crowd. I could not help but step back, gripped by fear. I hated to be surrounded by throngs of people. They were dangerous. They could trample you with the brute force of their ignorance. And I had to assure that no one could get close to Pheasant and harm him.

"Stay back!" one of the guards shouted, and pushed the crowd away from the corridor.

But still, waves of people rushed to us. Some climbed to the windowsills of the corridor and surged closer. "Your Majesty! Help us!"

"Open the gates, Your Majesty! Open the gates and let us leave the palace. Before it's too late."

"I have an elderly mother and my family to take care of!"

I put my hand on Pheasant's arm. "What are you going to do, Pheasant?" My hands were shaking, but I tried to stay calm.

"I need to take care of the rebels in front of the palace gates." He clenched his fists, and his eyes, even though bleary and tired these days, looked more resolved than ever.

Suddenly, I did not think it was a good idea. There would be many stray arrows, hidden daggers... "Perhaps—"

The sound of a gong rang out. It was only a night watcher announcing the hour of the night, but it sent a shiver through the crowd, and people began to scream.

"Ministers!" Pheasant shouted, raising his voice above the commotion. "I shall guarantee your safety, but you must all stay inside the palace... Ministers! For your own safety..." He thrust himself toward the crowd, working his way out.

I grabbed his sleeve. "You can't go to the watchtower now, Pheasant. It's too dangerous."

"My uncle will not succeed, Mei." He waved at the guards to clear the path among the ministers and rushed through the crowd. He walked so fast, his hat left shadows flying across the ministers' faces like a blackbird. "I will not let anyone die tonight."

"No. Wait! Wait for the General." I held up my skirt and ran after him. "Wait for me!"

"Go back, Mei," Pheasant shouted as he exited the compound. He disappeared from my view, and by the time I caught up with him, he was instructing a group of the Gold Bird Guards who had gathered in front of him. Armor clinked, and many shadows raced toward us. The Gold Bird Guards were ready to defend the palace.

He took a bow from a guard. "I will take the command from you here, Captain Pei. No. Hold your arrows! Do not shoot the protesters unless I give you my order. Do you hear me? All of you? Do you hear me?"

"But, Your Majesty—" the Captain protested. I could not see his face in the dark, only his bald head shining white in the reflection of the blades.

"This is an order! An order! Now follow me to the watchtower. All of you! Captains! Do you have all your men in position? Good! Now let's go. What are you waiting for? General! There you are!"

"Your Majesty, I returned as fast as I could—" The maroon cape flew down the path ahead of me. Behind him, more guards emerged.

I ran to greet him. "Did you find her, General?"

He pivoted to stop before me. "Luminous Lady. We followed the men reading the bulletins just as you instructed. Two were her spies. We found her nest, but she had already left."

"Left? How?"

He shook his head. "Someone had informed her before we arrived."

I bit my lip in frustration. "Where is she now?"

"We do not know. She could be anywhere. Even inside the palace."

How dare she return to the palace! But if she were here, I would find her and capture her myself.

"Your Majesty"—the General walked toward Pheasant as he stepped into a carriage—"I heard the rebels are out of control at the front gate. I shall take it from here."

"No. I shall take care of them. And you will take all the men you need and look after Luminous Lady, as we discussed earlier. Remember that. It's an order."

"Your Majesty, if the front gates are breached—"

"It will not happen! I shall hold it. I will lead my men. You must trust me, General!"

"Your Majesty—"

I could not let Pheasant face the danger himself. I brushed aside the General and hurried to Pheasant's carriage. "I'm coming with you."

"You can't, Mei." Pheasant shook his head. "You must look after Hong."

I stopped. Hong. My Hong. I had forgotten about him. I turned around and raced back to the yard. "Pheasant. I shall catch up with you in a moment."

His carriage rolled forward and disappeared into the night.

"Luminous Lady!" the General shouted behind me. "You must stay with me!"

"I will be right back!" I rushed into the library's yard. The vast yard sounded like a boiling pot with all sorts of cracklings and groanings as panicking ministers rushed to and fro. There were so many people, their dark heads rising and dipping, their arms flinging around.

I searched, straining to see through the dimness. I could not find my maids among the crowd. "Chunlu! Xiayu!"

No one answered. My voice was drowned out in the hubbub of noises.

"Hong. Where are you? Hong?" My hands shaking, I pushed through the crowd. I had a sickening feeling, being jostled everywhere I turned. I swore as long as I lived, I would never walk into a crowd again. "Hong! Hong! Where are you?"

Near the lion statue stood three shivering ministers. My Hong was not there. Opposite me were another group of ministers, wiping their eyes, their backs hunched; near them, a man with a bald head and large ears like fans dashed by. It was Captain Pei. What was he doing here? He should have left with Pheasant a moment ago. I was going to shout at him when a minister in a purple gown stumbled toward me, his hat nearly stabbing me in the eye. I ducked under his arm and drove him aside with my hand. When I straightened, the Captain was gone.

I turned around to search for my son again. "Hong, where are you?" Still, I could not see him or any of my maids. Perspiration ran down my forehead. Where was my child?

Strong hands grabbed my arm from the dark, and before I could cry out, before I could kick, a bald head appeared at the corner of my eye, a foul thing clamped over my mouth, and something hard and heavy knocked my head. Everything went dark.

35

PAIN. EVERYWHERE. ON MY ARMS, LEGS, AND IN MY HEAD and stomach. But I was still alive, and I was grateful for that, and the pain, the dull throb, was reassuring. It reminded me of my Oriole, of the Regent's upcoming attack, of why I was abducted here, and of what I must do next.

But I had not expected the darkness. I could not see anything. I could not see Hong either. I hoped, with all my heart, that he was safe with my maids.

Where was I?

I struggled to sit up but fell sideways. I was bound tightly, my arms tied behind my back. I had lost my cape, and my hair was falling near my ears. A filthy cloth was in my mouth. I shook my head, working hard to dislodge it, but I could not spit it out.

In the distance, I heard rumbling, shrieks, and the sounds of metal clashing. The Regent's attack. My heart tightened. I hoped the Gold Bird Guards were winning. I hoped Pheasant was safe. More determined than ever, I pushed myself up, balanced, and stared hard around me.

Tall shadows stood in front of me. Behind them draped a curtain of black sky. The wind carried the scent of fresh air mixed with dirt, resin, and the strong, fetid odor of something rotten. I was somewhere in a forest.

Some murmurs and faint rustling came from behind me. I jerked around. A few paces from me a fire flickered, near which hovered a dozen shadowy figures. Their heads bobbing, they raised some sticks with flat blades—shovels—and struck the ground. It was too dark to see their faces, but I could tell who they might be and whom they served.

All at once, anger burst from my stomach. That murderer! She had slipped through the General's hands, and now she had gotten me instead. I struggled again, trying to free my arms and spit the cloth out of my mouth.

"Bring her here!" a voice shouted, a voice I could never forget.

I thrust my head toward her. There! Near the fire appeared the large figure in a golden gown. Her phoenix crown stood on her head like a vulture. I breathed hard.

Hands clamped on my shoulders, and before I could resist, I was dragged across the hard ground. Finally, I reached the pit, where a group of tall figures gathered. There were a dozen of them, and they turned toward me. Some folded their arms across their chests, some held their weapons tied on their belts, and others leaned over the shovels, watching me. They were those rogue Gold Bird Guards, I could tell, for they all wore the same scarlet leather boots.

"Traitors!" I shouted, but my voice was muffled by the cloth in my mouth.

A man struck me. He had a bald head and ears sticking out like two round fans. It was Captain Pci. He had abducted me.

Pain shot through my bones, and my knees buckled. But I could not kneel or lie there for the Empress to kick. On my elbows, I crawled backward, inch by inch; all the while, I fixed my eyes on the woman who murdered my daughter. If only my hands were free...

The Empress walked toward me, her shadow enveloping me like a heavy cloak, and her white face flat like a gravestone. "Let her speak."

The traitor captain reached down and yanked the cloth from my mouth.

"Murderer!" I spat. "Murderer! You must die a thousand times!" But my mouth was numb and my words came out slurred.

"I heard you were looking for me, harlot," the Empress said, the fire lighting up her repulsive, closely set eyes. "So here I am. What will you do? I suppose you never dreamed of this, but I warned you, harlot, you are nobody. You mean nothing to me, and now this day has come. You, your son, and all your servants shall die."

I tried to sit up, and I would have torn her apart with my bare hands if they had not been bound behind me. But she had to die—on my terms. So I lowered my head and dove toward her. But someone caught me from behind and shoved me aside. I could not touch her. I screamed in frustration.

The Empress laughed, her voice shrill, disgusting. "Scream, scream, harlot. No one will hear you. No one will come to save you. You see this pit?" She grabbed my hair and pushed me down, forcing me to look at the pit. It was wide, round, and dark. "It used to contain serpents. What a pity they are no longer here. But all the same, I will kill you, set you on fire, and bury you here, and no one will ever know."

I thrust my body backward, away from the pit, and I put all my contempt and hatred into my voice. "Don't be so certain, murderer. You will not have your way. The forest knows, Heaven knows, and everyone knows." My voice was hoarse somehow, and even though I knew I must not give too much away, I could not help myself. I could not bear to see her so triumphant. "You will not have your way, murderer. The General shall come. Perhaps he is on his way here now, with his army, and Pheasant will come too. You will not succeed."

She thrust a torch near my cheek, the flame singeing my hair. "You think I am an idiot, harlot? How will the General know you are here? And Pheasant? I doubt he is still alive. The Regent surely beheaded him hours ago."

The Regent had broken into the palace? Pheasant was dead? A cold shiver ran down my spine, and my heart shuddered with fear. But I swallowed. I spat at her. "I do not believe you. You're a liar and a murderer. You are evil. You are a vile, demented, and barren monster!"

She struck me, and my head crashed against the ground. An acute sting cut my face, a sharp pain shot up from my wrists behind my back, and my neck felt as though it was about to break. The Empress was shouting something. I strained to hear. Nothing. I blinked, trying to sit upright while a wall of thick buzzing reverberated around me.

"Who said I was barren? I am not barren! I am fertile! You, you are the liar! You're the rumormonger. You ruined me!" She seized my robe and pushed her flat face close to mine, while her spittle sprayed my face. "Do you know what I have suffered all these years? Do you know how I have suffered? I have been his wife for nine years, nine long years, and he bedded me only once, on our wedding night. And you say I am barren? I am not barren. I am not barren!"

She threw me back to the ground, but I was so surprised to hear what she had said that I did not feel the pain. She was not barren? Pheasant had bedded her only once? That was ridiculous. I shook my head, laughing. I laughed so hard I had to stop to catch my breath.

"Why are you laughing? What are you laughing at, harlot?"

"Do you wish me to believe that? Once? Only once?" She always lied. "What happened to those full-moon nights when he summoned you? What happened to those nights before he became the Emperor? And you say he bedded you only once?"

Her chest rose and fell, rose and fell, and I could see a thick stream of breath puffing out of her stubby nose. "You know nothing. You know nothing! How could you know? He does not want me. He hates me. He despises me." She turned away sharply, so all I could see was her exposed thick neck. "He drank and drank and drank while I waited on the bed, watching the candles burning, watching the moon stealing away outside the window. He never called for me! He... he never touched me. I begged him... I put on those clownish silk dresses! I put a black stone in his wine to make him want me. I drank rainwater to be fertile. I did everything my uncle told me to do. He would not take me."

She was lying again. She had to be. No one could know what really happened inside their bedchamber, no one except Pheasant, but then I remembered, clearly, that she had begged me once to let Pheasant want her. I had just returned from exile then. But it did not matter now. Even if she was not barren, she was absolutely evil.

I struggled to my feet. "Ah," I said with relish. "Who can blame him? You are repulsive. Look at you. You are hideous. You are uglier than a toad. You are not a woman."

She moved toward me, her hand raised high, and I straightened, ready to take another blow. But it did not come. She swayed and fell to the ground with a loud thud instead. Holding her stomach, she rocked back and forth, shaking her head. She looked so pathetic that she reminded me of all those accounts of how weak she was, how tormented she was in her chamber. But I would not pity her, not after she had smothered my child.

"Don't say that... How can you say that?" Her voice was miserable, weak, so unlike her too. "It's your fault. It is. You stole him from me. You stole my happiness. You...you are the wanton woman. You were his father's concubine. You took him from me before he even married me. If it were not for you, he would love me, he would want me, and I would not have suffered this disgrace. What did I do? I did nothing. I did nothing wrong. I am his wife!"

"So you are his wife. But you are delusional. Pheasant will never love a woman like you. He will never love an ugly, evil woman like you."

She turned toward me, her hands clenched, but they were trembling, and there were tears in her eyes. I paused. For a moment, I did not know what to say. But her eyes, those small, closely set eyes, reminded me of what she had done to my beloved pet and cherished friend, and I wanted to say those words over and over and pierce her heart a thousand times.

"You smothered an infant. A six-month-old infant! Pheasant could never love a heartless woman like you. No one will love you. No one. No one!"

"No, no. You can't say that... Please don't say that..." She shook her head, covering her ears, and then as though she suddenly remembered something, she jumped up, shrieking. "You will not speak to me this way. You will not speak to me this way!"

I raised my chin. "You will not command me. You cannot command me, murderer."

"I shall kill you. I shall kill you!"

She turned around, grabbed a dagger from the man beside her, and dove toward me. She moved so fast I did not have time to dodge. A bolt of light glared in the air, and then it sank into my chest.

At first I felt no pain, and the force of her body, so powerful, drove me backward. I staggered, taking the dagger with me. She had stabbed the top of my chest, near my shoulder, missing my heart. The cold blade pierced my flesh, severed my veins, and excruciating pain burst in my body. All at once, I was giving birth to my Hong again. I was torn apart, I was leaking, yet, with my hands tied behind me, I could not staunch the flow. I stared at the dagger, where black blood gushed at a sickening speed. I shuddered. I felt cold and dizzy.

But I raised my head to the child killer. "You see? You cannot even kill me. You can only kill a child. A child! She could not even walk or talk!"

The Empress clenched her hands again. Her head dipped and rose as she breathed. "I did not want to."

"But you killed her. My daughter! What did she ever do to you? What did she do? You are a liar and a monster!"

She pointed her finger at me. "You made me do it! It was you!" She panted, and the phoenix crown fluttered, its wings spreading as though ready to fly. "I wanted to strangle you, but I saw her instead, her legs kicking on the bed. I picked her up. I held her, that little pink thing. I never thought a baby would look like that. I never thought of hurting her. She was so small, so soft, so precious. She smelled like milk. She looked like a dream. I wanted her. I wanted to love her, and she looked at me." The Empress looked down, holding out her arms as though she were cradling my Oriole, and her voice was eerily gentle, sending a chill down my spine.

I lost track of her voice for a moment. I felt weak and sank to the ground. But I shook my head. I had to concentrate.

"...She kicked her legs, smacking her lips. She had no teeth, only pink, bare gums. And those black eyes—oh, those eyes, so dark and so beautiful. I did not know what to do. I touched her cheeks. So soft and smooth. She was perfect, perfect. I wished I had made her. I wished she was mine. I wished I could take her and keep her forever."

And she did. She took her away from me. Tears wetting my face, I closed my eyes, and in my mind, I could see that moment, my child, so sweet looking and filled with life, smiling her toothless smile at the monster, not knowing the hands that held her would take her life. Why was I not there? Why did I not protect her?

I did not want to hear anything else. I did not wish to share my child, even the memory of her, with my enemy.

"She turned her head, this way and that, and her small hand tried to grab something. I think she was looking for my breasts. I let her. I took no offense. Do you see how kind I was to your child? I was kind! I was maternal. I cradled her like she was my own. I was born a mother!"

"No, no." I shook my head, but the movement pulled at the blade in my chest, and I felt it cut deeper into my flesh. I gasped. "No. You're not worthy. You will never be a mother. You are a monster, a child-killing monster."

"It's not fair. Not fair! Heaven has given me none but gave you two! What did I do to receive Heaven's wrath?" She lurched toward me. "I! The Empress of the kingdom! The chief wife of an emperor! I am noble and pious! But nine years! He would not bed me, and you, his father's concubine, took everything that belonged to me. You gave birth to one piglet and then another! I curse you. I curse your children. I curse Heaven! For you are blind. You are wanton. You are the one with a harlot's womb!"

Her voice cackled shrilly, piercing my bones, and I wanted to raise my head and shout back, but I was shivering, my teeth were chattering, and my lips were trembling. And the world spun again, and everything looked darker. So cold...

"So do you know what I did, harlot?" Her voice pierced me again. "I continued to hold her, that little thing. I held her close. I held her to my breasts while she cried, her small face scrunching and her legs kicking at my arm. I held her until she stopped."

Grief, hatred, and agony drowned me. Finally, I had heard what I wished to hear, but this was cruel. With her shrill voice, with her hateful words, she had killed my child twice. I wished I could spring up and strike her. I wished I could dig into her eyes and strangle her with my bare hands. "How could you? How could you..."

"You forced me to do it, and I hate you for it. I hate you, Pheasant, your child, and all of you! You are all spawns of malice, rodents bred from an evil womb. What innocence, what an infant! She would have grown up just like you, a harlot, seducing people's husbands and poisoning their wives. She would have produced more vile children, and they would all be like her. Those little things! So precious, people said. But it is a lie. A lie! Those little things, they hide their teeth, sharp and invisible. Then they grow, they bite, gnawing on your kindness and spill words of venom; they rake into your heart, sucking the nectar of your soul, and devour your flesh and bones. Those little faces, they change, those sweet voices, they change, and those sweet smiles, they change! They put on the skin of the evil, and they whisper, they plot behind your back, they hurt you, they devour you. They should all die. Die!"

"Enough." I felt tired, and I could not hold my head straight. A pool of blood was sitting on my lap and flowing down my hips, and the ground was sticky and slippery too. I needed to lean against something, a tree trunk, or lie down. I was going to pass out. "That's enough... You are evil. You killed my daughter. You cannot deny it now."

"I will not deny it. Yes, I smothered her. You heard me! What will you do? Look at you. You are going to bleed to death, and I shall bury you here, and you will bring this news to your grave to meet your daughter."

"No. Not yet," I said. "Because I have heard your confession, and so has everyone else."

"Who, who else?"

"Can you not see?" I nodded toward the dark forest. "They heard you—the forest, the wind, the trees, and the men behind them. They all heard you. They all heard your confession."

She turned sharply toward the darkness and froze for a moment. "What men? No one is here."

The traitor guards standing near the pit shifted their feet. Frowning, they glanced toward the forest as well.

It was time.

"General Li?" I shouted, gathering all my strength to raise my voice. "You may come out now." But my voice was not as loud as I had hoped, and it quickly dissipated in the air.

The men near me, however, jolted. "What? The General?"

"General Li is here?"

"Do not believe her!" the Empress shouted. "No one is here. Do not listen to her."

"You thought I was joking? You won't believe me? I told you they were here earlier, didn't I?" I said, and with all my might, I shouted, "You may come out now, General Li."

This was our agreement. He would follow my order. He would

serve me at my signal on this most important night, as we had discussed in Pheasant's library. But the night remained quiet, the trees still. The General should have answered me by now, and his guards should have leaped out from the forest. But I could not see any moving shadows or arrows whistling in the air.

Had the General betrayed me? My mouth was dry. An image burst into my mind. Her hair matted, one eye missing, crusts of blood covering her face. Jewel. How strange it was to see her again in this moment. We were both alike, she had said, women with dreams, women with their eyes drawn to the palace in the moon.

But there! A loud rustling came around me, and the General's voice, so loud and beautiful, filled the forest.

"Empress Wang! I am here. I have heard your confession. You murdered the little princess! You will be punished. Leave Luminous Lady alone. Do not harm her. All the men here, listen! Step back twenty paces, or I swear I will have your heads on stakes!"

Such a valiant and comforting voice. No wonder his enemies fled in fear on the battlefield. The General and his army, holding sabers, their golden breastplates shinning in the reflection of the torchlight, ran toward me in the shape of a crescent moon.

The Empress spun, and her phoenix crown dropped to the ground. "What is this? What is this?"

The men near the pit jumped to pick up their weapons as the General released a bloodcurdling cry. A bolt of silver light flashed in the air, and a man near me dropped to the ground.

I wanted to smile, but I could not, for every movement, even of my face, seemed to pull at the blade that had pierced my chest. "I told you so, didn't I? The General is here, with his army. Two hundred men. He surrounded you all while you spilled your venom for all to hear."

Her confession. The truth that I had so wanted.

"How did he find us? How? Harlot?"

I could not answer. I was so tired, I wished to sleep.

"Tell me, harlot. You will tell me!" She grabbed a blade from one of the rogue guards near her and lunged toward me, raising the blade high above her head. "How did he find us?"

I could not speak. She looked like a possessed giant from where I sat. She was going to kill me for sure, and the General was fighting the men on the other side of the pit. He was too far away to save me.

"Stop it, Empress Wang!" Apricot's familiar voice came to me. "Do not hurt Luminous Lady!"

"You." She spun around. "*Jianren, jianren!*" Despicable woman. "It's you! You told me where she was! You led me to her! You betrayed me!" The Empress turned away from me and dove toward Apricot's slim figure.

"Run!" I wanted to warn Apricot, but it was too late. The Empress raised her arm, the dagger glared in her hand, and Apricot froze, casting a long shadow across the pit, and then she slumped to the ground.

I jolted. "Apricot!"

A few paces from her, the General finally pivoted and grabbed the Empress's arm. He shouted, and his men swarmed around him to take that woman.

"Apricot!" With all the strength I could muster, I crawled to reach her. "Oh, Apricot."

She turned her face toward me. "Luminous Lady…I did what you told me." Blood poured from her mouth.

"You did. You did. I'm grateful. I'm grateful, Apricot. Thank you, good girl, good girl." She convulsed, and her lips curving into a smile, she became still.

If my hands had been free, I would have hugged her. If I had had enough time, I would have told her I was sorry I had beaten her.

"Are you all right, Luminous Lady?" the General asked beside me. "I told you this was risky. She could have killed you." He frowned at the dagger in my chest.

I could not speak. He was right after all.

The General ordered his men to spread around me. "You, guard us. Tie up the Empress. Subdue the traitors. Get them all. No one leaves here." He cut the ropes that bound my hands.

I flexed my fingers. My robe was soaked and sticky with blood, and my hands were chilled and numb.

"Now, stay still. Let me help you with this." He tore a piece of cloth from his cape, put it on his lap, and held the dagger on my chest. "This will hurt a little."

I had yet to say anything when he pulled the dagger out of my chest. I cried out, almost fainted. "I thought you would not come. But you did. You came. You saved me. Why, General? You always looked down on me."

"I don't look down on you." His hands working fast, he wound the strip of cloth around my chest.

"You never even cared to speak to me. You said you knew my father—"

"That is why you can be the only one who knows this."

I could not think with the pain. "What do you mean? Who else will know? Why does it matter?"

"The Regent is not a fool, Luminous Lady."

Then it dawned on me. The General had to keep his distance from me. If he had showed me any sign of favor, he would have attracted the Regent's attention, and the Regent would have discovered the connection between the General and my father, and he would have concocted stories of us, stories that would pin us together and bring death to both him and me.

"I see."

"You are your father's daughter, I can tell you that." He tightened the ends of the cloth and tied a knot on my shoulder.

I felt much better. "Thank you, General. Thank you for saving my life. Now, shall we go find Pheasant? Where is he? Is he all right? The Empress said—"

"Of course he's all right. He is still on the watchtower. There was a fight earlier, I heard," the General said, standing up. "The Emperor is holding it off, though. He has good archery skills. Many people were surprised. I heard he shot the Regent, and the rebels are retreating."

Pheasant's archery practice had paid off. "Is the Regent dead?" I asked with hope.

He shook his head. "We will find out."

"Take me to the watchtower."

"As you wish, Luminous Lady."

I looked around. Several of the General's men and the rogue guards were still fighting, and two guards were binding the Empress's hands behind her. She screamed, her hair whipping around her shoulders. But she had lost the battle, I could see.

I leaned over Apricot and placed my hand over her eyes, shutting them.

She was the secret and the most vital arrow I had unleashed. I had asked her to betray me, and she had gone to the Empress's uncle and told him where I was, and the Empress's uncle had in turn told the Empress, who then sent Captain Pei to abduct me. While the Captain took me, Apricot had followed, and the General, who had never let me out of his sight, followed me as well when I was taken to the Empress. While that evil woman, sure of her victory, delivered a virulent account of her crime and her hatred of children, she did not know the General and the guards, hiding near us, were listening to her every word.

For I knew even if I captured the child killer, she would never confess, and the only way to force her to tell the truth was to let her come to me, by offering myself as bait.

And that was what I had learned from the master Sun Tzu. That when your goal was too great, the best method to deceive your enemy was to make yourself a victim.

36

I PUSHED UP TO STAND. A FEW PACES FROM ME, THE General had trussed up Captain Pei, the rogue guards, and the Empress, and they were ready to herd them out of the forest.

"Stop, General. Give her to me." I tottered toward them.

"Luminous Lady—"

I picked up a sword near the pit and put it against the Empress's neck. I had to kill her. She had smothered my child, and I had to take her life in return. "She is mine."

"Luminous Lady, she is now a prisoner—"

He would take her and throw her in a dungeon. But she did not deserve that. She deserved death. I could not let her out of my hands. As long as she lived, I, and my child, would never live in peace. I should end her life and bury the threat underground. "No. She is mine." I pressed the blade harder against her thick neck.

"Go ahead." Her flat face was smeared with dirt and blood, and she looked like a dirty funeral wailer on a cursed burial site. "Kill me while you can, or I will kill you whenever I have the chance!"

"Shut up." I stabbed her. I could have finished her with a stroke, but I was too weak; my hands felt cold and numb; so did my legs. Drops of blood slid down her neck. She screamed.

"Mei!" Pheasant's voice came from behind me, accompanied by heavy hoofbeats. I turned around, and he swung off the horse near the pit and raced toward me. "Thank heavens you are all right!"

My heart warmed. Only hours ago, I had feared I would never see him again. "You missed a good confession, Your Majesty."

"That's what I heard. Everyone is talking about it now. Heavens!" He drew a sharp breath when he saw my bound chest. "What happened? Look at you!" He glanced at the screaming Empress. "She did that?"

I nodded.

"Let me take you to the physicians." He held my shoulders. "You look pale."

"She lost some blood," the General said beside me.

"Come. General, get her a stretcher. And call the physicians."

"Wait." I stopped him. "Why are you here? What about the palace? What about the Regent's army? I heard you shot him. Did you kill him?"

He shook his head. "I shot him in the shoulder."

I sighed. Of course, after everything that had happened, Pheasant would still spare his uncle's life. "Tell me what happened."

Pheasant nodded. "We had a brutal battle. The Regent was well organized. He had men attack our front gates with arrows and fire, and also had men climb over the wall. There were so many of them, Mei. It was very…disturbing. Our Gold Bird Guards did the best they could, trying to secure everywhere, but many were down, wounded. I almost thought we would lose. But then I spotted my uncle on horseback near a tent on Heavenly Street. I nocked my bow and shot him."

I sighed in relief.

"After that, the traitors and rioters backed off, and our Gold Bird Guards seized the chance and rallied. They were fierce and loyal fighters, and we pushed back as hard as we could. The enemy never broke through the gates. They are still outside the palace, but they will know not to fight when we return to the watchtower."

Pheasant had proven himself to be a capable leader. "So the palace is safe?"

He nodded. "The palace is safe. And now, even better, all the people in the palace know that you are innocent, that the Empress smothered our child and blamed it on you. Trust me, many guards will fight harder, and those guards who were fooled by my uncle, who knows? They might change their hearts again."

"What about the commoners who protested outside the palace?"

Pheasant sighed. "A good number of them were injured too—what a folly to join the revolt. But soon, all of them will hear the truth."

"Ah." I nodded.

"My uncle still has his mercenaries, but I don't believe they will have the resolve to attack the palace. In a matter of time we will defeat them. Now"—he touched my hand that held the blade—"you should let her go. The General will take her from here."

"No."

The Empress cried, "I do not need your pity, Li Zhi!"

Pheasant turned toward her.

"I do not need your pity." She was panting, and blood was dripping down her neck. "No, no, no. Not your pity. I will not have it. I will not have your pity! What have you given me in our nine years of marriage, Li Zhi? Nothing. You never even looked at me."

"Lady Wang," Pheasant said, his voice solemn. "You have brought this disaster to the palace. You have ended many innocent lives and put more in danger. You will be tried and impeached. You will face the consequences."

She laughed, shrilly. "Is that all you can say? Impeached, tried? Who cares about that? You are the worst kind, Li Zhi. You are not fit to be an emperor or a man! Do you know why? You turned me into this spiteful woman. I am the Empress of the kingdom, but a barren goat they call me in secret. My mother scolds me, my uncle resents me, and my servants laugh at me. I speak, but my words turn into the air. I have my own breath as my shadows! What did I do to deserve this? It's all because of you! You did this to me!"

Pheasant, looking dismayed, turned his face away. "I…"

I blinked. She was telling the truth—that Pheasant had bedded her only once and that she was not barren. Could this be possible? Was I responsible for her unhappiness?

"I was happy before I wed you. I was not pretty, but I was virtuous and honorable, and people bowed to me. 'The daughter of Wang,' they sang praise of me. I married you, and you gave me nothing but spite!"

"I never wished to marry you," Pheasant said quietly.

"I didn't wish to marry you either, Li Zhi. And I will never forgive you. Never. Or you"—she turned and spat at me—"or your progeny. So kill me now."

But this time I could not raise the blade. All these years, I had planted the tree of love with Pheasant, and we had cared for each other with determination and devotion, but our love had robbed the other women of the light they craved. It was not my intention, but sadly, it was our destiny.

"Virtue, my child, not vengeance," Tripitaka had advised me when he came to my Oriole's burial, and I had laughed at him. But I understood what he had meant.

I had to forgive her, for I had brought the darkness to her; I had turned her into a shadow. And Empress Wang, despite her twisted personality and her murderous heart, was not born a monster; she was made into one. Like many hapless women before her, she was simply a victim of her own fate.

I threw away my blade. "Take her away, General."

"You will not kill me? Why? Kill me, kill me!" She was hysterical.

"No, Empress Wang. I will not decide your fate. It's not in my hands." I leaned closer to Pheasant and held his hand.

The General steered her away, and laughing, she stumbled out of the woods, the torches spluttering around her, smoke surging behind her.

"Look." Pheasant pointed at the far edge, where many servants and ministers in purple and red robes appeared. They were shouting for me, their sound joyous.

"Your Majesty!"

"Luminous Lady!"

The servants and ministers came closer. Ministers Xu Jingzong and Minister Li Yifu were among them. They were Pheasant's ministers, but they had all come to see what had happened to me.

"We came as fast as we could," Minister Xu said, slightly out of breath. "I knew it! I knew she did it! I would have given my head to bet it was her. Of course she did it and blamed it on Luminous Lady. Luminous Lady? Are you… Thank heavens you are well!"

Minister Li, still impeccable with his manners, gave me a deep bow. "Heaven bless us! Now we know the truth! Only an evil woman like Empress Wang would kill a child and blame it on Luminous Lady."

The other ministers nodded. "It is truly brave of you, Luminous Lady, to give yourself up and face the Empress."

I motioned for them to stop. I did not need compliments, but I smiled to show my appreciation. "Ministers, if I am not mistaken, I believe you were all ordered to stay in the library's forecourt?"

"The palace is safe now, Luminous Lady," Minister Xu said, carrying the air of assurance and confidence that was vital in a minister of a high rank. "Besides, we believe there is someone else you will yearn to see."

Hong? Had they brought me my child? I had been so worried about him.

Pheasant squeezed my shoulder. "There he is."

The ministers stepped aside. Behind them came my four maids, and in Chunlu's arms was my sweet son, snuggling against Chunlu. He was sound asleep.

Minister Xu explained that the moment he heard the upcoming attack of the Regent, he had directed my maids and Hong to a safe chamber, hiding them from the crowd. That was why I could not find them.

"Thank you." I stroked my child's head. He looked so peaceful. I wanted to kiss him and hold him in my arms. But I did not wish to wake him, and I did not have the strength to hold him.

"Now, we must take you to the physicians," Pheasant said, offering me his hand.

I took his hand and walked beside him. I stumbled occasionally, and the ground felt as though it was floating, but I did not feel much pain.

When we reached the horse Pheasant had ridden, the servants spread out a stretcher. As I was ready to lie down, I tugged at Pheasant's sleeve. "Look."

He turned and followed my gaze.

Ahead of me, the sun was rising, its golden rays brightening the edge of the distant sky and throwing shining threads through the gap of the trees, and soon, the area where I stood was cloaked in a transparent, iridescent veil. Everything—the leaves, the branches, the ground—was illuminated. Everything sparkled.

And the moon was still there, still bright, placid, and shining, like an empty silver plate ready to accept gifts.

✦ ✦

When we returned to the palace, the attack of the rebels had already weakened, and when the General led the Gold Bird Guards to strike back, the commoners fled, and the Regent's men retreated to his ward. The crisis in front of the palace gates eased, and the next day, Pheasant ordered twenty legions of the Gold Bird Guards to surround the ward. The Regent's mercenaries cursed and shot arrows from inside the walls, and the Gold Bird Guards, unable to break into the building, laid siege to the ward, cutting off the supply to the mercenaries. Without sufficient food, the Regent soon tasted the bitter fruit of betrayal. His mercenary army revolted and abandoned him, and the General seized the chance, broke into the Regent's ward, and captured him.

Still, the Regent insisted on his innocence. He claimed he had no knowledge of the Empress's murderous act, and he had been fooled by the Empress just as everyone else was. In his loud and arrogant voice, the Regent stated that he had cared for Pheasant these years and devoted his entire life to the kingdom. Everything he had done, he said, he had done out of duty for the late Emperor, as it was Emperor Taizong who had decreed him to protect the kingdom and ensure its order and safety.

But in an unexpected move that would surprise everyone, Minister Li Yifu revealed to Pheasant that the late Emperor had not written such a will. The minister confessed that on the night of Emperor Taizong's death, he had been on his night duty in the imperial library when he saw the Regent slip into the dark hall, write the will, and press it with the dragon seal. The Regent then tucked the scroll into his sleeve and returned to the Emperor's chamber, where he announced it was a will written by the Emperor the previous year.

Fearing the Regent would exile him like the other ministers, the minister remained silent and kept the secret to himself. But now he said the people should know the truth.

Surprised, Pheasant asked the Regent if what the minister said was true, and for the first time in his life, the Regent lowered his head, unable to reply. Pheasant was astounded. He had never suspected his uncle's treachery, I realized, and although I had been certain the Regent had forged the will, I had not been able to prove it.

But Pheasant, the most benevolent ruler I would ever see, still did not have the heart to behead the Regent. Instead, he exiled him to a post in the remote south, providing him with a ration fit for a ninth-degree minister. Pheasant even indicated in his edict that the Regent's sojourn in the south was subject to recall if he proved remorseful.

But the old man was too proud to accept his defeat. Soon a message came that he had hanged himself near a stable in a horse rally post before he reached Yangzhou.

✦ ✦

I was placed under the care of physicians led by Meng Shen in the palace. While I lay in bed, Minister Xu Jingzong, keeping his promise, started the trial of Empress Wang in the Zhengshi Hall.

Many ministers, scribes, and eunuchs attended, and all the guards, even the General, who had heard the Empress's confession, testified.

The three Ladies came to the trial and gave their accounts as well. They recounted the cruelties they had suffered under the Empress these years and stated that the Pure Lady, in her confused state, had choked on a piece of cinnabar bark and died.

When all their testimonies were heard, Minister Xu declared the Empress guilty of murder. He proposed that the Empress's official title be stripped away and she be imprisoned for life, in the same kennel where she had kept the Pure Lady, though without the wolves.

When I heard the sentence, I remembered what the master Sun Tzu had said: "When one treats people with benevolence, justice, and righteousness, and reposes confidence in them, the army will be united in mind, and all will be happy to serve their leaders."

The Empress had lost her army a long time ago.

Soon, Empress Wang, or rather, Lady Wang, was sent to the kennel. A few days later, some eunuchs, who resented the Empress's harsh treatment of them these years, came to taunt her, and she threw herself at them but slipped in the mud. Her head crashed against the fence and bled. The wound became infected, and when we discovered it, she was already delirious, running a high fever. She died two months later.

Chancellor Chu Suiliang died a few months later too, ending his bold and overzealous life. That day I celebrated, hoping for a quieter and more peaceful life.

For the heir, Zhong, I did not punish him or seek the means to exile him. After all, he was only a pawn, and being so young, he could not yet fully understand the meaning of his actions. Pheasant decided to keep his heirship and allowed him to stay in the Eastern Palace. I had no objection. As long as the Empress was gone, he could not harm me. But I replaced all his tutors and retinue with people I felt more comfortable with. I would watch him, and if he turned out to be trouble, I would dethrone him.

I sought no punishment for the Regent's two brothers-in-law either. When I was well enough, I summoned them and told them I would forgive them, and if they were indeed men of learning, they would be given another chance to serve the kingdom.

I was eternally grateful to Minister Xu Jingzong for his stalwart belief in me and his service in impeaching the Empress. I asked Pheasant to promote him to Chancellor, replacing the loud Chu Suiliang. Upon my request, Pheasant also promoted the other ministers who had helped me.

I did not forget Tripitaka either. I was thankful for his advice—"The virtue of forgiveness would bear the fruit of your trees"—and I gave his pagoda and other Buddhist temples a generous donation, which they used to create splendid murals, sculptures of Buddha, bronze vases with Buddhist themes, and many paintings and poems.

Pheasant followed my donation with a decree that all religious houses were to receive a regular fund from the imperial treasury from that day on. He further indicated that all religions, regardless of their beliefs, were free to worship in our kingdom as long as they declared they would obey him. With his encouragement, more temples were built in the city. Divisions of Buddhism, such as Zen Buddhism and Niutou Buddhism, were created and recognized. Foreign priests who declared their faith in Manichaeism and Nestorianism also flocked to Chang'an. On a summer day, when I once rode on the streets of Chang'an, I glimpsed the arched buildings of Manichaean shrines, the flying eaves of Taoist abbeys, and many saffron walls of Buddhist temples.

✦ ✦

I recovered well under the care of my maids and the physicians. When summer came, I was able to walk and even laugh without grimacing or hurting my chest.

On a warm summer evening, when the palace celebrated the day of a feast with red lanterns, when the sweet scent of peonies and roses drifted in the Inner Court, when everyone in the palace, those with ranks and those without, stuffed their stomachs with fresh pears, apricots, and sweet, glutinous rice cakes rolled in sugar, Pheasant announced, with the presence of all my beloved ministers, that I, Luminous Lady, would become his chief wife. He proposed a formal ceremony take place to recognize my new status—the Empress of the kingdom.

There was loud applause, followed by thunderous cheers and happy shouts.

My steps steady, my heart filled with joy, I went before Pheasant's table and knelt, accepting the announcement.

Later, I went to my garden, and alone, I walked up Hope's bridge to visit Oriole.

✦ ✦

The surface of the stone looked clean, smooth, and shining, glowing in the sun. Near it, fresh green grass was growing. I sat down and brushed the nameless marker. My bulging stomach touched my thighs again. I was carrying another child.

But it was my Oriole whom I had gone to see. My daughter. Who came and went. But she was loved, and always would be.

I missed her. I missed her milky scent. I missed her gurgling voice. I missed her perfect black eyes like shining prunes and her plump cheeks. I missed having her snuggle right next to me as she slept, her arms stretching above her head. I wanted to listen, to remember the sound she had made, and to feel the joy of her gaze and the tightness of her grip when she held my fingers.

These were the only memories I had left of her. Her clothes had been taken away, her scent was gone, and even the image of her face, her smile, was fading in my mind.

I took out a doll I had kept in my pocket and placed it on the top of the stone. The doll had perfect black eyes and red lips, like my child, and like my child, she looked splendid, but small and delicate. Quietly, she sat there, mute, still, like a vision, like a sacrifice.

I thought of all the days my Oriole would miss: cloudy days, sunny days, the days with warm breezes, the days with chilly frost. And the seasons that would pass without her, the spring blossoms that would bloom without her, and the warm sunlight that would dance without her.

Children were birds, and mothers were trees, and no matter how far they flew, no matter how high they soared, they always craved the branches of the tree, and the nest, to rest.

The late Noble Lady's words. If what she said was true, then I hoped my bird would know that the tree would always be there, its roots deep in the earth, its branch of love spreading, growing, waiting, in every season and every year.

And I would tell her the scent of the blossoms in spring, the song of cicadas in the summer heat, the color of autumn's leaves, and the warmth of the sunlight during frosty days. I would tell her the shapes of the clouds, the echoes of the wind, and the reflections of the light. I would tell her everything I would see, everything I would know.

For my sweet daughter, you are not here, but you will never be gone. You can no longer speak, but I shall always hear your voice. You have melted into the wind, but you will never be forsaken.

For I shall always think of you. I shall think of you when the spring leaves sprout, holding morning dew, luminous like your soft skin. I shall think of you when the cloud of snow lingers on the eaves, wanders in the air, and fades on the earth. I shall think of you when the birds glide in the wind, their wings sweeping in the sky, and their trills, loud and clear, echo in the distant night.

O

AD 655

The Sixth Year *of*

Emperor Gaozong's Reign

of Eternal Glory

AUTUMN

37

BEFORE DAWN, MY MAIDS BEGAN TO DRESS ME, ADDING ON me layers of fabric in different hues, the formal crowning regalia. First they gave me an indigo underrobe embroidered with axes, pairing it with thick trousers; next they added a scarlet dress printed with feathers from twelve types of birds, a padded top, and a long, scarlet skirt; and then finally they put on me a glorious damask ceremonial gown with wide sleeves that reached my ankles. To finish, a golden shawl trimmed with fur was draped on my shoulders. On my feet, I wore indigo socks and a pair of high-heeled, boat-shaped shoes with curled tips.

I did not wear the traditional phoenix crown that had belonged to Empress Wende or Empress Wang; instead, I put on the wig Princess Gaoyang had given me. Tied to the wig was a gold chain that held a large round pearl, the size of an egg, which hung low to touch the center of my forehead. So from a distance, even if people could not see my face, they would see the pearl, shining like a luminous moon.

A special carriage, whose entire body was made of purple gold and wheels wrought with the same precious metal, waited for me outside the garden. I entered and sat on a silk cushion seat. The carriage had floorboards lacquered in indigo, and the ceiling was painted with five-hued feathers. Eight black stallions, caparisoned in splendid red and yellow cloth, pulled me to the front gates of the Outer Palace.

When I stepped out, waves of cheers broke out from the people who crowded on the Heavenly Street. I resisted the urge to look back and wave. The people of Chang'an had learned the truth, and they welcomed me. I wished to thank them, and I promised silently I would be a worthy empress for them. I would return their favor someday, and I would give them the security and prosperity that they deserved.

I walked down the vast street that extended all the way to the Taiji Gate. The Gold Bird Guards, in their magnificent uniforms of bronze breastplates and maroon capes, stood erect as I passed them. A chorus of music rose near me. First came the steady beat of drums, then the vibrant sound of flutes, accompanied by the solemn notes of chime bells and chime stones, then joined by the joyous sounds of *sheng* and *xia*, and finally, followed by the elegant melodies of *yangqin*.

My heart singing the same wonderful tunes, I entered the middle gate, the gate reserved for emperors and empresses, and treaded down the vast area before the Taiji Hall. I could see all the important people of the kingdom: the ministers in nine ranks dressed in purple, red, green, and indigo; the vassals in their tight, narrow-sleeved tunics; the khans in short skirts; the foreign ambassadors in tall hats; and the imperial family members in silk gowns. They knelt in the yard. It was a sight I would forever remember.

"The ceremony begins," the announcer, Han Yuan, called out near the Taiji Hall.

I had given him the special honor of being the announcer in hopes that he would remember my kindness and serve me well. How he truly felt about my crowning I would never know. But I should not worry about him. Today was my day.

In the far distance, I could see Pheasant seated on the golden throne on a platform in the center of the Taiji Hall. Standing on his right was General Li, the master of the ceremony, who held a golden tray, on which he had placed three items that would change my future: the Golden Imperial Genealogy Book, the Empress's seal, and the Empress's girdle.

I wished my father could be here to see the Genealogy Book. He would have been proud. The book recorded my family name, his name, his ancestors, my mother's name, and my mother's ancestors. With this recording, he would be forever known as the father of an empress. That had been his dream, and now his dream had come true.

When Tripitaka predicted my destiny twenty-four years ago, I never would have believed that this day would come. Now, seventeen years after Father's death, I would fulfill his wish. If I ever dreamed of Father, I would be happy to tell him I had not failed, that I had kept my promise to take good care of my family. Mother had retired from the monastery, and I had bought a large house for her in Chang'an, hired twenty servants to tend to her, and bestowed on her a generous annual stipend. She would never have to worry about food or money. She would have a life of comfort and leisure.

I had also searched for my older sister, who had moved to the south before I came to the palace. I located her, a widow in poor health, and bestowed a high-ranking title on her and some honored titles on her two children. I gave them permission to visit me and my children as often as they wished, and I would have my extended family surrounding me.

I did not forget even my half brother and his family. I gave them gifts and thanked them for providing for me and my family in the past.

As for my father's house in Wenshui, I retrieved it and set it up as a shrine, which entitled the local people to receive an annual stipend they could use.

Lifting my scarlet skirt, I ascended the stone stairs to the hall, and the large, round pearl slid from the center of my forehead to the side. I steadied it and continued to climb. The autumn weather was cold, but I did not feel the chill.

When I reached the top of the stairs, I paused. From where I was, I could see the throne in the center of the hall, the golden altar where wisps of incense rose to reach the ceiling, and my love, my friend, my emperor. He sat with his two hands on his knees, the golden sleeves draping to the ground. Like me, he was no longer young, and his eyes looked uneven, one high, one low, but he was still handsome and splendid.

Just yesterday, we had talked, reminiscing about our past. We had known each other when we were so young, and after this ceremony, we would be known as husband and wife, father and mother. We would face the kingdom as one.

"Kneel," the announcer shouted, and the music ceased. The moment of coronation began.

I could feel hundreds of eyes fixed on my back, yet I did not feel nervous. I belonged in the prestigious hall. I was destined to be part of this ritual. Dropping to my knees, I was ready.

"To Heaven!"

I raised my hands up to feel the sky, bent over, and touched the ground.

"To Earth!"

I spread my hands to the ground and touched it with my forehead.

"To the Emperor!"

I brushed my sleeves, the front of my ceremonial gown, and my skirt and prostrated before Pheasant. Acknowledging the three vital elements was essential in the ritual, but in my heart, I knew it was not enough, and silently, I recited, giving my gratitude to those who had put me up there:

To the ones who had given me life.

To the ones whom I had given life.

To the ones who had given their lives for me.

And there were so many. My child. Princess Gaoyang. Apricot. And Hope.

Han Yuan's voice rose beside me again. "Luminous Lady, you may now accept the three treasures."

I straightened. Next would come the most important part of the coronation.

"Now the Emperor confers the empress's girdle!"

Pheasant's golden robe appeared before me. "As the Emperor of Tang Dynasty, Emperor Gaozong, the ruler who is granted with Heaven's mission, the lord of all land and the seven seas, the third son of Emperor Taizong and Empress Wende, I now do announce you, the second daughter of the Wu family, the Luminous Lady of the Inner Court, the mother of Prince Hong, to be the Empress of the kingdom."

He took the empress's girdle, a broad golden belt encrusted with pearls, rubies, and gold, from the tray. Looking solemn, he tied it around my waist. I was surprised. He had breached the tradition. It was not his duty to tie the belt around me, and most importantly, such an act of open affection was too intimate to exhibit in public.

"Now the master of the ceremony confers the Golden Imperial Genealogy Book and the empress's seal!"

General Li, the man who had become the vital force of my support, stepped closer. He looked indifferent as usual, and his birthmark looked dark even in the daylight. I remembered what he had said on the watchtower: "A good sword serves his lord; a good swordsman believes in his lord." I owed him my eternal gratitude.

He handed me the Golden Imperial Genealogy Book, a golden scroll shining in the sunlight. Lowering my head, I accepted it. Next he presented me with the empress's seal, a large jade phoenix statue, the same size as Pheasant's jade dragon statue. Only two women before me had the fortune to hold it, Empress Wende and Empress Wang, and I was the third. It felt cold and heavy, but it fitted my hand perfectly.

"Now the Empress of the kingdom greets her people!"

Holding the book in my right hand and the seal in my left, I turned around, the golden girdle swaying around my waist.

The vast space before the hall was now crowded with people. On the right stood the ladies from the Inner Court, eunuchs, servants, and imperial families. In the center were the ministers, vassals, khans, and foreign ambassadors. On the left side stood the Gold Bird Guards in their shining breastplates and capes. At the four corners of the yard, near the stone bridges carved with reliefs, stood the flag bearers, standard carriers, the spear holders, and many others.

No one moved. All the people, their heads raised, stared at me, their eyes wide with expectation.

"Kneel!"

This time, all the ministers, the vassals, the ambassadors, the khans, the women with titles and without, the imperial family members, the guards, and the servants spread their hands on the ground and prostrated. To me.

I felt something hot rising in my eyes. I was thirteen when I first rode through the palace gate, and now I was twenty-nine. For sixteen years, I had been bowing and prostrating to the people who did not know my family name, living on their whims, following their commands, and now they were all hailing me, calling me, "Empress Wu, Empress Wu, Empress Wu!"

Somewhere a bell was struck. Once, twice, three times. Its solemn sound shook the complacent sky, driving away the wind of doubts and clouds of suspicion, and like a spell, it lingered.

In the distance, a bright moon was rising.

EPILOGUE

FIVE YEARS AFTER WU MEI WAS CROWNED EMPRESS, Pheasant suffered his first stroke, which robbed him of his vision. The blind emperor appointed Mei to be the coruler of the kingdom, beginning the reign of Twin Saints. But Emperor Gaozong's health continued to deteriorate, and soon he was paralyzed, placing the full duty of ruling the kingdom on Empress Wu's shoulders. Upon Gaozong's death, Empress Wu was named the Regent and was left with four sons and a daughter.

Empress Wu's firstborn, Hong, became the heir after Zhong abdicated before Emperor Gaozong's death, but Hong died young, and Empress Wu's other sons became victims of court intrigue. With her wit and determination, she fought against conspiracies, eliminated her enemies, and established her power in the court. After ruling the kingdom for over thirty years, she remained unchallenged. She decided to renounce the Tang Dynasty and founded her own dynasty, Zhou Dynasty, and declared herself the Emperor of the kingdom.

She was the first and only female in Chinese history to rule legitimately in her own name, her reign lasting until AD 705. She also formed her own Inner Court, populated with many male concubines, which would become the fodder for scandal after her death.

However, Empress Wu was an exceptional ruler. During her reign, the kingdom thrived in trade, architecture, religion, art, literature, and military expansion, and China blossomed into a golden age, unmatched in centuries.

Empress Wu ushered in a new era for Buddhism, helping the religion take root in China, and eventually Buddhism grew to be a rival of Taoism and Confucianism. She instructed the building of the Long Men Caves in Luoyang, which hosted a wealth of Buddhist art and featured a prominent statue of the great Buddha modeled after her own image. The caves remain a major part of Buddhist heritage today.

With her openness and tolerance, the kingdom's trade prospered. Many foreign merchants flocked from various regions via the Silk Route, Chang'an and Luoyang became the centers for trade, and in Canton, thousands of ships arrived daily.

Empress Wu was well-known for her insistence on reforming the Keju System, an archaic system the court used to find talents who would govern the kingdom. Valuing people's talent above their birth, she encouraged men and women—who had been perpetually excluded from learning—to study and learn. She administered exams in person and brought many talents to the court who otherwise never would have had the chance to serve the kingdom because of their birth. The most prominent figures often mentioned are the wise Judge Di Renjie and the Empress's Prime Minister, Shangguan Wan'er, the daughter of the Empress's enemy and also the first female prime minister in Chinese history. With Empress Wu's encouragement, people in the kingdom, young and old, took pride in studying literature, composing poems, ushering in the golden age of poetry in China.

Empress Wu also effectively reinforced the Equal Land System, giving men and women—again, who had never before been given any consideration—the equal right to share and cultivate the land, motivating them to work hard. Under her guidance, the kingdom's economy flourished, the population increased, and the kingdom's sophisticated culture and art became inspirations to neighboring kingdoms such as Korea and Japan.

According to historical record, the year when Empress Wu returned to the palace from her exile, the kingdom had a mere three million households. By the end of her reign, the kingdom's households had doubled to six million, with a total population of more than thirty million people.

Empress Wu was eventually overthrown by a military coup and

died in her eighties. The throne was briefly taken over by one of her sons, and then her grandson, Emperor Xuan Zong, who reaped the fruit of her reign. Under his rule, the kingdom was ripped apart by civil wars and later attacked by the Tibetans, Uigurs, and Turks. The Tang Dynasty never again saw the peace, prosperity, and vibrancy characteristic of Empress Wu's reign.

However, despite her contribution to the kingdom, her achievements were rarely acknowledged, and because she was a woman who defied male domination, violating the Confucian cardinal rule, she was subject to vilification by many Confucian historians in the coming centuries who labeled her a murderer, a tyrant, and a harlot.

Again, the story of Wu Mei is based on a historical figure, the one and only female ruler in China, Wu Zetian, also known as Empress Wu. All the male characters in the novels, except the eunuchs, are actual historical figures; the female characters, such as the Pure Lady, Empress Wang, and Princess Gaoyang, are real women who lived and are recorded in the history as well.

The exact location of the Buddhist monastery where Wu Mei was exiled, Ganye Miao, remains unknown, and no one seems to know how she returned to the palace.

The executions of Prince Ke, Princess Gaoyang, Fang Yi'ai, the monk Biji, and many others were recorded in history, but the friendship between Princess Gaoyang and Empress Wu is my imagination.

The journey of Tripitaka, also known as Tang Sanzang in Chinese, was most prominently fictionalized in the fantasy novel *Xi You Ji* by Wu Cheng'en. The monk's encounter with Wu Mei was also invented for the purpose of the books.

Some scholars believe that Empress Wu smothered her own child so she could become the Empress. I have portrayed the event quite differently in the book, showing Empress Wang to be the true culprit. During my research, I found that Wang Pu's *Tang Hui Yao*, perhaps the earliest and most reliable sources about the Tang Dynasty, does not mention the murder at all. *Ben Ji*, the main section of *The Old Tang Book*, written by Liu Xu in AD 945, almost three hundred years after the event, does not record the murder either. Both sources do indicate that Empress Wu's newborn daughter died suddenly. Most of the rhetoric of Empress Wu smothering her daughter comes from *The New Tang Book* by Ouyang Xiu, a devoted Confucian scholar, and from *Zi Zhi Tong Jian* by the conservative but influential Sima Guang.

I decided not to use Ouyang Xiu's and Sima Guang's references in my reimagining of Empress Wu's life, as the two historians' accounts were written in the eleventh century, almost four hundred years after the event, and in their accounts, the murder was narrated in extremely vivid detail that raised questions regarding its authenticity.

I also looked into the comments delivered by Empress Wu's peers for clues to her murder and discovered that her most vocal enemy, the poet Luobin Wang, who published an official proclamation denouncing her reign in AD 684 and concocted many sensational stories to discredit her, had also failed to mention the murder. It's my conclusion that had Empress Wu really murdered her daughter, this crime would not have escaped her enemy's eyes and would be more thoroughly documented.

Historical records do not mention that Duke Changsun Wuji forged Emperor Taizong's will.

READING GROUP GUIDE

1. Before Emperor Taizong's death, he gave an order to the Duke to exile all his women who had not borne him a child, about nine hundred of the women in the palace, to Buddhist monasteries, where they would pray for his soul for the rest of their lives. This is a convention that was followed by all palace women in China for almost two thousand years. What do you think about that practice? What would you do if you were a concubine and forced to leave your home?

2. Consider this decree and also the Regent's comments: "You must not give women too much freedom. They know not right from wrong. They are like dogs. They must be trained and chained. If you let them loose, they go wild." Can you get a glimpse of women's lives in ancient China? How do you think women in ancient China were treated? How were European women any different?

3. Discuss the character of the Duke (later the Regent), one of the major villains in the novel. What kind of a man is he?

4. Discuss the theme of power in the novel. How important is it? How do Mei, Pheasant, the Regent, and Empress Wang struggle to keep it in their hands?

5. Discuss how her experience as an exiled woman changes Mei's perceptions of love, power, and self.

6. Discuss the character Princess Gaoyang, her friendship with Mei, and how it changes Mei.

7. Discuss Empress Wang's character. Do you think she is evil? Do you pity her? Do you understand her motivations for her actions throughout the novel?

8. Talk about Mei and her pet, Hope. What impact does Hope have on Mei? How does Hope's death affect Mei? How do you think people in ancient China treated animals? Do you think people view and treat animals differently today?

9. Motherhood is a major theme in the book. How important is motherhood for Empress Wang, Mei, and the other female characters in the palace? How does it define their positions in the palace? How do they perceive motherhood? Do you think motherhood is an essential part of a woman's life?

10. Buddhism came to China from India, and its followers were mostly women at the beginning of the Tang Dynasty. How does Mei see the religion at the beginning of the novel? How does her perception change? What importance do you think religion has in the novel?

11. Princess Gaoyang said, "Fear is a roof... You cannot live in a pavilion built with fear, Luminous Lady. It gets smaller and smaller, hotter and hotter inside, until you cannot breathe." What do you think of this observation?

12. Compare Mei and Empress Wang. Discuss how their relationship worsens. At what point in the novel does Mei have power over Empress Wang? At what point in the novel is Mei lost?

13. Discuss the images of nature, birds, and animals in the story. Where do you see them in the novel? What are their significances? Why do you think Mei names her daughter Oriole?

14. Death is an important theme in the novel. Discuss each case of death. What devastating effects do they have on Mei and on Pheasant, and how does each death change them and their relationship?

15. After Mei hears the rumor that she has killed her own child, she reflects: "...for rumor had no grave and only bore seeds. It germinated in the air, thrived in the sun, and ripened in the shadows. It would not die in the rain and fly only higher in the wind." What do you think of this perception? How will you relate this perception to your own experience in the modern world dominated by social media and the Internet?

16. In the first book of the Empress Wu duology, *The Moon in the Palace*, Mei is unable to control her own destiny and is often manipulated. In the second book, however, Mei has learned how to subtly control other people and their ideas and use them for her own purposes. Where do you see those instances of her exerting her control over others in the novel?

17. In the first book, *The Moon in the Palace*, Mei is a young girl of exceptional intelligence, courage, and loyalty, but she still has many weaknesses and is also subject to temptations and court intrigues. In the second book, Mei has grown to be a mature woman. Compare the young Mei to the adult Mei. What are the qualities you see in the adult Mei? What are her weaknesses as an adult?

A Conversation with the Author

How old were you when you wrote your first story? What was it about?

I wrote my first story when I was in fourth grade. It was published in a local journal in China. I earned my first 6 RMB, which is equivalent to one dollar! It was a story of a girl investigating an ink stain on the classroom's wall.

What do you love most about writing?

I love to see how words form an image that transcends the banal reality, or how words join together to create a morsel of wisdom that tickles your mind.

What advice would you give to aspiring writers?

Characters are like needy mistresses; they need your attention and nurturing so they will live and thrive. Stay connected with them: know their needs, their wants, and their fears. When you feel the way they feel and see the way they see, you will know what the voice is in the first sentence of a scene, and you will also be able to channel their emotions throughout the scene. If you neglect them, they will abandon you, and a distance will grow between you and your characters, and when you want to write again, it will be hard to find the attachment you need. It will be difficult to understand the goal of a scene and how to construct it. The longer you neglect your characters, the harder it is to get back into the story again.

For me, it's essential to write every day, no matter what happens. Even one sentence a day is better than nothing.

Did you always want to be a writer, or did you start off in a different career?

It may be a cliché to say this, but I have always wanted to be a writer. It has been my dream since I was a child.

What are your favorite genres to read?

Honestly, the book's genre doesn't matter to me. I read broadly, and I enjoy reading many types of books. I like fantasy, sci-fi, mystery, thriller, family sagas, and, of course, historical fiction. I am, however, very fond of "a hero's journey" type of books.

What was the most challenging part when you were writing this novel?

Empress Wu's emotions, her sadness, grief, helplessness, and rage, were very challenging for me to write.

I was familiar with this part of the journey in Empress Wu's life, her exile, her return to the palace, and her rise to power. But still, to live through that journey was like nothing I had imagined before. I had to be completely submerged in the story, see the desolation of the monastery, and feel Mei's desperation. But as the writer, I also had to be above her experience, to be in control of her emotional arc, showing her resiliency and also keeping a steady pace so the plot would keep moving.

But then the hardest moment came after she returned to the palace. There were so many trials she had to face. As a mother myself, I considered it prohibitive to imagine the fate of her daughter and what Mei had to endure. So I tried to avoid writing that scene. I kept putting it off, but eventually, that section of story had to be written. To better prepare myself, I studied books about the grief process and reread Shakespeare's *King Lear* so I could feel the injustice and anger. But when I sat down to write, oh boy, I was still surprised. I was unprepared for the intensity of her anger, and from there, her emotions possessed me. Her shock, her grief, her anguish, her rage, and her hatred—they all poured out of me. For weeks, I couldn't get out of the emotional whirlpool, and I was extremely irritated and angry when she sought revenge but was unable to do anything to protect her family. I believe I yelled at my husband out of frustration many times, and when I went to pick up my kids at school, I was impatient and short-tempered. My usually fearless kids were very quiet. I think they were scared to see me that way.

What research or preparations did you engage in before writing this book?

After I finished writing the first book in the duology, *The Moon in the Palace*, I had completed the research about the world of the Tang Dynasty, and I had a clear picture of how the setting would be and how Mei would live in that environment. The major research I had to engage in for this book was for the character Tripitaka. He was an enigma himself, and he only spoke in metaphors. So I studied many Zen—Chan, in Chinese—poems composed in the legendary Chan period in China, which was dated from the mid-fifth century to the eighth century, as well as haiku written by well-known Japanese poets, in order to understand how the monk translated his thoughts into images and metaphors. I love that part of research because I have always been fascinated with Zen and the Zen poems. The masters' enlightening prose and images were very inspiring, and I was also awed at the deep meanings embedded in haiku's simple verse.

I also spent a lot of time fixing the details, such as the funeral preparations for the Emperor, the Buddhist conventions of meditation, and the specifics of the coronation ceremony. But it turned out I did not need that much detail in the novel, so I cut them out during revision.

Which character do you feel most closely connected to you?

I guess it's not a surprise that I feel connected to Empress Wu above everyone else. She is most endearing to me. I adore her resiliency and intelligence, and I am grateful to have the chance to explore her innermost thoughts.

In *The Moon in the Palace*, she is only a young girl, and her dreams and heartbreaks are related to her obligation and youthful desire.

But in *The Empress of Bright Moon*, she's a mature woman, a devoted mother, a valuable friend whose advice Pheasant relies on, and you can also see her poise, her foresight, her mind-set, and, of course, her growing ability to wade through the palace's dark water and take the control and lead, all the qualities that would make her a great ruler in the future.

This might be surprising, but another character I put in a lot of effort and feel sympathetic to is Empress Wang. She's scary, I know, and unpredictable—I wouldn't want her to be my enemy!—but if you look deeper, you can see she is a victim of the society and its stifling perceptions. I feel this connection to her because I have read many stories of Chinese women who, unable to conceive a child, dropped to the lowest level on the social ladder, and I felt I needed to look out for those women of disadvantage. So here she is, Empress Wang, a woman of great power, but because of her "barrenness," she is looked down upon, and she has little control of who she can be and what kind of a life she can have. But still, she has to assert herself, to hold on to what little is left for her. It is understandable that she is bipolar, subject to attacks of anxiety and depression, but also prone to violence. It is also inevitable that in her desperation, she would not be afraid to commit murder.

ACKNOWLEDGMENTS

As always, to my husband, Mark, for being here and for being true; to my shining stars, Annabelle and Joshua, for your sweet kisses and for hugging me like your favorite stuffed animal. And to my family and friends in China, I miss you.

To my editor, Anna Michels, my secret and most powerful ally, who provided me with keen perceptions and insightful notes that helped shape the book. Thank you, Anna. I can always rely on you.

To my two fabulous beta readers: my agent, Shannon Hassan, for your unwavering support, and my good friend Karen Walters, for telling me what worked and what did not. To my dear friend, Renae Bruce, for perusing the book with great enthusiasm each time I asked. Thank you!

I'm also most grateful to my outstanding team at Sourcebooks: editorial director Shana Drehs, for always being kind; production editor Heather Hall and copy editor Gail Foreman, for being amazingly thorough and sharp; the talented Laura Klynstra, for the enticing book cover; senior production designer Jillian Rahn, for the refreshing moon fonts; enthusiastic publicist Lathea Williams; the efficient marketing team; and everyone else at Sourcebooks who supported me. Thank you!

To Susan Blumberg-Kason and Jocelyn Eikenburg, who offered me generous support on my publishing journey. Thank you so much for all your help and emails!

Last but not least, my heartfelt thank-you to you, reader, for following Empress Wu's journey. Without you, her tears and her fears would have been washed away without a trace by the storm of history.

ABOUT THE AUTHOR

Photo credit: JCPenney Portrait Studios

Weina Dai Randel is the author of *The Moon in the Palace*, the first installment of the Empress of Bright Moon duology. Born and raised in China, she has worked as a journalist, a magazine editor, and an adjunct pr
history and
literature,
stories of (
cially wor
She is a m
Society an